THE MIRROR VISITOR
BOOK 3

# THE MEMORY
# OF BABEL

# Christelle Dabos

## THE MIRROR VISITOR
### BOOK 3

# THE MEMORY
# OF BABEL

*Translated from the French
by Hildegarde Serle*

Europa
*editions*

Europa Editions
214 West 29th Street
New York, N.Y. 10001
www.europaeditions.com
info@europaeditions.com

Copyright © 2017 by Gallimard Jeunesse
First Publication 2020 by Europa Editions

Translation by Hildegarde Serle
Original title: *La Passe-Miroir. Livre 3. La Mémoire de Babel*
Translation copyright © 2020 by Europa Editions

Library of Congress Cataloging in Publication Data is available
ISBN 978-1-60945-613-9

Dabos, Christelle
The Memory of Babel

Book design by Emanuele Ragnisco
www.mekkanografici.com

Cover and inside illustrations by Laurent Gapaillard © Gallimard Jeunesse

Prepress by Grafica Punto Print – Rome

Printed in Italy, at Puntoweb

# Contents

# VOLUME 2 RECALLED
## THE MISSING OF CLAIRDELUNE

Due to a misunderstanding, Ophelia is appointed Vice-Storyteller at the court of Farouk, the family spirit of the Pole. She plunges into the reality of Citaceleste and glimpses the corrupt souls behind the gilded illusions. Disturbing disappearances from among the nobles soon lead her to investigate—as a reader, this time—a blackmailer who claims to act on behalf of "GOD." Ophelia is herself targeted by him when Farouk counts on her power to unlock the secret of his Book, a coded text, of which every family spirit owns a copy, and which is all that remains of their forgotten childhood. It is a reading on which Thorn's life will ultimately depend, for he has been sentenced to death.

What Ophelia will discover goes far beyond what she had imagined. God really does exist. He is the creator of the family spirits, parent of all their descendants, master of the families' destinies, censor of their collective memories!

And above all, he can assume the characteristics and power of anyone whose path he crosses, something Ophelia and Thorn will learn at their expense when God visits them in prison. He tells them that the worst is still to come: the Other is far more formidable than he is . . . and it was Ophelia who had unwittingly released him during her very first passage through a mirror.

Thorn, who has himself become a mirror visitor thanks to his marriage, uses his new power to vanish into thin air.

Forced to leave the Pole and return to Anima, Ophelia is left, alone, with all her questions. Who is the Other? Was he really the one who brought about the Rupture? Why is he planning to cause the disintegration of the arks? And is she really destined to lead God to the Other?

But one question remains the most nagging of them all:

Where is Thorn?

# MAP OF THE COMPASS ROSES AND THEIR DESTINATIONS

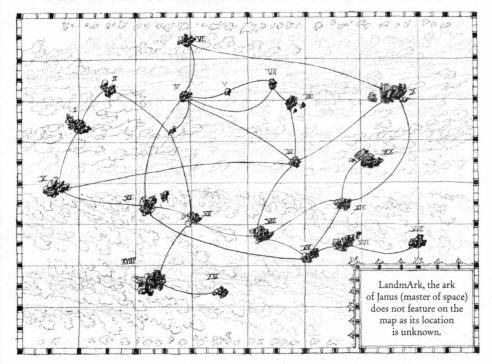

LandmArk, the ark of Janus (master of space) does not feature on the map as its location is unknown.

I.      Anima, the ark of Artemis (mistress of objects)
II.     The Pole, the ark of Farouk (master of spirits)
III.    Totem, the ark of Venus (mistress of animals)
IV.     Cylope, the ark of Ouranos (master of magnetism)
V.      Flora, the ark of Belisama (mistress of vegetation)
VI.     Leadgold, the ark of Midas (master of transmutation)
VII.    Pharos, the ark of Horus (master of charm)
VIII.   The Serenissima, the ark of Fama (mistress of divination)
IX.     Heliopolis, the ark of Lucifer (master of lightning)
X.      Babel, the ark of twins Pollux and Helen (master and mistress of the senses)

XI.     The Desert, the ark of Djinn (master of hydropathy)
XII.    The Tartar, the ark of Gaia (mistress of tellurism)
XIII.   Zephyr, the ark of Olympus (master of the winds)
XIV.    Titan, the ark of Yin (mistress of mass)
XV.     Corpolis, the ark of Zeus (master of metamorphosis)
XVI.    Sidh, the ark of Persephone (mistress of temperature)
XVII.   Selene, the ark of Morpheus (master of dreams)
XVIII.  Vesperal, the ark of Viracocha (master of phantomization)
XIX.    Al-Andaloose, the ark of Ra (master of empathy)
XX.     The Star, the neutral ark (seat of interfamilial institutions)

*Once upon a tomorrow,*
*before too long,*
*there will be a world that will finally live in peace.*

*At that time,*
*there will be new men*
*and there will be new women.*

*It will be the era of miracles.*

# THE ABSENT ONE

# The Festival

The clock was charging forward at full speed. It was a giant grandfather clock mounted on casters, its pendulum loudly marking every second. It wasn't every day that Ophelia witnessed a piece of furniture of this size rushing toward her.

"Please excuse it, dear cousin!" exclaimed a young girl, tugging on the clock's lead with all her might. "It's not usually so forward. In its defense, Mom doesn't take it out very often. May I have a waffle?"

Ophelia kept a wary eye on the clock, whose casters were still squeaking against the paving. "With some maple syrup?" she asked, plucking a crispy waffle from the counter.

"No thanks, cousin. Merry Tickers!"

Ophelia had responded half-heartedly, watching the young girl and her big clock disappear into the crowd. If there was one festival she wasn't in the mood to participate in, this was certainly it. Assigned to the waffle stand, right in the center of Anima's traditional market, she was seeing a never-ending procession of cuckoo clocks and alarm clocks. The continuous cacophony of tick-tocking and cries of "Merry Tickers!" reverberated against the large windows of the covered market. Ophelia felt as if all those clock hands were turning just to remind her of what she didn't wish to remember.

"Two years and seven months."

17

Ophelia looked at Aunt Rosaline, who had tossed these words out along with some piping-hot waffles onto the counter. She also found that Tickers put her into a dark mood.

"Do you think *madam* will reply to our letters?" Aunt Rosaline hissed, while shaking her spatula. "But then, I suppose *madam* has better things to do with her days."

"You're being unfair," said Ophelia. "Berenilde probably has tried to contact us."

Aunt Rosaline laid her spatula back on the waffle-iron, and wiped her hands on her kitchen apron. "Of course I'm being unfair. After what happened in the Pole, it wouldn't surprise me if the Doyennes were intercepting our mail. I shouldn't be complaining in your presence. These past two years and seven months have been even more silent for you than for me."

Ophelia didn't feel like talking about it. Just thinking about it made her feel as if she'd swallowed the hands of a clock. She hastened to serve a jeweler, adorned with his finest watches.

"Come, come!" he chided, when his watches all started frantically snapping their covers. "Where have your good manners gone, misses? Want me to take you back to the shop, do you?"

"Don't tick them off," said Ophelia, "it's me that has that effect on them. Syrup?"

"The waffle will suffice. Merry Tickers!"

Ophelia watched the jeweler move off, and placed the bottle of syrup, which she'd almost knocked over, back on the table. "The Doyennes should never have assigned me a festival stand. All I can do is hand out waffles that I can't even make myself. And even then, I've dropped half a dozen of them onto the floor."

Ophelia's pathological clumsiness was notorious within her family. No one would have risked asking her for maple syrup with all that clockwork around the place.

"It pains me to admit it, but for once I don't think the Doyennes were wrong. You're a fright to behold, and I think it's good for you to do something with your hands." Aunt Rosaline gave her niece a stern look, focusing on her drawn face, colorless glasses, and plait of hair so tangled that no comb could get through it.

"I'm fine."

"No, you're not fine. You don't go out anymore, you eat any old thing, you sleep at any old time. You haven't even been back to the museum," Aunt Rosaline added, solemnly, as if that particular detail were the most concerning of all.

"In fact, I have been back," countered Ophelia. She had rushed straight there on her return from the Pole, as soon as she'd got off the airship, before even dropping her suitcase off at home. She had wanted to see with her own eyes the cabinets stripped of their weapon collections, the rotunda stripped of its military aircraft, the walls stripped of their imperial standards, and the alcoves stripped of their ceremonial armor.

She had left the place distraught, and had never returned.

"It's no longer a museum," she muttered between her teeth. "Relating the past but refusing to relate war, that's lying."

"You are a reader," Aunt Rosaline rebuked her. "Surely you're not just going to stay with your fingers crossed until . . . until . . . In short, you must go forward."

Ophelia refrained from retorting that she wasn't crossing her fingers and that going forward didn't interest her. She'd done much research in recent months, without leaving her bed, nose buried in geographical tomes. It was *elsewhere* that she had to go, except that she couldn't. Not as long as the Doyennes were keeping a close eye on her.

Not as long as God was keeping a close eye on her.

"It would be better to leave your watch at home during

Tickers," Aunt Rosaline suddenly declared. "It's stirring up the others."

Some clocks had, indeed, flocked around the waffle stand. Ophelia instinctively laid her hand over her pocket, and then indicated to the dials to go and tick somewhere else. "That's typically Anima, that is. One can't carry an unruly watch around without sensing the disapproval of all those in the vicinity."

"You should get it treated by a clockmaker."

"I have. It isn't broken, just very troubled. Merry Tickers, dear uncle."

Wrapped in his old winter coat, his moustache heavy with melted snow, her great-uncle had just sprung out from the crowd. "Yeah, yeah, happy festival, tick-tock, and the rest of it," he mumbled, going straight to the other side of the stand and helping himself to a hot waffle. "It's getting ridiculous, all this bunkum! Festival of Silverware, Festival of Musical Instruments, Festival of Boots, Festival of Hats . . . Every year, a new booze-up in the calendar! Soon you'll see 'em celebrating chamber pots. In my day, we didn't spoil objects like they do now, and then they're surprised that they throw tantrums. Hide this, pronto," he suddenly whispered, handing an envelope to Ophelia.

"You've found another one?" As she slipped the envelope into her apron pocket, Ophelia felt her heart beating faster than all the festival's clocks.

"And no mere trifle, m'dear. Finding them's not too hard. Doing it without the Doyennes knowing, that's quite another matter. They spy on me almost as much as on you. Watch out, in fact," the great-uncle muttered, shaking his moustache. "I saw the Rapporteur, with her confounded sparrow, lurking around the place."

Aunt Rosaline gritted her long teeth on hearing their

exchange. She was perfectly aware of their little schemes, and although she didn't approve of them, fearing that Ophelia would get herself into more trouble, she was often their accomplice. "I'm starting to run low on waffle batter," she said, drily. "Go and fetch me some, please."

Ophelia needed no persuading to slip into the provisions store. It was freezing cold in there, but she was away from prying eyes. She soothed the scarf, which was getting restless on its peg, checked that no one was around, and then opened the envelope from her great-uncle.

It contained a picture postcard. The caption read, "XXII$^{nd}$ Interfamilial Exhibition," and the postmark dated back more than 60 years. As a worthy family archivist, her great-uncle must have used his contacts to get hold of this card. It was the photograph that interested Ophelia. The black-and-white image, tinted here and there with artificial colors, depicted the exhibitors' displays and the exotic curiosities along the aisles of a massive building. It was like Anima's covered market, but a hundred times more imposing. Pushing her glasses up on her nose, the young girl held the postcard closer to the light. She finally found what she was looking for: through the building's large windows, almost invisible in the fog outside, stood a headless statue.

For the first time in a long while, Ophelia's glasses colored with emotion. Her great-uncle had just brought her the confirmation of all her hypotheses.

"Ophelia!" called Aunt Rosaline. "Your mother's asking for you!"

At these words, she quickly hid the postcard. The surge of excitement that had overcome her instantly dissipated, to be replaced by frustration. It was even beyond that. The waiting, the endless waiting was digging a hole within her body. Each new day, each new week, each new month made that hole bigger. Ophelia sometimes wondered whether she wouldn't end up falling in on herself.

She took out the fob watch and lifted the cover with utmost care. The poor mechanism was suffering enough as it was, Ophelia couldn't risk any clumsiness. Since she had retrieved it from Thorn's belongings, just before being forcibly repatriated to Anima, the watch had never told the time. Or rather, it told a few too many times at once. All its hands pointed now one way, now another, with no apparent logic—four twenty-two, seven thirty-eight, five past one—and no longer the slightest tick-tock.

Two years and seven months of silence.

Ophelia had received no news from Thorn after his escape. Not a single telegram, not a single letter. She could keep telling herself that he couldn't run the risk of making contact, that he was a man wanted by the law, perhaps by God himself, but it was eating her up inside.

"Ophelia!"

"I'm coming."

She grabbed a pot of waffle batter and left the provisions store. On the other side of the stand stood her mother, in her enormous, flouncy dress.

"My daughter, who finally deigns to leave her bed! About time—any longer and you'd have turned into a bedside table! Merry Tickers, darling. Serve the little ones, would you?"

Her mother indicated the long line of children accompanying her. Ophelia saw among them her brother, sisters, nephews, second cousins, and the sitting-room clock. They weren't that "little" in her eyes. Hector had shot up so much in recent months, he'd more than caught up with Ophelia. Seeing them all like this, with their height, their flaming hair, and their freckles, she sometimes wondered whether she really belonged to the same family.

"I discussed your case with Agatha," Ophelia's mother said, leaning her entire bust over the stand. "Your sister agrees with me, you must think about finding yourself a job. She's spoken about it with Charles, and they both agree to you coming to work at the factory. Just take a look at yourself, my girl! You can't carry on like this. You're so young! Nothing still binds you to . . . you know . . . *him*."

Ophelia's mother had mouthed that last word without actually saying it. No one in the family ever mentioned Thorn, as if it were a shameful subject. In general, no one ever mentioned the Pole. There were days when Ophelia wondered whether all she'd lived through over there was actually real, as though she'd never been a valet, or a vice-storyteller, or a great family reader.

"Do thank Agatha and Charles, Mom, but it's a no. I can't see myself working in lace."

"I can have her with me at the archives," her great-uncle growled into his moustache.

Ophelia's mother pursed her lips so tight, her face looked like bellows. "You have a deplorable influence on her, uncle. The past, the past, always the past! My daughter must think about her future."

"Ah, that!" he said, with irony. "You'd like her to be as conformist as those nice little books in the library, hey? Might as well send her out into the sticks, your kid."

"I would particularly like her to give a favorable impression to the Doyennes and Artemis, just for a change."

Ophelia was so exasperated that she mistakenly handed a waffle to the family clock. It was no use—she could keep repeating to everyone that a Doyenne was not to be trusted, no one listened to her. She would have liked to warn them about so many more things! About God, in particular. And yet she'd spoken of him to no one; neither to her parents,

23

who endlessly questioned her, nor to Aunt Rosaline, who fretted over her silence, nor to her great-uncle, who was helping her with her research. The whole family knew something had occurred in Thorn's cell—the less informed thinking it was Ophelia who had been imprisoned—but no one had ever obtained the final word from her on this story. She couldn't utter it, not after what she'd discovered about God.

Mother Hildegarde had killed herself because of him.

Baron Melchior had killed for him.

Thorn had almost been killed by him.

The very existence of God was a dangerous truth. For as long as was required, Ophelia would keep the secret.

"I know you're all worrying about me," she finally declared, "but it's *my* life that this is about. I don't have to explain myself to anyone, not even to Artemis, and I don't give a damn what the Doyennes think."

"Much good that will do you, dear girl!"

Ophelia stiffened on seeing a middle-aged woman stealthily approaching the stand. She wore no watch, walked no clock, but sported an extraordinary hat, on top of which a weather vane in the form of a stork was spinning at full speed. Her gold-rimmed spectacles further enlarged two protruding eyes, which watched every move of the Animists in general, and Ophelia in particular. If the Doyennes were the accomplices of God, the Rapporteur was that of the Doyennes.

"Your daughter is a freethinker, my dear Sophie," she said, smiling benevolently at Ophelia's mother. "Every family has to have one! She doesn't want to return to her work at the museum? Let's respect her choice. She doesn't want to work in lace? Let's not force her hand. Let her fly with her own wings . . . Maybe she needs a change of scenery?"

In one movement, the Rapporteur's eyes and weather vane turned to Ophelia. She had to struggle to stop herself from checking that her great-uncle's postcard wasn't poking out from her apron pocket.

"You're encouraging me to leave Anima?" she asked, warily.

"Oh, we're not encouraging you to do anything at all!" the Rapporteur hastily countered, cutting off Ophelia's mother, whose mouth was already wide open. "You're a big girl, now. You're a free agent."

This woman definitely lacked subtlety; that was why she'd never be a Doyenne herself.

Ophelia knew only too well that the second she'd board an airship, they would have her followed and keep a close eye on her. She wanted to find Thorn, yes, but she had no intention of leading God to him. At such times, more than ever, she regretted not being able to use mirrors to leave Anima: her power, unfortunately, had its limits.

"Thank you," she said, once she'd finished distributing the waffles to the children. "I think I'd still rather stay in my room. Merry Tickers, madame."

The Rapporteur's smile became strained. "Our dearest mothers are doing you an immense honor—an immense honor, do you hear?—in concerning themselves with a small person like you. So stop with all your little secrets and confide in them. They could help you, and much more than you think."

"Merry Tickers," Ophelia repeated, drily. Suddenly, the Rapporteur jerked backwards, as if she had received an electric shock. She stared at Ophelia first with stupefaction, then with indignation, before turning on her heels. She rejoined a phalanx of old ladies in the midst of the procession of clocks. Doyennes. They merely nodded their heads as they listened to the Rapporteur, but the look they directed at Ophelia from a distance was frosty.

"You did it!" Ophelia's mother exclaimed, furiously. "You used that ghastly power! On the Rapporteur herself!"

"Not deliberately. If the Doyennes hadn't forced me to leave the Pole, Berenilde could have taught me how to control my claws." Ophelia had muttered these words while giving an annoyed wipe to the stand. She couldn't get used to this new power. She'd injured no one up to now—she'd cut no nose, sliced no finger—but if someone caused her to dislike them too much, it was always the same: *something* within her was triggered to push them away. And that definitely wasn't the best way to resolve a disagreement.

"You're not doing yourself any favors like this," hissed Ophelia's mother, while pointing a red nail at her. "I've had it up to my hat with seeing you lounging in your bed and defying our dearest mothers. Tomorrow morning you will go to your sister's factory, and that's the end of it!"

Ophelia waited until her mother had left with the children before leaning with both hands on the waffle stand and taking a deep breath. The hole she could feel inside her stomach had just got bigger.

"Your mother can say what she likes," muttered her great-uncle, "you can come and work at the archives."

"Or at the restoration studio with me," Aunt Rosaline added, encouragingly. "I know of nothing more gratifying than cleansing paper of its mites and mildew."

Ophelia didn't respond to them. She had no desire to go either to the lace factory or to the family archives or to the restoration studio. What she did desire from the depths of her being was to escape the Doyennes' vigilance in order to get to the place depicted on the postcard.

Where maybe Thorn was to be found at this very moment.

"First mezzanine."

"Gentlemen's bathroom"

"Don't forget your scarf—you're leaving."

Ophelia stood up so abruptly, she knocked the bottle of

maple syrup over on the stall. With cheeks burning, she searched among the kitchen clocks and pendulum clocks for the person who had whispered those three thoughts in her ear. He was already out of sight.

"What's got into you?" asked Aunt Rosaline, surprised, as she saw Ophelia hastily throwing her coat on over her apron.

"I have to go to the bathroom."

"Are you unwell?"

"I've never felt so well," Ophelia said, with a big smile. "Archibald has come for me."

# THE SHORTCUT

In truth, as Ophelia went discreetly up the stairs, along with her great-uncle, Aunt Rosaline, and her scarf, she hadn't a clue how Archibald had turned up here, right in the middle of an Animist festival, or why he'd asked her to meet him in the bathroom. "You're leaving," he'd told her. If he intended to make her leave Anima, wouldn't it have been better to meet up outside, as far away from the crowd and the Doyennes as possible?

"You should have watched over the stand," muttered Ophelia. "As soon as they notice that no one's doing waffles anymore, they'll be looking for us." She was talking to Aunt Rosaline, who was lugging, under both arms, all she'd been able to grab in the rush of leaving.

"You can't be serious," she said, indignantly. "If there's the remotest chance of returning to the Pole, I'm coming too!"

"And your work at the studio? What you were telling me about mites and mildew?"

"It's vipers and the depraved that Berenilde is confronting alone, since our departure. She's worth far more in my eyes than a piece of paper."

Ophelia felt her heart leap at the sight of Archibald, at the other end of the mezzanine. He was calmly waiting in front of the door to the restroom, wrapped in a patched-up old cape, his top hat askew. He wasn't even attempting to hide, which would have been a sensible precaution—however, even dressed as a tramp, he was the kind of man who attracted attention, of ladies in particular.

"It's not a trap, at least?" grumbled the great-uncle, holding Ophelia back by the shoulder. "That chap, over there, can he be trusted?"

Ophelia thought it best not to express her opinion on this. She trusted Archibald to a certain extent, but he certainly wasn't the most virtuous man she knew. She continued along the mezzanine walkway, avoiding showing herself at the railings. From here, all she could see of the festivities was a roiling sea of hats and clock dials, with much telling of time, winding of watches, and wishing of "Merry Tickers!"

"I did warn you, Madam Thorn!" Archibald called out, by way of greeting. "If you don't come to the Pole, the Pole will come to you."

He opened the door to the bathroom as though it were that of a fine carriage, and, with a flourish, invited them all to come in.

"What's going on here? Who is this individual?" Breathless from rushing up the stairs, her weather vane trained on them, the Rapporteur had just reached the mezzanine in a frenzy.

"Go in quickly," said Archibald, pushing Ophelia inside. Aunt Rosaline and the great-uncle hurried after her and skidded on the tiled floor, searching for an emergency exit. There was nothing but urinals around them. Ophelia would have liked to ask Archibald where they were supposed to escape; unfortunately, he was too busy preventing the Rapporteur from coming in, too. She'd been so quick, she'd managed to block the door with one of her boots.

"Dearest mothers!" she shrieked. "She's trying to escape! Do something!"

These words triggered mayhem inside the bathroom. With an appalling rumbling noise, the urinals, toilet bowls, and basins started disgorging all their water. The Doyennes' Animism was already at work. All public establishments obeyed their command, and the traditional covered market was no exception.

"We can't stay here forever," Ophelia shouted to Archibald over the din of all the water. "What's your plan?"

"To close this door." He had said this without dropping his smile, as if it were all just a minor hitch.

"And after that?" she insisted.

"After that, you will be free."

Ophelia didn't understand. She stared at the Rapporteur's hand, which had just slipped between the gap in the door; she knew Archibald well enough to know that he would never break a lady's fingers.

"Move over, sonny!" growled the great-uncle. "I'll sort out this pest, you help the girl to get away." With these words, he swept out of the bathroom, dragging the Rapporteur with him.

Archibald slammed the door, and silence descended with it. An eerie, baffling silence. All the water had stopped pouring out of the pipes. The cries of the Rapporteur could no longer be heard. All the tick-tocking of the festival had ceased. Ophelia began to wonder whether Archibald hadn't stopped time itself. When they went back out, there was no more mezzanine, or great-uncle, or Rapporteur, or market. Instead, there was a deserted shop in which one could make out rows of empty shelves. Judging by the strong musty smell, this business had been closed for a long time.

"Mind the step," warned Archibald.

Cautiously, Ophelia and Aunt Rosaline left the restrooms, stepping down onto the floor of the shop. They understood why when they glanced back: they had just come out of a wardrobe.

"How did you pull that trick off?"

"I called up a shortcut" said Archibald, as if it were obvious. "Don't be too impressed—it's only temporary. See for yourselves." He closed and then reopened the door of the wardrobe. Old bric-a-brac had replaced the men's restrooms. It made one wonder how three people could have emerged from such a confined piece of furniture.

"The market has gotten its restrooms back," Archibald added, looking delighted. "Imagine the look on the face of that weather vane woman when she'll find us no longer there."

Ophelia wrung out her sodden scarf and slightly opened the curtains of the shopwindow. The glass had misted up, but she could make out a little cobbled street, partly covered in snow, and full of muffled-up passersby, all endeavoring not to slip. Further down, under a pallid sky, a barge edged slowly along the half-frozen water of a canal.

"I recognize this place," Aunt Rosaline said, over her shoulder. "We're not far from the Great Lakes."

Ophelia was a bit disappointed. Their escape had been so phenomenal, she'd hoped for a moment to have left Anima.

"How did you pull that trick off?" she insisted.

Archibald was a very resourceful man, as capable of getting into people's heads as into ladies' hearts, but this, it really defied comprehension.

"It's a long story," he said, rummaging in the hole-riddled pockets of his cape. "It so happens that I've found myself some new opportunities, new ambitions, and new loves!"

He had declared that while triumphantly pulling out a bunch of keys. Ophelia studied him in the half-light of the shop. The last time she'd seen him, on the Citaceleste landing stage, he'd been but a shadow of himself. Today, a sun shone in

31

the sky of his eyes, and that brightness was very different to the bittersweet arrogance that was typical of him in former times.

Ophelia tensed up in spite of herself. Was it truly Archibald whom she was following like this? She'd had no dealings with God since their confrontation in Thorn's cell, but she didn't forget that he could assume any face he liked.

"How did you know where to find me?"

"I didn't," retorted Archibald. "I've just spent two hours in a freezing-cold ferry, and another hour asking my way in the streets of your little valley. When I finally located your parents' house, you weren't there. I can only summon a shortcut between two places I've already been to, so you made my life difficult! If you ladies would care to follow me," he continued, heading for the back of the shop.

But Ophelia no longer really felt like hurrying. "Why bring us here?"

"Is Berenilde with you?" asked Aunt Rosaline, in turn.

"And Thorn?" Ophelia couldn't help but add.

"Whoa, whoa!" Archibald said, laughing. "I brought you here because this is where I arrived. My calling up short-cuts has its limits. That dear Berenilde isn't with me, no. She doesn't even know I'm here . . . and she'll dismember me if I don't return to the Pole soon," he said, checking the time. "As for the elusive Mr. Thorn, we've received no news from him since his escape."

The hope that had risen in Ophelia at the appearance of Archibald collapsed like a soufflé. For one crazy moment, she'd thought that it was Thorn himself who had initiated the rescue. She glanced warily at the back of the shop, where Archibald was: it appeared to have been abandoned even longer than the front. "This is where you arrived? I don't understand."

Archibald tried several keys in the lock before producing a resounding click. "After you, ladies!"

Contrary to what Ophelia had imagined, the passageway didn't lead to a cellar, but to a rotunda as vast as a station concourse. A diaphanous, almost unreal light came through the cupola's high windows. The entire floor was a huge mosaic; it depicted a star, of which the eight corners pointed toward doors positioned like compass points. This place was as grandiose as the adjoining shop was grotty.

Several silver-plated signs reiterated the same message: WE WISH YOU A SMOOTH DOOR TRANSIT.

"A Compass Rose," murmured Ophelia. And judging by its scale, this was an interfamilial one. It was the first time Ophelia had set foot inside one of these. Shame it had to be just after being drenched in the restrooms—she made a squelching sound with every step, which wasn't the best look.

"I'd heard that there were some on Anima, but I only half-believed it." Even though Ophelia wasn't speaking loudly, the mosaic and the windows made the sound of her voice soar across the whole rotunda.

"There's only one of them," Archibald corrected, locking the door behind him. "And like every self-respecting Compass Rose, its location is confidential. It would have suited me if this one were a tad closer to your home."

At the center of the rotunda stood a counter, on which Ophelia was astonished to discover a little girl. Lying on her belly, she was drawing with utmost concentration. She was so quiet as to be almost unnoticeable.

"Ladies, you have before your eyes my new opportunities and my new ambitions," Archibald declared, gesturing proprietorially around the entire room. "As for my new loves, here they are!" He lifted the little girl from the counter and held her aloft like a trophy. "My dear Victoria, allow me to introduce you to your godmother and your godmother's godmother."

In her surprise, Aunt Rosaline dropped everything she'd

brought along with her: umbrella, muff, shawl, and waffle spatula. "Prams alive, Berenilde's little girl! And the spitting image of her, too."

Moved, and somewhat daunted, Ophelia considered the little girl, who stared back at her with big, light eyes. Berenilde's eyes. Otherwise, Victoria actually took more after her father. Her face was ethereally pale, and her hair, abnormally long for her age, appeared more white than blond. She also had that strange way of parting her lips without uttering a sound, recalling Farouk's interminable silences.

"She still doesn't know how to talk or walk," Archibald warned them, while shaking Victoria as if she were a talking doll whose mechanism was defective. "Her family power hasn't got going, either. But don't go thinking she's stupid—she already understands more than all my ex-sisters put together."

Aunt Rosaline frowned, suspiciously. "Does Berenilde at least know her child is here? You're still as irresponsible as ever!" she said, exasperated, on seeing Archibald's smile widen. "The child of a family spirit! Are you hoping for a diplomatic incident? Really, you're worth not a bean as an ambassador."

"I am no longer ambassador. It's my ex-sister Patience who now performs that function. My clan has crossed me off the register of the living, since you-know-what." Archibald mimed the cutting of scissors with his fingers. "Don't judge me too harshly, Madame Rosaline. Victoria has inherited a mother who would like to keep her in the cradle, and a father who can never remember her name. It's my role as godfather to offer her a stimulating life . . . And don't listen to all the spiteful gossips calling you retarded, young lady!" Archibald then declared, making Victoria's head disappear under his old top hat. "I personally predict for you that you will achieve great things."

Ophelia was overtaken by sudden emotion. Those weren't exactly the words her great-uncle had said to her about her engagement, but they were pretty similar. It suddenly struck her that had the Doyennes not meddled, she could have watched Victoria growing up, and also acted as a proper god-mother herself. She might even have already found Thorn, by this time. In any case, she wouldn't have spent two years clois-tered in her room while the rest of the world kept moving on.

"How does this Compass Rose work, and how far can it take us? I'd like to put as much distance as possible between the Doyennes and—"

The "me" never left Ophelia's lips. With a theatrical flour-ish, Archibald had just pulled back a curtain that had con-cealed a large round table behind the counter; leaning over it were Gail and Fox. They were busy taking notes and were both wearing, below their Russian fur hats, binocular magnifying glasses that made them barely recognizable. A large ginger cat, which Ophelia presumed to be Twit, was rubbing against their legs to get their attention, but they were each so focused that nothing seemed to exist for them beyond the table.

At least, so Ophelia thought until Fox gave her a wink, magnified by the lens, between note-taking. With his athletic frame, bushy eyebrows, and abundant red side-whiskers, he looked more than ever like a chimney.

"Hello, boss. We'll finish our calculations and be all yours. If we stop right in the middle, we'd have to go back over the itinerary from the start, and that would put my other boss into a bad mood."

"Stop with all your 'bosses,'" grumbled Gail, without rais-ing her binocular magnifying glasses from the table. "You're a trade unionist, talk like a trade unionist."

"Yes, boss."

The further the day progressed, the more Ophelia wondered whether she hadn't fallen asleep at her waffle stand and was now dreaming!

"My traveling companions!" declared Archibald, still balancing little Victoria on one arm. "We wouldn't make a very pretty picture, but that aside, we make a good team. I root out the Compass Roses, and they decode them. Seven of the eight doors here lead onto other arks, where other access points are to be found. Each Compass Rose is like this one in every respect: eight doors, a counter, a table of itineraries. You can't imagine how many transits we had to make just to get from the Pole to Anima, and I'm not talking about our wrong turnings."

Ophelia took a closer look at the round table and saw that its marble was entirely engraved with numbers, symbols, and lines of direction. The map of the Compass Rose network was like the most nightmarish of brain-teasers. Fox and Gail pointed out lines to each other, used measuring instruments, and then jotted down directions. They didn't touch each other, didn't look at each other, didn't speak to each other; and yet, from the way they stood close to each other, Ophelia *knew*. She looked away, suddenly embarrassed to be watching them like this, as though intruding on their privacy. Stroking Twit, who had turned to her for what he couldn't get elsewhere, she was disconcerted to see how much he, too, had grown.

She couldn't shake the unpleasant feeling of having missed a stair. An entire stairway, even.

"What's a trade unionist?" she asked Archibald. He had just put Victoria down, who immediately continued with her drawing on the counter.

"Oh, a new fad back at home. Compensatory rest, increased salaries, reduced working hours—it's as if old Hildegarde were more alive than ever, putting her crazy ideas into the heads of servants. Customs have greatly changed since your departure."

"You, too, have changed," observed Ophelia. "Are you going to explain to me how you go about calling up shortcuts and unlocking Compass Roses? I thought only the Arkadians were capable of doing so."

Archibald retrieved his top hat from Victoria's head and spun it around on his finger. "I've already spoken to you about Augustine, my great-grandfather. And the little fling he had with old Hildegarde. Do you remember?"

Ophelia looked at Archibald with amazement. She was still crouching in front of the cat, her hand suspended mid-stroke, not noticing that now he was scrapping with her scarf. "You and Madam Hildegarde? You would be her . . . "

"Great-grandson, yes," giggled Archibald. "Oh, it's a scandal that was carefully hushed up. I wouldn't have known about it myself had I not suddenly started performing magic tricks. It started last year, one afternoon when I was particularly sleepy, the day after a wedding—I'll spare you the details. I went into my bathroom; I landed instead in the courtesans' thermal baths. Just like that," he said, snapping his fingers, "from one end of Citaceleste to the other. And then I had the same experience again, and I set about creating transits more and more often. Give me a door, an enclosed space, and I'll summon a shortcut for you. That's how, one day, I came across an authentic Compass Rose. It was concealed in a fold within space and I . . . it's hard to describe . . . I sensed its presence, do you see? Don't ask me how it works, but if I turn a key in the lock of a door close to a Compass Rose, abracadabra, there we are! Any key of any door. It's a pretty far-fetched power that old Hildegarde passed on to me, that one, but I adore it."

While trying to separate cat and scarf, Ophelia had greatly to stretch her imagination to superimpose her memory of Mother Hildegarde on the man standing before her.

"And you'd never been aware of something so obvious before then?" Aunt Rosaline cut in, with her usual pragmatism.

Archibald tapped the teardrop tattoo between his eyebrows.

"It's the severing of the link with the Web that released my other family power. It was hibernating within me, patiently waiting for its time to come. And you, Madam Thorn?" he asked, point-blank. "What have you been up to these past two years?"

Ophelia opened, and then closed her mouth. Archibald had learnt to master a new power, Fox had become a trade unionist, but she, what had she spent her time doing? She'd remained imprisoned in an interminable parenthesis. No. It was even worse than that. She'd gone backwards, slipping into her old skin of solitary adolescent. She'd even put on weight, to top it all.

"I read," she finally replied.

"Right, enough of the small talk," Gail interrupted them, brusquely. "There's a more pressing question to be settled." She finally lifted her nose from the itinerary table and shook away the dark curls hindering her view. Her differently colored eyes, one black as night, the other blue as day, were inordinately enlarged by her binocular magnifying glasses. They may have been different, but they expressed the same cold rage as they looked deep into Ophelia's glasses.

"Does God exist?"

# THE DESTINATION

Time seemed to be holding its breath inside the Compass Rose. Ophelia, still tugging on her scarf to free it from Twit's claws, looked from Gail to Fox to Archibald to Aunt Rosaline, who all suddenly appeared to expect her to answer their every existential question.

"Before going any further," said Archibald, casually sitting on the itinerary table, "you must understand what has brought us all here. We're investigating the death of old Hildegarde. Apart from Thorn, you are the only person still alive to have witnessed her final moments. You're also the only one to know what was really behind that business of the GOD letters, in which she was implicated."

The word "GOD" echoed around the Compass Rose, which had the resonance of an ancient cathedral. That single mention made Ophelia remember Baron Melchior and his deadly blackmail; Mother Hildegarde sucked into her own pocket; the corpses in the Imaginoir; the fingers sliced off by Thorn.

Oh yes, she knew exactly what it was all about. She still had nightmares about it.

"And then there was Farouk's breakdown," Archibald continued, cheerily, as though telling a good joke. "The entire court witnessed his inexplicable behavior, and the way you brought him back to reason. You alone. With but a few words."

39

*"Your Book is but the start of your story, Odin. It's up to you alone to write the ending."* Ophelia remembered that, too, very clearly. Except that they weren't her words; they were God's words, uttered a very long time ago.

"Farouk hasn't been the same since," continued Archibald. "Lackadaisical and head-in-the-clouds, yes, but when it comes to the future of his family, he's showing himself to be almost . . . how can I put it? Almost concerned."

"Except it's the Mother we're talking about here," Gail said, losing patience. She walked around the table and pressed her magnifying lenses against Ophelia's glasses. Ophelia noticed that Gail had sewn—rather badly, in fact—an orange motif onto her flapped Russian hat. The orange was Mother Hildegarde's emblem. "Listen to me carefully, my dear. The Mother knew her days were numbered. She knew that something else exists, something not very pleasant, something bigger than the family spirits, something beyond all that." Gail thumbed over her shoulder to indicate the entire Compass Rose. "The Mother tried to talk to me, to prepare me, but me, I didn't listen to her. I just wanted to stay hidden in my corner. I was scared of ending up like the rest of my clan."

An abrupt silence followed these words, a silence inhabited by the deceased souls of all the Nihilists. Ophelia had wondered why Gail seemed so annoyed with her, but now she understood that it was against herself that her anger was directed.

"You broke my monocle," Gail grumbled. "For that, you owe me an apology. And me, I owe you thanks. Without it, I couldn't hide what I really am from others for long. It was the kick in the pants I needed. The Mother was like a family to me, and I'm tired of behaving like an ungrateful brat. So, I want you to tell me right now, face-to-face: does God exist, and is it because of him that the Mother is dead?"

"Yes."

Ophelia's response produced an immediate effect. Gail let out a volley of swearwords, Fox pushed his magnifying lenses up onto his forehead, Archibald burst out laughing, and Aunt Rosaline pursed her lips. Only Victoria continued to scratch away at her drawing with her pencil, unperturbed.

Ophelia straightened up her glasses, skewed by Gail. Before disappearing, Thorn had advised her to speak to no one of what she knew, but she didn't have the right to stay silent any longer. "Do you remember the Carnival Caravan?"

"The circus troupe?" Fox asked, surprised. "The one we visited with your little brother?"

"God was travelling in their midst, passing himself off as a Metamorphoser." Ophelia cleared her throat. The memory of what she'd witnessed that night, in Thorn's cell, still gave her the sensation of having swallowed sand. "He is much more than a Metamorphoser. God can reproduce the appearance, voice, and family power of all those whom he has approached. That's why he wanted to provoke a meeting with Mother Hildegarde—he coveted her mastery of space. And that's why Mother Hildegarde had entrenched herself in a non-place, behind a security cordon; she knew that whoever tried to cross that line would become more dangerous because of her. And that's not all," she continued, after another throat clearing. "God is the creator of the family spirits and, as such, considers himself the parent of us all. He imposes his law on us without our knowledge, with the help of men and women he calls 'the Guardians.' Oh, and a final detail," she hastened to add, with a tense smile. "Thorn's claws had no effect on him."

She paused for a moment to assess the impact of her words on her audience, but that was no easy task: everyone around her had frozen in astonishment. Even Archibald, who had been rubbing his hands with excitement, had finally stopped, mid-movement.

"I have put you all in danger just by speaking to you of this," continued Ophelia. "I don't know what your plans are exactly, but be extremely careful. The Guardians are the eyes and ears of God, across all the arks. It's impossible to determine with any certainty who is in his service, and who isn't. I'm telling you this because you are the people whom I trust the most."

It was Aunt Rosaline who was first to break the general paralysis. She crossed the room in a few energetic strides, long enough to calm herself down, her heels clicking on the mosaic and resonating right up to the cupola. Then she rubbed her forehead, sighing. "That's you all over, that is. When it comes to getting yourself into a fix, there are no half-measures."

Ophelia clenched her jaws. Her godmother didn't know how right she was. If God had told the truth, he wasn't the one to be most feared in the situation. There was the Other. That unidentifiable entity she'd freed from the mirror. That angel of the apocalypse who apparently broke up the world, and who, still according to God, was preparing to complete his work.

*"Sooner or later, whether you want to or not, you will lead me to him."*

Had a link really been created between Ophelia and this Other? The only memory she retained—a distant, confused memory—was that of her own reflection in the mirror of her childhood bedroom, on the night of her first passage through a mirror. Since then, contrary to what God had predicted, no ark had disintegrated. Sure, sections of earth sometimes went crashing into the void, but that could just as easily have been due to natural erosion. No, truly, the more Ophelia thought about it, the less she saw the point of panicking everyone with a story as nebulous as that of the Other.

She suddenly realized, from the way he was waiting, head

tilted to one side, that Archibald had asked her a question. "Sorry? You were saying to me?"

"That it was rather strange. On the one hand, you assert to us that God created the family spirits. On the other, you assert that he covets their family powers. To me, something doesn't feel quite right."

"There are many things that I don't understand myself," admitted Ophelia. "Why, for example, did God formerly say to the family spirits that they were free to make their own choices, only to make them his puppets today? For one reason or another, his plans have changed."

Archibald merely nodded with his chin. Sitting on the itinerary table, legs crossed and hands clasping knee, one might have thought he was just chatting about the weather. "And when he doesn't adopt the appearance of a mortal, what is God's face like then?"

"I've not seen it," replied Ophelia. "I don't even know if he's got one. What I do know, on the other hand, is that he has no reflection. And that he has a tendency to make slips of the tongue," she added, cautiously, "but I don't know to what extent that's a reliable distinguishing feature."

Archibald jumped off the table and exchanged a knowing wink with Gail and Fox, before returning to Ophelia. "Would you like to search for LandmArk with us?"

"LandmArk?"

"Old Hildegarde's native ark."

"I know that, but why LandmArk?"

"Because if Hildegarde knew about God, the odds are that her family does, too. You see, the Arkadians hold Compass Roses on every ark. They've been observing all that takes place across the world for generations. I believe they're extremely well-informed. The problem is that all the Arkadians have deserted the Compass Roses; we've not yet encountered a single one of them." With an eloquent flourish, Archibald opened a drawer at random and took out all manner of printed material—cards, stamps, passports, certificates—as if, now, they all belonged to him. "No problem, we'll go and look for them all the way to their home, if need be!"

"And you were waiting for me for that?" Ophelia asked with surprise.

Archibald shook his head, in a flurry of blond hair. "We didn't wait for you at all. In fact, we've been looking for them for a while. No, for the moment, we're feeling our way, experimenting, roaming. That's how we ended up finding the way to Anima. For technical explanations, it's your turn." Archibald bowed to Gail, who simply pushed him aside and banged the itinerary table with the flat of her hand.

"For weeks, now, we've been studying these coordinates! A whole load of blasted doors leading to twenty major arks, a hundred and eighty minor arks, and the myriad little islands floating around them. But not a *single* one that leads to LandmArk," she railed, glowering at the table. "On every occasion, the Arkadians have kept this itinerary secret. And it's impossible to get there by air."

Ophelia sympathized. LandmArk didn't feature on any maps. It was even said that the entire ark was concealed in a fold within space.

"There has to be some access to it," Gail continued, hammering the table with her index finger, "but we're going to need lots of time and application to find it. The Compass Roses are conceived like railway networks on a grand scale: there are direct lines, and hundreds of connecting lines. We must find the correct branch line."

"But haven't you already been to LandmArk several times?" Ophelia interrupted her. "I remember that you even brought back some oranges from there."

"That particular shortcut has disappeared," Archibald replied for Gail. "I can unlock a closed-down transit, but I can't reconstruct what has been destroyed."

Ophelia contemplated the round table, with its chaos of numbers, its maze of lines and symbols, for a long time. "Why?" she murmured. "Why go to all this trouble?"

Archibald's smile became more pronounced and the glimmer in his eyes intensified. Never had Ophelia seen him so determined. "It's pretty obvious. Hildegarde was a stubborn old mule who was forever causing me problems, but she was under *my* protection. If God is responsible for her death, then God will have to explain himself personally to me."

Gail spat on the ground as a sign of approval, and Fox automatically took out a handkerchief to wipe her mouth. "I wasn't particularly fond of the old bag," he sighed, "but what's important to my boss is important to me."

"I must now take this young lady back to her mother," Archibald declared, stroking Victoria's white hair. She had ended up falling asleep on the counter, still clutching her pencil. "You're in a Compass Rose, it's up to you to choose your destination, Madame Thorn! Would you like to stay on Anima with your family? Would you like to return to the Pole with your goddaughter? Or would you like to look for LandmArk with us?"

"The Pole!" replied Aunt Rosaline, without the slightest hesitation. "We're going to return to be with Berenilde, aren't we?"

Ophelia bit her lip. It would have been easy to say yes to Aunt Rosaline's request, or to Archibald's. She could have chosen to stay close to what was familiar to her, but that would have just deepened the void inside her. She was then seized by conflicting emotions, like those that churn the stomach when one gets on a train not knowing where it will take one, or whether one can turn back.

Ophelia gazed fondly at the stone table, engraved with the map of the Compass Roses and their destination arks.

ANIMA, the ark of Artemis, mistress of objects.
THE POLE, the ark of Farouk, master of spirits.
TOTEM, the ark of Venus, mistress of animals.
CYCLOPE, the ark of Ouranos, master of magnetism.
FLORA, the ark of Belisama, mistress of vegetation.
LEADGOLD, the ark of Midas, master of transmutation.
PHAROS, the ark of Horus, master of charm.
THE SERENISSIMA, the ark of Fama, mistress of divination.
HELIOPOLIS, the ark of Lucifer, master of lightning.
BABEL, the ark of twins Pollux and Helen, master and mistress of the senses.
THE DESERT, the ark of Djinn, master of hydropathy.
THE TARTAR, the ark of Gaia, mistress of tellurism.
ZEPHYR, the ark of Olympus, master of the winds.
TITAN, the ark of Yin, mistress of mass.
CORPOLIS, the ark of Zeus, master of metamorphosis.
SIDH, the ark of Persephone, mistress of temperature.
SELENE, the ark of Morpheus, master of dreams.
VESPERAL, the ark of Viracocha, master of phantomization.
AL-ANDALOOSE, the ark of Ra, master of empathy.
THE STAR, the neutral ark, seat of interfamilial institutions.

And, of course, the destination that didn't appear on the list: LandmArk, the ark of Janus, master of space.

Ophelia had studied them, these twenty-one major arks, in the confines of her room. She'd studied them, yes, but she felt as if she'd learnt nothing.

She pulled her great-uncle's postcard from her pocket. The

photograph had suffered during the episode in the bathroom, but on it one could still see clearly the majestic building of the XXII<sup>nd</sup> Interfamilial Exhibition.

"This is my destination," she finally declared, to everyone's surprise. "I must go to Babel. And I must go there alone."

# THE SEPARATION

Ophelia hugged the scarf tight as she contemplated the door before her. Archibald had barely closed it, with a final wink, when the light glinting through all the cracks had gone out. Ophelia turned the knob and cautiously pushed the door: plunged in darkness, a store cupboard had replaced the great rotunda of the Compass Rose. The path was closed, well and truly closed.

"I'm alone," Ophelia suddenly realized, staring wide-eyed into the dark recess. Alone in unknown territory, thousands of miles from home, with only a sixty-year-old postcard for reference. She'd dreamt of this moment for two years, and, now that she'd got to it, the thought made her dizzy.

Ophelia closed the store-cupboard door with resolve. She was afraid, yes, but she had no regrets.

She studied the location in which the Compass Rose had deposited her. A wan light filtered through the murky glass of an entrance door, defining the outlines of shovels, rakes, spades, and pots. Seemingly, a garden shed. Ophelia didn't know whose it was, but it would be best not to encounter its owner. Even on her own ark, Anima, where everything was shared, it wasn't the done thing to turn up at other people's homes unannounced.

Slipping through the shed's door as discreetly as possible,

she stopped short on the threshold: there was nothing outside. Nothing but whiteness, an unlikely and unyielding condensed whiteness. It was as if a giant eraser had made the outside world disappear, leaving nothing to be seen but a blank sheet of paper.

Ophelia looked around in all directions, feeling increasingly anxious. The shed, not adjoined to any building, was stuck in the middle of the void like a deserted little house. The air was so hot and humid that Ophelia felt stifled in her coat, and her glasses were already misting up. What if Gail and Fox had made a mistake in their calculations? What if Archibald, overconfident in his newfound power, had got it wrong?

"Where have you brought me?" muttered Ophelia.

"POLLUX'S BOTANICAL GARDENS."

Ophelia turned with a start. The voice—a disembodied voice unlike any she'd heard before—had risen up behind her, from inside the actual shed.

"Excuse me," Ophelia stammered, searching for whoever was speaking to her. "I lost my way, I didn't . . . "

"IT IS RECOMMENDED THAT VISITORS COME TO THE GARDENS DURING LOW TIDE," the voice interrupted. "EVERY CLOUD HAS A SILVER LINING."

Ophelia finally discovered where it was coming from. An articulated mannequin was standing against a wall, so stiff, so slender, and so still that it merged in with the silhouettes of shovels and rakes. The voice was coming, more precisely, from its stomach, which was punctured with little holes; its head had neither mouth nor nose nor eyes. The only item of clothing it wore was a cap like that of a stationmaster, with the words "guided visit" embroidered on it. She had only encountered a similar automaton once before: the mechanical butler of Lazarus, the famous explorer.

"Low tide?" she queried.

The mannequin didn't respond. Ophelia looked again at the whiteness beyond and realized that what she was seeing was an extraordinarily dense fog. She felt relieved. If she was in Pollux's botanical gardens, then she was in the right place. Pollux and Helen were the twin family spirits who ruled over Babel.

"When will it be low tide?" she asked, rephrasing her question.

"POLLUX'S BOTANICAL GARDENS ARE OPEN DAILY IN SUMMER FROM SUNRISE TO SUNSET," the mannequin replied, still standing to attention against its wall. "GOOD THINGS COME TO THOSE WHO WAIT."

It was still summer on Babel? Ophelia reflected that she should have studied her geographical guides more closely. She took out the postcard her great-uncle had given her and presented it to the mannequin, unsure how to proceed as it had nothing resembling eyes.

"Let's forget the tide. I have to get to the place where the XXII$^{nd}$ Interfamilial Exhibition was held. The photograph is a bit dated, but I believe the building still exists. Could you indicate to me where I—"

"POLLUX'S BOTANICAL GARDENS," the mannequin instantly replied.

Ophelia sat down on a stone pot. This mechanical guide did remind her of Lazarus's butler, encountered in the past: it only responded to basic instructions. She'd have to wait for the fog to lift; she'd have at least liked to know the time—she'd left Anima late afternoon, but there must be a time difference with Babel. The sweltering heat here was starting to make her thirsty.

Ophelia's eyes met those of her reflection in a broken pane of glass leaning against the wall. She considered for a moment her tinted glasses, her long, knotty plait, her twitching scarf, and was struck by the obvious: "I look far too much like me."

It had been hard for Ophelia to convince Aunt Rosaline not to accompany her, explaining again and again that together they would attract too much attention. But what if someone recognized her anyhow?

She started nibbling at the seams of her reader's gloves. Theoretically, it was highly unlikely that God had anticipated her arrival on Babel. She had followed that trail based on the slightest of clues: the golden mimosa, the headless soldier, and the old school. It was those three visions, triggered by reading Farouk's Book, that had led her here.

Three visions of which Ophelia had spoken only to Thorn.

According to her research, and unless she was mistaken, it was on Babel that the whole story had begun. The big story: that of the family spirits, the Books, God, and the Rupture. Maybe Ophelia could have penetrated those mysteries by following Archibald on his quest, but she would have had no chance of finding Thorn on LandmArk. No, if Thorn had reached the same conclusions as she had, and had succeeded in leaving the Pole—two things that Ophelia deemed him perfectly capable of doing—he had inevitably come to Babel.

Abruptly, she stopped nibbling her gloves, suddenly remembering that she had just the one pair left. "The fact remains, I look too much like me," she repeated, shaking her glasses to rid them of color.

Now the Doyennes had let her escape, God would soon be informed of the fact. If he had planted some Guardians on Babel, as he undoubtedly had, they would surely receive a wanted-person notification with a precise description. Ophelia would have to play it carefully to go unnoticed. She couldn't stop being nearsighted or small, but as for the rest . . .

She rummaged around the place and soon found some shears for trimming hedges. With resolve, she ineptly cut off her plait, which fell to the floor as heavily as a sheaf of hay. Ophelia checked the result in the broken pane and felt as if she now had a cohort of question marks sticking out of her head. Her hair, freed of its weight, had sprung into curls in all directions. She'd been growing it since childhood, but, curiously, when she threw that part of herself into a bag full of weeds, she felt nothing in particular. Nothing, apart from a sudden feeling of lightness. As though it weren't her hair she'd just cut, but the tie that bound her to her old life.

Next, she hid her coat under a pile of aprons; if it really was summer on Babel, she wouldn't need it. As Ophelia untied her scarf, it put up a fierce resistance.

"You're too recognizable. Don't be silly, I'm not abandoning you here. You'll stay with me, inside the bag." Ophelia released the straps of the knapsack Fox had given her. It contained dry biscuits, a siphon of sparkling water, and several items slipped in by Aunt Rosaline. As she stuffed the scarf into the bag, she let fall the false identity papers Archibald had made for her at the Compass Rose—back there, you could get absolutely anything falsified.

"My name is Eulalia," Ophelia repeated, while studying her papers. "I'm an Animist of the eighth degree and I've never set foot on my ark of origin." It would be credible as long as she avoided going into details. She knew from her great-uncle that she had a few distant cousins scattered on other arks.

She instantly felt a pang of guilt: she had left members of her own family without a word of explanation. She hoped, all the same, that they weren't too worried.

"My name is Eulalia," Ophelia repeated, pensively. Why *Eulalia*? When Archibald had asked her to choose a new name for herself, that one had come spontaneously to her lips. The more she thought about it, the more she deemed her choice ill-advised. The name sounded far too similar to her own.

Ophelia sought a more comfortable position for herself, between two sacks of grain. What about Thorn, she wondered, closing her eyes. Had he managed to create a new identity for himself after his escape? Was he at least living in decent conditions? Did he have enough to eat, he who had so little appetite?

She jumped when a burst of light hit her right in the face. She'd dozed off without even realizing it. Shielding her eyes, she saw, through the gaps between her fingers, the mechanical guide leaving the shed. The sun was streaming in through the door. Ophelia grabbed her knapsack and advanced into the light. She'd barely set foot outside before the heat took her breath away. In dispersing, the fog had unveiled a jungle of colors, an inextricable mix of leaves and springs, humus and fruits, birds and insects.

Although the wild beauty of the botanical gardens was spectacular, Ophelia couldn't appreciate it for long: assailed by unusual scents, she was hit with a sneezing fit that continued as she followed the mechanical guide through the ferns. Even without a coat, she was sweltering. The clammy air stuck to her skin and soaked her dress in perspiration. The wintry grayness of Anima was a long way away!

Through the tall grasses, Ophelia glimpsed the strange silhouettes of marsupials she'd only ever seen in books. The screeches of the monkeys, in the foliage, were like nothing she'd heard before.

"Where is the way out?" she asked the mechanical guide.

"THE TOUR OF POLLUX'S BOTANICAL GARDENS BEGINS AT THE ARBORETUM," it responded, walking straight on. "PLEASE KEEP TOGETHER."

Ophelia decided to give it the slip. As she was searching for the way she came across other mannequins who were clearing hedges and scraping moss from the paths' paving stones, stopping only to oil their joints. Each time she questioned them, they replied, "SLOW AND STEADY WINS THE RACE," and then, "ALL ROADS LEAD TO BABEL," which wasn't much help to her. There must be some Babelians here who weren't automatons, surely?

Ophelia went up some stone stairs that were dripping with bougainvillea. The higher she got, the more she gauged the scale of the gardens. They were divided into several levels, each one a veritable symphony of plants, trees, flowers, and fruits. At the lower levels, wisps of fog still clung to the palm trees.

It seemed incredible to think that, only yesterday, she was hanging around her bedroom in her nightdress. She'd spent so much time immobile, only venturing out to get croissants from the local baker for the family breakfast, that her muscles were already seizing up.

What concerned her more was the absence of mimosa. God's past was, in one way or another, linked to that tree. Ophelia had never encountered one in her life, but, since she'd had that vision of the tree, she'd researched it. Mimosas could be recognized by their clusters of golden flowers, and they grew only on very few arks. If the geographical guide hadn't been spouting nonsense, Babel should be one of those.

Ophelia finally found the botanical gardens' gates, majestic as those of an oriental palace. As she went through them, she felt as if she were leaving one world for another. A bridge as wide as a boulevard linked the gardens to a public market. Over there, a huge crowd undulated like a river between the stalls' tents. Some elephants and giraffes towered over the swarm of men, women, and automatons, as if this were the most natural of cohabitations.

Suddenly, the Tickers festival struck her as pretty tame!

She'd barely begun crossing the bridge before her head was

spinning from the aroma of spices. Dazzled by the sun, which was already high in the sky, she gazed all around her. Instinctively, her hand gripped the shoulder strap of her knapsack: the bridge she was on straddled the void. Ophelia had read, in her geographical guide, that Babel was splintered into several minor arks, but that hadn't prepared her for the spectacle unfolding before her. A multitude of floating islands bathed in a sea of unbelievably white clouds. Some were large enough to harbor a town. Others had hardly enough space to build a house. Architecture and vegetation were as one, as if the plants and stones were interwoven. The closest minor arks were linked to each other by a network of bridges and aqueducts; the furthest away were served by flying machines that Ophelia would have struggled to identify—they looked like winged trains.

She dived headlong into the crowd, and was immediately assailed by the cries of merchants, and a succession of fabrics, jewelry, lentils, beans, eggs, pimentos, melons, mangoes, bananas, and all manner of produce she didn't recognize. Her stomach was telling her she'd soon have to think about finding a meal.

"Could you direct me to this place, please?" she asked, showing her postcard to anyone she passed. With her small voice being drowned out by the surrounding hubbub, she asked her question increasingly loudly, without ever receiving a reply. Were these people ignoring her deliberately? They continued to look straight ahead, never lowering their eyes toward her.

Disconcerted, Ophelia went over to a fountain in which pink flamingos dipped their stilts. She dampened a handkerchief to cool her face, and downed a gulp of sparkling water. There, sitting on the edge of the fountain and stroking the scarf at the bottom of the bag, she took a moment to look closely at the market. The variety of skin tones, shapes, and accents was that of a cosmopolitan population; here, there wasn't just one, but several families. And yet they all seemed to form a single people in which Ophelia's role was that of intruder.

She decided not to linger any longer on this square. A patrol of men and women was cleaving the crowd. They wore breastplates over their tunics, and their spiked helmets, extended by neck-flaps, gave them a military appearance. They cast around them looks that, without being obviously menacing, were most disturbing: their pupils shone like gold. This supernatural glimmer betrayed their family power: eyesight so sharp that even a fly couldn't have escaped it.

Ophelia preferred not to deal with them. All that was close to authority was likely to be close to God. She crossed the market in the opposite direction and spotted a tram that ran on compressed air and was about to depart. It was plastered with advertising posters featuring a sun with the word "LUX" written in capital letters. The locals entered by punching tickets in a machine. Ophelia checked there was no inspector and hastened to board herself. She hadn't even caught her breath when a passenger rose from his seat to push her gently back onto the pavement. "Don't take it personally, *mademoiselle*," he apologized, politely. "You've not punched your ticket, you're not respecting the rules, I'm just doing my duty as a citizen."

"Listen, I absolutely have to get myself to there," Ophelia explained, brandishing her postcard. "Could you at least tell me how . . . " The door closed automatically, putting an end to the conversation. Ophelia's dismay turned into panic when she felt herself leaving along with the tram. The strap of her knapsack had got trapped in the door! She tugged on her bag with all her might, stumbled forward, was dragged the length of the pavement, until she could do nothing but let go.

"No!" she gasped, seeing the tram hurtle off on the tracks, bouncing her bag as it went.

The scarf was still inside it.

# THE WHAXI

Ophelia had run alongside the tracks at full speed. Soaked in sweat, covered in scratches, and stymied by a stitch in her side, she felt as if her lungs were on fire. After a bridge and a few streets, the tracks forked. Which branch had the tram taken? Which way had it gone? She looked around in all directions, searching for some indication. Nothing but a deafening maelstrom of locals, omnibuses, rickshaws, bicycles, animals, and automatons swirling around. When she raised her glasses, Ophelia felt giddy. The whole neighborhood had been conceived as a giant stairway, with each step being another street invaded by people and plants.

Despite the hubbub, Ophelia felt alone as never before. How would she get her scarf back? How would she reach Thorn? How could she have thought for one moment that she was ready to embark on such an expedition on her own? Aunt Rosaline, Archibald, Gail, and Fox had all recommended that she wait a little before rushing off, but she had heeded only her own impatience.

"Please," she shouted toward a rickshaw. "I'm looking for the tram that comes from the market." She had addressed the driver, but realized, when it lowered a faceless head in her direction, that it was a mannequin. Its passenger, dozing under the vehicle's awning, replied, sleepily, instead: "You should ask your questions to a guide, young lady."

"A guide?"

The passenger half-opened an eye, and his bulbous nose, in which a ring shone, suddenly inhaled, as though trying to sniff Ophelia from afar. "A public signaling guide. You'll find one at every crossroads. And since you're clearly not from around here, I'll give you some advice: dress yourself appropriately."

Ophelia watched the rickshaw move off. Her little gray dress wasn't exactly spotless, granted, but she was hardly going around stark naked. In the middle of the crossroads, she noticed a large statue-automaton with its eight arms all pointing in different directions; that had to be a public signaling guide.

"Er . . . the tram depot?" Ophelia asked it. Getting no response, she noticed a winding key, like that of a music box, inserted in the statue's pedestal. She freed the key from the encroaching foliage, and turned it several times.

"ASK ME A QUESTION," instructed the statue.

"The terminus of the market tram?"

"FORTUNE FAVORS THE BOLD."

"The lost-property office?"

"A GOOD DAY STARTS WITH A GOOD NIGHT."

"The XXII[nd] Interfamilial Exhibition?"

"A BIRD IN THE HAND IS WORTH TWO IN THE BUSH."

"Thanks anyhow."

Disheartened, Ophelia leant against the pedestal of the statue. Her sole possessions were now Thorn's watch and the old postcard. She no longer had either identity papers or a change of clothes, and her poor scarf was again on its lonesome in this unfathomable city.

And what if someone found the bag, Ophelia wondered, furiously rubbing her eyelids. And what if someone handed it in to Pollux's family guard? And what if God learnt that an animated scarf had been found on Babel? She'd only just arrived, but Ophelia felt she'd already jeopardized all her chances.

"Judging by your reaction, the experience was pretty disappointing."

She put her glasses back on, astonished to hear a human voice addressing her. An adolescent was seated right in front of her, arms resting on a chair of carved wood, in the shade of a large parasol. The dazzling white of his clothes brought out the bronze hue of his skin. There was something strange about him that Ophelia couldn't quite define. In truth, he would have seemed more at home in a tearoom than in the middle of the public highway. He was observing Ophelia with such curiosity that he paid no attention to the torrent of townsfolk around him.

"The public signaling guide," he finally explained, indicating the statue-automaton. "You have to give it the precise address of your destination, otherwise it won't understand you. And without wishing to offend you, *mademoiselle*, I think your accent's a bit too much for it."

The adolescent spoke himself with the typical Babel accent, which was both mellifluous and refined. Everything about him was gentle: his antelope eyes, his long, silky black hair, the fine features of his face, even the satin of his clothes. Ophelia was probably older than him, but, right now, she felt like a child before him.

"I've lost my bag and my papers," she said, in a croaky voice she wasn't proud of. "I don't know what to do. It's my first time on Babel."

The adolescent turned with difficulty in his chair, and Ophelia was struck again by the indefinable strangeness he emanated. "Take that avenue, go right to the end of it, and cross the bridge," he said, pointing eastwards. "From there you'll see a very large edifice looking like a lighthouse; once you've spotted it, you can't get lost anymore."

"And this edifice, what exactly is it?"

The adolescent smiled, faintly. "The Babel Memorial. It's over there that the XXII$^{nd}$ Interfamilial Exhibition was held. That's what you were asking the guide about, isn't it? *Pardonnez-moi, mademoiselle*, I couldn't stop myself from listening to you. My father says that curiosity is a 'fine flaw,' but I always tend to meddle in what's none of my business. And to talk too much, also," he admitted, apologetically, "but I get that from my father as well. On the subject of your bag, I'm sure you'll find it again soon. Honesty is a civic duty on Babel."

Ophelia was overcome with gratitude. This young man had restored all her courage. "Thank you, sir."

"Ambrose. Without the 'sir,' *mademoiselle*."

"O . . . Eulalia. Thank you, Ambrose."

"Good luck, *mademoiselle*."

He hesitated a moment, as if wanting to add something, then changed his mind. Ophelia crossed the junction against the traffic, to outraged cries from the cyclists and rickshaw drivers, but she couldn't resist looking back. She felt as if she'd missed an important detail. She understood what it was as she saw Ambrose struggling to maneuver his chair.

It was a wheelchair. He'd got stuck between the cobbles.

Ophelia immediately turned back, prompting a fresh wave of disapproval, and leant with all her weight on the chair to release the wheel. Ambrose looked up at her in surprise, thinking she'd already be long gone.

"It's ridiculous," he said, with an embarrassed little laugh, "I get caught out every time. That's why I'd never make a good whaxi."

"A whaxi?"

61

"A whistle-for taxi, *mademoiselle*. Anything that can move and take a passenger. You don't have them where you live?"

As Ophelia merely nodded evasively, Ambrose considered her with renewed curiosity. "I helped you. You helped me. We're friends."

This declaration was so spontaneous, Ophelia couldn't help but shake the hand he held out to her. It was at that very moment that she knew why this adolescent seemed strange: he had a left arm where his right arm should have been, a right arm where his left arm should have been. And judging by the bizarre angle of his babouches, his legs were similarly reversed. It was the most unusual disability Ophelia had ever encountered in someone—as if Ambrose had also been the victim of a mirror accident.

"If you're happy to have me as your driver, Mademoiselle Eulalia, jump on!" He turned a crank fitted to his chair, producing a prolonged clanking of gears. Ophelia perched awkwardly on the rear running board and almost fell as soon as Ambrose lowered the handbrake, propelling the chair forward. She felt the road's every cobble unrolling beneath her. On several occasions, she had to step down and release the wheels from potholes, while Ambrose raised the springs of his chair by turning the crank. The large parasol, badly attached to the back of the seat, creaked noisily in the wind, drowning out Ambrose's gentle voice as he chatted away. It was a pretty uncomfortable journey, but Ophelia stopped thinking about it the moment the chair launched onto a bridge between two arks, and Ambrose pointed into the distance with his inverted hand.

Between the infinity of the sky and the sea of clouds, a huge, spiraling tower, topped with a glass dome, stood on a floating island barely big enough to support it. An entire side of the building jutted out into the void, but so perfect was the architectural equilibrium, the whole edifice remained upright all the same.

"The Babel Memorial," declared Ambrose. "It's our oldest monument, half of it dating back to the old world. It's said that all of humanity's memory resides within it."

"Humanity's memory," Ophelia repeated to her deepest self. At the thought that Thorn might have made his way there, she felt a drumming in her chest. She leant over the seat to be heard by Ambrose, of whom she could only see waves of black hair. "Only half?"

"Part of the tower collapsed with the Rupture, but it was rebuilt by LUX centuries ago. I like going to the Memorial, there are thousands of books there! I adore books, don't you? I could spend my days reading them, on whatever subject. I attempted to write one once, but I'm as hopeless an author as I am a whaxi driver; I always get sidetracked. Don't go thinking the Memorial is some sort of old, dusty library, Mademoiselle Eulalia. It's at the cutting edge of modernity, with familio-theques, transcendiuses, and phantograms! And all thanks to LUX."

Ophelia hadn't the slightest idea what familiotheques, tran-scendiuses, and phantograms were, but the word "LUX" rang a bell. She then recalled that it was printed on all the advertising posters on the tram.

"And a headless soldier?" she asked. "Is there one there?"

Ambrose lifted his lever abruptly, braking so suddenly that Ophelia banged her head on his. "You mustn't use that word in public, *mademoiselle*," he muttered, giving her a surprised glance over his shoulder. "I don't know about where you're from, but here we have an Index."

"An Index?"

"The Index Vocabulum Prohibitorum. The list of all the words we're forbidden to say out loud. All those that have to do with . . . you know." Ambrose indicated to Ophelia to lean closer so he could whisper in her ear. "The war."

Ophelia's every muscle tensed. So, the taboos imposed by God also held sway on Babel.

"I daresay you meant the old statue, at the entrance to the Memorial," Ambrose continued, his tone lighter, as he got his chair moving again. "It's as ancient as the site."

"And how does one get to it?"

"In a birdtrain, *mademoiselle*." Before she could even ask what a birdtrain was, he went on: "But if you want to visit the Memorial or get your bag back, first you'll have to get changed. You won't be allowed entrance anywhere in that outfit."

"I don't understand," Ophelia said, frowning. "In what way is my dress a problem?"

Ambrose burst out laughing. "I invite you to my place, *mademoiselle*! There are two or three things I must explain to you."

Ambrose's residence bore no resemblance to what Ophelia would have expected the home of a whaxi driver to be like. The wheelchair moved along a portico, between the columns of which shimmered pools of water lilies. The further into the residence they went, the more distant became the sounds and smells of the street. A squad of mannequins, in servant livery, approached and opened up the high doors of the property to them. The cool of the interior prompted a sigh of relief from Ophelia; the nape of her neck, uncovered by her new haircut, was burning hot.

She stepped down from the running board and looked, nonplussed, around the atrium. Statues and automatons, marble tables and telephonic equipment, climbing plants and electric lamps all rubbed shoulders in a singular marriage of antique refinement and modern technology. This place on its own epitomized the anachronistic character of the whole city.

"Is this where you live?"

"Me and my father. Mainly me, in fact. My father isn't often at home." As he said this he indicated a full-length portrait that had pride of place on the largest wall. It depicted a man with long white hair and small, rose-tinted spectacles, through which eyes full of mischief sparkled.

"That's Lazarus, the famous ark-trotter," exclaimed Ophelia. "That man is your father? I met him once."

"I'm not surprised. Everyone knows my father and my father knows everyone."

She noticed that there was more melancholy than pride in the smile Ambrose directed at the painting. It couldn't be easy to find one's place in a life as full as that father's. "And you have no other relatives here?"

"Neither family nor friends. None that isn't an automaton, at least."

Ophelia observed the mechanical butlers, who were busy removing the parasol, rather ineptly, from the wheelchair. She tried to imagine herself growing up in the midst of these faceless bodies, whose stomachs occasionally let out a "CON-STANCY IS THE FOUNDATION OF VIRTUES," or a "BREAD ALWAYS FALLS ON THE BUTTERED SIDE."

"I told my father that the sayings weren't that effective," Ambrose sighed, "but he's as stubborn as a dromedary."

"He's the inventor of the city's automatons?" Ophelia asked, amazed. "I knew he marketed them, but I didn't realize he'd created them."

"He's one of the powerless, but he's no less of a genius. My father owes his status as a citizen solely to his own merit."

"Your family must be very important."

Ambrose frowned, as though struggling to understand Ophelia. "It's my father who's important, and even then, he's far from being as important as the Lords of LUX. But why

THE MEMORY OF BABEL

would I, myself, be? I haven't succeeded in finding my useful-
ness to the city. I'm just a kept man."

He had uttered the last two words with a shame that made
it pretty clear how degrading it was. He sped off in his wheelchair, between the inner columns, and, with forced gusto, continued to speak without pausing for breath, as though hoping
to fill the great empty spaces of his home with his voice:

"Before being a whaxi driver, I tried all kinds of little jobs,
and each one ended in failure. I'm not a manual person, you
see. Even using a typewriter seems awfully tricky to me. I often
tell myself that, had I been a Son of Pollux, I would have at
least had a heightened sense at my disposal. If, here and now,
a good fairy asked me what I'd like to be, I'd reply without
hesitation: a Visionary! It must be fascinating to see microbes
with the naked eye, don't you think? Or then an Acoustic. It's
extraordinary all that can be learnt about the world around us
merely with ultrasound. Even being an Olfactory, a Tactile, or
a Gustatory wouldn't have displeased me, but no, I had to end
up with my hands the wrong way round. My father is forever
telling me that my mere existence makes me someone of great
importance to the city. He's certainly the only one to think so."

As Ophelia followed Ambrose, somewhat dazed by his chat-
tering, she found it increasingly hard to understand this society in which throwing a stranger off a tram was approved of,
providing for the needs of one's child wasn't, and no one cared
if a young lady went alone to the home of a young man. It
seemed to her that neither the Pole nor Anima nor her guide-
books had really prepared her for Babel. This world followed
rules that were totally different from those she knew.

This feeling changed to certainty when Ambrose led her
into an elegant dressing room and opened the carved shutters
of the closets, adapted to wheelchair height. All the clothes,
neatly folded, were as white as those he was wearing.

"What you must understand, Mademoiselle Eulalia, is that here, people are exactly what they appear to be. Just as we have a civil code and a penal code, we have a very strict dress code. My father and I, for example, are legally obliged to wear white. It's the non-color of those without powers. Are you one of them?"

"Er . . . I'm an Animist. Of the eighth degree," added Ophelia, thinking of the false identity papers she'd lost.

"Of the eighth degree? With a family power that's so diluted, you can wear white, too. You're slight, but I'm not very big, either. My clothes will be almost your size."

"Because it will be less shocking for me to wear men's clothing?"

Ambrose, who was unfolding a long, white tunic, looked up at Ophelia, startled, before cracking a half-smile. "Forgive me, I'm not like my father, who knows the customs of the other arks. We don't differentiate between the sexes here. I infer that, where you're from, men don't wear clothing like yours?"

Ophelia had to stop herself from imagining Thorn in a little gray dress. "No, indeed."

"That's interesting. However, Mademoiselle Eulalia, the main problem with your dress is that its style doesn't feature in our dress code. Not respecting that code in public is seen as an act of provocation. Which is, of course, greatly disapproved of."

Ophelia raised her eyebrows. She would never have imagined that this old thing, which buttoned her up from ankle to chin, would one day make her seem like a bad girl.

"The sartorial details vary depending on age, profession, and civil status," Ambrose continued, while rummaging in his closets. "Citizens don't wear the same colors as noncitizens, for example."

"Noncitizens," Ophelia repeated, recalling reading a

passage about that in her geographical guide. "They're the ones who live on Babel, but don't descend from Pollux?"

"That's not entirely accurate," Ambrose said, smiling indulgently. "The Sons of Pollux are, indeed, automatically citizens. They can vote, elect, and be elected. But it's also possible to become a citizen through merit, like my father. That's been the case since Babel entered into commercial alliances with the other arks. You must have noticed in the street, there are plenty of different families living here: Florins, Totemists, Cyclopeans, Alchemists, Heliopolitans! And those without power," he added, this time half-heartedly. "We are the 'Godsons of Helen.' Madame Helen, being unable to have descendants, became the official godmother of all those who aren't Sons of Pollux. She will be yours, too, for as long as you remain on Babel."

Ophelia really hoped not. The last time she'd been the ward of a family spirit, it had almost cost her her life.

"Returning to our clothes," said Ambrose, diving back into his closet, "you have to understand that every adornment, every jewel, every accessory adds very specific layers of significance. It's a language in its own right! If your stay on Babel must be extended, I advise you to get completely to grips with it in order to avoid misunderstandings. And beware, the dress police carry out regular checks."

Having always thrown on the first garment that came to hand, Ophelia would now have to make a concerted effort if she wanted to melt into the background on Babel. "And what happens if one dresses other than the code allows?"

"One has to pay a fine to the city. The greater the offense, the heavier the fine."

She knocked over the pile of the clothes that Ambrose had heaped into her arms. It was galling to note that, even without having hands the wrong way around, she was the clumsier of the two of them.

"Stay here overnight," suggested the whaxi driver, noticing the light fading through the casements. "We'll start the search for your bag first thing tomorrow morning."

"And the Memorial? Wouldn't it be possible to go there today?"

Ambrose's eyes widened, the whites standing out against the dark surface of his skin. "It would be closed by the time we got there. The place seems to mean a lot to you. What are you seeking, exactly?"

"It's personal." Ophelia regretted her snappiness when she saw Ambrose's smile disappear.

"Forgive my indiscretion. Please follow me, *mademoiselle*, you must feel like freshening up and resting. Are you hungry? Would you care to share my table?"

Ophelia picked up the clothes scattered on the floor, and then turned her glasses to the chair that was already moving toward the door with a mechanical purring sound. "Ambrose?"

"*Mademoiselle?*"

"Why are you helping me?"

The chair's wheels came to an abrupt halt, screeching on the checkered marble, but Ambrose didn't turn around. From where she stood, Ophelia could see his inverted hands tightening on the armrests.

"Because you're not an automaton."

# THE MEMORY

Ophelia wasn't sleeping. She was opening and closing Thorn's watch without looking at it, just to hear the familiar clicking of the cover.

Click click. Click click. Click click.

Curled up, she had thrown off all the bedsheets, and was staring myopically at the splashes of light shining between the gap in the mosquito net, unable to determine where the stars began and the lamps ended. The breeze swept through the open window, wafting the fresh scent of eucalyptus around the room. The crickets' chirring rippled the surface of night.

Click click. Click click. Click click.

Ophelia was shivering. The sun had burnt the skin of her face, and yet she was freezing cold. Tonight, the void deep inside her had taken on breathtaking proportions, as though it weren't just Thorn who had disappeared from her life, but also a part of herself. She felt the night air on her nape, where, before, there had been her long, unruly hair, her lazy old scarf, and sometimes, on rare occasions, Aunt Rosaline's rather rough caress.

Click click. Click click. Click click.

And what if Ophelia had got the wrong ark? If there was no connection between the Memorial's decapitated statue and the headless soldier of her vision? If her only lead was a dead end?

Click click. Click click. Click click.

She still wasn't sleeping when dawn made the sky blanch and the foliage hum, but the daylight restored her determination. "I'm going to get my scarf back, research at the Memorial, and find a small job," she declared to the mirror in her room. She ran her fingers through her curls, which had doubled in volume overnight, forming a wild halo around her face. Babel's sun had turned her cheeks crimson.

Putting on her new clothes demanded great perseverance, despite the assistance of a mechanical servant. She had to fold and wind a long toga over her tunic in such a way as to pass a panel between the legs and leave one shoulder uncovered. A clasp, waistband, and belt held the whole thing in place, but Ophelia had the feeling that, with one false move, the whole arrangement would come apart, and the fabric fall around her feet.

She felt more awkward than usual when she met up with Ambrose under the entrance portico. Relaxing against the back of his chair, he had closed his eyes as if to savor the morning air rising from the lily pools. The wind made the voile of his turban flutter. His golden profile, with its long lashes, was so refined, it made one forget the strange deformity of his body. He didn't open his eyes immediately as Ophelia approached, but his lips turned into a smile.

"I like hearing your footsteps in the house, Mademoiselle Eulalia."

That was all Ophelia needed to feel ashamed. Of having felt alone while close to someone far more alone than she was. Of asking him questions without ever answering his. Of having given him neither her real name nor her true story. Of having no intention to remedy this.

Ambrose peered at Ophelia through the half-light of the portico, and nodded approvingly. "Congratulations, you've now become a true Babelian. I have a surprise for you. Jasper?"

A mechanical butler stepped forward from the mannequins lined up before the front door. Ophelia rushed over to him as soon as she saw what was hanging from his articulated arm.

"My bag? But how?"

"Last night I sent a telegram to the Municipal Tram Company," said Ambrose. "I reported the loss of your belongings. A courier came early this morning to drop them off here. I did tell you that honesty was a civic duty here. What is it?"

Ophelia had suddenly frozen, clutching the wide-open bag, her glasses turning blue. "My scarf's not there," she muttered. "Was it also returned to you? It's three-colored, quite long, a bit lily-livered."

Ambrose seemed disconcerted by Ophelia's reaction; he had hoped she would burst with joy. "*Eh bien*, there was nothing else. Are your papers missing, too?"

"No. They're here." Her throat was so tight, her voice was strangled. Someone must have opened the bag and the scarf had escaped. Or worse: it had been stolen.

I must go looking for it, thought Ophelia. "Stick "missing" posters on all the walls, question people, scour every nook and cranny.

No. She couldn't do that. When she'd hidden the scarf, it was precisely not to attract attention. As harsh as this decision might be, she had to stick to the plan.

"I'm so sorry," stammered Ambrose. "You seem to attach importance to this object."

Ophelia avoided looking him in the face as she slipped on the strap of her knapsack. How could she have made him understand that the scarf was much more than an object? How could she have explained to him that she had given it life, and that she owed hers to it in return?

"Thank you," she said, in a choked voice. "You have been

of considerable help to me. Right now, I must go to the Memorial."

After an awkward silence, Ambrose turned the crank on his chair. "I'll drive you, *mademoiselle*. On you get."

The sun was rising over Babel, cutting through any lingering morning mist with its great blades, and casting the arcades' shadows onto the cobbles. Ambrose's chair moved from dark, little lanes to vast, light squares, avoiding the jungle of the gardens and the dust of the building sites. Perched on the rear running board, Ophelia looked gloomily at the crowd around them. Among all these togas, kaftans, tunics, shawls, harem trousers, belts, babouches, turbans, parasols, where was her scarf?

None of the marvels Ambrose was showing her could shake her gloom; neither the great cascades of the Pyramid nor the monumental statues of Helen and Pollux nor the agora, with its imposing amphitheater nor the power exchanges in the city center, where the top engineers of all the arks gathered daily.

Ophelia's interest was solely directed at the sun-shaped LUX emblem, engraved in the marble of every building, stuck on the columns of every forum. She had even noticed it on the inside of her toga, embroidered in gold thread.

"Who is . . . LUX?" she asked, out of breath. She was pushing Ambrose's chair to help him up a seemingly endless incline. It was no easy task: she kept skidding on the needles that the umbrella pines, shaken by a searing wind, rained down on the cobbles.

"A very ancient institution, *mademoiselle*. They are patrons who make their wealth available to all enterprises deemed of public service. True philanthropists!"

Ophelia rubbed off, on a cobble, a blob of resin stuck to her sandal. Philanthropists whose signature was on every wall of the city, all the same. "I deduce that they're pretty influential."

"One could say that, yes. They preside at the Mint, at the Familistery, and at the Court of Justice. The Lords of LUX are not merely at the service of the city, *mademoiselle*. They *are* the city. Sir Pollux and Lady Helen themselves take no important decision without consulting them. It is also they who instigated the Index I told you about. You know, the ban on mentioning anything to do with . . . *eh bien* . . . the war," he whispered, very quietly.

Ophelia didn't need to know any more to understand that the Lords of LUX were to Babel what the Doyennes were to Anima: Guardians in the service of God. If their grip on the ark was as absolute as Ambrose's explanations led one to believe, she'd have to be doubly vigilant to escape their notice.

Deep in these thoughts, she jumped when she was hit in the face by a feather so large that it flicked loudly against the lenses of her glasses. The slope they had just ascended opened onto a huge terrace overhanging the void: beyond the wide, stone balustrade, the sky stretched out endlessly. The terrace extended into a railway bridge, on which a train awaited, with the clouds its sole destination. The last passengers were hurriedly piling into the carriages.

"We're right on time," said Ambrose, with a smile for the platform clock. "Let's hurry to get on."

Ophelia struggled to do as he said. She couldn't tear her eyes away from the gigantic, winged creatures perched on the roof of the train. A Totemist, identifiable by his night-dark skin and golden hair, was circulating among them to check their harnesses. "Are they Beasts?"

Ambrose waited until he had managed to get his chair into the nearest carriage before answering Ophelia. "Chimeras, *mademoiselle*," he said, inserting their two travel cards in the on-board machine. "They have the strength of the condor and the docility of the canary."

The stationmaster blew his whistle, and the scratching sound of the birds' talons on the train's roof reverberated across the metal. Since all the seats were occupied, Ophelia instinctively clung onto Ambrose's chair. "But a train, isn't that a bit heavy for birds?"

"Of course it is," Ambrose replied, to her extreme consternation. "They don't carry it, they propel it. The birdtrains are made to be weightless. The worst thing that could happen to us, if these birds stopped flying, would be to remain suspended in the middle of the sky. It won't happen," he assured her, indicating a shaven-headed woman milling around the passengers' seats. "There are always Cyclopeans on board to control the gravitational fields. Reassured, *mademoiselle*?"

"Almost."

Ophelia leant against a window as the train glided through the air, emitting metallic grating sounds. She glimpsed the powerful beating of a wing up above, and the slow swirling of the clouds down below. The experience reminded her of the flying sleighs of Citaceleste, although this was even more impressive.

Seeing that the birdtrain didn't plunge into the void, she finally relaxed and looked around at the other passengers, who, with the indifference of regulars, paid more attention to their books than to the view. She found them all surprisingly young and serious, so focused that no one spoke to anyone.

"Students," whispered Ambrose. "This birdtrain will serve the five academies and the virtuosos' conservatoire before reaching the Memorial. We thus have time ahead of us. Did you know that several attempts have been made to explore the void between the arks?" he asked her, straight off. "It seems that no living being can remain there for more than a few hours. The deeper one goes, the worse it is—even birds don't risk it. There's sufficient oxygen, but even so, it's physically intolerable. My father tried it out for himself, with a space-suit he invented. He wanted to take a photograph of the world's core, you know, where there are those perpetual thunderstorms. He lasted six hours and thirty-nine minutes. He admitted to me that they were the most challenging six hours and thirty-nine minutes of his entire life. As if, down below, there was a force that hadn't wanted him. Don't you find that extraordinary, Mademoiselle Eulalia? Our whole planet seems to want to remind us that, before, all that emptiness was filled up. My father thinks it's a shame because it would be much quicker for him to travel from one ark to the next by crossing the void in a straight line, without having to respect the curvature of the old world."

"Really?" Ophelia said, politely. In truth, she was far too preoccupied with seeing the headless soldier to listen. Ambrose contemplated the sky through the window with a childlike fascination, and his inverted hands gripped his chair with excitement.

"Indeed, did you also know that the arks don't respect the laws of gravity? All the celestial bodies each move in relation to the rest, depending on their forces of attraction. All, except for the arks. They keep to the same position among themselves and all turn together, at exactly the same rhythm, as if they still formed one and the same celestial body. It's what scientists call 'planetary memory.'"

Ophelia wondered what those scientists would think if they discovered that the shattering of the world was due to an apocalyptic creature trapped in a mirror.

Ambrose continued talking enough for two, only falling quiet once they had arrived at their destination. Ophelia shaded her glasses from the sun as she tipped her head back to take in the Memorial tower. Its size was so overwhelming, its glass dome so dazzling, it looked like a lighthouse destined to illuminate the world. The little ark that served as its perch was ludicrously out of proportion by comparison; it seemed totally mad to have rebuilt, above the void, the half of the tower that had previously collapsed. Hundreds of monkeys leapt between the creepers entwining the carved stones, and then disappeared into the surrounding clouds.

Ophelia moved along the forecourt until swallowed up by the Memorial's shadow. The decapitated statue was there. It stood exactly as depicted on the postcard, just in front of the great picture windows of the entrance.

"Is that what you were looking for?" asked Ambrose.

She didn't reply immediately. Now that she was seeing the statue close up, it was blindingly obvious. It didn't resemble the headless soldier of her vision. It didn't resemble a soldier at all. It barely resembled a man. It was now but an undefined form, ravaged by erosion and shrouded in creepers. The wrought-iron tip of its boot stuck out from the greenery, shinier and lighter than the rest of its body.

"It's a public monument, isn't it?"

"It is, *mademoiselle.*"

Ambrose had seemed disconcerted by Ophelia's question, and he was even more so when she handed him her knapsack, and then took off her gloves. Once she'd checked that there was no one but them on the forecourt, she rubbed her palms together to remove any sweat. When she approached the statue, a feverish shiver coursed down her spine, as happened whenever she was about to go back in time. She breathed deeply, and with each inhalation, little by little she forgot herself. She forgot the apprehension, the heat, she even forgot the reason for her being here, and when empty of herself, she placed her hands on the statue's boot.

The Memorial's shadow ebbed away like a tide, while the sun moved in reverse in the sky. Day gave way to night, today became yesterday, and time exploded beneath Ophelia's fingers. They were no longer her fingers. They were hundreds, thousands of other fingers stroking the boot of the statue, day before day, year before year, century before century.

For luck.

For success.

For healing.

For a laugh.

For growth.

For survival.

And suddenly, as Ophelia was dissolving into this crowd of anonymous hands, she found her own hands again. Or rather, hands that were hers without being hers. And it was through eyes that were hers without being hers that she looked at the statue. In gleaming metal, the soldier proudly brandished his rifle beneath the flowering mimosas, his head blown off by the shell that had destroyed the porch of the school behind him.

*Once upon a tomorrow, before too long, there will be a world that will finally live in peace.*

"*Mademoiselle?*" Ambrose asked, concerned, moving his chair closer.

Ophelia contemplated her hands, really hers this time, as they shook uncontrollably. It had happened again. She had penetrated God's past as if it had been her own past. She raised her face to the Memorial tower, standing there instead of the school destroyed by war. The mimosas were still there, bordering the central path; Ophelia hadn't recognized them because, quite simply, it wasn't yet the flowering season.

The headless soldier. The golden mimosas. The old school.

"It's here," she murmured.

Here that she would tread in God's footsteps. Here that she would tread in Thorn's footsteps.

78

# THE VIRTUOSOS

Ophelia was used to being small. And yet, when she entered the Memorial, she felt tinier than ever before. Inside, the tower took the form of a monumental atrium, encircled by the floors in parallel rings. The sun came through the cupola's countless windows, making the bindings of the books, glasses of the readers, and metal of the automatons gleam. The silence here was so intense that a page turned had the effect of a thunderbolt. Ophelia felt dizzy when she noticed that there was neither staircase nor lift; visitors accessed the various floors by taking large, vertical corridors. There were reading rooms available right up to, and on, the ceilings. Seeing all these people and all these archives upside down was an experience even crazier than traveling with the help of public restrooms.

In a heartbeat, Ophelia felt herself vibrating in unison with the thousands of ancient objects surrounding her, and then reality hit her: Where to begin her research?

"Do you have a preferred side, *mademoiselle*?" Ambrose whispered, as quietly as he could.

"A side?"

"One half of the Memorial is dedicated to Babel's heritage, and the other half to the heritage of the other arks. Here, all public buildings are divided in two." Ambrose indicated the copper gutter tracing a demarcation line on the ground across the entire diameter of the tower. This line underlined the temporal difference between the original part of the building, all in ancient stone, and the part that had been rebuilt after the collapse linked to the Rupture.

"It's Babel's past that interests me," said Ophelia, turning to the oldest half.

As they were making their way towards one of the vertical corridors, Ophelia looked up at a statue-automaton that, bolted to its plinth, was endlessly bowing and then straightening up its top half to welcome visitors. An inscription indicated that it depicted the first LUX patron to contribute to subsidizing the Memorial. *Because knowledge serves peace*, the commemorative plaque pompously declared.

Looking up even higher, Ophelia saw a gigantic globe of the old world that was floating weightlessly under the glass dome. An intact world. A forgotten world. A world whose secrets she had the firm intention of extracting.

She tensed up when she saw Ambrose's chair going onto a curved ramp that enabled one to tilt gently from the horizontality of the hall to the verticality of a corridor. In a few seconds, he started to move as naturally as anything up the wall, without even losing his turban on the way.

"*Mademoiselle?*" he whispered, when he noticed that Ophelia wasn't following him.

"I . . . I've never done that before."

"Take a transcendium? It's child's play. Walk straight ahead, without questioning anything."

Ophelia had expected to feel her stomach protesting along with her center of gravity, but at no time did she have the sensation of leaving behind terrestrial gravitational pull. The transcendiums could be gone up and down as easily as one walks up and down an ordinary corridor. She still felt pretty strange when, after a few steps, her eyes fell on the hall she'd left down below. It was as if the whole tower had upended itself.

"The transcendiums and the topsy-turviums are the work of the Cyclopeans employed by the Memorial," said Ambrose, whose chair was sliding along the marble with a clanking of gears. "That's Babel for you: as soon as a foreign invention pleases us, we adopt it and adapt it."

Ophelia jumped. Somewhere in a fold of her toga, Thorn's watch had suddenly opened and closed on its own, with an exclamatory click-click. Had her handling of it ended up animating it?

Distracted, Ophelia bumped into a sweeper standing in the middle of the transcendium. He was so tall, so slim, and so bearded that he resembled his broom.

"I feel bad every time I see him," admitted Ambrose.

"The sweeper?" she asked with surprise, while checking the watch had calmed down. "Why?"

"My father has always fought against the servitude of man by man. The Memorialists should replace that man with an automaton, as they've done with the rest of the maintenance personnel."

Ophelia realized that, indeed, wherever she turned her glasses, Lazarus's mannequins were there, discreet and omnipresent, polishing the cabinets and dusting the books.

Leaving the transcendium was as disconcertingly easy as entering it had been; one just had to follow the curve in the ground leading to that floor. Ambrose guided her through the labyrinth of books and archives. The visitors around them were perfectly silent, each applying themselves assiduously to their research.

Ophelia envied them. She herself hadn't the slightest idea what she was looking for. She'd hoped that the mysterious memory she shared with God since her reading of Farouk's

Book would clarify itself by her visiting the Memorial. Nothing of the sort. Apart from its ancient stones, the building probably hadn't retained a great deal of the school in which the family spirits had once lived. It was now nothing but a shell; the life form that had inhabited it had long been replaced by a different one.

At the end of some shelving, Ophelia stopped in front of a poster:

> The Good Family seeks virtuosos.
> Are you a Memorialist at heart?
> Do you have a gift for tracking down information?
> Are you passionate about history and the future?
> Become a FORERUNNER in the city's service.

"That's for Sir Henry's reading groups," whispered Ambrose. "They recruit all year round." He raised his hand—the left one that was on the right—and Ophelia raised her glasses up to the ceiling of the floor above. Dozens of students in uniform were sitting there, heads down. They were in reading cubicles and were busily taking notes.

"Are they all virtuosos?"

"Apprentice virtuosos," corrected Ambrose. "There are several guilds. Those ones are Forerunners—specialists in information. It's been more than a year now that I've seen them working up there for the Memorial catalogue. They spend hours and hours reading. I don't know how far they've got, but I hope they will soon be finished; one can't borrow any books for the moment, just consult them here."

"Shush!"

One of the students had interrupted his reading to look down—or up, depending on the point of view—in Ophelia's and Ambrose's direction. He frowned when he saw they were wearing white togas. "You powerless folk have no business being here."

"The Memorial is accessible to everyone," Ambrose replied gently to him. "We are Godchildren of Helen."

"Powerless folk shouldn't even have the right to utter the name of Lady Helen," the student retorted.

Ophelia had noticed that the Babelians aspirated their "h"s hard, but this one had said the name of Helen as if he wanted to fill himself entirely with it. As if it belonged personally to him.

Ambrose turned the crank of his chair and moved off with a mechanical purring sound. He continued with his guided tour as if nothing noteworthy had occurred. Ophelia looked at him more than she listened to him. Being called powerless in public was thus that usual for him? His father was the inventor of all the automatons around here; he could have used his name to put that student in his place.

"You're a decent person."

Ambrose was so startled by Ophelia's spontaneity, he almost lost control of his chair. "It's rather that I detest conflict," he stammered, with an embarrassed smile. "I realize that I've again imposed my presence on you, *mademoiselle*. I'll let you visit the Memorial as you like. I'm off to look at the invention patents on the top floor; they always succeed in making me dream. Meet in the hall at midday?"

"Will do."

When she found herself wandering alone around the shelves and cabinets, Ophelia suddenly became aware of how nervous she felt. She kept delving into her toga to grasp Thorn's watch. Whenever she crossed a man who was a bit taller than average, she couldn't stop herself from looking back as she passed, with a frantic pounding in her chest. It was absurd. Even if Thorn had already been to do research at the Memorial, it was unlikely that he would be there at that precise moment.

And maybe it wasn't such a bad thing, she thought, crossing some guards for the third time. The Memorial was under close surveillance; not an ideal meeting place for two fugitives.

For a long time, Ophelia roamed the various rooms as she happened upon them. She looked closely at the collections—paintings, sculptures, ceramics, goldwork—but none of them seemed to have belonged to the old school. There were no military archives, either, as if even here, where the memory of humanity was supposed to reside, nothing remained of the wars of the past.

I'm reasoning like an occasional table, Ophelia chided herself. If this place had formerly been a school, it was in the juvenile section that she'd stand a chance to find something. She consulted the plan of the building, and took two transcendiums. Each time it was a strange experience to be walking sometimes the wrong way, sometimes upside down.

Once she was in the gallery for young readers, Ophelia read the labels on the shelves: "Alphabets and Primers"; "Rudiments of Learning"; "Civic Education"; Allegories of Old"; etc. She came across a class of schoolchildren who were remarkably calm for their age. As for her, she didn't feel remotely calm. The more she scanned the shelves, the more she felt her anxiety rising. What if there was, quite simply, nothing to be found? If God had taken care not to leave the slightest trace of his past here? If Thorn had reached the same dead end? If he had left Babel a long time ago? Had he even set foot on it?

While her head was swirling with doubt, Ophelia crashed straight into a trolley in front of her. The books stacked on it were sent flying, and, to add to the confusion, she dropped her own bag, whose contents spread across the floor.

The man pushing the trolley didn't get angry. He merely sighed and gathered up his books with resignation.

"I'm so sorry," Ophelia whispered, kneeling beside him, despite her toga.

"You shouldn't be, *mademoiselle*. I alone am at fault."

The man had said this with disillusion in his voice and a stoop, as if he carried the weight of the sins of the world on his shoulders. A badge saying "assistant" was pinned to his uniform. Ophelia retrieved her personal belongings, but they had got so mixed up with the children's books that she found her fake identity papers caught between the pages of one of them.

"But of course. You again, always you."

A woman had sneaked up like a cat. Her badge indicated that she worked at the Memorial as a "senior censor." Her ears, slender and triangular as a cat's, were pricked up with contempt. An Acoustic.

"Throwing books on the floor. Books I had entrusted into your care. It's an offense as much to my hearing as to my work." The Memorialist spoke in a very low, almost inaudible voice, as if she couldn't bear the sound of it herself.

"Forgive me, Mademoiselle Silence," replied the assistant, still returning the books to the trolley. Ophelia wanted to intervene, to explain that the fault was hers, but the Memorialist cut her short:

"You are, and you will remain forever, a subordinate; you have no ambition. But that is not my case, so for pity's sake, don't tarnish me with your incompetence. Take that trolley over to my department, and don't drop another thing."

"Yes, Mademoiselle Silence."

The assistant loaded on the remaining books and proceeded along the corridor, his head so sunken, it seemed about to disappear into his body.

The Memorialist's ears immediately swiveled toward

Ophelia, swiftly followed by her eyes. "As for you, open up your bag."

Ophelia gripped the strap tightly. This woman inspired such dislike in her that, as a precaution, she moved back. It really wasn't the time for her claws to show themselves.

"Why?"

"Because I'm ordering you to."

"There's nothing in my belongings of interest to you."

The Memorialist made a suspicious, somewhat disgusted face, and Ophelia then became aware of the state of her bag. From having dragged it around and lost it, she had turned this perfectly respectable piece of luggage into a disgusting, tattered thing.

"That, little powerless one, is for me to decide. Since we no longer lend out books, we've seen no end of pilferers. Open your bag."

Ophelia felt a drop of sweat roll down her neck. Obeying would mean showing her false papers, and that wasn't something she wished to do to a professional archivist, and a suspicious one at that.

"Maybe you would prefer me to call security?" The Memorialist had whispered her question while tugging the chain on her uniform to reveal a whistle at its end. Just as Ophelia was wondering how to get herself out of this situation, there was a resounding crackling noise. The woman dropped her whistle to block her ears. Barely had the racket subsided than a booming voice, amplified by a megaphone, reverberated throughout the corridors:

"Wake up, citizens! This Memorial's just a massive joke! They're amputating our past! They're amputating our language! Down with the Index! Death to the censors!"

"*Him* again," muttered the Memorialist, looking offended. She turned her attention away from Ophelia, who took advantage of the diversion to scarper. The readers had all lifted their noses out of their books with shocked expressions, as the voice through the megaphone chanted, "Death to the censors! Death to the censors!" before giving way to an abrupt silence. Either the agitator had been stopped, or he had run away.

Out of breath, Ophelia returned to the atrium, where Ambrose was already waiting for her. Sitting nonchalantly in his wheelchair, with a half-smile, he didn't seem bothered by the incident.

"It's Fearless-and-Almost-Blameless," he explained. "He always has to come and disturb the peace of this place. He barks a lot, but he doesn't bite. He didn't scare you, I hope?"

Ophelia merely shook her head. If she uttered a word right then, right there, her voice would betray her distress. This visit to the Memorial was a disaster. Her bag weighed her down as if it were her own morale slung on her shoulder.

Ambrose observed her with his gentle, antelope eyes. "You know, *mademoiselle*, the Memorial isn't somewhere one can visit in half a day. I've been coming here regularly for years, and there are still a whole load of things that are unknown to me." He raised his face, with a meaningful look, and Ophelia followed his eyes. The gigantic terrestrial globe that was gravitating above them was plunging them entirely in its shadow. "It's not simply a decorative globe," Ambrose continued, in a dreamy murmur. "It's the Secretarium. Within it are stored all the collections that are not accessible to the public—the rarest and oldest. They say there's a strongroom inside it, and in there can be found the 'ultimate truth.' Of course, it's a tall tale to make kids dream, but I do believe that the strongroom really does exist."

Ophelia's heart, which, just a moment before, had been heavy in her chest, started to beat like crazy. "The ultimate truth?" she whispered.

Ambrose threw her a sidelong glance, disconcerted by the emotion coloring her glasses. "As I told you, it's just a tall tale told to children, it's not to be taken seriously."

Ophelia, on the contrary, took it very seriously. "How does one enter this Secretarium?"

"It's impossible, *mademoiselle*," Ambrose replied, becoming even more disconcerted. "It isn't even open to citizens. Only the Forerunners have access to it. And there again, only the most virtuoso among them."

Ophelia contemplated the globe, which, at this moment, had superimposed itself so perfectly on the midday sun that it was producing the effect of an eclipse. It was linked to no floor of the Memorial, was furnished with no gangway, and allowed nothing to be seen of the secret rooms it harbored. A sudden thought returned her to the students in the reading cubicles, and the recruiting poster.

"In that case, I'll be a virtuoso," she declared, to Ambrose's astonishment.

# THE APPLICATION

The birdtrain took off. Ophelia had a final look at the statue of the headless soldier, guarding the entrance to the Memorial, surrounded by mimosas. She made him a promise. The next time she came to see him, she'd be ready.

"The virtuosos are a true elite," insisted Ambrose, who had boarded with her. "The Good Family is the conservatoire that everyone on Babel dreams of getting into. Believe me, *mademoiselle*, over there they only accept applicants with a unique talent. They're highly selective."

"They recruit Forerunners all year round, don't they?"

"The Forerunners are the top specialists in information. And you . . . *eh bien*, you're not the most well-informed person I know."

Ophelia was only half-listening to him. Her attention was focused on the double ark, partly shrouded in wisps of the clouds that kept getting bigger on the other side of the window. The Good Family was such a huge conservatoire that, on its own, it took up two floating islands, linked by a bridge.

As the birdtrain neared the landing stage, Ophelia checked that she really did have her false papers on her. "I'll entrust my bag to you," she said to Ambrose. "It made me seem like a scruff at the Memorial, and I'd rather not repeat the experience."

"Count on me, *mademoiselle*."

Ophelia hesitated. She would have liked to take the adolescent's inverted hands into her own, and tell him how grateful she was for the kindness he'd shown her from the start. She couldn't. It was always like this with her—the slightest emotion, and she fell apart. "You are . . . a good whaxi driver."

The statement drew a smile from Ambrose, a brief flash of white light against the bronze of his skin. "And you an unexpected client. Your bag and I, we'll be waiting for you at my father's. Good luck, *mademoiselle.*"

Once she'd alighted, Ophelia returned Ambrose's wave; he was encouraging her through the window as the powerful beating of the chimeras' wings carried him off.

The entrance to the Good Family was at the other end of the platform that served as a link between sky and land. It was framed by two statues that were so colossal, Ophelia had to shade her eyes from the blinding sun to make out their faces from the ground. A woman and a man. Probably Helen and Pollux.

She followed the seemingly endless paved path that led straight to the main building. This evoked a cathedral of the old world, with its filigree-carved façade, flying buttresses, and stained-glass rose window. It all had such majesty: the white dome of the observatory; the great marble stairs; the buildings styled like ancient temples; and even the stature of the hundred-year-old trees that shaded the path entirely. An army of automatons were busy maintaining the gardens and cleaning the windows. The conservatoire was an actual town in its own right. The students who frowned at Ophelia as she passed by all wore elegant midnight-blue uniforms, embellished with silver. Ambrose was right: this place wasn't accessible to ordinary folk.

Once Ophelia had climbed the steps to the main building, she could read the motto on its pediment:

## PRESTIGE AND EXCELLENCE

She had barely set foot on the marble floor of the reception hall before a man politely indicated that she should turn back. "Forgive me, young lady, but you can't enter."

"I've come regarding the request for applications."

The man seemed disconcerted. He glanced warily at the white toga and Ophelia's reddened skin before showing her back to the door. He pointed out to her, on the other side of the estate, the vast bridge that straddled the void. "You have come to the wrong ark, young lady. This is where Pollux's virtuosos reside. You must go over to the building for Helen's virtuosos."

Ophelia really didn't fancy any more walking. Her sandals hurt her feet, and her nape was roasting once again in the sun. No exotic illusion at the Pole's court had ever made her this hot. She crossed the bridge, long and wide as an avenue, and reached the twin ark. It was as if the builders had duplicated here all the buildings on the other side, before stripping them, one by one, of their grandiose style. Marble had been replaced by rough stone, stained-glass windows by frosted glass, and no embellishment enhanced the overall appearance. There were no automatons, either.

If the buildings were made in the image of Babel's family spirits, Pollux was king of the esthetes, and Helen queen of the ascetics.

Even the weather was less radiant, and Ophelia was soon engulfed in a rising tide of clouds that had appeared from nowhere. Hindered by steam clinging to her glasses, she struggled to find the stairs to the administration department.

On the pediment, the motto of Helen's virtuosos differed from that of Pollux's:

## MAKING KNOWN AND KNOW-HOW

This time, Ophelia wasn't turned away upon entering. An attendant at the reception examined her papers without a word. She then led her to a study room where two other applicants, a man and a young girl, were each bent over a desk.

The attendant supplied Ophelia with writing materials. "Copy out the different definitions of the word 'definition.' Find a synonym for each one, and copy out their definitions, too. It's just a simple exercise to check your knowledge of the alphabet."

Ophelia looked at the dictionary that had been handed to her. She would have preferred a glass of cold water.

As soon as the attendant had closed the study-room door, the man brought his desk closer to that of the adolescent girl. "And so, you were saying?"

"My mother forced me to come here," the latter hissed, angrily turning the pages of her dictionary. "Me, I asked for nothing, I never ask for anything, I'm always the one who obediently does what is expected of her. And . . . and . . . "

"And?" the man encouraged her.

"And my mother, she became a citizen solely on her own merit. Now she wants me to follow in her footsteps. To do better, even. She's forever repeating to me that I must become a virtuoso, while, at the same time, calling me useless. And . . . and . . . "

"And?"

Ophelia looked up from her dictionary, having lost her concentration. The man was still moving his desk closer to his young neighbor. He was eyeing her greedily, hanging on her every word, as though there was nothing in the world more fascinating than what she had to tell him.

"And apparently they give you a hard time here," the

adolescent continued, needing no encouragement. "And you have to study night and day, and even that's never enough. And the more you apply yourself, the more they humiliate you. I'm fed up with being humiliated. No," she added, sounding different, suddenly seeing the light. "I'm fed up with my mother. I've no reason to be here."

With these words, the adolescent crumpled her sheet of paper and left the study room, slamming the door. Looking triumphant, the man put his desk back in its place and, sensing Ophelia's flabbergasted eyes on him, blew her a kiss with his fingertips.

"Don't judge me too harshly, *mademoiselle*. Our test starts right now, doesn't it? That's the tough law of competition."

"You influenced her," she acknowledged, eyebrows shooting up.

"I'm a Pharoan, charm is my family power. I entice others, irresistibly, to confide in me. I wouldn't want to discourage you, *mademoiselle*, but I'm the greatest extractor of information in all of Babel. The ideal Forerunner!"

Ophelia was relieved to hear the attendant calling the man for his interview. She hadn't been able to stop herself from finding him charming, proof that his power was formidable. If he managed to seduce the examiners with the same ease, she didn't stand much chance.

She tried to return to her dictionary, but struggled to get on with the exercise. She had lost her concentration. Initially, the path to access the Memorial's Secretarium had seemed straightforward. Now, the doubt cast by Ambrose and the Pharoan was having its effect. Who was she even to hope to join Babel's elite?

She attempted, somewhat in vain, to smooth her unruly curls. Maybe she shouldn't have cut her hair with shears after all.

Ophelia was called by the attendant, who took her sheet of paper and showed her into a new room. A pair of examiners sat in the hatched light of louvered shutters, both behind an imposing marble table. The man had slanted eyes that betrayed great intensity, and the woman was deathly pale, verging on blue; they weren't descendants of Pollux, but everything about their appearance showed that they were no less citizens of Babel.

"Take your place."

The seat indicated by one of the examiners, on the other side of the table, was a stool with intertwined legs. Ophelia knocked it over trying to sit on it. As a first impression, it was just great.

"Your name?"

"Eulalia," replied Ophelia, straightening up the stool.

"Do you have references? A letter of recommendation? Professional experience?"

"No."

Mentioning her work at Anima's museum and her being in service at the Pole's court was out of the question. If she wanted to escape God's attention, here she had to be Eulalia, just Eulalia. And Eulalia had no past.

"Young lady," the woman continued, "you must understand that the Good Family is an establishment specializing in the perfecting of family powers. We accept people of all ages and all backgrounds, but it is rare, extremely rare, that we take on those without power. You are going to have to be convincing."

"She's not powerless."

The man had replied in Ophelia's place, to the latter's surprise. He linked his hands on the table and focused his slanting eyes, black and shiny as ink, on her.

"I detect several family powers amalgamated within her.

94

And not very evenly distributed. Don't be so anxious," he added, more gently.

An Empathetic from Al-Andaloose. It was a family that Ophelia didn't know well—she would have been hard-pressed to locate their ark on a map—but she knew at least one thing: their power allowed them to connect to the power of others. Rigid on her stool, she hoped she wouldn't be too transparent to this man.

"So you are of mixed race?" concluded the woman, to Ophelia's relief. "Normally, powers from different lineages rarely work well together. But maybe not in your case. We are listening, young lady. In what way would you make a good Forerunner? What are your skills?"

Ophelia was well aware that she was starting with a definite disadvantage in the eyes of the jury. "My dominant family power is Animism."

"Animists are not common on Babel. Are you able to animate any object?"

"Particularly objects I know well."

"You would be able to repair material damage?"

"I can heal my glasses in a few days."

"Would you be capable of creating perpetual movement?"

"Movement, yes. Perpetual, no."

The man and woman exchanged a look. Ophelia suspected as much. To have the slightest chance of becoming a virtuoso, she would have to play the talent card, and thus run the risk of revealing her real self. "The Forerunners are the top specialists in information," Ambrose had said.

"I'm a reader."

"A reader," repeated the woman. "Yes, I've heard about that particular aspect of Animism. You perceive 'certain things' by touching objects, is that it?"

From the tone of her voice, Ophelia could tell that she

didn't take that power very seriously. If the man's role was to be empathetic toward applicants, this woman's was to be insensitive towards them. The bluish tinge of her skin was characteristic of the Selenites, a people who controlled the conscious and subconscious forces present in every human being. It was pointless to seek to flatter, cajole, or bewitch a Selenite. One had to convince them, period.

Ophelia pushed her glasses up her nose and scanned the room, with its austere furniture, potted plants, pneumatic tubes, and serried punch cards, before settling on a cabinet in which trophies glimmered. Among them, some appeared particularly old.

"Are they the property of the Good family? If you give me permission, I would like to evaluate one of them."

"You have our permission," said the man.

"We will choose one for you," specified the woman.

They selected a trophy on which the gold had faded considerably. There was no plaque on it, no inscription. It was impossible to guess who had won it, and for what.

It was a perfect choice.

Ophelia took off her gloves and took the trophy in her hands. She was instantly overwhelmed by a skepticism that wasn't hers; it corresponded to the state of mind of the woman as she had taken the trophy out of the cabinet. It lasted but a fraction of a second as the tide of time carried her further and further back. She felt herself passing from hand to hand. The trophy was being shown as an example. It was being stolen to infuriate the management. It was being polished with utmost respect. It was being vandalized in rage. And then suddenly there was a burst of applause and booing; satisfaction mixed with embarrassment; and, muttered into the ear, inaudible to the rest of the crowd, a hate-filled whisper: *Everyone will soon forget you, you powerless thing.*

Ophelia placed the trophy on the table and looked the two examiners straight on. "It's a first prize for excellence awarded to a virtuoso. Not any old virtuoso: a powerless one. Today it is held up as an example, but this prize was highly controversial at the time. Originally, there was a plaque," she added, pointing at the base of the trophy. "It was torn off by a rival in a fit of jealousy. On it was written: 'Awarded for the great merits of your theoretical and experimental research on the analytical machine.'"

The two examiners exchanged another look, but made no comment. They were both so impassive, Ophelia couldn't tell whether she'd made a strong impression on them, or not. She didn't even know what an analytical machine was.

The woman returned the trophy to the cabinet, and handed Ophelia a fountain pen. "We ask all applicants to sign the register. Before doing it yourself, I would like you to read this pen."

Ophelia gripped the gloves she was about to put back on. "You expect me to supply you with information about the other applicants?"

"It will be your final test."

"I can't read a possession without the consent of its owner."

"The Good Family is the owner of this fountain pen, as it is of these trophies," the woman said, gesturing at the cabinet. "There's no difference."

Ophelia contemplated the object for a long time; a ray of sunlight, suddenly escaping through the shutter, bounced off the gold of its nib. Her final test.

She buttoned up her gloves. "I'm sorry, madame, there is a difference. These trophies belong to the past. The future of their owners doesn't depend on what I might divulge about them."

The woman pursed her lips, and it seemed to Ophelia

that the network of her veins became even more prominent beneath the bluish pallor of her skin. The ray of sunlight, swallowed by a cloud, went out like a flame on the nib.

"Sign and go, young lady."

"Should I leave you a contact address? I'm currently staying at the son of Mr. Laza . . . "

"That will not be necessary," the woman interrupted her.

As Ophelia was scribbling a clumsy "Eulalia" on the applications register, she felt a lump rising in her throat. The examiners each wrote down a grade on the same piece of paper, which was then slipped into a cartridge and sent to a different department via a pneumatic tube.

As soon as she got out, she dived into the closest restroom and splashed water on her face.

She hadn't been able to stop herself. Once again, her professional ethics had had the upper hand. She had just let slip away her only chance of accessing the Memorial's Secretarium, of researching into the "ultimate truth," of unmasking God, of finding Thorn again, and all out of consideration for whom? Applicants who didn't hesitate to use their own powers to get rid of the competition.

"Mademoiselle Eulalia?"

She had barely left the restroom when a young girl had approached her. A student, going by her uniform.

"Yes?"

"Kindly follow me, please. Lady Helen would like to converse with you."

Ophelia was no expert on family spirits. Out of the twenty-one in existence, she had known only two up until now, and both those encounters had left her with a memorable impression. When she entered Lady Helen's office, she knew that this occasion would be no different.

The chair the family spirit was sitting in was linked to

a tentacular mechanism. Dozens of articulated arms were humming away, one opening the drawer of a filing cabinet, another raising the cover of a hoist, and another emptying the contents of a pneumatic tube. Some were gathering pending correspondence to the left, others collecting dealt-with correspondence to the right, and all without a lull.

The first thing that struck Ophelia, once the surprise of this mechanical ballet had faded, was that Helen didn't remotely resemble the statues one saw of her in the city, standing magnificently to the right of Pollux. Her nose and ears were elephantine, as though the gigantism afflicting her had concentrated on those parts of her anatomy. In general, nothing seemed normally proportioned in this family spirit. Her head was too large compared with her body, her fingers too long compared with her hands, her bosom too generous compared with her torso. She looked like a huge caricature brought to life.

Ophelia felt her stomach lurch when Helen stamped a paper, placed it on the pile of dealt-with correspondence, and then slowly raised her eyes in her direction; they had completely disappeared behind an optical appliance of crazy complexity. Her slender fingers, similar to a spider's legs, removed two detachable lenses from among the dozens that were stacked on her huge nose, as if that would allow her better to see the little visitor who was standing on the other side of her desk.

The student escorting Ophelia closed the door, and turned the spoked handle several times; it was as if she were closing a vault from the inside. The thousand and one little sounds that filled the conservatoire—pounding of feet, raising of voices, banging of doors—were instantly smothered under a triple layer of silence. Now that Ophelia thought about it, owing to the luminous globes, there wasn't a single window in the office; merely a strange periscope that descended from the ceiling.

"Howard Harper."

Helen's voice had suddenly reverberated against all the marble and metal in the room. It was a voice so grating, so drawn out, so sepulchral that Ophelia wondered for a moment whether she was attempting to call up a spirit.

"That was a time when the powerless still had family names," Helen continued, systematically articulating each syllable. "Today they have all sunk into oblivion. All apart from one: Harper. Even I, endowed with an appalling memory, know that particular name. And you, young lady, do you know it?"

"No, madame," replied Ophelia, puzzled. Where was this conversation leading her? Was this the usual procedure for every applicant?

"Howard Harper is the man who contributed to building the place you are in right now," said Helen, leaning heavily against the back of her chair. "Before him, this little ark was nothing but a jungle shrouded in clouds, and only one virtuoso conservatoire existed: that of my brother and his dear offspring. I, myself, was never able to have children. Of all the family spirits, I'm the only one to be infertile . . . and that's not the only defect to afflict me," she added, with an ironic tone that made her voice even more grating. "Howard Harper is the one who showed me a different path. He was my very first Godson."

"The trophy," murmured Ophelia.

Helen considered her through her stack of lenses. The golden glint of an eye, tiny as a star, so distant did it seem, shone from the other side. "The trophy, yes. With a bare minimum of education, you would have immediately identified its owner. I listened to your so-called evaluation from here, and I found it woefully incomplete. Lack of historical knowledge, absence of dates, anecdotes devoid of relevance: your family power is interesting, but you, young lady, you are an ignoramus. If you had fallen into the trap of the examiners by reading the fountain pen, you wouldn't even be here in my office."

Ophelia squeezed her hands tight behind her back. She had received all manner of insult during her life, and of much greater cruelty, but this one hit her straight in the heart. Reading objects was the one field in which she was gifted. Being criticized for her abilities awoke in her a sensitivity whose existence she'd not even suspected.

"I am not from here, madame. I couldn't have known . . . "

Helen made a gesture of annoyance. Her fingers were so huge, the draft sent all the papers on the desk flying. "Of course you should have known. That is the whole difference between the amateur and the professional. Ignorance, when one possesses a power such as yours, is an unacceptable fault. So my role will be to remedy that."

Ophelia, who was squeezing her hands ever tighter, suddenly relaxed her grip. "You are accepting me as a virtuoso?"

A mechanical arm opened a drawer, took out a piece of paper, and handed it to Ophelia. It was an official document of enrolment to the conservatoire. Helen's lips curled into an ogress's grin that revealed a horrifying number of teeth. "I am not welcoming you into the Good Family, young lady. I will do so in three weeks' time, if you are still among us by then. You will have to do a great, great deal of catching up before even hoping to become a Forerunner."

# THE TRADITION

Ophelia was in such a hurry to tell Ambrose the good news that she slipped on the doorstep of the administration department. The tide of clouds had turned into a downpour, the steps into a cascade. The smell from the vegetation, already strong in the sun, had become heady in the rain.

"Where are you going, apprentice?"

She raised her glasses, streaked with water, toward the figure standing at the top of the entrance steps, under the glass canopy. It was the student who had accompanied her to Helen's office. Squalls were making the panels of her frock coat flap like silver-embroidered standards. She pointed to the arcaded gallery adjoining the administrative building. "We're going that way. All the conservatoire's outbuildings are linked by covered walkways. We'll be sheltered."

"It's just that I have to get back to town," said Ophelia, whose toga was becoming more drenched by the second. "I wouldn't want to miss the last birdtrain."

"You're coming with me. You're to undergo an initial assessment. It's the tradition."

The rain fell even harder on the cobblestones, smothering the voice and silhouette of the student. Ophelia had to resign herself to trekking back up the stairs, against the flow of the water. "Now? But I've only just been accepted."

"You're starting your probationary period. You must not leave the conservatoire premises for the next three weeks, except with Lady Helen's special permission. Without it, she will consider you to have given up, and you won't be given a second chance. Having said that, if you want to go home," the student said, turning on her heels, "no one here's going to stop you."

Ophelia followed her along the walkway. She'd barely had a chance to feel jubilant, and already she'd been brought back down to earth. So she'd have to remain three whole weeks on this little ark? Couldn't she do her research at the Memorial's Secretarium before this time limit?

And Ambrose, she suddenly thought, wringing out the soaked panels of her toga, wouldn't he worry when she didn't return? "It's somewhat of a prison-like approach."

"Hmm?" The student half-turned, as if surprised to find Ophelia behind her. "You signed an agreement, apprentice. Lady Helen is offering you board, lodgings, and a future. Tradition requires that, in exchange, you follow her instructions without asking questions."

Ophelia reflected that she should have read the agreement more carefully before signing it. She wiped her glasses and looked at the student's profile, emerging from her long, tawny hair. Livid complexion, half-closed eyelid, fixed eyebrow, nondescript nose, flat mouth: her face was like her voice, devoid of expression. This impassivity contrasted with the flamboyance of her freckles. She was on the tall side, very slender, and her fitted frock coat emphasized her lack of curves. The complete opposite of Ophelia.

"Are you an apprentice, too? You haven't told me your name."

"Hmm?" went the student, roused from her reverie. "I'm called Elizabeth. From today onwards, we're rivals, you and I. Sworn enemies, one might say."

During the silence that ensued, Ophelia had ample time to hear the rain beating down on the glass of the arcade.

"I'm joking," Elizabeth finally added, a few steps later. "I'm an aspiring virtuoso, which places me, hierarchically, above the apprentices. We'll be neither rivals nor enemies. I'm in charge of the second division of Forerunners. If you have any questions, it's to me that you must address them. Congratulations, in fact."

She was speaking in a distant voice, without a shadow of a smile. Even the melodious Babel accent fell flat from her mouth.

"And what is your family power, Elizabeth, if it's not indiscreet to ask?"

"Hmm? I don't have one."

Ophelia's eyebrows twitched. "I was told that the powerless were very rare here."

"I'm currently their sole representative at the conservatoire. I had only two predecessors: Howard Harper and Lazarus."

"Lazarus, as in the Lazarus of the automatons? I didn't know he'd been a virtuoso." Ambrose had neglected to tell her, which raised a new question. Why had he tried to discourage her from joining the Good Family when his own father had followed that path?

"Everyone should know that. Particularly a Forerunner. Let's hurry up now, apprentice."

Ophelia couldn't have been keener to do so, but of the two of them, it was Elizabeth who walked slower. The aspiring virtuoso was forever slowing down to pull a notebook out from her frock coat and jot things down in it, which she always ended up crossing out, while muttering between her teeth. This young girl was certainly a queer fish.

Ophelia soon noticed that Elizabeth was far from an isolated case. A cohort of shaven-headed Cyclopeans was running along the ceiling of the galleries while loudly reciting physics formulae. A young Totemist girl was walking straight ahead, nose in a book, cloaked in a swarm of mosquitoes, buzzing around her but never biting her. There was even an old man conjuring up electric arcs between his fingers while sniggering in a rather senile way.

All of these people wore the same midnight-blue-and-silver uniform. Were they all, then, future virtuosos?

Elizabeth climbed a series of stairs leading to a particularly imposing residence. Built all on the vertical, it hugged the edge of the ark, and its ramparts, spreading like wings of stone, served as a frontier between land and sky. Gigantic sculpted elephant heads, incorporated in the building's facade, looked so stern that they prompted not a smile.

"This is the Hall of Residence," explained Elizabeth, scribbling something new in her notebook. "It's where you will sleep, wash, take your meals, and do your chores. Don't expect to find automatons to clean for you; there's a whole load of them for the Sons of Pollux, but Lady Helen insists that, here, we do everything for ourselves."

Ophelia looked up high enough to crick her neck. The Hall of Residence was designed like the Memorial, but more modest in size: it had a vast atrium around which the stories circled like a planet's rings. Floors, walls, and ceilings were all turned into rooms. The apprentices up on high were debating some aspect of rhetoric with their heads upside down; those down below were calling for silence to concentrate on their homework. Some were pushing trolleys of laundry along the vertical corridors, others were carrying out unfathomable experiments in cubicles reserved for practical work. The whole atmosphere was buzzing, like a beehive, resonating with accents from the four corners of the world.

Ophelia's chest tightened. Even here, even now, she couldn't stop herself from looking for the tallest and least talkative of them all. And what if Thorn had taken the very same path as her? If he had used the Good Family to infiltrate the corridors of the Memorial?

"Does the conservatoire have many virtuosos?" she asked Elizabeth.

"Hmm? Yes, rather. There's the company of Forerunners, the company of Lawyers, the company of Scribes, the company of Guardians, and plenty of others, too. Each company is made up of two divisions: the Godchildren of Helen here, and the Sons of Pollux over there." Elizabeth had indicated, to underline the last word, a large balcony that enabled one to make out, through several layers of rain, the cliff of the neighboring ark.

"Why live separately if we're following the same apprenticeship?"

"Because it's the tradition."

Ophelia wondered whether conservatoire students received a bonus every time they repeated this mantra. Elizabeth was chewing her pencil rubber, dreamily, eyes lost in her notebook, long hair following her undulating walk. In the experiment cubicle of a topsy-turvium, there was a puff of smoke and exclamations, to which she paid no attention whatsoever. She didn't seem that keen to make conversation.

That wasn't the case for Ophelia. "It was a poster in the Memorial that brought me here. I discovered they wanted Forerunners for their reading groups. I'd like to apply. I'm certain it would be right up my alley."

Elizabeth gave her a sidelong look. She had stopped walking and chewing her pencil. Her eyes had turned from vague to piercing as arrows. "Relinquish all your certainty." Even her voice had changed, suddenly resonant, deeply concerned. "Who do you think you are, you who speak of our cause so lightly? Your talent is but a bent rod that will have to be straightened. Sir Henry's reading groups demand a know-how that your hands don't yet possess, that they will probably never possess."

Ophelia clenched her fists so tight, her gloves creaked. It was the second time today that someone was knocking her professional pride, and she clearly wasn't lacking in it. Over the top of her notebook, in the midst of the university hubbub, Elizabeth continued to study her, with neither hostility nor friendliness, as though expecting a rebellious reaction from her.

The young Animist released her breath and relaxed her clenched fists. She understood. A good citizen, and even more so a virtuoso, didn't cling to what made him or her an individual. The interest of the group had to come before personal pride. "You're right. The more I discover the world around me, the more I realize how little I know it."

Elizabeth's half-closed eyelids lowered even more, and Ophelia thought she caught a glimmer of satisfaction between her eyelashes.

"An admission for an admission: I, too, feel pride. I love the city, love the Memorial, and love the Good Family. I tend to expect others to demonstrate the same devotion. And to respect my work."

"You work for the reading groups?"

Elizabeth stuck her notebook against Ophelia's glasses. It was covered in a jumble of numbers and letters. "Algorithms, functions, iterative structures, conditional structures," she translated. "It's the reading groups that are working for me. I'm in charge of the new catalogue. The readers encode the database I've created, for Sir Henry's use. Most of the Memorial's ancient documents are neither dated nor authenticated, so we need faultless evaluations. I'm working right now on a system of perforated cards that would enable Sir Henry to deal efficiently with those myriad pieces of information."

Ophelia lowered her eyes, despite herself. The lessons in humility suddenly made total sense. Elizabeth was perhaps not far from her in age, but she was ahead in a way not quantifiable in years.

"Lady Septima has three weeks to prepare you," continued Elizabeth. "If you do exactly what she tells you, and toe the line with her, then you may have a chance of joining our ranks."

"Lady Septima," Ophelia repeated, trying to memorize the name. "I thought it was Sir Henry who was in charge of the reading groups."

Elizabeth's mouth suddenly twisted into a smile that struggled to find its place on her expressionless face. "He would be pretty incapable of doing so. Sir Henry is an automaton. He never leaves the Secretarium."

Ophelia would have to get used to the idea: on Babel, automatons were members of society in their own right, and some of them could be called "Sir." Just as she was about to ask some questions on the Secretarium—how one entered it, in particular—she changed her mind. Show too much curiosity, and she would end up arousing suspicion, and she'd lacked enough subtlety for today. "Thank you," she said, instead.

Elizabeth shrugged her shoulders, and went over to a noticeboard standing in the middle of the atrium. A mechanical arm was writing out words in chalk:

*The apprentice Eulalia is expected at the interfamilial amphitheater.*

"We didn't hurry enough," said Elizabeth. "You should already be in uniform. Quick, let's get a move on," she added, not hastening in the slightest.

She led Ophelia to the Hall's cloakroom to find a uniform in her size, and unfolded a mechanical screen. The shirt, frock coat, trousers, and boots had so many fastenings, Ophelia couldn't see the end of them. Her breathing was restricted the moment she buttoned up her frock coat; here was an outfit that didn't leave much room for curves.

Elizabeth showed her the silver braiding on her midnight-blue sleeve. "Pay close attention to stripes. An apprentice virtuoso has only one band on his or her uniform. An aspiring virtuoso of the first degree, like me, has two bands. An aspiring virtuoso of the second degree has three bands. One band for each year at the conservatoire."

Ophelia refrained from saying that she had no intention of staying that long. As soon as she had access to the Memorial's Secretarium, or as soon as she had tracked down Thorn, ideally both of those, she would take her leave.

She tackled the endless laces on her boots. Elizabeth's boots were spurred with two little silver wings, at ankle level.

"That's the emblem of the Frontrunners. You will get your wings if you complete your three weeks on probation."

*If*, Ophelia noted, putting Thorn's watch into a pocket of her frock coat. Not *when*.

"This assessment I have to undergo, what does it consist of?"

"Hmm? Oh, you'll be put through all sorts of tests. It's rather painful, many applicants can't withstand it. Even though it remains rare, some die from it." Elizabeth's eyelids vaguely lifted on seeing Ophelia's glasses turn yellow on her nose, and then she added, flatly: "I'm joking. There have never been either deaths or injuries. See it more as a game."

Ophelia hadn't been too sure until now, but this time she was certain: her heart rate didn't appreciate Elizabeth's sense of humor one bit. She closed the clasp on her belt, finally ready, and felt a lump in her throat. Throughout the day, she had tried not to think about it, to stay focused on all these new things she had to take in. Now that she could feel this strange garment on her, she couldn't manage it anymore. She took a deep breath, trying to stifle the sudden emotion rising from deep inside her, but she couldn't stop herself from seeing the scene repeated: the bag snatched away by the tram, and the scarf with it. Why had fate allowed her to get one back and not the other?

"Are you following me, apprentice?" Elizabeth called out, folding up the mechanical screen. "I'm taking you to your assessment."

"Coming." Ophelia coughed to clear her voice. Weakening was a luxury she couldn't allow herself. She would require all her concentration to pass her tests.

Elizabeth left Ophelia at the door to the interfamilial amphitheatre. It was semicircular and its tiers could easily accommodate around a hundred people. That was a lot of seats for a single apprentice. A man in a toga guided her to the front row, where writing equipment already awaited her.

"It's the tradition," was all he said by way of instruction.

Ophelia dried up at the first question: *List the methods of dating, relative and absolute, that you know.* The rest of the questions were all along the same lines, on increasingly specialized concepts and historical methodologies, and there were entire pages of them. "See it more like a game." Well, it was certainly nothing like a game of cards. She was starting to feel the effects of her previous insomnia, and her empty stomach soon filled the amphitheatre with highly embarrassing rumbling sounds.

When she finally handed her work in, engulfed in the abyss of her own ignorance, the man in the toga asked her to follow him. Ophelia was shown into an elegant laboratory where an old lady asked her to remove her uniform—when she'd had

such difficulty putting it on—and then examined her rigor-
ously from head to toe, tongue included. She made her do a
whole series of movements, sometimes with the right hand,
sometimes the left, which Ophelia found baffling.

"It's the tradition," said the old woman. She then gave her a
new outfit, plainer and looser than her uniform, and requested
that she go to the stadium, outside, when she was ready.

Evening was closing in. It was becoming very dark and very
humid when Ophelia got there. She couldn't believe her ears
when an instructor ordered her to run fifteen laps. "It's the
tradition."

On Anima, the only sporting activities were swimming,
dancing, and mountain climbing, and Ophelia had never
done any of them. After just one lap, she felt as if her lungs
were about to burst. Her tunic and hair were sticking to her
as if she'd plunged fully dressed into a bath. The rain had
stopped, the stadium had become a giant swamp populated
by frogs. She had to finish her run at a limp, a stitch stabbing
her in the side, under the disapproving eyes of the instructor.
He made no comment, however, returned her uniform to her,
and simply declared that the assessment was over.

Ophelia followed the path of the Chinese lanterns suspended along the walkway arcades, paying no attention to
the moths bumping into her glasses. She felt in great need of a
bath and a meal, but when she reached the Hall of Residence,
a deafening silence reigned in the vast atrium. Everyone had
long been in bed.

Taking a transcendium, she swung from the vertical position to the horizontal. Fatigue gave her a real impression of
fighting against the terrestrial forces of attraction, as though,
at any moment, she risked falling from the wall and crashing
to the floor.

After wandering around the topsy-turviums, wondering

where she was supposed to go, she went up to the top floor, just beneath the cupola's stars, where a single circular corridor led to several doors. Hanging over each one was a wrought-iron sign bearing the name of a company.

Ophelia went through the Forerunners' door.

Inside it was so very dark that she banged into several beds, triggering a chain reaction of drowsy grunts, before finding one that was vacant. She placed her uniform on what she supposed was a chair, and unlaced her boots in the dark. All she could hope now was that her stomach's moaning wouldn't wake up the entire Hall.

Ophelia had barely lain down before she heard stifled laughter in the darkness. There was no mattress on her bed. "Of course," she thought, clasping Thorn's watch close to her. "Tradition."

# THE RUMOR

Ophelia leapt from cloud to cloud, above an old world that was still intact. She wasn't interested in the towns, the forests, the oceans of the past flashing by beneath her feet. She sought only to reach the birdtrain flying across the sky. She could just see the scarf caught in its door, and a familiar silhouette behind one of its windows. Thorn's silhouette. Ophelia was just catching up with the birdtrain when, suddenly, the clouds under her feet started groaning.

She half-opened an eye to peer through the bent glasses she'd forgotten to take off to sleep. It wasn't the clouds groaning, but the springs of her bed. It took her many blinks to remember where she was and why. The heat was oppressive. The window, bright with morning, cast a limpid light over the dormitory. It was an austere room, with visible beams, a strong smell of hot stone, wrought-iron furniture, and a single screen to assure privacy. A screen that Ophelia wouldn't be needing: there was no one left here but her. The other beds that she'd banged into during the night had been replaced with study desks.

If a bell had rung, she hadn't heard it. In fact, the only bell she was hearing right now was the one chiming inside her skull. She would need a whole urn of coffee to make it shut up.

Ophelia dragged herself off the springs of the bed, to the

sound of her every vertebra protesting. She felt like an automaton that had been taken apart, screw by screw, and then reassembled any old how. It was no great surprise to see that her uniform had gone from the chair. Probably down to the same jokers who had thought it amusing to remove her mattress.

With a yawn, Ophelia thought: "I've been Berenilde's valet, Farouk's plaything, and Baron Melchior's prey; a tasteless prank isn't going to intimidate me."

Keeping on her stadium outfit, still caked in mud, she pulled on a cord hanging from the wall. With a mechanical hum, her bed rose until neatly slotted into the wall alcove, while a desk, through an ingenious telescopic process, unfolded itself in its stead. It was just like those books in which the illustrations open out and then close up as one turns the pages. Ophelia would have marveled at it had that bed not put her through torture.

The rest of the Hall turned out to be as deserted as the Forerunners' dormitory. Ophelia encountered no one in the refectory, where she made do with the remains of some cereal; or in the cloakroom, where she looked for a new uniform; or in the communal showers, where she hurriedly soaped herself. She checked the noticeboard, but the mechanical arm had written no instruction in chalk. She was almost certain she was supposed to be somewhere else, but she didn't know where.

For an information specialist, it was a great start.

As she was roaming the walkways, in search of someone to advise her, Ophelia couldn't help but think of Ambrose. She imagined him alone, surrounded by his father's automatons, waiting for news of her. He must really think her the queen of ingratitude, a profiteer ready to leave one benefactor for another offering more. Ophelia would have readily improvised using a mirror to pay him a flying visit—although the distance was probably too great—but she hadn't yet found a single one at the Good Family. Helen seemed very keen not to encourage vanity among her students.

In fact, it wasn't such a bad thing. Strong as the temptation might be, it was better not to reveal that she was a mirror visitor. She'd already taken enough of a risk in revealing her talent for reading objects.

Ophelia finally found some other apprentice virtuosos in the amphitheater where she'd had her assessment the previous day. All was so silent that, when she had pushed open the door, she had at first thought the place deserted. She saw no lecturer on the rostrum, but all the students were busy writing. They were wearing earphones. No one looked up from their shorthand as Ophelia, as unobtrusively as possible, tried to find herself a place on the top tier.

Once seated, she understood that a radio was incorporated within each unit. She slipped on some earphones, heard nothing, twiddled a few knobs, still heard nothing. When she asked her neighbors how to use her radio, they gestured to her to be quiet. With perseverance, she finally found the frequency modulator and succeeded in catching some broadcasts. Dozens of broadcasts, each on a different frequency. They were exclusively university lectures recorded live in the city's academic institutions; how could she know which one she was supposed to follow?

Ophelia lowered the sound and stopped trying. She had come to Babel to do research, not to study. She wiped away the trickle of sweat already running down her neck, resisting the urge to take off her too-tight frock coat. She studied the apprentices sitting in front of her, one by one. Thorn was not among them, but that in itself wasn't surprising. If he had reached here in advance of her, as she supposed, she would be more likely to find him among the aspiring virtuosos; going by stripes on uniforms, there wasn't one of them in this amphitheater.

At first, Ophelia had thought the silence total, but that wasn't the case. Above the scratching of fountain pens on paper, above the rustling of voices in earphones, above the chirring of the cicadas outdoors, she could hear some whispering. It was going on in the row below hers. Apprentices were leaning over to each other, allowing glimpses of nervous expressions. Ophelia wouldn't have paid them much attention had the word "Memorial" not suddenly reached her. She switched the sound of her radio off, and, without removing her earphones, leant forward slightly on her desk.

They were all speaking with the same accent, very different to that of Babel, but just as musical:

"I had a premonition. Didn't I tell you that, yesterday?"

"Shut up. We all had a premonition. The trouble is, we should have foreseen what, where, and who, but didn't manage to do so."

"It's surely not that serious, is it? It's just a rumor. They always exaggerate, do rumors."

"Oh *sí?* And why have today's readings all been canceled?"

"No complaints from me. I can't see a book anymore without feeling nauseous."

"You're forgetting the automaton." The apprentice had pronounced it "owtomatin," but Ophelia, who was leaning further and further on her desk, immediately understood the allusion to Sir Henry. "He'll make us work twice as long to catch up."

"You don't find it a bit too much of a coincidence? The little new girl turning up, and this incident at the Memorial?"

"*Basta.* She's watching us."

At these words, all the whisperers replaced their earphones and returned to their shorthand. All apart from a pretty, boyish girl who turned around, unashamedly, to stare at Ophelia with obvious curiosity. On her face, illuminations shone like inlays on a carnival mask.

A sonorous voice immediately boomed across the amphi-theater with the force of a rumble of thunder: "Apprentice Mediana, eyes forward."

The boyish girl returned nonchalantly to her work, and Ophelia pretended to do the same, not without glancing at the gramophone horn that was fixed to the ceiling. She hadn't noticed it, that one, no more than she'd noticed the periscope that turned its cyclops eye now to the right, now to the left. She had taken the absence of a lecturer as evidence of trust, a sign that the conservatoire treated its students as responsible young people. Big mistake. They were all under surveillance.

As soon as the voice from the horn announced the end of the radio lessons, much later on, Ophelia hurried to catch up with the whisperers on the stairs outside. Now they were stand-ing, she could see the wings pinned to their boots. As she'd suspected when listening to them, they were all Forerunners.

"I'm 'the little new girl,'" she said, introducing herself with sarcasm. "Forgive me for inviting myself to your confab, but I believe mention was made of m—"

"Sorry about your glasses," one of them suddenly inter-rupted her.

"Pardon?" The remark so threw Ophelia that she missed a step and descended the rest of the marble staircase on her backside. The Forerunners stepped over her, one after the other, without a glance. Now she herself could only half-see them; she'd lost one of her lenses in her fall. As she was feeling around for it on the steps, her body humiliatingly sore, an illuminated hand held out what she was looking for.

"Mediana, of the second division of the company of Fore-runners," the boyish girl formally introduced herself. "But that you already knew, didn't you? My cousins' predictions cause almost as many accidents as they prevent. Beware, *signorina*, they do take advantage somewhat."

Her accent made her pronounce each word with a sensual purr. Cautiously, Ophelia took back her lens. "The Forerunners are all from your family?"

"A good number of them. We, the Seers of The Serenissima, have information in the blood."

"Ah. And you can see the future, too, Mediana?"

"No, with me it's more the past. A bit like you, little reader, but our skill is different."

So, noted Ophelia to herself, Mediana, as a Forerunner worthy of the name, already knew what her family power was.

"What were you talking about with your cousins? What happened at the Memorial?"

With overt familiarity, Mediana laid a finger on Ophelia's mouth, inciting her to wait. Apprentices continued to flow around them, as carelessly as a river around a rock. When there was no one but them left on the stairs, she brought her face close to Ophelia's, so close that the latter could see each illumination, despite her missing lens. Mediana had a rare beauty in which were combined, with infinite subtlety, curved lines and angular forms—an allure that could enchant both men and women.

"I'm going to try to help you gain precious time, little reader. Lady Helen should never have accepted your application. My power is worth at least ten times yours, and I have perfect mastery of the ancient languages. You are condemned to be a prisoner of my shadow, as are all the other Forerunners. Don't think my cousins like me any more than you do. Friendship doesn't exist at the Good Family, because only the best remain."

"I—"

"Say nothing," whispered Mediana, pressing her index finger to Ophelia's lips. "Just listen, *signorina*. Violence, even in its most trivial form, is severely punished on Babel. You will suffer no physical mistreatment among us. But believe me," she added, her hot breath brushing Ophelia's skin, "there are all sorts of torment. Go home, forget the virtuosos and forget the Memorial. It's my destiny, not yours."

Ophelia was less shocked by these words than by the tone in which they were said. A sincere, deeply apologetic tone. Through her half-glasses, she watched Mediana walk down the stairs with a mixture of strength and grace, the illuminations on her skin glinting in the sunshine.

"I've been Berenilde's valet, Farouk's plaything, and Baron Melchior's prey," she repeated to herself, while returning her lens to its frame. An empty threat isn't going to intimidate me.

With her lower back smarting from her tumble down the stairs, Ophelia followed the Forerunners at a respectable distance. Whether they wanted her or not, they were now members of the same company; she would impose her presence on them for as long as she needed to be one of them.

They all crossed the impressive bridge that linked the ark of Helen's virtuosos to that of Pollux's, and then continued to one of the conservatoire's outbuildings. Two floors up, Ophelia discovered a laboratory that was the epitome of estheticism, all high ceilings, brass, and velvet. The room was bathed in the rainbow light of a rose window and the balmy breeze from the overhead fans. The precious-wood tables displayed the very latest in instruments for experiments.

When Ophelia, unsure, took a seat at the bench, she realized that the number of Forerunners around her had doubled. The division of Helen's Godchildren had joined that of the Sons of Pollux in a swirl of uniforms and a surge of accents, which stopped the moment a woman closed the laboratory door.

"Knowledge serves peace," she declared.

"Knowledge serves peace," the apprentices all repeated in

unison, holding fists on chests and banging winged heels of boots together.

The woman approved without a smile. Judging from her bronze skin, black hair, and blazing eyes, she was a true Babelian. The gold braiding on her uniform was as dazzling as the look she directed at Ophelia.

"Apprentice Eulalia, I am Lady Septima, and I will be your specialization teacher. The results of your assessment yesterday have been passed on to me. They are not brilliant. I prefer, however, to judge for myself whether you are worthy or not of becoming a Forerunner. To be worthy does not mean to *succeed*." This time, Lady Septima's eyes took in the entire laboratory, drawing into their blaze the face of each apprentice. "Today, there are many of you, but only two among you, one Son of Pollux and one Godchild of Helen, will ultimately be able to rise to the rank of aspiring virtuoso."

Lady Septima's eyes had lingered, possibly unconsciously, on an apprentice who resembled her too much not to be a member of her family. As for Ophelia, she better understood certain things. *Only the best remain.* This conservatoire had made rivalry its cornerstone.

"My work," Lady Septima continued, returning to Ophelia, "consists of turning the crude mineral that is your family power into the purest of diamonds. And that is not all. The corporation of Forerunners, of which I am overall in charge, has been conferred the honor of revising the Memorial's catalogue. Those who are worthy of joining the reading groups, and they only, belong at the conservatoire. You have three weeks, Apprentice Eulalia, to convince me that I am not wasting my time on you. Do you have any questions?"

Ophelia gritted her teeth hard to hold back all those that came to her. How could one gain the right to enter the Secretarium? Does it really have a strongroom? Does it harbor any vestiges of the old school? And what is it, this ultimate truth that your glorious Memorial refuses to divulge to the public?

It would have been unwise, not to say dangerous, to reveal the true object of her visit. "Why were the reading groups canceled today?" she simply asked.

This curiosity was legitimate. At least, Ophelia had thought so before realizing that everyone around her had frozen, as if the ceiling fans had suddenly flung an icy wind over the laboratory. Only Mediana was biting her lip so as not to burst out laughing.

As for Lady Septima, she remained unperturbed. She just toned down, with a mere flicker of the eyelids, her fiery gaze, directing it not at Ophelia in particular, but at each apprentice.

"I have no comment to make on the affair you all have in mind. Pay no attention to the rumor that's going around. The *Official Journal* will tell you all you need to know tomorrow. Remember that for you, Forerunners, it must be your sole source of information. And now, I would like each of you to examine the sample before you, applying the regulatory procedure," she added, in a tone that brooked no response. "You must have identified the object to which it belonged and written a full report by the end of the class. Apprentice Eulalia, you will touch nothing today; simply observe your classmates to see how they proceed."

If Lady Septima had hoped to obtain Ophelia's utmost concentration, it was a total failure. While all the apprentices carefully studied their samples with the laboratory instruments, she wasn't remotely inclined to watch them doing so. All she could think of was that rumor. What had actually happened at the Memorial? Was there a chance, even the slightest one, that it was connected to Thorn? Had he been in trouble while she remained there, twiddling her thumbs?

Ophelia was drawn from her thoughts by the sense of eyes

burning into her. At first she presumed it was Mediana still shamelessly staring at her, but the Seer was totally immersed in her work. No, this time it was another apprentice; the one Lady Septima had silently singled out during her talk. Sitting on the other side of the bench, he had already finished typing up his analysis report. His Visionary's eyes were boring into her, so she felt caught in the beams of two incandescent lamps, as if she were a new sample to be analyzed. A golden chain linked the arch of his brow to his nostril. Ophelia hadn't yet learnt all the subtleties of the Babel dress code, but Ambrose had spoken to her of this type of jewelry; this young man belonged to a family that was highly placed within Pollux's lineage. There was no doubting it now—he was Lady Septima's own son.

Ophelia returned to his stare with equal curiosity. Getting to know him would have been a good strategy with regard to her plans, but she dropped the idea almost as soon as she'd had it. The relentless intensity with which the young man was staring at her wasn't merely a sign of interest. It was distrust.

"Put away your equipment, leave your samples on the bench, and hand your reports in to me before you go," instructed Lady Septima at the end of the class. "Sons of Pollux, you are to go to the gymnasium for your sensory training. Godchildren of Helen, you are to return to your ark and to mind what you say. No more rumors for today, understood? Stay with me, Apprentice Eulalia," she added, holding Ophelia back by the shoulder. "I would like to discuss one or two things with you."

Once everyone had left her laboratory, Lady Septima closed the door and turned to Ophelia with stonelike rigidity. "Apprentice Eulalia, are you bored among us?"

Ophelia tensed. This woman made her feel uncomfortable. And yet she was very calm, and almost as small as her.

"I don't understand."

Lady Septima looked at her. No, *look* was the wrong verb for such eyes. She dissected her. Penetrating the loose lens of Ophelia's glasses, she calculated the dilation of her pupils; probed inside her veins; measured her blood-flow rate; delved into the intimate chemistry of her organs; examined, one by one, every molecule of her body.

"You remained idle for the entire duration of my class."

"Because you asked me to touch nothing." Ophelia felt sweat soaking her gloves. She had only just noticed, now that they were standing close to one another, the emblem that Lady Septima wore as a clasp on her cape. A sun with the word "LUX" engraved within it.

This woman, on whom Ophelia would depend from now on, was a sentinel of God.

Lady Septima pulled on a glove as golden as her uniform. Delicately, between thumb and index finger, she picked up the minuscule sample that had remained at Ophelia's place on the bench. Her red eyes examined it in the light.

"Let's see . . . This metal is composed of more than three-quarters tin, just under a quarter lead, and a tiny part copper," she murmured. "This alloy was created . . . *eh bien* . . . three centuries ago, maybe even four. A variant of bronze, but with an entirely distinctive makeup. That is reserved for the manufacture of organ pipes."

Ophelia felt, much despite herself, a rare admiration. Sons and Daughters of Pollux were known for their highly developed senses, but Lady Septima would have made the best microscope on Anima blanch. So this was what Visionaries were really capable of.

"Why do you think I left this within your reach?" the teacher asked, returning the fragment to its velvet pad

It was a test, Ophelia realized. And she'd failed it.

"You could have tried to impress me, to show me what your reader's hands are capable of," Lady Septima persisted, her tone measured. "You did nothing of the sort. Either you lack daring, or you lack curiosity. What, in your opinion, is the foremost quality of a Forerunner?"

Ophelia almost retorted that she didn't think she lacked either daring or curiosity, in her own way, but refrained at the last second. *Become a FORERUNNER in the city's service!* the recruitment poster had proclaimed. It was now that the true test was taking place. "Obedience."

Lady Septima broke into a fleeting smile of approval. How could a woman with such fire in her eyes send such shivers down one's spine?

"That, indeed, is the correct answer, but I would like to be sure of its sincerity. Take your place on this," she requested, pulling a stool in front of the stained-glass window.

As Ophelia was sitting on it, Lady Septima made a sign for her to stop. "Not like that, apprentice. Standing."

With great stiffness, Ophelia hoisted herself, awkwardly, up on to the stool.

"Perfect," Lady Septima said, appreciatively. "You will remain like that until you receive permission to leave."

"And my apprenticeship?"

"During your period of probation, your every day will be broken down into four periods: theory, practical, training, and chores. Theory and practical are done for today. So consider this little exercise as training."

With these words, Lady Septima pulled the cords of the fans to stop them and closed the door behind her. Ophelia found herself alone among the test tubes and the scales, in the dazzling light of the rose window. Without the fans, the laboratory gradually turned into a furnace. Having already played at being a servant, Ophelia knew it was hard to remain standing still for a lengthy period, but this was the first time she was trying it on a stool: it was impossible for her to stretch her legs, impossible to change position, impossible to shift her body weight more to one side than to the other. All her muscles were straining to maintain her balance, but they were aching due to the night without a mattress and the fall on the stairs. The numbness spread, like slow petrifaction, from her calves up to her hips, from her lower back up to her shoulders. Ophelia focused on the rose window's colors sliding across the precious wood of the laboratory, as the sun gradually moved in the sky. Sweat was trickling under her trousers and she felt the increasingly urgent need to go to the toilet.

She fell backwards onto the floor. The stool, overcome by the exasperation of her Animism, had suddenly launched into a tap-dancing number.

As Ophelia was searching for the lens from her glasses, which, sneakily, had taken advantage of the situation to escape again, anger exploded inside her. A kid! Even far from home, even after all these years, she was still, and forever, being treated like a kid.

She watched the stool galloping around the laboratory, and suddenly thought back to the periscope in the amphitheater, to the words that it was forbidden to utter, to that collective memory locked away in the Secretarium. It wasn't she who was the kid. It was the whole of humanity. They were all, absolutely all, kept in a state of infantilism by God and his Guardians.

"I've been Berenilde's valet, Farouk's plaything, and Baron Melchior's prey," she repeated to herself, once she'd halted the stool and got back on to it. "I'm not going to give Lady Septima any excuse to distance me from my objective."

The sun was fading from the laboratory when the door was at last reopened. Ophelia blinked several times to make the beads of sweat clinging to her eyelashes fall. Elizabeth was standing right in front of her, expressionless behind her constellation of freckles.

"So, your first day? Still determined to remain with us, Apprentice Eulalia?"

"Still." Ophelia's voice was croaky due to thirst.

"As the person in charge of the second division of the company of Forerunners, I release you from that stool."

The phrase was so pompous, Ophelia thought she was making fun of her. So she was astonished when she offered her hand to help her get down, and then gave her a siphon of water, brought specially for her.

"That was the good news," Elizabeth said, watching her drink and cough all at once. "The bad news is that you've incurred a reprimand for having mislaid a mattress and a uniform. You will get twice the chores of the others to repay your debt."

"They were mislaid for me."

Elizabeth merely blinked slowly. "It's tradition. You'll have to be more vigilant. By the way, I have a telegram for you."

Ophelia's heart missed a beat. She impatiently unfolded the little blue paper Elizabeth had just handed to her.

CONGRATULATIONS. AMBROSE.

She turned the telegram over. That was it. The voluble, inexhaustible Ambrose had no other message for her. Ophelia felt something tighten inside her. Had she just lost the only friend she'd made on Babel?

"I seem to be going from blunder to blunder." Her avowal had slipped out almost despite herself, while she was putting the stool back in its place. For a moment, she feared it would lead to a lot of indiscreet questions, but Elizabeth asked not one. She had already got her notebook out again to scribble code in it.

"The only real mistake is that which one doesn't remedy."

As Elizabeth concentrated on her notebook, Ophelia studied her waxen face at length. As a character, she was hard to figure out, but what she had just said to her was the most reassuring thing she had heard all day.

"Elizabeth?"

"Hmm?"

"What happened at the Memorial today?"

"Oh, that?" Elizabeth said, crossing out another lot of code. "Mademoiselle Silence died."

Ophelia's eyebrows shot up. Mademoiselle Silence? That name rang a bell . . . Wasn't it that of the Memorialist with the sensitive ears? That tyrannical woman who wanted to search her bag?

"Her body was found this morning in the Memorial," continued Elizabeth."When I arrived there, like every morning, to work on my database, I was immediately asked to return to the conservatoire. They told me that it was an unfortunate accident, and that poor Mademoiselle Silence had fallen from a library ladder."

"Fallen from a ladder," repeated Ophelia, who had expected something a little more scandalous. "That's really unlucky."

Elizabeth concurred, distractedly, chewing the end of her pencil. "Yes, that's what Mademoiselle Silence must have thought just before dying. I barely had time to see her body. Her face, mainly. I didn't think a fall could leave you with an expression like that."

"What expression?" murmured Ophelia.

Elizabeth lifted her lampshade eyelids, revealing eyes as inscrutable as the codes in her notebook. "An expression of abject terror."

Until that moment, Ophelia had convinced herself that nothing she would experience here would remind her of the Pole. It was now clear to her that she had underestimated Babel.

# JOURNEY

Mommy had put her to bed even earlier than usual. Like every evening, she had taken her temperature, twice; given her a drink after first tasting the water; combed her long, white hair; and tucked her in, checking that she wasn't cold. Like every evening, she had observed her for a long time from the bedroom door, hesitant yet smiling, before resolving to pull the door to and withdraw, with a rustle of dress.

And now, Victoria was staring up at the ceiling.

Mommy hadn't closed the door—she never closed the door, regularly peeping into the bedroom to reassure herself that all was well—and distant voices were rising from the drawing room. The house was often filled with silence, sometimes with music, almost never with voices.

Victoria had no desire to sleep at all; she wanted to be with the voices. Her sheets were tucked so tight, she could barely wriggle her toes. If she were an ordinary little girl, she would have struggled crossly, she would have called her mother, screaming and crying, but Victoria wasn't ordinary.

Victoria didn't speak. Ever.

Victoria didn't walk. Ever.

That is to say, the Other-Victoria. The true Victoria got out of bed, put her feet on the ground, and went over to the almost-closed door.

128

She hesitated and, as Mommy had done earlier, she looked back toward the bed. A little girl was lying in it, eyes staring up at the ceiling. Her face, lips, and hair were as white as the pillowcase. Victoria knew that it was her in the bed, and out of it. She felt neither fear nor surprise at that. Rather, she felt at fault, a bit like when she tried to get down from her chair on her own, and Mommy darted toward her looking terrified.

Victoria didn't hesitate for long; the call of the *journey* was always strongest.

She slipped into the corridor. She felt so light, so much lighter than the Other-Victoria! As light as in the warm bathwater. And just as when she ducked her head under the water, prompting panicked cries from Mommy, she saw objects differently: their forms had become blurred, their colors smudged. Victoria could neither grab them nor move them. She looked at a large wall mirror that didn't return her reflection; its surface resembled a whirlpool, just like when Mommy pulled the plug to empty the bath.

Victoria bounced on each step of the big staircase, like a soap bubble, drawn by the voices in the drawing room. Just as she was crossing the hall, she heard someone else behind the front door, which was still open.

She took a quick look outside.

At first she saw only the autumnal trees, stirred by the wind. It was raining. It rained nearly every day, and even though that rain didn't wet you, Victoria still preferred the sun. Her eyes followed the flight of a bird in the sky, but she knew it wasn't a real one. Nothing was really real outside the house. Mommy had told her so. Victoria wondered what real rain, real trees, and real birds might look like. Godfather hadn't taken her to see them, and she'd never dared leave the house during her *journeys*.

Victoria suddenly saw a hole. An enormous hole right in

the middle of the garden. Here, there was neither grass nor tree nor rain. There was nothing but a dusty, old wooden floor. Right opposite, a couple were sitting on the steps. The Funny-Eyed-Lady and the Big-Ginger-Fellow. Godfather's friends.

Neither of them noticed Victoria as she approached. They were talking, but even when she got as close as possible, their voices remained distant and distorted.

"He's taking his time, that slowcoach!" moaned the Funny-Eyed-Lady. "LandmArk won't find itself, and I can't stand this manor. It's swarming with illusions—I don't know where to look anymore." She spat out in the direction of the big hole.

Victoria stepped back. Once, she had walked in front of the Funny-Eyed-Lady during a *journey*; doing so had instantly returned her to the position of the Other-Victoria, in bed. Although the Funny-Eyed-Lady couldn't see her, she was very peculiar.

The Big-Ginger-Fellow rested his elbows on the step behind his back. Victoria thought his smile strangely greedy, as if he suddenly wanted to gobble up the Funny-Eyed-Lady. "As far as I'm concerned, I know exactly where to look."

The Funny-Eyed-Lady tilted her cap, and the hole disappeared from the garden just as her face did. "I'm really serious, Foster. Since Mother Hildegarde died, I don't feel I belong here anymore. Neither at Citaceleste nor anywhere else on the Pole. That the toffs hate me, I can handle—I feel the same about them. But to see all our old mates groveling like grubs before me, it makes me sick. The cowards! They want to call a strike, to challenge, to demand . . . and then they kowtow to the first aristo they encounter. How d'you think we're going to overthrow God if we can't be bothered to take the revolution to a few marquises? So, what's Mr. Unionist got to say about it? You do realize, just being seen with me makes you be seen as a traitor?"

The Big-Ginger-Fellow placed his hand on the Funny-Eyed-Lady's head and drew it close to him. "I say that the first to say one word against my boss, just one, I'll smash his teeth in. And I'm really serious, too, Gail."

The Funny-Eyed-Lady said nothing more, but Victoria glimpsed a smile under the peak of her cap. She'd never seen Father and Mommy behave like this, and that thought produced a sort of pain in her other body, the one that had stayed in the bed.

She turned around and then noticed Twit on the banister. He was staring at her with his big yellow eyes. Victoria had never stroked Twit—Mommy thought cats far too dangerous—but she'd always wanted to. As she raised a timid hand toward him, Twit spat. He sped away so fast that the Big-Ginger-Fellow and the Funny-Eyed-Lady both got a start.

Victoria ran back into the house, sure she'd made an unforgiveable mistake. For a moment, she was tempted to go back to being the Other-Victoria, in bed and sleeping, as Mommy had told her to, but as soon as she heard the harp, she forgot her fright.

Once again, the call of the *journey* was strongest.

She went into the drawing room. She slowed down on seeing Great-Godmother pressed to a window, arms crossed and frowning, looking up at the clouds. Victoria didn't yet know her well. Her stern looks and yellow skin intimidated her.

Luckily, Mommy was there. She was sitting beside the harp and her lovely tattooed hands flew from one string to another, like the fake birds in the garden. Victoria went closer to cuddle her, but Mommy didn't see her. Her music was as hazy as her body was.

To Victoria's delight, Godfather was there, too, sprawled across an armchair. He was flicking through some envelopes as if they were a pack of cards. "More and more and more marriage proposals! Not yet three years old, and already she's considered the finest match on the Pole. We'll turn them all down, of course?"

His voice was distorted, too, and Victoria had to strain to hear it properly. Mommy continued to play the harp without replying to him.

"You're never as fine a musician as when you're furious with me," Godfather added, his smile as wide as the split in his hat. "I returned her to you safe and sound, didn't I? She remained within the Compass Rose. I know you're not at all keen on the Citaceleste, but you can't keep your daughter locked away in this manor house forever. Believe me, I tried that approach with my ex-sisters, and they've become more outrageous in two years than I've been for my entire life."

Victoria didn't know what Godfather was talking about— too many complicated words in one go—but she didn't care. He had messy hair, cheeks all golden with beard, and held himself appallingly on his chair. She loved him to bits.

"Come now, Berenilde," he insisted, flapping the envelopes as he would a fan. "I'll soon be embarking once more on my journey, let's not part on bad terms."

Mommy burst into laughter as melodious as her harp. "Your journey? Roaming from Compass Rose to Compass Rose in search of an ark you know to be out of your reach? What you call a journey, I, personally, call an escape."

Godfather's smile widened. Victoria climbed the chair to touch his ill-shaven skin and prickle her fingers, but to her great disappointment, she felt nothing at all. "Oh, I'm starting to understand. It's not my escapade with your daughter for which you reproach me, is it? What you can't accept is that I returned without our little Madame Thorn."

Mommy's hands flew faster and faster across the strings,

but Victoria sensed something was wrong. Mommy had told her once, while tucking her up in bed, that she possessed big, hidden nails that she wouldn't hesitate for a second to use if someone tried to harm them. Victoria had sometimes almost felt them, those nails, when Mommy was cross.

She could see them now.

A shadow was forming all around Mommy: a shadow bristling with claws, claws even scarier than those on the bearskin hanging on the rack in the library. The shadow was as terrifying as Mommy was beautiful.

"Where is she?" she asked, calmly. "Where is Ophelia?"

Great-Godmother turned around from the window and exchanged a look with Godfather, who winked at her.

"You can ask the question again and again," he said to Mommy, "the answer will remain the same. She made us promise not to reveal it to anyone. Not even to you. Isn't the specialty of the Web to protect its secrets?"

"Your clan disowned you, Archie." Mommy had spoken these words very affectionately, but Victoria saw the shadow bristling with claws spread wider. Godfather burst out laughing. So he couldn't see it, Mommy's fearsome shadow?

"Touché!" he said, throwing the pile of envelopes onto a coffee table. "And yet, whether you like it or not, dear friend, I will keep that secret preciously. Ophelia asked me to give you just one single message. A promise. She will find Thorn."

The shadow around Mommy disappeared like a puff of smoke. She pressed both hands on the harp strings to silence them. That silence was almost as loud as a scream. And yet, Mommy was as calm as usual. "There was a time when I had mastered the rules of the game perfectly, even if learning them could prove a cruel lesson. The rules are no longer the same today. The new clans impose their reforms on us, and the servants complain behind their masters' backs. I avoid the court like one of the disgraced; I've dismissed all those who served me. As for our Lord . . . he does try, you understand? He really tries, and they, they all take advantage of him. He's continually harassed by his ministers. I haven't seen him for weeks, and yet, I remain here and I write to him every day. Do you know why, Archie? Because he needs it. He needs me, and maybe even more, he needs his daughter. But the truth is, I'm terrified," Mommy added, in an even softer voice. "I'm terrified because the world I thought I knew is but a cog among thousands of others, within a mechanism that is beyond me. That mechanism stole Thorn from me. I refuse to let it get hold of my daughter. The universe beyond these walls has become too dangerous for us. Stay here, please. Don't leave us all alone, my daughter and me."

Victoria could feel, in her other body, on the next floor, a sob rising to her throat. She understood nothing of this conversation, but part of her sensed, dimly, that Mommy was unhappy, and that it was, in a way, because of Father.

Father was terrifying. Far more terrifying than Twit. Far more terrifying than Mommy's shadow. On the rare occasions Victoria had seen him, he'd not had a single word, a single gesture, a single glance for her.

Father didn't love her.

Leaping from his chair with two pirouettes, Godfather emptied the dregs of a carafe into a glass. "By cutting my thread, the Web condemned me to eternal solitude. Honestly, you might be used to it, but I don't know how you can put up with staying here, day after day. Immobility has become intolerable to me!"

Godfather guffawed, as if he'd just said something very funny, and Victoria thought how he himself would have made the best father in the world.

He drank half of his glass, then offered the other half to

Mommy. "I have many vices; ingratitude is not one of them. I lost my whole family, but I've gained another one in exchange. You had every right to choose a new guardian for your daughter, and you kept me, despite everything. Believe it or not, what I do today I do also for you, for Victoria, for Ophelia, and, even if it galls me to say it, for Thorn. And for you, too, Madam Rosaline."

Godfather winked again at Great-Godmother, who rolled her eyes, although Victoria found her at once much less yellow and much more pink. He then took off his big, holey hat, mumbling, "Ladies!" and left the drawing room with a little jig.

Victoria suddenly longed to leave her other body in the bedroom and follow Godfather out of the house, to go with him to see the real trees and the real birds.

"He's not entirely wrong," Great-Godmother suddenly said, in her funny accent. "You're not alone, Berenilde. I've just crossed half the arks to be back with you, and I have the firm intention of imposing my company on you. But just look at this weather!" she said, with exasperation, slapping her hand on the window. "It's more depressing in your place than inside a pickle jar. You going to have to buck up, starting with a good sweep. What would Mr. Thorn say if he found your manor shrouded in dust?"

Mommy let out a little laugh, and seemed the first to be surprised. "He would refuse point-blank to come in."

Victoria returned to being the Other-Victoria in bed. She yawned and closed her eyes, worn out by her too-heavy body. Outside, the rain had stopped. If Great-Godmother really could bring back the sun, it was worth staying at home a little longer.

# THE GLOVES

A violent gust of wind shook the ladder. Ophelia dropped the spent bulb she had just unscrewed from the top of the lamp. She clung to the rungs, waiting for the squall to stop, before pulling a new one out of her haversack. Bulbs from Heliopolis contained the light in its pure state. They required neither firing by gas nor powering by electricity, and they didn't burn the fingers when handled. They were screwed on merely to prevent them breaking at the first gust of wind. The city had adopted them with the same enthusiasm it had shown toward the transcendiums from Cyclope. With her eyes shut tight to avoid being dazzled, Ophelia handled the bulbs carefully so as not to break them all—she had no desire to be even more indebted to the Good Family. Every hour she lost on extra chores wasn't being devoted to her apprenticeship. And she didn't have much time left.

"Apprentice Eulalia, quicken your pace."

Ophelia turned to look at the megaphone at the top of the watchtower. There was a whole team of supervisors observing every corner of the conservatoire using the network of periscopes, and they were ruthless.

Ladder under arm, she walked along the wall to the next lamp, reciting her last radio lesson out loud. Phenomenology, epistemology, biblioteconomy, synchrony, diachrony . . . every time she went to the amphitheater and put on her earphones, it was as if she were putting a funnel into each ear through which a stream of unpronounceable words poured. Far from feeling increasingly erudite, she felt even more ignorant. Anima's museum hadn't prepared her for this.

And yet those lessons were feasible when compared with those given by Lady Septima. Ophelia spent hours in the laboratory doing endless readings to hone her skills, sometimes to the point of feeling nauseous, but her teacher was never satisfied: "Your hands lack precision."

She energetically screwed the dazzling bulb into its lamp. She had three days left to prove to all of them that she was fit to join one of Sir Henry's groups. She would practice all night if necessary, but she would achieve her goal!

The wind carried the distant sound of the gong. Dawn, at last.

"Apprentice Eulalia, your chore is completed!" the voice from the megaphone announced. "Please return to your division."

Ophelia climbed down her ladder, not sorry that was over. But she couldn't resist a final look at the sea of clouds above the wall. The lofty tower of the Memorial, perched on the edge of its tiny ark, was barely visible in the crystalline limpidity of the morning.

Eighteen days already. Eighteen days since Mademoiselle Silence had met her death over there, and no one even mentioned it anymore. The city's *Official Journal* had concluded that it was an accident; the rumors had stopped; and the reading groups had resumed. The matter was considered closed.

But not for Ophelia. A woman had died in dubious circumstances shortly after her arrival in Babel, at the location central to her search; this couldn't be a mere coincidence. Had Ophelia not been retained at the conservatoire by the internal rules, she would have already gone over there. A little more patience. She would access the Memorial's Secretarium in the end, and, at the same time, the answers she was seeking.

Ophelia walked along the covered arcades, where remnants of fog lingered between the columns, and then passed under the portico of the Hall of Residence. The apprentices were already debating on the walls and ceilings of the atrium. Here, perpetual disagreement reigned, with some forever suspecting others of stealing their ideas. As soon as tempers were rising, the Hall's megaphone would request calm, and everyone would obediently dive back into their work. It sometimes seemed to Ophelia that the conservatoire of virtuosos was more about taming than education.

She went to the cloakroom to swap her overalls for her uniform, and was confronted with a group of Totemists all getting undressed. Her sister Agatha, who subscribed to the *Gazette of Fashion Across the Arks*, had once told her, between cheeky giggles, that the women and men of Totem had the world's most beautiful bodies. Without being a specialist in the subject, Ophelia had to agree. The Totemists greeted her with smiles as bright as their skin was dark; she did her best to return them without seeming embarrassed. The Good Family was a co-educational establishment right down to the basics of daily life. Either one put one's modesty aside or one surrendered one's place to someone else.

She opened the locker labeled with her name, unfolded her screen, and took off her work overalls. How she longed to put her gloves back on! She had only one pair, so, to preserve them, she didn't wear them to do her chores. All contact with objects, however fleeting, clouded her perception with a chaotic array of visions. Even when it was her personal effects, she inevitably plunged back into her own past, her old emotions, her obsolete thoughts.

As she put on her uniform, she focused on the present, and realized she was having less and less difficulty doing up her buttons. This frock coat, which had constricted her stomach when she arrived, now allowed her to breathe freely: she had lost weight, and it wasn't just down to the obligatory laps of the stadium or the vegetarian food in the canteen. There was something else, in this conservatoire, on this entire ark, that hollowed out her body and put her into a permanent state of stress.

Ophelia quickly checked that that there was no one but her left in the cloakroom. The Totemists had gone. She emptied her locker of all her exercise books—a real jumble of notes—and removed the false bottom protecting the opening to her hiding place. With her belongings continually disappearing, she'd finally taken drastic measures.

The gloves were no longer there.

She rummaged deeper, banging herself in the process. Her false identity papers were there, and Thorn's malfunctioning watch, but her gloves, which she knew for certain she had put away here before leaving, had vanished. "There are all sorts of torment," Mediana had warned her.

Ophelia closed the locker door. This time, it was too much.

"Nothing to do with us."

All the Seers had chanted these five words in unison the very moment Ophelia had entered the dormitory, before even letting her ask her question. They always anticipated her reactions, and that wasn't the least annoying of their little habits. They were all getting ready with even more care than usual, glossing their goatees with brilliantine, and polishing the wings on their boots. Ophelia had learnt more about personal grooming in two weeks around these boys than in all her years surrounded by women.

"Where are my gloves?" she asked all the same.

"Is that blame I detect in your voice, *signorina*?"

Ophelia looked up at the ceiling, where Mediana was doing endless gymnastic exercises. "My mattress, my uniform, my boots, my notebooks—all that, I put down to a dubious sense of humor. My gloves, that's theft. If you're afraid of competition, fight cleanly."

"Keep it down," Mediana said, extending her long, supple body. "You're going to put Zen off."

She indicated a woman, delicate as an oriental doll, leaning over her desk. Her pretty, porcelain hands were exerting pressure around a musical box that was visibly shrinking, and whose tune was getting higher and higher. She stopped only once the musical box was the size of a thimble and produced a buzzing like that of an insect. Then, reversing the process, she widened her hands as if carefully stretching an invisible elastic band. The box began to mushroom.

Ophelia aside, Zen was the only Frontrunner in the division not to belong to Mediana's family. She was a Colossus from Titan and, as such, could modify the mass and size of objects. She specialized in making micro-documents, a very useful skill for the storing of information, and trained endlessly to miniaturize increasingly complex objects. Zen would have been the best in her field had she not been afflicted with an overanxious nature: the slightest irritant completely threw her.

"I need my gloves," Ophelia insisted, her voice hard. "They were made of very rare, very special leather, the only sort capable of shielding my power."

Mediana pushed out like a spring to free herself from the ceiling's gravity, and landed in front of Ophelia with a graceful somersault. With the countless illuminations covering her skin, she looked like an acrobat primed for a display. "You may have lost them. Want me to look into your past?"

Ophelia shrank away when Mediana wanted to place a hand on the nape of her neck. Her cousins could foresee, at short notice, all that they were about to witness, but her power was even more indiscreet. She could tune into the memory, conscious or repressed, of anyone whose backbone she touched. She was the Forerunner par excellence, from whom no secret was safe.

"I did not lose them," Ophelia said, categorically.

"On Babel, dishonesty is severely punished by law. When it comes to making accusations, Apprentice Eulalia, best to think twice."

Ophelia clenched her jaws. What was Mediana really trying to tell her? That she had seen through her false identity? The tomboy was superior to her in height and muscles, but there was nothing threatening in her tone. She had the art of disguising every warning under a veneer of friendliness.

"I just want my gloves back," insisted Ophelia. "If you show goodwill, I will, too."

Mediana turned away, shrugging her shoulders, and, across the dormitory, everyone lost all interest in the subject.

Ophelia felt her hands shaking. It had happened once to her, having to wait a whole day bare-skinned until the Anima glove-maker had fashioned her new pair. She'd almost gone mad. Wearing ordinary gloves had just made things worse, obliging her endlessly to read her own emotions as they seeped into the fabric.

She wouldn't be able to stay in Babel if she didn't find a solution, fast.

She jumped on hearing the Hall's megaphones: "Examination of conscience! All companies are called to the gymnasium! Examination of conscience!"

Zen buried her oriental doll's face in her hands, groaning.

141

The musical box, which she had just returned to its original size, was now totally out of tune. "That'd be right," she moaned, "I've botched the decompression."

The Seers in the dormitory calmly finished sprucing up their uniforms, more elegant than ever. Of course, they had anticipated this surprise summons.

Ophelia was so distraught at the loss of her gloves that she just followed the flow of apprentices through the gardens without even caring what the examination of conscience might entail. Around her, everyone was checking that their frock coats were correctly buttoned, collars turned down, company insignia in the right place. Ophelia had already been several times to the twin ark, for communal lessons with the other division of Forerunners, but it was the first time she was going inside the gymnasium. It was a huge stadium of glass and steel that bore no comparison to the muddy one in which she ran her daily laps.

The companies lined up in serried ranks, Pollux's virtuosos to the right, Helen's virtuosos to the left, in almost perfect symmetry. Only Ophelia disrupted the visual harmony as she tried to find her way amid this maze of uniforms.

"Over here, apprentice. Put yourself behind me."

It was Elizabeth who was indicating a place to her in the row of Forerunners. Ophelia positioned herself, avoiding flattening her hands against her trousers and succumbing to another uncontrollable reading.

"I must speak to you urgently, Elizabeth. They've taken my reader's gloves. Without them, I can no longer work in the right conditions . . . "

"I told you to be vigilant, apprentice."

Her tone was final. Ophelia silently contemplated the tawny hair that cloaked Elizabeth's lanky figure. This aspiring virtuoso might be in charge of Helen's Forerunners, but she never got involved in their disagreements. Ophelia wouldn't find an ally in her, either.

As she thought fast, desperately seeking a solution to her problem while stifled by the mugginess of the gymnasium, she detected the reddish glow of eyes out of a corner of her glasses. It was coming from the row of Pollux's Forerunners, just to her right. She didn't need to turn to know whose they were. Once again, as ever, it was Octavio, Lady Septima's son. He had not spoken once to Ophelia, despite all the hours spent together in the laboratory, but he never missed a chance to look scornfully down at her—not the easiest task since he wasn't very tall himself. Octavio's powers of observation were superior to his mother's, which was saying something. He could date any sample that passed under the rays of his eyes, and, apparently, had, so far, never made the slightest error when evaluating.

Ophelia could have gladly done without his repeated signs of attention, particularly as there was nothing flattering about them. Octavio wasn't looking at her in the way a young man might look at a young woman. He was keeping watch on her. If his being a Son of Pollux hadn't obliged him to live in his own dormitory, Ophelia was convinced he would have spent his nights sitting at her bedside.

Sometimes, she had the unpleasant feeling that it was God himself spying on her through those eyes.

Carefully avoiding Octavio's insistent stare, Ophelia took a look around. Her size forced her to stand on the tip of her boots to get an overview. The Good Family was gathered in its entirety: apprentices of all companies, first-degree candidates, second-degree candidates, specialization teachers, administrative staff. Also present were the Lords of LUX, their displays of gold decorations glinting in the light the glass let though, like veritable living suns. Lady Septima stood among them, small, silent, calm. Inexplicably imposing.

Among all these faces, Ophelia saw only the one that was missing. She had finally come to accept it, even if with far more disappointment than she cared to admit: Thorn wasn't among the Good Family.

She felt alone in the middle of this throng of uniforms. When she had lived through testing times in the past, she had always been able to rely on solid support. Today, she no longer had Aunt Rosaline, or great-uncle, or Berenilde, or Fox, or Gail, or Archibald, or scarf by her side. Apprentices were allowed a visit, but who could she have invited? She had bombarded Ambrose with telegrams, and his only response had been:

YOUR BAG IS STILL WITH ME. SHOULD I SEND IT TO YOU?

Suddenly, all the apprentices stood to attention, raising fists to chests. The banging together of their heels produced a burst of sound that reverberated against all the glass. This time, Ophelia didn't need to stand on tiptoe to see who had just moved onto the rostrum. Helen's elephantine figure towered over the assembly, her optical appliance surveying every face. Her limbs were all so unbelievably ill-proportioned, one wondered how she managed to keep her balance. Ophelia understood how when she heard a high-pitched squeaking against the floor of the gymnasium: Helen's enormous dress was stretched around a crinoline on casters.

Another family spirit accompanied her. It was Pollux himself. The lines of his body and face were as harmonious as his twin's were chaotic. He needed no apparatus to correct the range of his sight, and his eyes blazed like beacons out of his dark skin. Yet it was his smile that struck Ophelia the most: a smile full of kindness, which she had never witnessed from Helen, or Artemis, or Farouk.

"My dear children, thank you for all gathering here."

Pollux's voice was deep, warm, mellifluous, like the rich resonance of a cello. A father's voice. With his eyes, he embraced the entire assembly of apprentices, as if they were all his descendants, irrespective of skin color or power.

"Twenty-one family spirits," thought Ophelia, "but each one unique."

"You are the apple of our eyes, both my sister's and mine," continued Pollux. "You are not all destined to become virtuosos, but you represent no less the future of the city, each in your own way, whatever position awaits you there once you leave the conservatoire."

Ophelia frowned. Lady Septima was standing to the back of the rostrum, among the Lords of LUX, and her lips were moving at the same time as Pollux's. She was watching him out of the corner of her eye, as a teacher would a pupil from whom a perfect recitation was expected.

The young Animist observed the profiles of the apprentices around her. They were lapping up this speech with such fervid expressions, it was clear that, for each of them, the only position in the world worth having was that of virtuoso. Only one within each division, however, would attain that honor.

On the rostrum, Pollux's smile widened. "I can hear your hearts beating. They gladden my own. Thanks to your parents, and thanks to the parents of your parents, we are living in an era of peace and prosperity such as the old world never knew. A peace and prosperity that you are preparing yourselves, in turn, to protect."

Pollux allowed a long silence to descend, such as Ophelia had rarely heard in a packed room. The kind of silence that always gave her an irresistible urge to cough. She resisted the even stronger desire to raise her hand and ask him to tell them, indeed, a little more about this old world. They were made to learn by heart the history of the various technologies, the geological formations, the linguistic evolutions, and even the smallest ramifications of the great interfamilial tree, but no reference was ever made to the state of humanity before the Rupture.

"And now, my dear children, I would like to speak to you . . . speak to you about . . . " Pollux broke off. He had forgotten the rest of his speech. In a fraction of a second, the charismatic father figure seemed as lost as a child. He exchanged a look with Helen, who made very sure not to come to his aid, enormous lips resolutely pursed, telescopic glasses turned elsewhere.

Ophelia noticed the way Lady Septima moved her lips once again, from the back of the rostrum, and the way Pollux instinctively turned toward her. This family spirit was a puppet. A gigantic, magnificent puppet.

"Ah, yes," said Pollux, reviving his broadest smile. "My sister and I would like personally to thank the LUX patrons who subsidize this conservatoire. They endeavor to instill into each of you the very essence of citizenship. A citizenship that, of its own accord, curbs its least noble, most subversive instincts. My dear children, it is your turn to speak now: confess!"

Ophelia was taken aback. Who had to confess what?

At the end of the very front row, an apprentice took it upon himself to step forward and declare in a loud voice: "I solemnly swear that I have not lied, or cheated, or stolen, or in any way contravened the law of the city."

"Good," Pollux responded, with utmost gentleness. "If anyone has an objection to make, let them speak now."

No one made an objection. The apprentice returned to his row, and his neighbor in turn stood forward to make the same declaration. And so it continued, with each member of each division of each company. Occasionally, one or another would publicly admit a fault, like the boy who wasted food by not finishing his plate, or the girl who had secretly copied a friend's notes because she had been inattentive in class. The head of the company would then propose a punishment, and Pollux would nod his chin to approve it.

Ophelia was astounded. She understood what pushed the guilty to denounce themselves when she witnessed the first challenge. An apprentice lawyer had just sworn that he had respected the law and a hand instantly shot up in the crowd: "Objection! I heard him say a word forbidden by the Index."

Whispering spread across the entire gymnasium, and Pollux's kindly smile faltered, as if he had just been personally struck right in the heart.

"Apprentice, what is your response to this objection?" It was Helen who, for the first time during the assembly, had just spoken, her sepulchral voice extinguishing the murmuring. She manipulated the detachable lenses of her optical appliance to see the accused clearly. It was one of her Godsons.

"I protest," said the apprentice lawyer. "It wasn't really . . . "

"Either it is, or it isn't," Helen cut in. "Did any other witnesses hear the forbidden word being uttered?"

Several hands went up. Ophelia could see the ears of the apprentice lawyer, two rows in front of her, turn crimson. She was feeling pretty uncomfortable herself. This examination of conscience was turning into a public trial.

"I offer my sincerest apology," stammered the apprentice lawyer. "I may have once said, during a rhetorical debate, that it was pointless to fight, but it was obviously to be taken figura—"

"You have tripled your guilt," Lady Septima instantly intervened. "By having committed a sin, by not having admitted it, and by having committed it once again. The choice of punishment is yours, Lady Helen, but all I can suggest to you is quarantine."

"Amen to that," Helen approved, impassively. "Apprentice, you are put in quarantine starting from right now. For forty days, you will be allowed to speak to no one, and no one will be allowed to speak to you. You are temporarily excluded from all group activities and deprived of all your privileges. No leave. No visits. No letters. You will follow your lessons in silence and will only have the right to speak if a superior asks you a direct question."

Ophelia saw the apprentice lawyer's ears go from bright red to very pale. Her own were buzzing like beehives. She had felt alone earlier; she didn't dare even imagine how lonely he would feel. Punishing someone that harshly for using the verb "to fight"? Was that what working for peace meant? Ophelia turned her glasses in all directions, but there was no one in the ranks who would protest. She forced herself to contain her emotion when her eyes met those of Octavio, who was watching her through his long, black fringe.

The examination of conscience resumed and Pollux, who had already forgotten the incident, regained all his fatherly bonhomie.

When Ophelia's turn finally arrived, her heart was pounding so loud, she hoped neither Helen nor Pollux could hear it from the rostrum. Her dormitory colleagues had gone before her, and none of them had confessed to stealing her gloves. What would happen if she raised the matter now, in public? She felt she had no right to cause a scandal, not with false papers in her locker.

"I solemnly swear that I have neither lied nor cheated nor stolen nor contravened in any way the law of the city." Ophelia's small voice didn't carry far, but she was relieved when Pollux smiled at her without asking her to repeat herself.

"Good. If anyone has an objection to raise, let them speak now."

Ophelia saw a hand go up to her right. The blood in her veins caught fire. It was Octavio. He had fixed his red-eyed gaze straight ahead, causing the gold chain to quiver against his cheek.

He knew.

He knew and he was going to denounce her.

"This is not an objection, but a request," Octavio announced, his tone measured. "Apprentice Eulalia needs new gloves. They are tools, and are indispensable for her to pursue her apprenticeship. Given that she is still in her probationary period, I'm asking on her behalf for exceptional leave so that she can go into town."

From the rostrum, Lady Septima gave her son an even more incandescent look than usual. If she was disconcerted, Ophelia, herself, was completely staggered.

"Leave granted," Helen declared, simply. "Next confession."

Ophelia chewed her lips, longing for the end of the examination of conscience. As soon as the apprentices were authorized to fall out, she made a beeline for Octavio.

"Thanks."

The word had, unintentionally, sounded mistrustful. He had helped her. Now she wanted to know what he wanted in return.

Octavio arched his eyebrows, so black and well-defined that they resembled two circumflexes. He was the spitting image of his mother: the slightest changes of expression became imposing on him. He had no need of height or muscles. His charisma sufficed. "It's the conservatoire's interest that I defended, not yours. If you must fail to become a virtuoso, it must be due to a lack of competence, not equipment." And without allowing Ophelia time to respond, he continued, matter-of-factly: "When you go into town, go to the home of Professor Wolf. He should be able to help you."

"Professor Wolf?" Ophelia repeated, increasingly disconcerted. "Is he a glover?"

"No, an Animist. Not born and bred, but a reader, like you. You won't have any difficulty finding him. When he's not researching at the Memorial, he shuts himself away at home."

Ophelia heard nothing more after that. The racket in her chest had drowned out the rest of the world.

# THE READER

Ophelia didn't feel the burning sun bearing down on her. Neither did she hear the buzzing of the flies around her. Nor see the sea of clouds that the gondola with a sail she sat in was slowly cleaving through. All her attention was focused on a single, recurring thought: she was going to meet another reader, a reader who wasn't born on Anima, a reader who was doing research at the Memorial.

'It can't be Thorn,' she repeated to herself, over and over again. 'My Animism made him a mirror traveler, not a reader.' And yet Ophelia couldn't stop herself from wondering. Hadn't her own claws shown themselves belatedly, weeks after the marriage?

With a professional flourish, the Zephyr sailing the gondola gently deflected the breeze to draw alongside the quay smoothly, and then lowered the mechanical gangway. Ophelia disembarked with the other passengers without having to pay for the crossing. For that day, the Good Family had given her a perforated card she just had to insert into the ticket machine of any public service. It was an illusory freedom: inserting the card allowed the conservatoire to check that students weren't out and about beyond the times permitted by their leave. Ophelia had been allowed three hours to do what she had to do. No more, no less.

She pushed her glasses up on her nose. The island she had just landed on was at the edge of the archipelago surrounding Babel, whose aqueducts and rotundas could be seen as distant silhouettes distorted by the heat of the afternoon. The splendor of the city hadn't extended this far. The houses were all piled up, one against the other, like a single block of granite, with not a garden or fountain to soften the general effect. Neither were there cobbles on the roads, whose red dust, lifted by the wind, sizzled like embers. There was, however, an entire population of dodos waddling around the street, with the gait of obese pigeons.

Until then, Ophelia had asked her way to public signaling guides, but here she found no statue-automaton even remotely resembling one.

"Professor Wolf's house, please?" Ophelia had addressed a passerby, who looked her uniform up and down before pointing out the direction to her without saying a word. She soon noticed that the locals turned as she passed, looking hostile. They all wore togas and turbans that would have been white had the surrounding dust not turned them red. They were the powerless. She was struck at seeing so many youngsters among them, sullen and idle, playing dice on the doorsteps. They were a startling contrast to the hyperactive automatons of the city center.

Ophelia had to keep asking the way until she finally reached a dilapidated building shrouded in creepers. A toucan, perched on the handrail of the front steps, screeched loudly as she approached, and a dozy old lady opened the door. Ophelia's uniform had the effect of a bucket of water on her.

"*Mademioselle*?" she asked, staring wide-eyed.

"I'm looking for Professor Wolf." Ophelia hadn't managed to stop her voice betraying the emotion she had, however, been trying to curb since her conversation with Octavio. That was a hope she just mustn't allow herself.

"I'm his landlady," the old woman replied, now looking bored. "He has his own entrance around the back, but I don't mind warning you: he's an awkward customer, that lodger."

Ophelia ignored as best she could the cramp that had just wrenched her stomach. "Is he at home?"

"Oh, yes, *mademoiselle*, that he is. Even a bit too much, in fact. He never goes out any more since his accident. What a shame, such an intelligent man!"

Another cramp gripped Ophelia's stomach. "His accident?"

"It's not for me to tell you, *mademoiselle*. Just go around the house and knock on his door. Maybe he'll open to you. Maybe not."

Ophelia went to the back of the building. The creepers were even more abundant here than at the front, to the extent of having entirely covered the closed shutters of the ground floor. A veritable plant prison.

'A hiding place,' Ophelia couldn't help but correct, swallowing what little saliva she had left. There was no plaque, no letter box to indicate the identity of the place's occupant.

She jumped. Barely had she neared the door than the knocker had struck it to announce her arrival. It had animated itself.

The smallest noise, from the other side of the door, indicated that someone had lifted the spyhole cover. Ophelia stretched as high as she could to be seen. After a long silence, the door opened barely a crack, restrained by a chain. The man didn't show himself. He said nothing, either. Only his breathing—tense, deep—testified to his presence.

He was waiting.

Incapable of uttering a word herself, so tight was her throat, Ophelia slipped the Good Family's administrative reference through the crack. She saw long, gloved fingers snatch it before disappearing into the darkness.

153

A rustling of paper. Another interminable silence.

The man slammed the door shut, released the security chain, and opened to Ophelia.

Barely had she set foot in the hall when the door closed itself behind her. The many bolts instantly slid into place themselves with a series of resounding clicks. Still dazzled from the sun, Ophelia and her glasses took a while to get used to the nocturnal atmosphere that prevailed inside. For now, the man was just an anonymous shadow, tall and stiff as a hat stand. The floorboards creaked beneath his wary steps. His eyes, like two small, nervy sparks in an oven, kept darting back and forth, from the paper he was holding to the uniform of his visitor.

"Gloves, h'm? There's an uncommon request."

Ophelia agreed, forcing herself to smile politely. Professor Wolf was gradually revealing himself to her. His hair, eyebrows, and goatee were as black as his skin was pale. Lines furrowed his forehead and around his mouth, giving him the appearance of a prematurely aged forty-year-old.

It wasn't Thorn.

She had spent the day forbidding herself from hoping. So why did she suddenly feel like leaving with a slam of the door?

"Are you mute, as well as everything else?" Professor Wolf's accent was neither entirely Babelian nor really Animist, but a singular mix of the two. Perhaps because he no longer left his home, he didn't respect the city's dress code: his suit and his gloves, also black, resembled those worn by the scientists at Anima's great observatory.

"No," Ophelia finally muttered. She didn't know what his "everything else" referred to, and she didn't care. This man wasn't Thorn, nothing he might think of her interested her.

"If I'm to believe your document, you are yourself a reader," Professor Wolf continued, curling his lips on the last word. "A reader who goes about with bare hands, moreover. What have you done with your gloves?"

Ophelia wondered what business it was of his, but she needed him too much to be disagreeable. "They were, unfortunately, mislaid. I am here for your help in procuring me a new pair. The Good Family will take care of all expenses." And I'll repay that debt in extra chores, she refrained from adding.

Professor Wolf looked skeptically at Ophelia's hands. His extreme stiffness was accentuated by a wooden brace enclosing his neck and, combined with his pointed chin, made his head look like a pickax. Was that due to the accident the landlady had mentioned?

"Follow me," he barked, begrudgingly.

The professor led Ophelia from the hall to the living room, where the same twilight prevailed. The daylight glimmered weakly through the slits of the shutters. The air was unbreathable. The room's fan dispersed neither the sweltering heat nor the musty smell. Behind the dusty windows of the stacked-up display cases, one could just make out bones and fossils, making her feel as if she had entered a particularly morbid cabinet of curiosities. She was disconcerted when the chairs, tables, and chests drew back as she passed, like timid animals; Professor Wolf must truly have a wary nature for his Animism to have permeated his furniture to this extent.

Ophelia's surprise increased when she discovered, among the finds from archeological digs, a very impressive collection of military weapons. "Your research is on the wars of the old world?" She realized too late that she had let slip the forbidden word. Professor Wolf, busy rummaging in a drawer, threw her a dark look.

"And what's next? You're going to denounce me, perhaps? The law forbids the possession of weapons, not historic artifacts." Exasperated by his neck brace, which prevented him from leaning with ease, the professor pulled the drawer out of its chest and emptied the contents onto a table. "War," he continued, lowering his voice, "is generally associated with the notion of the border. The Rupture totally shattered the borders, but did wars cease for all that? For your information, little lady, peace is a purely theoretical concept. There are, and there always will be, conflicts, whatever semblance they take. You need only go out there, dressed in your provocative uniform, to see it for yourself."

Ophelia thought back to the powerless who had stared at her with a mix of disdain and envy.

For the first time in a long while, she felt as if she had before her someone sensible to talk to. The disappointment she had felt on meeting him disappeared. "I agree with you."

As he extracted a measuring tape from the jumble on his table, Professor Wolf knitted his thick, black brows and produced the faintest of sardonic smiles. "Well I never. A distant member of my family, a reader what's more, turns up at my place and shares my vision of the world. My lucky day, it would seem!"

"You don't believe me," Ophelia responded. "Since I crossed your threshold, you haven't believed me for a single moment. Why?"

The professor unrolled the measuring tape with a sudden flourish, as if it were a whip. "I told you, little lady, it's war out there. An Animist father, a powerless mother: I've never been accepted by any community. My entire existence is a web of conflict, so my principle is to consider every human being as a potential adversary. Your hand at my eye level," he instructed, drily.

Ophelia lifted her arm to allow him to take her measurements, but it wasn't an easy process: the measuring tape, also contaminated by its owner's wariness, was wriggling to avoid touching a perfect stranger.

"So, the old world intrigues you?" Professor Wolf asked, without dropping his sarcastic tone. "Perhaps reading a few of my fossils would interest you?"

Ophelia bit her tongue. The tape was gripping her hand so tight, it was bruising her skin. "Fossils can't be read," she replied, "any more than raw materials and living organisms can. I really am who I claim to be. If you really want to put me to the test, set me a less obvious trap."

The professor's face creased into a mocking smile, and then he wrote out the measurements on telegram paper. The simple act of writing was an amazing feat, with his neck brace preventing him from tilting his head. Ophelia had the, perhaps misguided, feeling that she'd just scored a point.

"I want to join Sir Henry's reading groups at the Memorial. I was told that you yourself are doing research over there?"

The professor's pencil slipped on the paper. To Ophelia's surprise, his hand had started to shake. "I was doing some," he corrected, between his teeth.

"Why did you stop?"

"For a reason that concerns only me."

"You must still know the place well."

"Enough never to set foot in there ever again."

Professor Wolf scowled, as if he'd said too much. He rolled his telegram inside a cylinder, which he slid into the compartment of a tube, and pulled a lever; the telegram was instantly sucked into the pipe. "There. I've sent the order for your gloves to my personal supplier. He will get directly in touch with the Good Family to deliver them to you in a few days' time. Satisfied?"

Ophelia hesitated. There were questions she was dying to ask, on the Secretarium in particular, but persisting would just make this man even more suspicious than he already was. "Could you lend me an old pair you don't use anymore? I've

THE MEMORY OF BABEL

been reading everything I touch since this morning, I can't last several days like this."

Professor Wolf pursed his lips, as if about to refuse point-blank, but then, with an exasperated sigh, changed his mind. "Give me a moment. Just don't touch anything."

He went up some stairs that were as creaky as he was, leaving Ophelia alone in the middle of the collections. She walked along the military weapons, stopping before the warm breeze from the fan. She got a slight shock when she came across a dusty mirror fixed to the wall. She hadn't looked at herself in a mirror since entering the conservatoire. It took her a few seconds to get used to this little woman in uniform, with cheeks like peaches and curls like question marks. Without her invasive long hair, prim dress, and old scarf—her heart sank, painfully, at that thought—she barely recognized herself. Showing herself openly to the world was her best disguise. A disguise even more effective than Mime's livery, behind which she had long hidden in the Pole.

As Ophelia went up to an old photograph of an archaeological site, she scared a wastepaper basket, which leapt aside to avoid her. It couldn't have been emptied for a long time, as it was overflowing with balls of paper, some of which spilt onto the floor. Ophelia hastily picked them up, but one gave her such a shock, it took her breath away.

Fear. Pure fear. Professor Wolf's fear.

Ophelia looked at the crumpled letter she'd dropped to the floor like a hot potato. If Professor Wolf had contaminated this paper with his fear, it meant he'd been wearing gloves when he'd touched it; no experienced reader would handle a letter with their bare hands, unless they wanted to assure themselves of the honesty of its sender.

In other circumstances, she would never have permitted herself to go any further, but her curiosity this time was stronger than her conscience. Before realizing what she was doing, she smoothed out the paper in the weak light from the shutters.

*Dear colleague,*

*I was sad to hear of your accident. That fall in the stairs could have broken your neck entirely! It's fortunate, for you as for all of us, that you emerged unscathed. I hope to have the pleasure of seeing you soon at the Memorial at the academic meetings: your research may not meet with everyone's approval, but it is no less of fundamental interest to our discipline.*

*On that subject, I studied the sample you sent me. Its composition is fascinating! Dating it caused me problems, but my evaluation ended up reaching the same conclusion as yours. May I ask you from which document your sample was taken?*

*Please accept, dear colleague, my sincere good wishes,*

*Signed: your devoted friend and colleague*

Ophelia's fingers were shaking with the terror Professor Wolf had felt on reading these lines. She didn't understand the reason, and she didn't get time to look deeper into it. The man's steps could be heard on the stairs.

She crumpled the paper and threw it into the basket, but her clumsiness made her miss her target completely.

"Here," said Professor Wolf, once downstairs, presenting her with some black gloves. "No point returning them to me, I won't use them again."

Ophelia pulled them on, avoiding looking him in the eye. She felt so shaken by her reading, so guilty for having betrayed her professional code, that she couldn't stop her voice from wobbling: "Th-thank you."

Professor Wolf jutted out his jaw, further elongating his chin, as his eyes, wary once again, darted around all four corners of the room. Ophelia had hoped that his neck brace would prevent him from seeing the ball of paper on the floor, but his eyes finally fell on it. His face instantly became a combination of astonishment, terror, and fury.

"I'm sorry," Ophelia said, impulsively. "The letter had fallen. I just meant to pick it up. I shouldn't have . . . " She didn't get to the end of her sentence. Professor Wolf had grabbed her arm to fling her against the wall mirror, which shattered into a thousand pieces.

"Filthy little spy!"

"No!" she cried, painfully straightening up while almost seeing stars. "I'm not your enemy, I sincerely want to understand what happened to you."

Beside himself, the professor grabbed her by the frock-coat collar and hoisted her up off her feet. For someone who had a dislocated neck, he wasn't lacking in strength.

"All of humanity is my enemy," he hissed between his teeth. "Go and join Sir Henry's reading groups, little snooper. I hope you enjoy it. Get out of my home!" he ordered, suddenly letting go of her.

Ophelia rushed into the hall. The door drew back its own bolts to let her through, and then slammed shut behind her, ejecting her from the place with the force of a catapult. Ophelia fell to her knees in the building's courtyard, heart pounding against ribs. When she raised her glasses, still blue with fright, her eyes met those of the landlady, who was sweeping in the sun, her toucan on her shoulder.

"I did tell you, *mademoiselle*. An awkward customer, that lodger."

# THE UNLUCKY CHARM

One by one, Ophelia pulled at the tips of Professor Wolf's gloves, which were too long for her fingers. She had visited that man in search of answers, and left him with even more questions—along with a fine collection of scratches. What could have persuaded him not to pursue his research at the Memorial? What was that sample he had evaluated? Why had the response of his colleague terrified him to that extent? Did that fear have anything to do with the fear that had gripped Mademoiselle Silence as she met her death?

A heavy downpour battered every window of the birdtrain. Ophelia closed her eyes, suppressing the emotion that was choking her. The image of the scarf, wandering the streets of Babel like an abandoned dog, obsessed her, day in, day out.

No. Don't dwell on it. Forge ahead.

She reopened her eyes when she felt the birdtrain veering toward a belvedere. It was the fifth academy it served; soon it would be the conservatoire. Some students got off into the rain, pulling their hoods up; others got on, shaking their raincoats. As at every station, Ophelia checked there wasn't a boy in a wheelchair among them. She was missing Ambrose. Missing his friendship, his kindness, his chattiness. She didn't understand why he had suddenly become distant, barely replying to her telegrams, never visiting her, but it concerned her.

No. Don't dwell on that either.

Through the sinuous trails of raindrops on the window, Ophelia looked at the Memorial tower in the distance. Somewhere between those walls there was the Secretarium. And within that Secretarium, a strongroom. And in that strongroom, the "ultimate truth." What if it were that very truth to which Mademoiselle Silence and Professor Wolf had gotten too close? And what if Thorn had put himself in danger to uncover it? It was frustrating to know she'd have to get off at the next station, rather than continue the journey over there. Her three hours of leave were coming to an end. The gondolas' slowness had made her lose precious time; indeed, she'd nearly missed her birdtrain. To be expelled from the Good Family over a missed connection, two days before the end of her probation period, would have been too ridiculous.

Ophelia returned to pulling at the floppy fabric of the gloves at the tips of her fingers. A sigh rose up from deep inside her, but it was her neighbor on the banquette who let it out it in her stead. She gave him a questioning look. He, too, was contemplating the window splattered with rain, but with a guilty expression, as if personally responsible for the bad weather. His profile, with its shaggy pepper-and-salt hair and long, pointed nose, recalled the snout of a hedgehog. He looked familiar to Ophelia, and she understood why on seeing the "assistant" badge pinned to his uniform. "The man with the trolley," she murmured.

After a moment's hesitation, the assistant tore his eyes from the window. *"Pardon, mademoiselle?* Are you speaking to me?"

Ophelia gave him a polite smile. This hadn't really worked with Professor Wolf, but surely this assistant wouldn't throw her out of a birdtrain in full flight, would he? "We've already met, sir. In the Memorial's youth department. I had knocked over the books on your trolley, and you . . . well, you received a reprimand because of me."

"Ah, those books!" stammered the assistant. "That seems so long ago to me." With head sunk between shoulders, he showed a sudden, intense interest in his hands, clasped together on his knees, and said nothing more. He seemed desperately alone. As alone as Ambrose, surrounded by his father's automatons. As alone as Professor Wolf, triple-locked into his apartment.

As alone as me, Ophelia couldn't help but think.

"Eulalia," she said, introducing herself.

"*Quoi?*" the assistant asked with surprise. "Oh, um . . . me, I'm Blaise." He rubbed his nape uneasily, like someone unaccustomed to civilities. "I . . . Your uniform . . . Apprentice virtuoso?"

Ophelia felt a smile, a real one this time, come to her lips. It wasn't every day she encountered someone even more awkward than her. "Forerunner."

"I'm impressed."

Blaise seemed sincere. His eyes, with their black, moist, hedgehog-like pupils, had widened, as if he'd just been told he was sitting beside a Lord of LUX.

Outside, the rain doubled in intensity against the windows, propelled by a westerly wind. The lightning tore through the silence, throwing a bright light across the students' faces, but not one lifted their nose out of their textbook. Babel's public transport was always excessively quiet, and for good reason: the conductor imposed a fine at the slightest disturbance.

Ophelia couldn't help glancing anxiously up at the ceiling, with a thought for the chimeras towing the carriages through the thunderstorm.

"On probation," she felt obliged to specify. "I'd love to work at the Memorial, like you."

"Like me? I wouldn't wish that on you," Blaise said, pointing at his "assistant" badge. "For years now, I've been returning to shelves what I'm told to return; there's nothing prestigious about it."

"The Memorial's collections are really impressive. They must demand a formidable amount of work, no? Especially if one includes the Secretarium," Ophelia added, as innocently as possible.

"I've never set foot in there," Blaise sighed, much to her disappointment. "It's far too important and far too confidential a department for the likes of me."

"And you don't take part in the reading groups, either?"

Blaise let out an incredulous laugh, which he stifled with his palm as he caught the disdainful look of the conductor. "The automa . . . *pardon*, Sir Henry's groups?" he asked, very quietly. "They'd have to be mad to accept me."

Ophelia didn't understand what lay behind this remark, but chose not to pursue it. She'd finally found a reasonable person to talk to; she must make the most of every minute of the journey. "I heard about Mademoiselle Silence," she whispered, watching for Blaise's reaction out of the corner of her eye. "It must have been a terrible shock."

At the precise moment she spoke that last word, she was suddenly shaken on her seat. A gust of wind, more violent than the others, had rocked the whole carriage, this time prompting cries of surprise across all the banquettes.

"Keep calm, citizens!" shouted the conductor. "Just some light turbulence. Our Totemist has total control of his team."

Ophelia pushed up her glasses, thrown to the very tip of her nose by the jolt; she saw several students around her picking up the textbooks they had dropped. As for herself, she wasn't at all reassured. She had instinctively clung to Blaise's arm, and he was staring at her hand with a flabbergasted expression, as if it were the first time he was seeing one in such an improbable place. Finally, he tapped it, clumsily, with his fingertips, an apologetic smile at the corner of his mouth.

"This sort of thing often happens with me. The gloves you're wearing," he hastily continued, before Ophelia could wonder what he'd meant, "they're Wolf's, aren't they?"

"How do you know they're . . . You know Professor Wolf?" Ophelia stammered, increasingly surprised.

Blaise rubbed his large, pointed nose with embarrassment. "I recognized his smell on you. I'm an Olfactory, you see? Wolf is a regular at the Memorial. Or rather, he was," he added, with a lump in his throat. "Before his accident."

Ophelia noted that he called him just Wolf, without his title. They were certainly rather more than mere acquaintances. Just as she was thinking this, Blaise checked with a nervous glance that the conductor wasn't paying them any attention.

"Can I make a confession to you, *mademoiselle*?"

"Er . . . yes?"

Blaise leant over, shyly, and, over the racket of the rain, whispered in a low voice: "It was me who killed Mademoiselle Silence."

Ophelia felt her stomach lurch, and it was no longer due to the rocking of the carriage. She mouthed "Why?" unable to emit the slightest sound. Blaise withdrew again and slumped on the banquette, plunging his fingers into his already tousled hair, his features strained with guilt.

"That's not the question, *mademoiselle*. Ask yourself rather *how*." He gave Ophelia a worried look, as if he feared she would suddenly smash the window and leap into the void to escape him. "I . . . I bring bad luck."

"Ah." Ophelia could find nothing better to say in response. It was one of the most unexpected admissions ever made to her.

"I'm serious," Blaise insisted, staring with wide, tormented eyes. "The book trolley, Wolf's accident, Mademoiselle Silence's fall, this torrential rain: it's all really me, you understand? It's been that way since the day I was born. I defy all the statistics. People who are *très* competent have studied my case."

Blaise's words went straight to Ophelia's heart. They echoed those of Thorn, two and a half years back: "You have a preternatural predisposition to disasters." She opened her mouth, but a roar cut her short:

"Shame on you, lambkins!"

Ophelia and Blaise turned around. The students were all exchanging stunned looks. As for the conductor, he had already seized his fine book and was searching, banquette to banquette, for whoever had dared to break the rules. He couldn't find him.

The voice rose up again, from nowhere and everywhere at once, louder than the thunder outside: "Yes, absolutely, lambkins! Look at you, with your fine uniforms! Look at you with your goody-goody textbooks! Look at you with your oh so proper language! And you dare to claim you're the youth of Babel?"

Ophelia blocked her ears to avoid being deafened. She'd heard this tenor voice before. It was that of Fearless-and-Almost-Blameless, the day she'd visited the Memorial.

"Me, I'll tell you what you are," the voice continued. "Accomplices! Conspirators of silence! Dictators of right-thinking! If you still have a semblance of pride, citizens, repeat after me: down with the Index and death to the censors! Down with the Index and death to the censors! Down with the Index and d . . . "

The voice turned into a very shrill, crackling noise, piercing Ophelia's eardrums. Eventually, the conductor had found a radio set under a seat, turned up to full volume, and had smashed it to pieces with his heel. Silence descended once more, heavy with rain, wind, and storm.

"The incident is over, citizens," the conductor declared, categorically. "Next stop, the Good Family!"

With ears still ringing, Ophelia looked at Blaise, who had stood up from the banquette to allow her to leave her seat. He shrugged his shoulders, fatalistically.

"As I told you, Mademoiselle Eulalia. I bring bad luck."

Ophelia stood up, trying to get her balance in the swaying. She looked at what remained of the radio set, which the conductor was picking up at the other end of the carriage. The voice still resonated within her: "Death to the censors!"

"Mademoiselle Silence was actually the senior censor, wasn't she?"

Blaise raised his eyebrows, which were as pepper-and-salt and shaggy as his hair. "Eh? Yes, but . . . *eh bien* . . . you surely don't think . . . "

"I don't yet know what I think," Ophelia whispered, as quietly and quickly as possible. "The only thing I'm almost certain of, Mr. Blaise, is that you're not responsible for what happened to Mademoiselle Silence and Professor Wolf. I even think that meeting you here, in this birdtrain, has been really lucky for me."

Blaise stared wide-eyed. The corners of his mouth quivered, like a flickering candle flame. "It's the first time in my life that I've heard someone say that to me."

"The Good Family!" announced the conductor.

Ophelia shook the hand Blaise had politely held out to her, despite the encumbrance of her oversized gloves. "I have the firm intention of joining the reading groups," she told him. "We'll see each other again soon at the Memorial. In the meantime, take care, and ask yourself what really killed Mademoiselle Silence."

167

From the landing stage, Ophelia's eyes followed the silhouette of the winged train as it continued on its path across the sky. The rain had stopped the moment it had pulled away from the ark. 'I mustn't,' she thought, with determination. 'Offering my friendship to a Memorialist would be unreasonable. Dangerous, even."

She was forced to admit, realizing she suddenly felt less alone, that it was already too late.

# THE WELCOME

The articulated arms kept moving, like tentacles, around the principal chair. They were endlessly sorting the Good Family's papers, and their perpetual motion made Helen's stillness behind the imposing marble desk even more striking. The giant woman was staring at the file she was holding with her long, spidery fingers.

Ophelia felt as if she'd been waiting an eternity for her verdict. She turned her attention to the desk lamp, which emitted a flickering light. She had screwed and unscrewed so many bulbs during the pre-morning chore, she had to control her urge to change this one.

Helen's cavernous voice gave her a start. "Going by Lady Septima's report, you deigned to make some effort during your three weeks of probation."

Ophelia suppressed the words that came to her mouth. She wouldn't describe two hundred hours of radio lessons and applied readings, not to mention all the chores, as "some effort," but so be it. "I did my best, madame."

Helen lifted her elephantine nose from her file. In the midst of the mechanical ballet of her chair, she recalled one of those ancient goddesses with several arms, half-woman, half-monster, of whom one still found sculptures on Babel's oldest walls. "Is doing your best enough? Lady Septima isn't impressed, either, by your evaluations. You lose yourself in the subjectivity that permeates objects, but history is a science that demands rigor. We don't practice vagueness here, we require *context*. You have shown signs of progress, I read it in your file. However, virtuosos mustn't be good in their field; they must be excellent." Helen's mouth cracked into a grimace as wide and toothy as that of an abyssal fish. "Calm down, young lady, your heartbeats are hurting my ears."

"I will become excellent," promised Ophelia, who was totally incapable of calming down.

"I have two questions for you, apprentice. Here is the first: what have you learned during these three weeks of probation?"

Ophelia had to admit that she'd expected something a little more concrete. In her head, she formulated all sorts of fine sentences, searching for the one that would most pleasing, but Helen interrupted her, abruptly:

"Don't think. Reply to me now, with total sincerity, in as few words as possible. What have you learned?"

"That I know nothing."

The statement had almost sprung from Ophelia's lungs. It wasn't exactly what she had intended to say, but Helen gave her no chance to expand on it, going straight to her second question:

"Why do you want to become a Forerunner?"

"I . . . In fact, I thought—"

"Why?" Helen's voice was now more sepulchral than ever.

"To put my hands in the service of the truth."

"In the service of the truth," repeated Helen. "Might it not have been good form to say 'in the service of the city'?"

Ophelia allowed herself a moment's thought, recognizing that she'd been given a chance to go back on her words, and then decided to follow her instincts. Helen wasn't Pollux. Helen wasn't the puppet of Lady Septima and the Lords of LUX. Helen thought for herself and made her own decisions.

"You asked for a sincere answer."

Helen then directed her optical appliance at Elizabeth, who was standing to attention near the door, so silently that Ophelia had forgotten she was there.

"Remind me who you are."

"I'm . . . I'm in charge of the second division of Forerunners, *madame*. I coordinate the reading groups."

Ophelia couldn't resist giving Elizabeth an astonished glance. In the three weeks she'd been around her, it was the first time she'd detected any uncertainty in her voice. Outwardly, however, she still had the same expressionless face, unhealthily pale behind its freckles, with the heavy eyelids of a sleepwalker.

"That I already know," Helen stated. "Why, otherwise, would you be attending this interview? What I want to know is your name."

"Elizabeth."

These four syllables, stiffly articulated, reinforced Ophelia's impression. It was almost a distress call.

Helen hit the piston keys of a keyboard. A mechanical arm instantly extended, telescopically, to open the flap of a writing desk at the back of the room. Ophelia was astonished to see that, on it, there was a giant book with pages as thick as skin.

No, not a book. A *Book*, with a capital B. Helen's Book.

Ignoring it, the mechanical arm opened one of the writing desk's many drawers and pulled out a register, which it placed on Helen's desk.

"A good system for a bad memory," Helen commented, not without irony, as she flicked through the register. "Elizabeth, Elizabeth, Elizabeth . . . Ah, yes, you are the one without a power. Your virtuosity is with databases. Oh? It's to you that I owe my personal consulting system? Yes, I seem to recall, now," she declared, closing the register. "I think I can trust in your judgment. Do you think the apprentice here present is worthy of interest for the reading groups?"

The silence that ensued made Ophelia feel uncomfortable. If her acceptance into the Good Family depended on Elizabeth's opinion, it didn't bode well. The division leader didn't raise her nose from her algorithms often enough to know the apprentices she was in charge of. Her devotion to the city and the Memorial made her blind to the rest of the world.

At least, that is how Ophelia saw her, so she was amazed to hear her reply:

"I think she is worthy of interest, period, *madame.*"

Pensively, Helen tapped the marble of her desk with her fingernail. Once, just once, Ophelia would have liked to meet her eyes, but she knew that was impossible: without her corrective appliance, this family spirit saw people as but a galaxy of atoms. Just as the room's compressed-air door stopped her from hearing the muttering, sneezing, grumbling of the students of her conservatoire.

With a resounding creak of leather, Helen leaned forward in her chair, and her enormous bosom followed suit. Her disproportionately long fingers placed a box in front of Ophelia. "Welcome to the Good Family. Be sure to close the door as you leave, you two. Your heartbeats are deafening."

A moment later, Ophelia was following Elizabeth down the stairs of the administration department, hugging her box. She felt a combination of relief and disbelief.

"What you said to Lady Helen, did you truly think it?"

Elizabeth stopped in the middle of the stairs, her hand resting limply on the banister. "Of course not. You are now indebted to me and I intend to take advantage of it."

During an uncomfortable silence, all that could be heard were the typists of the administration department, as fast and noisy as sewing machines.

Elizabeth ended it by raising her half-closed eyes at Ophelia. "I'm joking. Of course I thought it. You'll hear no one telling you so here, but you're pretty talented with your hands. As a reader, at least."

Indeed, Ophelia had inadvertently dropped her box, which tumbled down the marble steps. Elizabeth picked it up, opened it, and took out two little silver wings. Without a word, she kneeled at Ophelia's feet to pin them on to her boots. Her face had remained impassive, but her gestures had become caring. Almost maternal.

"You are one of us, Apprentice Eulalia."

Ophelia felt more touched by these words than she would have expected to be.

"Elizabeth . . . Lady Helen didn't want to hurt you. Her memory . . . " Ophelia only just held back the end of her sentence. *Her memory was torn away by God, along with a page of her Book.* She couldn't reasonably reveal such information to a Forerunner. It would have been dangerous for them both.

"She didn't forget your name deliberately," she said instead.

"I know that." Elizabeth had said these words with a sigh. Sitting down in the middle of the stairs, she wrapped her arms around her knees. Her face showed no emotion, but her slumped body, its lack of contours accentuated by the light from the windows, betrayed her overwhelming melancholy. "I know that," she repeated, quietly, as though to herself. "That's what the family spirits are like. The truth is that before arriving here, I was totally lost. A girl without powers and without purpose. Lady Helen gave me a home, a family, a future. She means so much to me, while I mean nothing to her . . . It's not her fault, she is condemned to forget everything all the time. It's for that reason that the Memorial is so important."

The evening gong sounded, and, as though turned into watch springs, Elizabeth's legs unfolded to stand her up. "I must go without delay to the Secretarium at the Memorial. Sir Henry is expecting me there and, for him, a minute late is a minute too late."

"Will I meet him soon? As a new member of the reading groups, I'd like to introduce myself to him properly."

What Ophelia mainly wanted was a pretext for entering the Secretarium, but Elizabeth slowly shook her head.

"Introduce yourself to the automaton? Believe me, he's not some tourist attraction, and he doesn't care a fig who's working for him. Despite all the respect I owe him, he's only an assemblage of calculations, analyses, and steel. One must, however, acknowledge that he transformed the Memorial's catalogue. We live in the best of worlds," she suddenly declared, solemnly standing to attention. Let's see to it that, together, we make it even better, Apprentice Eulalia."

Elizabeth gave Ophelia's hand a quick shake and left, allowing her no time to react. Which wasn't such a bad thing, really. It was unlikely that she would have appreciated Ophelia's opinion.

Once she was alone on the stairs, it suddenly hit Ophelia that she'd succeeded. She'd become an apprentice virtuoso.

She left the administration building and hurried along the walkway between the columns, pushed along by the searing evening wind. She marched so determinedly, monkeys scattered as she passed. The silver wings attached to her boots produced a metallic ring that punctuated her strides. Each step forward was a step toward God. A step toward Thorn.

"Well done."

The haughty voice made Ophelia slow down, and then turn back. She had passed by Octavio without noticing him. Leaning against a column, in the midst of the creepers, he merged with the shadows that the setting sun was ushering across the gallery. Only his glowing red eyes indicated his presence.

"Thank you," Ophelia said, cautiously.

It was unusual to see him alone. There was always a swarm of apprentices in his wake, ready to applaud his every achievement, as if student rivalries in no way applied to him; it was, of course, Lady Septima they were flattering, through him. Even the gallery's megaphones went quiet in his presence. If he had been someone else, the voice of a supervisor would have soon requested him to return to the quarters of the Sons of Pollux.

"Are those gloves to your satisfaction?" he asked.

Ophelia opened and closed her hands several times, softening the new leather covering them. "They were delivered to me today. I'll be able to continue my apprenticeship in a good position. I owe you one." She had been deliberately familiar. The time for formality was over. From now on, she considered herself the equal of the other apprentices in her company; that this one was Lady Septima's son made no difference to her.

Octavio dragged himself out of the column's shadow. The sun's oblique rays lit up the bronze of his skin, the silver on his uniform, and the gold of his eyebrow chain as he advanced through the gallery. And yet that light was very pale compared with the incandescence of his eyes.

"More than you think, Apprentice Eulalia. Was your visit to Professor Wolf edifying?"

The question had the effect of a poisoned arrow on Ophelia. How naive she'd been! It wasn't simply for the sake of some gloves that Octavio had instigated that encounter. "Well played," she muttered. "I really believed that you'd helped me out of a concern for fairness."

"Oh, but I did. What happened to the professor could happen to others. I thought it fair that you know about it."

Ophelia tensed even more. From the start, a mutual mistrust had hovered between them, as formless and silent as fog.

Now more than ever, she wondered to what extent Octavio wasn't more God's accomplice than his mother was.

"What happened to him?" she asked, pretending to be surprised. "Are you referring to his accident?"

She knew that there was nothing accidental about Professor Wolf's injury, but acknowledging that would be like admitting that she'd pried into his private life, and that was precisely the trap she mustn't fall into.

Octavio studied her with an attention at once sustained and distant, much as he submitted the laboratory samples to the scrutiny of his eyes.

"The dilation of the pupils, the duration of eye contact, the frequency of eyelash fluttering," he whispered. "Our eyes say more about us than any speech could. And yours, Apprentice Eulalia, tell me that you're lying. You lie all the time and to everyone. Even that gesture," Octavio added, seeing Ophelia nervously straighten her glasses, "tells me a great deal about you. My mother sees you as just a clumsy rookie who, sooner or later, will end up losing heart. I, myself, know that nothing will stop you because you are here for a precise reason. A personal reason, totally unconnected to the interests of the city."

During a long silence, the gallery was invaded by the twilight clamor of the birds. Ophelia felt an insect settle on her cheek, but made not the slightest move to chase it away, for fear of betraying herself even more. "Why allow me to remain in the Good Family if you deem me unworthy of being there?"

Octavio's skin furrowed at the corners of his mouth. "The better to keep an eye on you."

He turned on his heel and walked off, his Forerunner wings catching the last ray of sun as it sank behind the jungle. Night fell abruptly, dark and muggy.

He knows nothing, Ophelia repeated to herself, watching

the boy's shadow disappear into the darkness of the walkway. He knows neither my real name nor my real motives. He has suspicions, but he knows nothing.

"Apprentice Eulalia, you are requested to return to your division!" the gallery megaphones ordered. She turned toward one of the watchtowers that surrounded the gardens. Binoculars glinted from it, like a cat's pupils in the dark. Now that Octavio was gone, the supervisor on duty had miraculously regained her sight and voice.

Ophelia set off once more with a resolute step. She would let no one spoil her victory.

She found an empty dormitory, on her return to the Hall. Her colleagues weren't back yet. The reading groups alternated during the day between Pollux's Forerunners and Helen's; because the time of the sessions could vary between six o'clock in the morning and eleven o'clock in the evening, they had their own airship at their disposal.

Ophelia unfolded her mechanical bed and fell onto it, fully clothed. Tomorrow, she thought, looking out to the Memorial, shining like a lighthouse through the mosquito screen on the window. Tomorrow, it will be me who's over there.

She must have fallen asleep without realizing it, because, when she reopened her eyes, her division colleagues were there. Around her bed. They hadn't lit the lamps and were all standing at her bedside, contemplative and silent, as though attending a funeral vigil.

She immediately wanted to get up, but dozens of hands held her down on the mattress and gagged her mouth. None of them hurt her. Their actions were methodical, implacable.

"My cousins have a riddle for you, *signorina*," Mediana's smooth voice whispered in the darkness. "What happens here to all those who receive their wings?"

With her glasses skew-whiff, Ophelia made out rather than

saw her face. Incapable of moving or speaking, she was too astonished to be afraid.

"You will swear allegiance to Mediana," predicted all the Seers in a single, united whisper.

"I'd like to show you something, *signorina.*" Mediana had just turned on a flashlight, which lit up all the precious stones set in her skin. She made a sign to Zen, who had remained in the background until now. Her oriental doll's face was contorted with anxiety, and yet she obeyed the silent command unhesitatingly. She opened the drawer of the bedside table until it came right away from it.

"Look, little reader," Mediana gently instructed.

The Seers' hands immediately sat Ophelia up on the bed, using no force at all, to make her head lean to one side. She felt like a marionette. At first, she saw nothing but the bottom of a drawer she had never used. Suddenly, she noticed them: minuscule shadows, caught by the flashlight.

"Your mattress, your uniform, and your gloves," Mediana specified, with a slightly apologetic smile. "It's not theft, you see. They've been there all along, in your drawer."

Ophelia looked up at Zen, who instantly looked away, ashamed.

"Yes," said Mediana, "it is she who miniaturized them. Oh, she took no pleasure in doing so, believe me. No more than my cousins are taking pleasure in manhandling you right now. Do you know why they are doing it all the same? Because I asked them to. All those here present hate me, and see how they obey me!" The flashlight's beam accentuated the half-masculine, half-feminine features of her illuminated face, making her at once a queen and a king. "Do you remember what I told you, when we first met? There are a thousand ways to torment someone without inflicting the slightest physical suffering on them. You have made the choice to remain among us, *signorina*, so I'm going to explain to you exactly what is going to happen."

Mediana's melodious accent had become hypnotic. Ophelia had to admit that she had obtained her fullest attention. The dormitories were among the few places shielded from the surveillance periscopes, and Elizabeth slept in an individual room, at the other end of the Hall. She mustn't count on any assistance.

"Only one apprentice in this room will become an aspiring virtuoso, and it will be me," Mediana continued, in a whisper. "I have dreamt of being a Forerunner ever since I was old enough to pronounce the word. I will die with wings on my feet. As from tonight, you will put your little hands on the back burner. Impressing Lady Septima is strictly prohibited. You will keep a low profile, keep to yourself, and seek to please just one master: me. If you relinquish first place to me, I won't be ungrateful," she said, sensually rolling each "r" in her sentence. "When the time comes, when I have reached the top, I'll make you my assistant."

"But . . . I thought . . . it was supposed to be me," Zen stammered, as she was replacing the drawer.

Mediana smiled without even glancing at her, all her attention being focused on Ophelia. "Favoritism isn't approved of in Babel. I've already promised posts to all of my cousins, I'm hardly going to employ two assistants."

One of the Seers finally removed the gag from Ophelia's mouth, giving her a chance to respond. She needed no persuading:

"Keep Zen as your assistant. I'm not interested."

Mediana directed her flashlight's beam straight at her glasses. Ophelia was too dazzled to see her expression, but a rustling of uniform indicated to her that she was moving. A winged boot came down right on her hand, at the edge of the bed. The pressure was minimal, and entirely painless, but Ophelia couldn't extricate herself from it, and was forced to remain still. An act of pure domination.

"You didn't listen to my cousins, *signorina*? You will swear allegiance to me. Repeat after me: 'I will do all that you ask of me.'"

Ophelia said nothing. To go to such lengths, this Seer must really think that Ophelia had the potential to overshadow her. In a way, it was pretty flattering. However, when she was no longer blinded by the flashlight and could see Mediana's eyes shining with covetousness, she got really worried.

"Turn her over."

Acting as one, the Seers flipped her on to her stomach. It was done without brutality, without insult, without obscenity, and yet, with her head plunged forcibly into the pillow, Ophelia had rarely experienced something so violent. Much as she struggled, she couldn't put up any resistance to these arms that were doing with her as they pleased. Why weren't her claws coming out to repel them?

"Calm down," breathed a whisper against her ear. "I won't take long."

Anxiety turned into panic in Ophelia's stomach. Mediana had often teased her with her family power, but it had always remained merely words. Just as readers had no right to touch objects without the permission of their owners, Seers couldn't delve into the past and future of someone without their consent. It was much more than a rule of etiquette; it was a family taboo, the sort one wouldn't break lightly.

It was with an exasperating sense of powerlessness that Ophelia felt a hand sliding under her collar and stroking her nape. An icy chill tore down her back, where the spinal cord branched out. Once, in the past, a Chronicler had subjected her to a memory search; Ophelia had felt like a boring book whose pages one skims through.

What Mediana made her endure was not comparable. Ophelia was invaded from within by an intrusive presence, burning with curiosity, keen to absorb her most private self. Her life immediately began to scroll backwards, in the form of kaleidoscopic images, as though a slide projector had started up inside her head. Octavio's red eyes. Elizabeth pinning the wings to her boots. Ambrose's wheelchair stuck between the cobbles. The cutting of the hair in the garden shed. Archibald handing her the false identity papers. The spectacular escape from the public restrooms.

It wasn't only images. It was every thought she'd had, every emotion she'd felt. Ophelia bit into the pillow, resisting this invasion of her memory with all her might, but she couldn't prevent the inevitable. Thorn finally sprang up in the course of a memory. He appeared to her as clearly as if it were yesterday, in the middle of his prison cell, constricted in his too-short shirt, struggling to stay upright due to his broken leg.

Facing God.

Ophelia returned to the present moment as soon as Mediana let go of her nape. She tried, with difficulty, to catch her breath against the pillow. Her glasses were digging into her skin. Her shirt was soaked in sweat.

"*Bene, bene, bene!* I knew you were a secretive little one, but then that! That!" Mediana's voice was weaker, as if this trip in time had physically tested her, but she was exultant. "Don't worry, *signorina*. Your secret . . . All your secrets will remain mine as long as you are a nice, obedient girl. No one, not even my cousins, will know what brought you to Babel and who you really are. You just have a few words to say."

Ophelia swallowed. She felt nauseous. She would have liked to spend the rest of her days buried in this pillow, but the Seers turned her back toward Mediana as soon as the latter snapped her fingers.

"I'm listening."

Ophelia heard herself reply in a tiny voice, as though she were listening to another person: "I will do all that you ask of me."

Mediana smiled at her and planted a kiss on her forehead.

"*Grazie.* Welcome to the Good Family."

# SURPRISE

"Popping a pie in the oven, come on, it's hardly a big deal!"

"Take a good look at these hands, my dear. Are they, in your opinion, the attributes of a commoner?"

"Don't put on your grand airs. I've lived with you long enough to know that you're built the same as ordinary mortals, top to bottom, in front and behind."

"I would ask you not to be vulgar in front of my daughter."

"Your daughter's hungry."

"I received the education of a court lady. I serve one of the finest teas in all of Citaceleste."

"Well, if it's with tea you think you'll meet her needs, she's not about to walk normally soon. In pepperpot's name, Berenilde! I'm your friend, not your maid. I'm not going to run this manor myself, at sleeve's length!"

Squeezed into the baby high chair, now too small for her age, Victoria's eyes followed Mommy and Great-Godmother as they ran from window to window to get rid of the smoke. On the dining-room table, a dish covered with a black crust was giving off a very unpleasant smell.

The house had changed since the arrival of Great-Godmother. Looking stern, she cut open the crust of the dish to examine what lay beneath. "Burnt to a cinder. And our larder's growing bare. You should write to Mr. Farouk."

Victoria coughed, bothered by the smoke. Mommy immediately rushed over to her to flap her fan in front of her face.

"I write to him every day, Madame Rosaline, but I do so to
support him, not to importune him. Never will I stoop so low
as to beg."

"Who said anything about begging for our food?"

Great-Godmother put her fists on her hips. She always
looked angry, Great-Godmother, but she never really lost
her temper. Victoria no longer found her at all intimidating.
Father, on the other hand, terrified her, and even though she
didn't really understand the conversation, she hoped there
was no question of getting him to come to the house.

Father didn't love her.

"What I'm talking to you about is *deserving* our food," continued Great-Godmother. "Let's get out of here, offer our services, show them what we're made of!"

Between two flutters of the fan, Victoria saw a dimple appear
in Mommy's porcelain skin, just at the corners of her lips. It
was a different smile from the ones before. A smile that had
appeared from one day to the next, just when Great-Godmother
had. A smile that made Victoria want to smile, too.

It wasn't the house that had changed; it was Mommy.

"Well, there's a brilliant idea, Madame Rosaline! I'm sure
all the nobles will be ready to cover you in diamonds so you
repair their bits of paper."

Great-Godmother frowned, but a bell rang in the house
as soon as she unclenched her teeth. "Were you expecting a
visit?"

"No. Let's go and see who it is."

Victoria wasn't displeased when Mommy snatched her
from that too-narrow chair and took her in her arms. The
dimples were still there, at the corners of her lips, but she was
trembling like the pearls of her earring.

They went to the music room and Great-Godmother made straight for a cupboard that Victoria knew was the front door to the house. There was another one, right at the back of the fake garden, but no one used it apart from Godfather.

"It's Madam Cunegond," said Great-Godmother, as she clamped her eye on the spyhole in the cupboard. "By Jove, she's really aged!"

"Has she come alone?"

"As far as I can see, yes."

Mommy, who was gripping Victoria so tight it was winding her, relaxed her hands with relief. Even if she didn't speak of it often, everything that went on outside the house worried her. And yet Victoria would have so loved to walk around out there! Her adventure with Godfather was a long time ago, now. The days felt long to her, and she found her little *journeys* here less and less satisfying. She had explored everything to be explored.

"You can let her in," Mommy finally decided.

"Really?" Great-Godmother asked, amazed. "The actual sister of Baron Melchior? I've seen you turn away every visitor, refuse every parcel, but opening your door to a Mirage whose brother was killed by your nephew, that doesn't seem unwise to you?"

"We've always stood together, she and I. Times have become difficult for the Mirages. Illusions are no longer well perceived, the era of frivolity is over. Since she became bankrupt, Dame Cunegond lives alone, I know not where, but above all, not a word about that in front of her—keeping up appearances is all she has left. Open to her, Madame Rosaline."

Great-Godmother turned the key of the cupboard. A tinkling of jewelry and a smell of perfume, even stronger than that of the burned pie, instantly swept into the music room.

"Good day, ladies!"

Victoria felt her heart race with excitement. The Golden Lady! Every time she came to the house, it was a real party. She called Victoria "my little dove," and always had surprises for her: showers of cherries, acrobatic bear cubs, dancing dolls, and many other illusions, too. So Victoria was very disappointed when the Golden Lady didn't even glance at her. She only had eyes for Great-Godmother, as her wide, red mouth stretched from ear to ear.

"You, here! So the rumor was true?"

"What rumor?" muttered Great-Godmother.

"The one announcing the departure, or, I should say, return of our little reader!" The Golden Lady turned in all directions, making the golden pendants on her veil tinkle, as though looking for someone else in the music room. Victoria, thinking it was her, hoped she would finally notice her in Mommy's arms, call her "my little dove," and blow confetti into her hair.

"Don't look for Ophelia, dearest friend," sighed Mommy. "The rumor's wrong, I myself don't even know where she is."

"What a shame!" The Golden Lady was smiling, but Victoria thought she saw her fingers, with their long, long red nails, clenching.

"May I offer you some tea?" said Mommy, in her sweetest voice. "In exchange, I'll take all the news from the court you'd care to give me!"

"I'm not staying," said the Golden Lady. "In fact, I was hoping to find our ex-ambassador at mine. I mean, at yours."

Victoria looked up at Mommy, sensing her arms slacken. She, too, seemed disappointed.

"It's just that, you see, Archibald isn't here any more often than Ophelia is."

"Why are you looking for him?" asked Great-Godmother.

"It so looks, I mean, it so happens that he ordered an illusion from me and never announced his intention to purchase it. If you could at most indicate to me where to reach him, he's so elusive!"

The Golden Lady had always been a bit strange, but she was even more so today, and that intrigued Victoria, greatly. Perhaps it was because of her mouth. She hesitated over every sentence she uttered, as if she'd had too much of what Mommy called "illusions for grown-ups."

"I'm so sorry, my dear Cunegond, you find me as in the dark as you," said Mommy. "Archibald must still be hanging around in goodness knows which Compass Rose! He'll be back. He always comes back."

The Golden Lady had listened to Mommy with the utmost attention. Her thick, tattooed eyelids had opened wider, along with her smile. "In that case, I'll be back, too." With those words, she left through the cupboard, just as she had arrived.

Victoria followed her without even thinking. The long-awaited surprise hadn't come to her, so she would come to the surprise. She left her heavy, stupid body behind, in Mommy's arms, to leap outside, light as a thought.

She skipped behind the Golden Lady, who kept twisting her ankles on the street's cobbles, not suspecting she had company. Victoria had already been out into the street a few times, but never on a *journey*. It was completely different. The sounds made by the Golden Lady's heels and pendants had become hazy. The lampposts rippled, as if turned into rubber, and their light became a large white blot against the darkness. Victoria saw the same carriage passing and re-passing in the road, seconds apart; when she *journeyed*, she sometimes saw or heard things double, so it didn't surprise her.

The sky here was no more real than it was at the house. Mommy had told Victoria that one had to go along many roads and many stairs to see it, but that it was so cold, that sky, that it would instantly turn her fingers to ice.

Victoria never felt really cold or really hot when she *journeyed*, but she'd go to see the sky another day. The Golden Lady had just disappeared into a lift at the end of the road, and Victoria had to hurry to get into it, too. Huddled in a corner of the lift, she watched her with increasing curiosity. The Golden Lady was no longer smiling, but the way she held herself was very funny: sometimes, she tilted her head excessively to one side, or then scratched her hip by stretching her arm behind her back.

Looking down, Victoria suddenly noticed her shadow. Or rather, her shadows. The Golden Lady seemed to have lots of them, swarming around her feet like living creatures. Were they one of her surprise illusions? Victoria hadn't noticed them earlier, these shadows, with her other body's eyes.

She followed the Golden Lady out of the lift and had to walk behind her for quite a while—fortunately, Victoria didn't get tired on *journeys*—before entering a tiny house with her. The place looked like the little studio to which Mommy would retire for a couple of hours a day to do her embroidery. There were dummies' busts, a large blackboard covered in chalk-written notes, and a counter twice Victoria's height.

But not an illusion anywhere.

The Golden Lady closed the door behind her and picked up the receiver of a telephone on the counter. Victoria hoped something more interesting was going to happen soon; she was starting to get bored.

"Change of plan," the Golden Lady said into the receiver. "Our little runaway isn't here, either. But I'm going to longer a bit linger. Linger a bit longer. No, my child, I prefer to remain discreet. This Madame Cunegond isn't yet coffee table—comfortable—but she may open more doors for me than anticipated. Tell all my dear children to remain vigilant. Every day counts."

Victoria couldn't understand a thing the Golden Lady was saying; her words reached her as though through water, and yet she was starting to feel a little uneasy. The Golden Lady's mouth didn't hesitate at all anymore. Victoria had followed her this far because it had seemed a fantastically fun adventure, but, in fact, she wasn't having that much fun. She could just make out, in the Other-Victoria's ear, Mommy's tiny voice, fretting—"the little darling gets increasingly lost in her daydreams"—and could feel, like the lightest touch, her warm hand stroking her hair.

She was just about to return to having Mommy's warm skin against hers when the Golden Lady pulled aside a drape behind the counter to go into a back room. Victoria's curiosity meant she couldn't resist following her. The call of the *journey* was, once again, strongest.

She froze when she saw the Golden Lady leaning over a Second Golden Lady. She wasn't seeing double, as with the carriage in the road. This Second Golden Lady was reclining on a large, white carpet and staring wide-eyed, a smile of pure joy on her lips, her veil and its pendants spread around her like a beautiful golden puddle.

Red water was trickling out of her nose and ears.

She was watching, without seeming to see them, bodies as transparent as the smoke from a hookah pipe, totally naked, half-woman and half-man, who were whispering words against her lips that only she could hear.

Victoria understood nothing of what was unfolding before her eyes.

With a single gesture, the First Golden Lady shooed away the naked bodies floating around the Second Golden Lady. "That illusion was perhaps a little too strong for you," she told her. "You, my poor children, are such fragile creatures!" With her red-taloned hand, she closed the Second Golden Lady's tattooed eyelids. "Rest in peace, my dear, your death was not in vain. Thanks to your face, I may succeed in swirling the wave. Saving the world."

With these words, the First Golden Lady slowly raised her head toward Victoria. She didn't seem to see her, but she was squinting and staring at the corner of the room where she was, as if she sensed her presence. All her shadows immediately began to writhe and slither under her feet, as if wanting to hurl themselves at Victoria.

"And you, my child? Would you also like to help me save the world?"

The next moment, everything had disappeared: the two Golden Ladies, the white carpet, the back room. Victoria had returned to being the Other-Victoria at the house. She was strapped once more into the too-narrow baby chair. Mommy, smiling, was holding a spoonful of jam out to her.

Victoria opened her mouth to scream. Not a sound came out.

# THE SLAVE

Ophelia took off her glasses and gave her stinging eyes a long rub. After so long staring at text, she could see printed words even with her eyes closed. As she stretched in her chair, she looked up at the ceiling. Or rather, at the ground. Visitors were walking upside down there, moving silently between the library shelves. She always found it strange to think that it was she who was up above, and they who were down below.

She closed her book, and then checked, one last time, the catalogue entry she had just written. No print date, no mention of a publisher, and some worthy unknown by way of an author: evaluating this monograph had been a real headache, forcing her to keep switching between ocular reading and manual reading. She opened the compartment of the phantogram and saw, with relief, that nothing new had arrived. She couldn't have handled one book more.

She glanced furtively through the latticed partitions separating her reading cubicle from her neighbors'. The Seers were bent over their books, in the haloes of the lamps. Of Zen, hidden behind her piles of ministerial archives, all one could see was a porcelain forehead beaded with perspiration.

Only Mediana sat with arms crossed in her cubicle. She

was watching Ophelia with amused curiosity. "You've finished your quota, *signorina*? Me, too. Let's go and do our holes
together."

Ophelia gathered up her index cards. As if she had the
choice . . .

They deposited the catalogued books on the counter of the
Phantoms, who, in truth, were hardly ectoplasmic. Endowed
with impressive girths and brick-red coloring, they owed this
name to their family power, which allowed them to transform
any object from a solid state to a gaseous one, and vice versa.
Once "phantomized," the most voluminous documents could
circulate by pneumatic tube, so it was possible to dispatch an
entire collection of encyclopedias from one end of the Memorial to the other, in the blink of an eye.

Ophelia flipped from the ceiling to the wall, and from the
wall to the ground, before taking one of the eight transcendiums serving the atrium. She didn't check whether Mediana
was following her; she could hear her boots clicking behind
her. It was a taunting sound that accompanied her perma-
nently, wherever she went, pursuing her even in her nightmares. Since this Seer had placed her hands on her, her life
had ceased to be her own.

The sunlight pouring through the rotunda disappeared as
soon as Ophelia moved into the shadow of the Secretarium.
The gigantic globe of the old world floated weightlessly above
the hall, as close and as inaccessible as it was in her dreams.
Much as she passed, back and forth, beneath this globe, she
couldn't spot an opening in it. There was but one possible
means of access: a gangway that led from the northern transcendium to a door that blended in so well with the illustrations on the sphere, it was invisible from the ground. The
gangway was guarded by a sentry, relieved every three hours;
it was deployed with the aid of a special key, of which very few

individuals at the Memorial possessed a copy. Lady Septima only entrusted hers to her son, and, on more rare occasions, to Mediana and Elizabeth, when Sir Henry required their services.

Ophelia would have loved to know what had to be done to get into the good books of this automaton, who directed the reading groups without ever leaving his Secretarium. She still hadn't met him, but once or twice she had chanced to hear the echo of his mechanical step on the lower floors of the globe, when the database—the punched cards of which were all stored in the Secretarium—broke down. Sir Henry gobbled up bibliographical references as a greedy pig does pastries. The rate of cataloguing he imposed on them was intolerable, and the entries never detailed enough for his liking. Ophelia couldn't count the times she'd had to start some work from scratch again, after it had been returned to her stamped, in big, red letters, "incomplete."

Lazarus had created his automatons to put an end to the servitude of man by man. Ophelia would have had one or two things to tell him.

She squinted. A cloud in the form of a snake flew through the air, went into a long spiral, and entered the terrestrial globe from the top. One could only see the glass tubes of the phantograms in the sunlight. They allowed documents to be sent straight into the Secretarium. For one crazy moment, Ophelia wondered if that might not be the best way for her to access it. The house rules strictly forbade the phantomization of human beings—only the most experienced Phantoms were capable of turning themselves into vapor without risking their lives—but she was desperate.

"As long as I'm alive, you'll never go up there," Mediana whispered to her, pinching her chin to turn her eyes from the globe. "Let's make a detour, my *vescica* is fit to burst."

Ophelia followed her under the peristyle and waited

outside the door to the restrooms, as would an obedient dog. Never had she felt so humiliated. Her anger with Mediana didn't, however, compare with that she felt with herself. She exchanged a stern look with her reflection, on one of the mirrors she could see through the half-open door to the toilet stalls. She had compromised Thorn, no more, no less.

"I'm not going to beat about the bush. You are not productive."

Hearing Lady Septima's voice ringing through the peristyle's arcades, Ophelia stood to attention. In her haste, she scattered all her index cards at her feet. Not saluting a teacher, or, even worse, a Lord of LUX, meant instant punishment: she'd learnt that lesson through chores and detentions. It was not, however, to her that Lady Septima had just spoken, but to the old sweeper of the Memorial, who was methodically dusting each flagstone on the floor.

"It is the subsidies generously granted by LUX that maintain this building. Our Memorialists rely entirely on automatons' orders. Accept it, their productivity is a hundred times yours."

Ophelia raised her eyebrows, as she gathered up the cards she'd dropped. Lady Septima was waving a file under the nose of the sweeper—she was as short and muscular as he was tall and thin.

"We are grateful for your loyal and faithful service, old man, but it is time to make way for the future. Sign this paper." Lady Septima was the embodiment of authority, her eyes and gold braiding making her blaze like a sun. And yet the sweeper simply shook his head.

Ophelia felt an instant, irresistible liking for him. Inside the pocket of her uniform, Thorn's watch opened and closed its cover with a resounding click. The impertinent noise made Lady Septima swivel round.

"Apprentice Eulalia, do you not have work to do?"

If Ophelia's hands hadn't already been occupied picking up her cards, she would have squeezed the watch tight to stop it reoffending. It was becoming animated with increasing frequency, snapping its cover all over the place. For a poor, broken mechanism, it wasn't short on repartee.

"I do, madame."

"You don't look as if you do. I was proud of your slight progress at the end of your probation period. You have slackened lamentably since then. Do not rest on your wings—they can be withdrawn from you at any moment."

Ophelia held Lady Septima's piercing gaze through the dark rectangles of her glasses. If this woman was as observant as her family power predisposed her to be, she would have suspected what was going on within the division of Helen's Forerunners.

Maybe she did know about it.

"I will see to it that Sir Henry increases your reading group's quotas," Lady Septima declared, moving off with a military step. "Your colleagues will be most grateful to you, Apprentice Eulalia."

A group punishment—Ophelia really needed that. Even so, she couldn't refrain from giving a quick smile to the sweeper, who turned his big beard almost imperceptibly toward her without stopping his meticulous dusting.

"I'm going to end up thinking that you like being punished, *signorina*."

Ophelia's muscles all tensed at once. Having just come out of the restrooms, Mediana had leaned against her back with all her weight, so as to keep her kneeling in the middle of the scattered cards on the floor. Ophelia couldn't see her smile, but could imagine it from the feline purring of her voice.

"Watch out," she whispered in her ear. "Jinx straight ahead."

Ophelia looked up, mortified. Blaise had abandoned his returns trolley right in the middle of the atrium to make a beeline for her. Mediana backed away as he got nearer. The assistant's bad luck was notorious: wherever he was, whatever he was doing, a bookshelf would always collapse, or a lamp explode, as he passed.

Blaise crouched down to help Ophelia pick her up her cards; in his haste, he banged his forehead against hers. "Mademoiselle Eulalia," he greeted her with a hesitant smile. "I tried so hard . . . You were never . . . *Bon*, I'm pleased to speak to you at last."

It was, indeed, the first time they were speaking since their encounter in the birdtrain. And for a very good reason: Ophelia had scrupulously avoided bumping into him at the Memorial. She absorbed herself in her cataloguing when she heard his timid step close to the reading cubicles; she turned back whenever she came across his trolley around the corner of a corridor. He seemed so anxious to engage in conversation, he whose company everyone shunned, that she despised herself a little more every time she avoided him.

"Sorry," she muttered, not daring to look him in the eye. "My apprenticeship takes up all my time." She silently implored him not to persist, to leave it at that. How could she make him understand that he mustn't confide in her anymore? Sensing, out of the corner of her glasses, Mediana's thrilled interest in the two of them was unbearable.

Blaise leaned even further, his moist, hedgehog eyes obstinately searching for hers. "Mademoiselle Eulalia, if you would just accept to grant me even but a moment . . . "

Ophelia took her cards out of his hands with such brusqueness that Blaise wouldn't have looked more shocked if she'd torn his heart from his chest. "Sorry," she repeated. She couldn't be more sincere.

He raised his shaggy eyebrows, dumbfounded, and then a flash of understanding crossed his eyes. A painful understanding. "No," he said, slowly moving backwards. "It's I who am sorry."

He went off again with his trolley, back hunched, but not without accidentally wheeling it over the foot of a visitor in the wrong place at the wrong time. Right then, Ophelia would have liked to have her formerly long hair back again; the disadvantage of short curls is that one can't hide behind them.

"Aha, might I have missed a passing fancy among your countless secrets?" Mediana whispered to her, leaning on her shoulder. "Your poor husband, if he knew . . . "

Ophelia couldn't contain the deep dislike she felt any longer. Her claws had proved powerless before a dozen assailants, but they repelled Mediana with no trouble at all. The tomboy steadied herself with a pirouette and burst out laughing, as if she had just experienced a mere amorous rebuff.

"Ah, yes, I was forgetting. A little bit Dragon, our Animist."

"One word more," Ophelia said, through gritted teeth, "and I will put a stop to this blackmail myself."

Mediana's smile twisted into a pout of sincere sorrow. It always went like that with her. One moment masculine and insolent, the next sweet and feminine, as if she wore two carnival masks in turn. "I think it's time we had a little talk, *noi due*. Let's go and do our holes."

In the Memorialists' jargon, "doing holes" consisted of turning the handwritten entries into punched cards for Sir Henry's database. With the card-punchers being noisier than typewriters, a soundproof room was specially allocated to them in the basement, so as not to disturb the readers' peace. The ideal place to speak away from eavesdroppers.

"First, let's check your work." Mediana had said these words as soon as she had turned the wheel of the compressed-air door and reassured herself that there was no one else in the card-punching room. Perched on a stool, she went through Ophelia's index cards, one by one. "You've improved," she noted, with an appreciative whistle. "Your contextualizations are increasingly precise, *bravissima*!" She unscrewed the cap of a fountain pen and started crossing out every entry that Ophelia had spent hours cataloguing. "This should render your results a little less satisfactory."

"Sir Henry will return it all to me, once again."

Mediana's eyes started to shine with the same brilliance as the precious stones set into her skin. The more Ophelia's glasses darkened, the more Mediana's face lit up. "It's funny, you speak of him as if you feared angering him."

"I do not believe that an automaton can get angry," Ophelia retorted, in a muted voice. "But that's not the case with me. Only the best accede to the Secretarium; by preventing me from doing well, you're making me waste my time. I didn't come all the way to Babel to be a slave to your caprices."

"Yes, I sense that you're finding the situation rather tricky," Mediana sighed. "So I'm going to reveal to you why I care so much about becoming a Forerunner." She returned the cards to Ophelia and placed her own on the stand of a card-puncher. This machine resembled an actual piano, with its winding stool and fine ivory keyboard. The noise it made at every touch, on the other hand, wasn't particularly musical. "Because the Forerunners know everything about everybody," Mediana sang out, above the din of the punching. "And it so happens that I've developed a real addiction to secrets!"

Sitting at her own machine, Ophelia couldn't help but admire the dexterity with which Mediana's fingers danced across the keys, without the slightest hesitation. As for her, she was still far from mastering the basis of the code invented by Elizabeth; with her clumsiness not helping, she was often obliged to start all over again due to hitting the wrong key.

"There are few domains in which you don't excel," Ophelia acknowledged, reluctantly. "You're already way ahead of all of us, so why alter our results?"

Mediana smiled more sweetly as she slid another blank card into her punch. "Do you honestly think I would be where I am now thanks to my talent alone? My family power allows me to absorb not only the memories of those I touch, but also their knowledge. Do you know the reason why I managed to get into the Secretarium? Because Sir Henry and Lady Septima were in urgent need of a translator of ancient languages. And do you know why I suddenly became excellent at ancient languages? Because I laid my hands on many, many specialists. And allowed them, in return, to lay their hands on me."

Mediana had added that last sentence so airily, while tapping away on her keyboard so cheerily, that Ophelia wasn't taken in for a second. What this pretty tomboy had sacrificed to satisfy her appetite for knowledge had cost her more than she wanted to let on.

"And was it worth it?"

"All secrets are worth it. If it were just up to me, I'd spend my life in the Secretarium's galleries, extracting its every mystery. You've already heard talk of the 'ultimate truth,' haven't you? I have the firm intention of discovering one day what it is. That having been said, your own secrets aren't bad, either, *signorina*." Mediana paused her punching and, this time, shot a deadly serious look at Ophelia. "I'm going to be frank; some of your memories are very hard to interpret. I couldn't make any sense of that fellow who can switch heads. I know at least one thing: you have put Babel in a very tricky position, your husband and you. The city has signed commercial treaties with all the arks, Anima and the Pole included. It is no place of refuge for runaways and fugitives of your sort. If LUX discovers who you are and who you seek, the risk to you is great. And that's nothing compared with what will happen to your husband once caught. Babel advocates nonviolence, but, believe me, you wouldn't want to know what goes on in their correction centers."

Ophelia's fingers slipped on her keyboard. She would have to throw away the card she was punching and replace it with a blank one. "So what next?" she said. "You're going to denounce me?"

"No, *signorina*, but I would like you to understand that you're in no position to complain. My blackmailing displeases you? Put up with it."

"And what if I were to read your personal belongings without your permission? If I were to blackmail you over your own secrets?"

"I defy you to find a single one that would be more awkward than yours," Mediana said, her smile tinged with kindness. "Let's be serious: to whom, you or me, would Lady Septima give more credit?"

Ophelia stared at her crossed-out cards on the stand, breathing deeply, in and out, to disperse the grayness shrouding her glasses like smoke, to the point that she couldn't see. She felt trapped. So, was she condemned, week after week, to punch incomplete cards? Should she give up looking for Thorn to protect him?

Mediana returned to her card-punching with the grace of a concert pianist. "You hate me. You all hate me. And the saddest thing is that you don't hate me because of what I discovered about you. You hate me because you sense, deep down, that I am the person who understands you the most in the whole world. I stuck to your recent memories, *signorina*, but if I had gone right back to your birth, I would know you better than you do yourself."

"You don't know me."

Ophelia hadn't managed to stop her voice, when saying these words, sounding like a warning. Mediana's arrogance, her gall in taking control of her life, set her every nerve on edge.

"Oh, but yes, I do know you," Mediana gently insisted. "The absent one who haunts you, I know how afraid you are that you will never find him. And I know," she added, after an eloquent silence, "how equally afraid you are of succeeding in doing so. You hate being treated like a child, but in front of a man, you remain an inexperienced *bambina*."

Ophelia's fingers began to shake so hard, she had to wedge them between her knees. The fleeting image of Mediana punching holes into her own tongue crossed her mind. The rest of their encoding session went by without a single word, both of them concentrating on their keyboards.

Mediana had soon finished her work, whereas Ophelia, totally preoccupied by what had just been said, continued to struggle with hers.

"A present."

She contemplated, with incomprehension, the two cabaret tickets Mediana had just placed on her stand.

"I'm not as cruel as you think I am. I was being sincere, you know, when I told you I'd like, one day, to have you as my assistant. It's in my interest to take care of you, and you're very edgy. Tomorrow, it's Sunday. Take your leave, hit the town, and get yourself over there."

The thought of escaping Mediana's clutches for a few hours was appealing, but Ophelia really didn't like her obsession with controlling her schedule. "No thanks," she declined, drily.

"It wasn't a suggestion. You have no idea how many people I had to blackmail to obtain that address. You're going there, *punto e basta*."

201

"Why?"

Mediana placed her punched cards in the hoist. Her expression, behind her illuminations, had become enigmatic. At this moment, more than ever, she seemed to be wearing a carnival mask. "Let's say, to simplify, that it's not a respectable place. Up until now, I haven't put a foot wrong, you understand? I'm not too keen to flaunt myself over there, but they say certain things are going on in the place. Compromising things. Go there not in uniform, preferably accompanied, and you'll attract less attention. Gather information for me, and I shan't be ungrateful."

"You'll release me?"

"No, but we'll proceed to an exchange of information."

"What information could you possibly have to offer me?" Ophelia stiffened when Mediana leaned slowly, sensually, over her, almost making her lose her balance on her stool.

"That tall oddball who serves as your husband," she whispered, right into her ear. "I've already come across him. Here, at the Memorial."

With a voluptuous flourish, she plucked the tickets from the stand and tapped Ophelia's glasses with them; the glasses paled to transparency.

"Go over there for me, *signorina*, and I'll tell you more."

# THE PROHIBITIONS

The entrance to the great people's bazaar looked like the pediment of a glass-and-steel temple. From the shadow of a statue of a sphinx, Ophelia watched the crowd, a colorful, shifting mosaic of men, animals, and automatons. The contrasting smells given off made the scorching air even more unbreathable.

It was entirely futile, but she couldn't help looking out for Thorn. For months now, she had endlessly constructed hypotheses, which she tempered with "if" and "perhaps." And the thought that she was actually following in his footsteps, if Mediana hadn't lied to her, made her chest pound. It was a chaotic heartbeat, exacerbated by hope and impatience, that caused her inner emptiness to echo.

And yet, even though it was hard for her to admit it, Mediana was right: she was also afraid. Although she was forever thinking about her reunion with Thorn, she never imagined how it would turn out *afterwards*.

Suddenly, she saw him. Not Thorn, of course, but the other man she was waiting for.

Blaise was stumbling through the crowd, barely recognizable in his civvies. His large babouches, pantaloons, and flapping smock sleeves were so many excuses for getting into a tangle at every step. He had covered his face with his hand; as an Olfactory, his sense of smell doubtless found the mingled odors of the bazaar highly offensive. He was squinting, blinded by the sun, but as soon as he moved into the shadow of the sphinx, he was relieved to find Ophelia there, as arranged.

"Bademoiselle Eulalia!" he exclaimed, still holding his nose. "I bust adbit I didn't believe it, even after receiving your bessage. This appointbent was so unexpected! I . . . *en fait*, I thought you were angry with be."

"Before you go any further, I must warn you," Ophelia said, hastily. "I know you wanted to speak to me, but please, don't tell me anything about your private life. My own no longer belongs to me and I can't promise to protect yours. And I also want you to know this," she added, showing him her cabaret tickets. "If you come with me, I'll probably expose you to trouble."

Blaise was so taken aback by this declaration, he stopped holding his nose. He readjusted his turban, as if wrestling with himself, and then gave a faint, timid smile. "*Eh bien*, this makes a nice change for me. Usually, it's rather me who exposes others to trouble. Where are we going?"

Ophelia was so overcome with gratitude, she tried to find the words to convey it. She couldn't find them. Whenever she was moved, they treacherously escaped her.

"In fact, I was hoping you would be able to tell me that. I've asked several public signaling guides and not one knows the address of this cabaret. All I know is that it's somewhere around this area."

Ophelia handed the tickets to Blaise, who almost instantly frowned. "Are you sure the address indicated isn't a mistake?"

"Why?"

"Because it's that of the ancient baths, and they've been closed for a millennium. The traders set up their stalls in the ruins. If . . . *eh bien* . . . if you'd care to follow me, I'd be delighted to show you."

Blaise's skin had become even more florid than normal, but Ophelia was too preoccupied to notice it. What if these cabaret tickets were a mean prank?

Entering the people's bazaar was like walking into a firework display of textiles and spices. The central market was so cluttered, it was almost impassable. Blaise stammered apologies all around him every time a pot shattered, a stall collapsed, an automaton jammed, a bicycle skidded, or a zebu bolted, as if he really were responsible for every incident in the market.

"What was it you wanted to tell me yesterday?" Ophelia asked him. "If it's not too personal, I mean."

"*Quoi?* Oh, yes, it was about the death of Mademoiselle Silence," Blaise whispered, leaning closer to her. "I followed your advice and did my own investigation. I wanted to verify whether . . . whether I was to blame, yes or no."

"You discovered something."

Blaise nodded his head nervously, knocking his turban off-balance once again. "According to the medical examiner, the fall from the ladder isn't the cause of death. Mademoiselle Silence had apparently died before falling. Of . . . of a massive heart attack."

Ophelia felt her own heart hammering her ribs. She remembered Baron Melchior's kiss on her hand, the treacherous illusion he had instilled into her body, the unbearable pain that had ripped through her chest.

No. He was dead. What had killed the missing of Clairdelune and what had killed Mademoiselle Silence were two separate matters.

"I cause many accidents," Blaise continued, not noticing her distress, "but I've never made people ill. I . . . I'm starting to think that you were right, that perhaps I'm not to blame. All the more since I discovered something else."

He seemed torn between relief and anxiety, two conflicting

emotions that distorted the already tormented features of his face.

"Something else?" Ophelia asked, with surprise.

"Mademoiselle Silence was senior censor," Blaise reminded her. "Among all the works in the Memorial, a senior censor decides which conform to the city's outlook, and which don't. If one of them is questionable, he or she can decide to transfer it to the reserved section, or . . . *eh bien* . . . proceed with its destruction, pure and simple."

Ophelia thought, bitterly, of her museum, on Anima. "And what kind of senior censor was Mademoiselle Silence?"

"The radical sort," Blaise suddenly whispered, very quietly, as though the formidable ears of his superior could hear him from beyond the grave. "She hunted down, relentlessly, all the works she deemed harmful. At the first sign of any ambiguous words, the book went *directement* into the incinerator. We lost some unique editions due to this purge. The Lords of LUX issued several warnings to Mademoiselle Silence, as you can imagine: they subsidize the Memorial to develop its collections, not to throw them into the flames. It was no good, she always ended up resuming her excessive behavior. Until the revision of the catalogue, at least."

With a movement familiar to him, Blaise made Ophelia step to one side; they thus avoided a lantern that, incredibly, had unhooked itself from a store awning just as they were passing beneath it.

"The introduction of Sir Henry's reading groups changed everything," he continued, as if nothing had happened. "Mademoiselle Silence was strictly prohibited from destroying any more works. This intensely annoyed her, and, believe me, I often had to pay for her foul moods."

"I do believe you. I met her only once, and the memory is still painful."

"It's precisely that occasion that I wanted to get to," whispered Blaise. "The day when I . . . when you . . . *bon*, the day when the book trolley tipped over."

"Yes?" Ophelia encouraged him.

"Those . . . those books, Mademoiselle destroyed them. Despite the prohibition. Just prior to dying. When she gave me the order to remove them, I swear to you I had no idea the fate she had in store for them," Blaise stammered, as if fearing censure. "I was just supposed to transport them to her department for her to examine them."

To Ophelia, it seemed as if the merry bustle of the bazaar, its exotic aromas, its eye-catching knickknacks, had suddenly become distant. She knew, with absolute certainty, that continuing this discussion would be to venture onto an isolated and dangerous path, a path that decent citizens didn't take. "Go on," she said, all the same. "Why did she destroy those books? What was so distinctive about them?"

Blaise rubbed his large, pointed nose, bothered by the smoke from an incense stall they were just passing. "They were just tales for children! They were published after the Rupture, and described the beginnings of the new world. They were very fine editions, but, *honnêtement*, they were starting to gather dust. Our young readers never borrowed them."

"From what you're saying, the tales weren't particularly subversive."

"Oh, they made a few allusions to the 'hm-hms' of the old world," Blaise said, coughing to avoid saying the word "wars," "but with metaphoric and pacific intent. They were rather naive, even, from what little I recall. I have no idea what possessed Mademoiselle Silence to target them, despite orders."

"Because of their author, perhaps?" Ophelia suggested.

"Long dead and long forgotten," Blaise said, with a shrug. "A certain 'E. G.'"

"Erjay?"

"'E. G.,'" Blaise repeated, trying to modify his accent. "Just the initials. Might as well say anonymous. I did some research on him, but there's no other known work by him, apart from these tales. Very few were printed, and we held perhaps the last remaining volumes at the Memorial. Such beautiful books!" he sighed. "Lost forever!"

"So, the last thing Mademoiselle Silence did before her death was to burn the tales of an unknown writer," Ophelia recapped. "It's pretty strange."

"*En fait*, I've kept the strangest for last. The place where Mademoiselle Silence's body was discovered . . . That library ladder she fell off. . ." Blaise suddenly put his hand to his nose, as if a smell from the past, stronger even than all those of the bazaar, had just turned his stomach. "Oh, Mademoiselle Eulalia! If you had smelt it, that terrible stench . . . The reek of abject fear. Her corpse," he said, after taking a deep breath, "was found exactly where the books by our mysterious E. G. were shelved. I mean, before they were removed. All that remained were empty shelves, but she still had to go and inspect them, in the middle of the night, without rhyme or reason!"

"That determination speaks volumes," Ophelia acknowledged. "But it doesn't explain the terror that gripped her at the moment of dying. Do you think . . . Do you believe there could be some link there with the Secretarium?"

"The Secretarium?" asked Blaise, surprised. "I can't really see the connection. Mademoiselle Silence had no more access to it than I do. I know there are rumors circulating about that place, but they're nothing more. Here are your ancient baths, Mademoiselle Eulalia!"

He had just passed under an arch that led to a side street. The steel and glass of the market gave way to stone and water. The remains of columns formed a circular gallery, open to the sky, around a pool that didn't look too clean. The fruit sellers who had set up shop there were forever chasing away wasps with mechanical rackets.

Ophelia now better understood Blaise's reaction on seeing her tickets. This place bore no resemblance whatsoever to a cabaret. The thought that Mediana had made a fool of her made her furious in a way she had rarely felt.

And then, she spotted it. On the other side of the pool. A round sign, battered by the wind, was swinging above a rusty, old door. Ophelia had to bang into many stalls and skid on much rotten fruit to reach it.

"You think this bight be it, bademoiselle?" asked a surprised Blaise, holding his nose again, unable to bear the smell any longer.

She didn't reply. She was observing. The sign had lost its paint, washed out by sun and rain, but its form was undoubtedly that of an orange. Of course, it could be a coincidence, but Ophelia's instinct whispered to her that it wasn't. She banged the door's knocker, crushing her fingers in the process.

A spyhole opened almost immediately.

"What may I do to help you?" a little voice inquired.

Ophelia showed her tickets, and, after the click of a lock, the door opened on a child. He was wearing just a simple loin-cloth, doing justice to his chocolate-hued skin; being barefoot on cobbles scorched by the sun didn't seem to bother him. Politely, he ushered them in, turning the key behind them. On the other side of the door there was a small courtyard, open-air and ill-paved, which might have once served as a changing room for the ancient baths.

Without a word, the child lit a gas lamp, one of many hanging around the entrance. He handed it to Blaise, who took hold of it looking traumatized, as if he'd just entrusted him with a stick of dynamite.

"Follow the arrows," the child said, indicating an entrance on the other side of the courtyard. "I wish you, *Messieur-Dames*, a happy sauciness!"

Ophelia and Blaise plunged into the darkness of a staircase that led deep underground. The tropical temperature of the outside world began to plummet. A hundred and thirty steps later, it had become freezing, as they arrived at the beginning of a vast, subterranean corridor. Ophelia shivered all over. She was wearing the toga and light sandals Ambrose had given her the day she'd arrived in Babel; not exactly suitable garb for exploring cellars.

"*Mon Dieu . . .* " muttered Blaise. The light from his lamp had just revealed an arrow, barely visible among the graffiti, which had been chalked onto a wall. Except that it wasn't a wall; it was human bones. Dozens, hundreds, thousands of tibias and skulls, placed one on top of the other like bricks.

Catacombs.

"Whatever you do, don't stay close to me," Blaise warned. "I'm likely to set off a landslide at any moment."

Their steps resounded like explosions in the silence of the ossuary, as they went deeper into the tunnel.

"Animists' family power only works on objects," whispered Ophelia. "This basic principle means that, logically, I should be incapable of reading organic material. When I was an adolescent, I got the chance to have a prehistoric necklace in my hands. It was made of human teeth, Mr. Blaise, and yet I read it just as I would have read any other necklace. I didn't question it too much at the time."

The tone of her voice was distorted by the reverberations of the place; she sounded like a foreigner. She rubbed her frozen arms and looked at Blaise, walking awkwardly ahead. "At what moment?" she asked him. "At what moment do we cease to be humans and become objects?"

Blaise continued to make his way in silence, carrying the lamp at arm's length to spread its light as far as possible. When he finally replied, it was in a different voice from usual, deeper, calmer, and without the slightest stutter: "Some humans are objects while they're alive, Mademoiselle Eulalia."

Ophelia was struck by this insight, but Blaise didn't get a chance to elaborate. The ossuary had just opened onto a large, vaulted room.

It was full of people.

Men and women were swaying their hips ecstatically under orange-shaped lanterns. Those who weren't dancing had taken over the bars and pedestal tables, sitting one against the other. One on top of the other, in some cases. They were clinking glasses, smoking, gesticulating, chatting, hugging, fighting . . . without making the slightest sound. Ophelia felt as if she were watching a gathering of mime artists.

"Such soundproofing can only be the work of an excellent Acoustic," Blaise commented, impressed. He turned off the lamp and studied the silent spectacle unfolding before them, much as he would have tried to analyze a painting that had come to life. He then took off his turban. Awkwardly, he placed it on Ophelia's curly head and unwound the fabric so as to cover half of her face. "I don't know what has brought you here, *mademoiselle*," he whispered to her, "but this is no place for an apprentice virtuoso. If Lady Helen hears where you have been today, she will have no option but to expel you from her conservatoire."

"But . . . what about you?" Ophelia stammered from under the fabric, while trying to straighten her glasses.

Blaise broke into a joyless smile and pressed the slender tip of his nose. "Can you see me wearing a veil with a profile like this? *Ne t'inquiète pas!* I'm just an assistant, I have no reputation to protect."

211

Barely had they moved into the subterranean room than the silence was shattered. Ophelia was jostled by a whirlwind of dancers, musicians, smokers, wrestlers, artistes, and gamblers, not one of them taking any notice of her.

Miraculously, Blaise found them a table where they wouldn't get trampled on. He apologized effusively when the chair he offered to Ophelia gave way under his weight, and then asked her a question that she didn't hear due to the surrounding hubbub.

"Are you looking for something specific?" he repeated, raising his voice.

With her head swathed in his turban, Ophelia looked around her. Her eyes were assailed with movement, her nostrils with absinthe, her ears with jazz. Mediana had sent her to gather compromising information. She was spoilt for choice. Alcohol, tobacco, dueling: Ophelia had been in Babel long enough to know that everything going on and everything being consumed in this cabaret was illegal. The game of darts on its own would have meant prison for all those taking part in it. It was as if all the tension accumulated aboveground in the city—the right-thinking, the taboo subjects, the countless rules of good conduct—was released in the cellars. Rarely had Ophelia felt so intrusive: she was here to spy on them, but, really, she would have preferred to be one of them.

And then there were the oranges. They were everywhere, forged into every wrought-iron table, printed on every lampshade. Once again, Ophelia couldn't help but think that this wasn't the fruit of coincidence.

She jumped when a man approached her, opening one side of his coat. An impressive collection of books burst out of every pocket: detective novels, erotic journals, revolutionary manifestos. Prohibited books only. She shook her head as respectfully as possible to decline. In any case, she would have struggled to pay him. As an apprentice virtuoso, she received, weekly, a paltry sum in the form of a punch card, but it only gave her access to a precise list of public services. The black market was certainly not one of them.

Her eyes met Blaise's. They were both so stiff and starchy on their chairs, in the midst of all these forbidden pleasures, that they ended up bursting out laughing. Ophelia hadn't laughed like that for an eternity, but she became serious again when she noticed Blaise looking intently at her. He was sitting with his hands folded on the table, twiddling his thumbs nervously, as though hesitating. Without his turban, his pepper-and-salt hair stuck out in all directions. His black eyes shone with a timid, slightly concerned, brightness.

He finally decided to articulate two syllables, which, although drowned by the music, could easily be read from his lips: "Thank you."

Ophelia was then struck by a sense of awful misgiving. By making a date with a bachelor, wasn't she misleading him as to her intentions? She had rapidly felt close to Blaise, and had known the feeling was mutual, but at no time had she envisaged the possibility of a misunderstanding over the nature of that closeness.

"There's . . . um . . . something I must admit to you."

Blaise cupped his hand around his ear to convey to Ophelia that he couldn't hear her. She picked up a playing card from the many carpeting the floor and, on the edge, where nothing was printed, she wrote a message that turned her glasses crimson. It was infuriating to realize how right Mediana was.

THERE'S A MAN IN MY LIFE.

Blaise tried to make out the spidery scrawl in the orange light of the table lamp. His straggly eyebrows shot up high enough to turn his forehead into an accordion. He remained like that for some time, playing card in hand, unable to look away from it, putting Ophelia through torture.

Then he wrote a reply on the opposite edge.

IN MINE, TOO.

Ophelia had to read these three words several times to be sure she wasn't mistaken. When she raised her glasses back at Blaise, he was kneading the rubbery skin of his face, seemingly awaiting her reaction with apprehension, as if the rest of his life depended on it. Ophelia wasn't prone to great demonstrative outbursts, but she couldn't stop her hand springing towards his. For the first time, Blaise's tormented features relaxed. She found him handsome. Their fingers clasped clumsily, firmly. A friendship sealed.

"May the sauciness be with you, citizens!"

The dancers froze, the laughter died, and the musicians silenced their instruments. Everyone turned to the stage, from where the voice had erupted, like the roar of a lion. A voice that Ophelia had recognized without a second's hesitation: that of Fearless-and-Almost-Blameless. It was the first time she was seeing him in the flesh, this elusive rebel, and she couldn't believe her glasses. The individual standing behind the footlights was so puny, so balding, so ordinary, she could have passed him a hundred times without ever noticing him. One couldn't but wonder where he got his thunderous voice from.

He pointed up at the high, vaulted ceiling. "Above our heads live the lambs!" he exclaimed. "A great docile herd that bleats whatever those hypocrites of LUX ask it to bleat. A herd whose freedom is curtailed with every new law, every new code, and yet still it bleats!"

Anarchic applause and whistling rose in the room, stopping as soon as Fearless-and-Almost-Blameless spoke again:

"Down here, citizens, we become free voices again. We say

all that we think just as we think it. We are not the model little pupils, we're the little brats of Babel!"

An eruption of joy set the room alight.

"Down with the Index!" Fearless concluded. "Death to the censors!"

Ophelia kept shrinking into her chair. This cabaret was the haunt of the public enemy of the city and all its supporters. What would they do if they discovered that two representatives of the institution they hated the most were seated at a table in their midst?

"Let's go," she mouthed in Blaise's direction, rising discreetly from her chair.

At first, she didn't understand why he insisted on remaining seated, stiff as a statue. It took her a moment to notice that the child who had opened the door to them had now joined their table. And that he was pointing a pistol at them.

"Grant us the honor of staying a little longer, *Messieur-Dames*," he said, with extreme politeness. "My father will receive you in his dressing room, if you would care to follow me."

# THE WILD BEAST

Ophelia had already had the opportunity to visit a diva's dressing room, at the Family Opera House in the Pole. The one to which she and Blaise were forcibly led bore no resemblance to it. There was no velvet, no carpet, no mirror, no wardrobe to be found here. There was, on the other hand, some impressive radio-communication equipment, and, pinned to the walls, detailed maps of each minor ark that made up the city of Babel.

With the pistol, the child calmly indicated a bench, on which Blaise and Ophelia were only too willing to sit. For a small boy with dirty feet, he had persuasive manners.

"My father will be with you when he's finished his speech. That can take time—he finds it hard to stop once he gets warmed up. I'll put the radio on for you, to fill in the time." The child turned the knob on a radio set, and it immediately broadcast the solemn music of a symphonic march. He whistled along to it and waved his pistol like a conductor's baton.

I'm *vraiment désolé*," Blaise whispered, eyeing the firearm like someone seeing one for the first time. "My bad luck has struck again."

"In fact," said Ophelia, "I think we were more foolhardy than unlucky. It is I who apologize to you for dragging you into this business."

She began to think hard. How could they get out of this trap unscathed? They were now somewhere within the maze-like cellars, and a child had a gun trained on them. An attempt to escape seemed problematic.

Ophelia looked more closely at the dressing room. The radio-communication equipment and the maps on the walls appeared to have been installed here in haste; it wasn't a place that had been occupied for long. She noticed some sepia photographs leaning on the radio-communication instrument panel. On the oldest and palest of them all, a pair of young women clasped each other, cigar in mouth and glass in hand. Ophelia pushed away the scarf of her turban to be sure she was seeing clearly. One of them was wearing a polka-dot dress of totally inimitable bad taste.

Mother Hildegarde!

It was extraordinary to find her here, in Babel, in a spectacularly younger and lovelier version. And it confirmed the intuition that had struck Ophelia on seeing the cabaret's sign in the form of an orange.

"Ah," the child suddenly said, stopping his whistling. "Here's my father and his bodyguard."

The dressing-room door had indeed just opened on to Fearless-and-Almost-Blameless. He was wiping his streaming face, as if his stint onstage had exhausted him. The gigantic proportions of the saber-toothed tiger accompanying him were those of a Beast. One wondered by what miracle such a creature managed to fit through the door frame. With such a bodyguard, this man could indeed allow himself to be afraid of nothing and no one.

Fearless gave the sign to his wild beast to sit, and to his son to leave. Then he leaned over the radio that was still broadcasting its symphonic march. Ophelia thought he was going to turn it off so they could talk, but instead he increased the

217

volume and parked himself up on the radio set as if it were a seat. He placed a forefinger on his mouth to indicate to everyone to keep quiet and concentrate on the music.

Ophelia had experienced some unusual situations in her life. Listening to the radio in the same room as a saber-toothed tiger would now be up there with them.

A long time went by in this eerie way when, suddenly, the radio malfunctioned, repeating the same musical passage twice. Fearless instantly turned the knob to cut the sound, as though that was what he'd been waiting for from the start.

"Echoes are a *vrrraiment* fascinating phenomenon," he said, with a very strong Babelian accent. "Our scientists are capable of lighting up towns and sending men into the sky, and there's not a single one—not a single one, do you hear me?—who's ever been able to explain that particular quirk of nature. Since I've launched into the subtle art of radio-piracy, I've heard plenty of duplicating wavelengths like the one you just heard. At first, I found it *vrrraiment* tiresome, but then I ended up becoming fascinated by the subject."

Fearless's voice was so sonorous that, even without raising it, he seemed to be roaring every sentence. Ophelia wondered, not without some apprehension, what he was driving at.

"I've done a whole load of experiments on echoes," he continued, unperturbed. "Have you ever seen duplicated images on a photograph? Have you ever heard your own words continually returning to you through a telephone receiver? I have. Countless times. And yet I've never been able to understand what an echo is, and what conditions trigger it. I have, however, made a *vrrraiment* interesting discovery."

He had adopted a confidential tone, but his voice, unsuited to whispering, carried absolutely everywhere.

"For a few years now, the frequency of these phenomena has increased exponentially. There are more and more echoes, more and more often, in more and more places. Would it interest you to know my conclusion on the subject?"

Ophelia nodded her head stiffly. In truth, she was having all the trouble in the world following what Fearless was saying: the bench was shaking due to the quaking of Blaise, who couldn't tear his eyes away from the saber-toothed tiger. If she was scared, he was petrified.

"I deduced that it was the entire universe endeavoring to send us a message," Fearless declared, bombastically. "A vital message. An urgent message." He then tapped his temple, theatrically, and put on a fearsome voice: "'Think for yourself, you stupid little man, instead of foolishly repeating what you hear!'"

His throat then let out a laugh that reverberated throughout the surrounding catacombs. Ophelia was awestruck. How could such a puny body produce such an explosion of sound?

The next moment, Fearless had returned to being serious and was scrutinizing his two guests without the slightest congeniality. "Eulalia, eighth-degree Animist, recently admitted to the conservatoire of the Good Family as an apprentice Forerunner," he recited, half-heartedly. "Blaise, third-class Olfactory, assistant at the Memorial of Babel," he continued. "Don't ask me how I know this. The only question worth asking, here and now, is: what on earth are two lambs like you doing in the wild beasts' den?"

Matching gesture to words, Fearless laid a hand on the enormous head of the tiger. The mighty purr that ensued made Blaise's cheeks turn the same gray as his hair.

Ophelia's heart was also in her boots. The wild beast's size was so out of proportion to that of the dressing room, she found herself obliged to tuck her feet under the bench so as not to tread on its tail. In her mind, she ran through all the possible replies that came to her, but none seemed wise.

"I also knew Mother Hildegarde."

Fearless barely batted an eyelid. "*Vrrraiment*? Is that name supposed to mean something to me?"

Ophelia glanced at the photographs lined up on the radio console. Had she been on the wrong track? Were the oranges and the polka-dot dress mere coincidences?

A blink of an eye later, she understood her mistake. "Maybe not that name, but that's what she called herself where I met her. Meredith Hildegarde. Her real name must have had a more Arkadian ring to it. She had three passions: architecture, cigars, and oranges."

"Doña Mercedes Imelda. A remarkable woman." Fearless had said these words without flinching, but without hesitating, either. He reached over to the console and grabbed one of the frames. "This young *demoiselle* beside Doña Imelda," he said, placing his finger on the other woman, "is my great-grandmother. I knew her less well than I would have liked, but she made a mark on my childhood. She, like Doña Imelda, was a free spirit such as one no longer encounters. One must admit, they still knew how to have a laugh in those days! There were already killjoys to teach you to speak proper and walk straight, but not like today. Not like today." He put the frame back in its place, and then drilled his penetrating gaze into Ophelia's glasses. "My great-grandmother left us half a century ago. At a *vrrraiment* great age. I therefore have my doubts that you ever knew Doña Imelda in person, lambkin."

Ophelia clenched her fists. "I grant you that I'm small, but I'm definitely no lamb. Listen," she insisted, seeing Fearless break into a mocking smile. "Mother Hildegarde was, without doubt, a very old lady, but she had a constitution of iron and a mind of steel. She would even still be alive if . . . if she hadn't . . . "

Ophelia couldn't say it. That body sucked down into her

pocket, the dislocating of limbs, the cracking of vertebrae . . . It was impossible for her to evoke that memory without seizing up. It was her emotion, even more than her words, that seemed to make Fearless decide to swallow his skepticism.

"Do you know why the orange is a *vrrraiment* important fruit?"

She hadn't expected that particular question. "Er . . . it cures scurvy?"

"It's a very ancient legend," said Fearless, crossing his legs on his radio transmitter. "I heard it from my great-grandmother, who herself heard it from her distant ancestors. The story goes that the angels were living in the gardens of Knowledge, while humans were groveling in the dark caves of Ignorance. And that's how it remained for millennia. One day, however, a man—or a woman, depending on the version of the story—entered, by accident, the gardens of Knowledge. A poor peasant, lost and famished. He saw golden apples. He picked one. Barely had he taken a bite out of it than his mind opened. Suddenly, he became aware of his ignorance, of the ignorance in which all his fellow humans were kept. He stole other golden apples, distributed them to the men and women, and, together, they emerged from the caves of Ignorance to discover the world. 'Golden apples,'" continued Fearless, after a long, dramatic pause, "is the name our ancestors gave to oranges. And that's why it a *vrrraiment* important fruit. That's why people such as Doña Imelda and I have made it our rallying sign. It's the symbol of all those who want to free themselves from the ignorance in which we're forcibly kept. Between you and me, *mademoiselle*, I can see no difference between the angels of the legend and the Lords of LUX."

He had spat out that last word with such loathing that his tiger snarled and let out a growl that made Blaise fall off the bench.

Ophelia wondered to what extent Fearless was aware of the existence of God, as Mother Hildegarde had been. The question almost slipped out when she suddenly remembered why she was there. There was nothing, absolutely nothing, of what was being said at that very moment, in that dressing room, that she would be able to hide from Mediana, if the latter decided to delve into her memory.

With resolve, she unwound the turban that was hiding her face and looked Fearless straight in the eye. "You wanted to know the reason for our presence in your cabaret. The truth is that I was asked to have a good look and listen around it. I give you my word that Mr. Blaise has nothing to do with any of this. I therefore suggest to you that we stop our exchange right now and each go our own way. In fact," Ophelia added, as an afterthought, "you should look for a new address for your cabaret."

Fearless, sitting astride the radio set, considered her for a long time in silence, and then threw back his head and let out a howl of laughter. All the glass in the frames shattered to pieces.

"Did it not occur to you that it would be *vrrraiment* simpler to set my tiger on you? I am Fearless-and-Almost-Blameless! Where does the 'Almost' come from, in your opinion?"

"But I thought . . . Mother Hildegarde . . . Doña Imelda," stammered Ophelia.

"But seriously, what were you expecting? That I open my arms to you, crying 'the friends of my friends are my friends'? Grow up a bit, little girl."

Fearless had lost all his bonhomie. He eyed Ophelia with a scorn he didn't attempt to conceal. At this moment, he was no longer the great rabble-rouser with a tenor's voice. And neither was he an insignificant-looking little balding man. He was a third individual, an entirely different one.

A wild beast who had made fear his ally.

From an inside pocket of his tunic, he pulled out some tickets to his cabaret. "You came to me because I accepted that you do so. I was hoping for someone else, if truth be told. Your charming colleague, for example. Mademoiselle Mediana. There's a girl who's incapable of minding her own business, no? Being predatory runs in her blood! If, one day, she were to enter the ranks of LUX, she would make a formidable adversary for me."

Fearless observed a silence during which Ophelia had ample time to hear her heart, and that of Blaise, pounding.

"In one hour," he continued, "everything will have disappeared: the sign, the tables, the stage, the equipment in my dressing room. Not because you advised me to do that, little girl, but because it's my way of life. The cellars of Babel offer infinite possibilities and it's me, only me, who decides where I go and who comes to see me."

Fearless got up and his tiger copied him, with a muscular stirring of fur.

"I won't kill you. I don't attack lambs, only wild beasts interest me. Merely convey the following message to Mademoiselle Mediana." He lowered his voice until it was reduced to the sound of distant thunder. "He who sows the wind shall reap the storm."

# THE COMPASS

"Are you . . . used to that sort of thing?"

Those were the first words that Blaise managed to utter, once back at ground level. He had leant against one of the ancient baths' ruined columns, breathing in deeply through his nose, under the disdainful gaze of the fruit sellers. His pantaloons, soaked in sweat, had lost all their fullness.

Ophelia went to the closest fountain to get some water for him to drink. The searing heat of the bazaar, buzzing with people and flies, offered a stark contrast to the catacombs.

"I'm sorry," she said, handing a beaker to Blaise. "Really sorry." That was all she could say, again and again. All that she'd experienced in the Pole—the Clairdelune dungeons, the Knight and his hounds, Farouk's tantrums, the countless assassination attempts, not to mention her encounter with God—had hardened her to intimidation. But that was part of her own life, not Eulalia's.

Blaise looked at her, goggle-eyed. "Any more and my heart would have packed up. *Mon Dieu!* It's him, isn't it? It's him who killed Mademoiselle Silence?"

"I don't know." And that's what exasperated Ophelia. Had she met him in other circumstances, Fearless could have taught her a great deal. "Will you be alright?" she asked, concerned.

Blaise nodded, but that head movement alone made him

regurgitate all the water he'd just swallowed. "You . . . you must find me very emotional, Mademoiselle Eulalia," he said, shamefully wiping his mouth. "The truth is, I have a cat phobia. That one was . . . particularly large."

"I'm really, really sorry," Ophelia muttered, as the bazaar gongs rang out. "My leave is coming to an end. I must return to the Good family, and deliver my message, and . . . and . . . "

"And claim my compensation," she thought to herself. Much as she wanted to stay with Blaise, the need to know what Mediana had to tell her about Thorn, that was urgent.

"We'll have to do this again," she tried to joke. "Without the saber-toothed tiger."

As she returned his turban, now like an unraveled ball of wool, Blaise contorted his lips into a grimace that was probably meant to be a smile. *"Eh bien*, another time, maybe?"

"So sorry, again."

Ophelia would have liked to add something more intelligent, but once more, the words escaped her. She crossed the bazaar at a run, tripping on carpets and bumping into passersby. She was sure this meeting with Blaise would be the first and last. She was equally sure that it was best that way.

So why couldn't she bear the thought?

With every stride, anger made her blood boil. Mediana had deliberately put her in danger. She hadn't hesitated to make use of her most intimate secret, to play with her most fragile hope to satisfy her own curiosity. Now that Ophelia had fulfilled her part of the deal, she had an ominous feeling about it.

*He who sows the wind shall reap the storm.*

"If Mediana has lied to me," she thought, clenching her jaws, "if she's made it all up about Thorn, I'll make sure that I myself become that storm."

As though reflecting her inner state, the sky became increasingly oppressive. A miasma of clouds lowered above Babel, but

225

it was a storm without lightning, or wind, or rain. Ophelia struggled to catch her breath as she went up the slope, fringed with umbrella pines, that led to the belvedere; those daily laps of the stadium hadn't yet made an athlete of her.

She sighed with relief when she saw she'd arrived just in time. The birdtrain coaches were in the process of landing on the platform tracks, carried by the powerful beating of the chimeras' wings. Soon, passengers were pouring out of them. Ophelia boarded one, inserted her card in the ticket machine, and looked for a seat. It wasn't easy: the students of all the academies spent their Sundays in town, and always waited until the last birdtrain to return to their lodgings.

Barely had Ophelia sat down when she heard, on the other side of the window, a mechanical clicking that made her jump up. A wheelchair, maneuvered by an adolescent with dark skin and white clothes, was moving off along the platform, in the midst of the passengers who had just alighted. Ophelia rushed to the nearest door and leaned over the step.

"Ambrose?"

He had heard her. Ophelia knew that from the way his shoulders had shuddered at the sound of his name. He had heard her, but he continued on his way without turning around.

Ophelia never shouted. But she couldn't help the imploring cry that burst from her lungs: "Ambrose!"

She saw the inverted hands grip the levers of the wheel-chair, as though fighting the desire to halt it, but unable to make that decision. Ophelia wanted to run over to him, look into his eyes, ask him what she'd done to anger him, beg him not to leave her to face alone all that she still had to face.

That second of hesitation cost her the chance. The conductor closed the carriage door. She looked disparagingly at

Ophelia's toga and sandals, their whiteness lost to the dust of the catacombs.

"One does not make a spectacle of oneself on the public highway, powerless one. Draw attention to yourself once more, and I'll book you."

As the birdtrain sped along the tracks and laboriously took flight again, Ophelia sat back in her seat. Wearily, she removed her glasses, leaned her forehead against the window, and stared at the hazy clouds swirling in the void.

She felt downhearted.

Her ominous feeling had become a certainty. Mediana would tell her nothing at all. Blaise would want to have nothing more to do with her. He would withdraw his friendship, just as Ambrose had before him. Ophelia wouldn't gain access to the Secretarium, wouldn't discover more about God's past, wouldn't find Thorn. She would forever be a slave to blackmail, and spend the rest of her days punching little holes in cards.

It was the conductor's voice, through the birdtrain's loudspeakers, that jolted her out of her torpor: "Apprentice Virtuoso Eulalia, member of the second division of the company of Forerunners, is requested to present herself at the front of the train."

Ophelia put her glasses back on and got up, under the students' curious gaze. She was as surprised as they were. She elbowed her way through the succession of carriages to reach the inspectors' compartment. The conductor, in the middle of repeating her announcement into the loudspeaker, stopped on seeing her arrive.

"What do you want, powerless one?"

"You called for me. I am Eulalia."

"You're an apprentice virtuoso? You're an apprentice virtuoso," she repeated, this time as a statement, having noticed the Good Family-stamped card Ophelia was handing her. "I imagined you to be more . . . less . . . anyway, it's good news to have found you at last, Mademoiselle Eulalia. I've been making this announcement repeatedly, for two hours."

"Two hours? Why? What's going on?"

The conductor took off her cap and wiped a handkerchief over her pink, egg-shaped head, shaved the Cyclopean way. The air was even more stifling inside the train than out. "My only instruction is to take you to the Memorial. Lady Septima—glory to LUX!—has summoned you there very urgently. I don't know what you've done, but it seems like a serious matter."

Ophelia, struck suddenly by the obvious, felt her legs go weak. Mediana hadn't sent her to the cabaret to make use of her, but to get rid of her. She'd denounced her to Lady Septima, no less!

Ophelia risked expulsion. Or worse, prison.

She quelled the panic and anger surging up inside her, and did some quick thinking. If Lady Septima wanted to see her at the Memorial, not the conservatoire, it was to avoid having to involve Helen. Perhaps Ophelia would have a chance by pleading her case with the principal.

"I must get off first at the Good Family," she said, with all the confidence she could muster. "I'm in civvies, I can't present myself to Lady Septima not wearing the regulation uniform."

The conductor seemed to reflect on the matter, then grabbed her loudhailer: "Your attention please. Exceptionally, this train will not be stopping until the Memorial. We would ask you to bear with us; we will stop at each academy on the return journey. The Birdtrain Company will supply confirmation of the delay to anyone requesting it. You, Mademoiselle Eulalia, stay right here, like a good girl," the conductor instructed, after hanging up her loudhailer. "If you have a clear conscience, like all decent citizens, you have nothing to fear."

Ophelia sat on the foldaway seat assigned to her. The trap had closed. She clasped her hands together, on her thighs, to try to conceal their shaking.

She looked around for a way of escape, knowing full well she wouldn't find one. All the train's doors opened onto the void. There were no mirrors onboard, and even if there were, would she still be able to pass through them? Since her arrival in Babel, not a single day had passed without her lying to someone, about her identity or her intentions. This deception was greater than all the playacting she might have done in the past. It wasn't merely a disguise, as Mime's livery had been; it was a second skin that, day after day, had become second nature. After continually thinking of herself as Eulalia, could she still claim to be Ophelia?

The journey to the Memorial seemed both horribly long and abominably short to her. Her worst fears were confirmed when saw a troop of vigilantes awaiting her on the landing stage. They weren't armed—the very word was an offense—but they didn't need to be. They were all Necromancers, masters of temperature, capable of paralyzing with cold at a mere glance. They were also first-rate manufacturers of freezers.

They escorted Ophelia without uttering a word to her. As they passed the statue of the headless soldier, she felt like a criminal being led to a court-martial. Once through the Memorial's big glass doors, she was overwhelmed by the silence reigning within. This quiet bore no resemblance to the usual whispering of readers; it was a total absence of sound. The great circular galleries on each floor were all deserted, giving the entire place the feel of an abandoned temple. The cloak of clouds bearing down on the rotunda cast its shadow over every nook and cranny. The suspended globe of the Secretarium, whose metal usually glinted in the sun, today looked more like a dead planet.

The Necromancers made Ophelia take the northern transcendium. She tensed upon seeing, in the middle of the huge vertical corridor, a small figure with red-glowing eyes. When Ophelia had gotten close enough, she was surprised to see that it wasn't Lady Septima, as she had at first supposed, but her son, Octavio. He was watching her through the long, black strands of his fringe and his eyebrow chain. He exuded such suspicion that Ophelia felt condemned before having even been tried.

"You're keeping everyone waiting, Apprentice Eulalia."

She didn't respond. She knew that, from now on, her every word could be used against her. She would say nothing for as long as she didn't know of what, exactly, she stood accused.

She thought Octavio was going to take her to the private room, where Lady Septima and the Lords of LUX had their headquarters, on the top floor of the Memorial, but instead, he took out a key from inside his uniform. Ophelia couldn't believe her glasses when he inserted it into the lock on a post, which then sprang a metal gangway over to the Secretarium. That *terra incognita* she'd been barred from when playing the model pupil, she was being invited into it, now that she'd fallen from grace? It was unbelievably ironic. She followed Octavio onto the spiral stairway that allowed one to swing from the horizontal position of the transcendium to the vertical position of the gangway. Barely had Ophelia set off down the latter than her hands clutched both handrails. She didn't suffer from vertigo, but they were more than one hundred feet above the ground, and the thought of walking on a gangway that could be lifted by the mere turn of a key didn't really reassure her. She glanced back at the Necromancers, who, having remained in the transcendium, were now standing perpendicular to her.

The closer Ophelia got to the weightless globe, the more she gauged its giant proportions. The red-gold coating of the earth's crust dipped wherever there were oceans, and defined in relief the contours of continents. The reinforced door that Octavio opened, somewhere within a southern sea, was a perfectly respectable size, and yet it gave the impression of being a tiny keyhole.

Ophelia went through it, to the other side.

All that her imagination had conjured up of this inaccessible sanctuary was immediately shattered. The interior of the Secretarium was an identical copy of the interior of the Memorial. Galleries, served by transcendiums, were tiered in rings around a well of natural light. There was even, suspended between its atrium and its cupola, a terrestrial globe that was the exact replica of the one containing it. The architects had designed the entire place like a nest of dolls!

In the galleries to the right, thousands of antiquities glimmered from the length of glass-fronted cabinets, illuminated by the cold bulbs of Heliopolis. In the galleries to the left, entire rows of cylinders turned on their axles, humming continuously. Ophelia knew that, around each cylinder, a punched card was rolled, and that each punched card replicated a document. The whole complex combination of cogs and gears resembled the workings of a hurdy-gurdy.

"It's true that you're coming here for the first time," commented Octavio, who was closely observing her every reaction. "The Secretarium, like the Memorial, is divided into two twin parts: the rare collections are stored in the eastern hemisphere, and the database in the western hemisphere."

"And this?" she asked, pointing at the globe floating above them. "A second Secretarium?"

In spite of herself, Ophelia had broken her self-imposed silence.

"Just a decorative globe," answered Octavio. "Ah, here comes the head of your division."

She felt a surge of hope on seeing that Elizabeth was, indeed, crossing the atrium in their direction. She appeared more solemn than ever to her. Her tawny hair rose like a cape with her every step, and her face was even less expressive than usual.

"Anything new?" Elizabeth had addressed this question solely to Octavio.

"Nothing to report. No one entered the Memorial, or exited it, with the exception of Apprentice Eulalia."

"Very good. Let's go."

Ophelia followed them, battling the vertigo that had beset her. Maybe it was the oppressiveness of the clouds over the cupolas, but she was starting to feel short of air. It wasn't her descent into the catacombs that was behind this summons. It was something else that was even more serious.

Thorn's watch, afflicted by her nervousness, snapped its cover from inside a pocket of her toga. The question was no longer whether Mediana had betrayed her, but to what extent.

They stopped in front of a compressed-air door. "We are not authorized to enter with you," Elizabeth explained, after opening it. "All that takes place in there is highly confidential. Good luck."

"Luck doesn't exist," Octavio chipped in, coldly. "We alone are the authors of our destiny. But that," he added, in a hushed voice, "Apprentice Eulalia already knows."

Ophelia knew nothing at all, and that was precisely the problem. With wary steps, she entered an austere room, seemingly designated for consulting documents. It boasted, as its sole piece of furniture, a large lectern made of precious wood, over which Lady Septima was leaning.

"The door," she ordered.

Ophelia turned the steering-wheel-shaped handle until the lock clicked. It was so cold inside, she felt as if she were locking herself into an ice store. Her bare feet, in their sandals, started tingling, painfully, all over.

"Step forward." Lady Septima had issued this command without hesitation. Calm and distant, as ever. Slowly, she turned eyes blazing like two beacons in the dimly lit room toward Ophelia. "Do you like jigsaw puzzles?"

Ophelia blinked. This wasn't the interrogation she'd prepared herself for. Cautiously, she approached the manuscript on the lectern that Lady Septima was indicating to her. It was old, judging by its state of decay. The faded letters running across the page, in the few legible parts, were those of an unknown language.

It was the pages of notes lying on the other leaf of the lectern that particularly caught her attention. "Mediana's translation," she acknowledged. "Why are you asking me about this, rather than her?"

Lady Septima didn't reply. Ophelia then felt every muscle in her body, which she'd been clenching since her birdtrain journey, relax to the point of making her unsteady. The anger she'd built up against Mediana evaporated in an instant.

"What's happened to her?"

Lady Septima dropped the grin that had been stretching her mouth, ridding her face of any trace of personal feeling. "A division almost entirely composed of Seers, and not one among them capable of seeing the future of their own cousin. They bring shame on all the Frontrunners. In short," she said, rallying herself with a lift of the chin, "Sir Henry demands to be provided with a replacement at a moment's notice. Even if I have serious reservations about you, one has to admit that you are the fittest candidate for this work. The least incapable, anyway. You will have to prove yourself worthy of the honor that LUX is granting you, Apprentice Eulalia. I'm going to inform Sir Henry of your arrival," she added, marching off. "You can cast a look at the manuscript, but do not, for any reason, touch it. Handling a document of this value is done according to a protocol that you have not yet mastered."

Lady Septima entered a lift at the back of the room; it rose with a grinding of gearwheels as soon as she operated the lever.

Once alone, Ophelia leaned with both hands on the lectern and stared at length at the manuscript without seeing it. Waves of conflicting emotions crashed within her, making her glasses turn every possible shade.

Relief. Incredulity. Exultation. Distress.

Distress? After all Mediana had put her through, was it really possible that Ophelia felt concerned about her fate? She had become a Forerunner in order to find herself exactly where she stood right now; her real research could finally begin. She should have been overjoyed, so why was she terrified?

It was an imperious click-click from within her toga that distracted her from her turbulent thoughts. Ophelia tugged on the chain of her watch in order to examine it. Now, the cover wouldn't stop opening and closing, as if in the grip of an epileptic fit. Click-click! Click-click! Click-click!

"Alright, calm down," Ophelia muttered, as much to herself as to the watch. She blocked the cover with her thumb, but the hands immediately took over, spinning around in a frenzied waltz. At regular intervals, they all stopped at once, pointing, again and again, at the same time.

Thirty minutes and thirty seconds past six.

Ophelia turned to the lift, as its gearwheels had started up again. Sir Henry might be an automaton, but it wouldn't make a good impression to wrestle with a broken-down fob watch in front of him.

She blinked. The hands had suddenly changed time, now all pointing obstinately at exactly midday.

No. The hands weren't indicating the time. They were indicating a direction.

Thorn's watch wasn't, never had been, broken down. It had quite simply turned itself into a compass. A compass of which the three needles, at that very second, were pointing at the arriving lift.

The lift door opened onto Lady Septima and Sir Henry.

Except that Sir Henry wasn't an automaton.

Sir Henry was Thorn.

# THE SCARECROW

# THE DISCOVERY

Thorn stood in a corner of the lift, so excessively tall that his head touched the ceiling. His steely eyes, slashed by the long facial scar, were focused on a document he was busily flicking through. He paid not the slightest attention to Lady Septima as she showed him Ophelia, rooted to the spot in the middle of the cold room.

"Our latest recruit, *monsieur*. I will personally see to it that she proves equal to the situation."

The rules required Ophelia to stand to attention, trot out the traditional greeting—"Knowledge serves peace!"—and state her particulars, or risk severe punishment. She found doing so impossible.

From the moment Thorn had appeared, all thought had abandoned her. She clutched her fob watch with both hands: it was solid, it was tangible, it was real.

Lady Septima pursed her lips, interpreting her silence as an untimely attack of shyness. "Apprentice Eulalia joined the second division of the company of Forerunners fifty days ago. Not much going on in the head, but her hands show potential."

Ophelia wasn't listening to her. Lady Septima no longer existed. There was only Thorn, still at the back of the lift, frowning, deeply absorbed in some chart. His silver-blond hair was meticulously combed back; his face, long and angular, perfectly shaved. He was wearing an impeccably white shirt that, over both forearms, became work gauntlets, with built-in dials, gauges, and various other measuring devices. It was the emblem pinned on his chest, over his heart, that held all her attention. A sun.

All this time, she'd been looking for a fugitive. She'd just found a Lord of LUX.

With one step behind another, Ophelia backed into the most dimly lit corner of the cold room. Even if her seething blood prevented her from thinking, one thing was perfectly obvious to her. Whatever would occur, when Thorn's eyes finally met hers, would have irreversible consequences.

"We're taking too long over the projected schedule. The Genealogists will end up demanding explanations." Thorn had spoken these words with the Babel accent, devoid of any Northern lilt, just like a native of the city. And yet Ophelia would have recognized his voice out of a thousand. The resonance of a double bass, solemn and sullen, that echoed through her inner emptiness, shook her to the core, welled up to her throat, choked her.

Thorn's voice after nearly three years of silence.

Ophelia jumped when he closed his document with a sharp snap.

"Furthermore, I need the Necromancers here urgently. The temperature and the level of humidity are becoming too high in the eastern hemisphere of the Secretarium. We are losing staff, let us avoid also losing collections."

Thorn's attention shifted directly from his charts to the old manuscript on the consulting lectern. As he crossed the cold room, a sinister creaking accompanied his every step. Ophelia hadn't noticed it until then, but now it stared her in the face: an iron frame, articulated like a skeleton, caged one of his boots from ankle to knee. The leg that had been broken during his time in prison.

*The automaton.*

Rarely had Ophelia felt so stupid. She had taken literally what had only ever been a tasteless nickname. Tasteless, and yet entirely apt. Thorn leant stiffly over the lectern, and then turned, methodically, between the metallic fingers of his gauntlet, a page of the manuscript.

"Does your recruit know ancient languages?" He had addressed Lady Septima as if the person in question wasn't in the room. This dreadful habit, which so exasperated Ophelia at the time of their engagement, today felt more than welcome to her.

"She doesn't know them, *monsieur*. However, I feel she is still capable of taking over from Apprentice Mediana. She's an Animist. A reader."

"Here we go," thought Ophelia, whose glasses were growing bluer before her very eyes. "He's going to turn toward me. He's going to recognize me."

Thorn did no such thing. He merely examined the page, nibbled by time like old lace, that he held with his fingertips. "Would she know how to restore the missing text?"

"No, *monsieur*," Lady Septima declared, with the assurance of the teacher who knows her pupil better than the pupil knows herself. "On the other hand, she could reconstruct the substance of it by penetrating the thoughts of those who have read it. Ideally, of the person who wrote it."

Ophelia was struck by the way her fiery eyes stared at Thorn's caliper, as though trying to melt down the metal. Lady Septima seemingly treated him with the respect owed by a member of LUX to a peer, but she didn't consider him her equal. Which, to Ophelia, didn't bode well.

If Lady Septima detected the slightest reaction between Sir

Henry and herself—a movement of surprise, however small—
she would instinctively be suspicious, and their false identities
would be blown apart, thought Ophelia.

She forced herself to breathe in slowly. To still the turmoil in
her heart. Return her glasses to transparency. Relax the muscles
in her face. Straighten her shoulders. She couldn't stop her
body from shaking, but never mind. She was in a cold room,
in a toga and sandals; shivering was a normal physical reaction.

All that remained was to hope that Thorn wouldn't choke
on seeing her.

"Where is Apprentice Mediana now?" He had asked this
half-heartedly, while leafing through the translation notes.
The lectern's lamp cast a cold light on his profile, making
the steep slope of the nose, the furrow of the long scar, and,
between the narrow half-opening of the eyelid, the focused
eye, all shine.

"She was transferred, *monsieur*."

"Will she resume her work here one day?"

"Giving an opinion on the matter would be premature."

"Mediana is alive" was the only coherent thought Ophelia
could muster at this point in the conversation.

"And what are your thoughts on the case of Mademoiselle
Silence now?"

"I don't understand your question, *monsieur*."

Thorn turned from the consulting lectern. "One apoplectic
attack within our ranks is what I call a regrettable incident.
How would you describe a second one?"

"A regrettable coincidence, *monsieur*."

They were both impenetrable, but Ophelia detected a
tension that was gradually building. If Thorn's expression
remained inscrutable, that of Lady Septima betrayed disgust.
At no moment had she deigned to look up at him, insisting
on staring at his crippled leg. Did she even know that the

man before her was endowed with a phenomenal memory and ferocious claws? He was two heads taller than her, but she saw him as a greenhorn who would forever be inferior to her, and not just due to their age difference. Ophelia realized that she behaved the same way with the old sweeper, Helen's Forerunners, and even Mediana. All those who weren't Pollux's descendants were, for Lady Septima, merely the necessary parts for the smooth functioning of a machine, and it was advisable to replace them when they became deficient.

"We will have to increase the pace of the reading groups," Thorn finally declared. "The Genealogists are growing impatient, and neither you nor I wish to see a surprise inspection by them. Particularly right now, with these sort of . . . coincidences."

It was the second time the Genealogists had come up; if Ophelia had no idea who they were, she at least understood that they were at the apex of the LUX hierarchy. And that Thorn didn't want to have dealings with them.

"All leave will be suspended until further notice," Lady Septima said, banging her heels together. "The readings will start earlier and finish later."

"As long as it's not to the detriment of the detail. Your students still produce too many inaccuracies, and I'm not talking about the encoding errors."

Lady Septima assented, but her face had hardened. Ophelia was suffering agonies. Thorn clearly didn't realize that offending this representative of God, here and now, was the last thing that, in their position, they should be doing.

As was to be expected, Lady Septima sought someone on whom to take out her annoyance. She didn't have to look far. "Apprentice Eulalia, are you just going to stay forever twiddling your thumbs? Stop causing me trouble and prove to Sir Henry that you will live up to his expectations."

Ophelia felt as if her blood had suddenly stopped circulating through her body.

Thorn had finally turned toward her.

He had turned toward her and his eyes expressed nothing. Neither surprise nor bafflement. The neutral look that a stranger would direct at any other stranger.

"I will not disappoint you," she declared.

Ophelia was relieved not to hear her voice crack. She even surprised herself by handling, without shaking too much, the attention being focused on her, as if she were no longer really herself. Because she was no longer really herself.

"I am Eulalia," she repeated to herself, "and the man in front of me is Sir Henry."

It was as simple as that.

Thorn's long arm snatched Mediana's notes from the lectern, and stretched to give them to Ophelia, covering the distance between them without needing to make even a step in her direction.

*The automaton.*

"You have three days to learn this translation off by heart, and be trained in the handling of ancient documents. After which you will come right here, every evening, after the reading groups. Three days—have I made myself quite clear, apprentice?"

Thorn's words fell down on her like hailstones. He wouldn't have been more convincing if they had never met. So much so, in fact, that, as she clutched the pages of notes in her hands, she was gripped by an overwhelming doubt.

Had he even recognized her?

# THE SUSPICION

"I have nothing . . . to tell you."

"She was . . . our colleague. I have the right . . . to know."

"You're . . . putting me off."

Ophelia was running with some difficulty in the dust of the stadium. It was six o'clock in the morning, the least hot and least muggy time of the day, but her lungs were already on fire. It gave her meager comfort to see that Elizabeth, although used to the daily circuits, was struggling enormously to put one foot in front of the other. On her head, the aspiring virtuoso had an extraordinary radio-hat that was spluttering out the repeat of a scientific program; it was supposed to help her to maintain her rhythm, but the weight of it slowed her down more than anything.

"Where is Mediana?" Ophelia insisted. "Where have they . . . taken her?

"It's confidential. I can't . . . divulge . . . that information . . . to an apprentice."

Unable to keep going, Elizabeth stopped in the middle of the track. She was bent double, panting, with one hand stopping her radio-hat from falling off, and the other pressing a stitch in her side. Her complexion, usually wan, had reddened so much that it merged with her freckles. From spending her days sitting in a chair, her nose buried in her code, she had ended up with the physical constitution of an old lady.

Ophelia had tracked her down to the stadium to get some answers. For three days now, she'd been confronted by a wall of silence in her dormitory, three days of getting strange looks from a distance, with no word of explanation. Her patience was starting to run out and Elizabeth was the only one, out of the whole company of Forerunners, who wouldn't be able to shake her off.

"Can you at least tell me what happened?"

Elizabeth unfolded her body as if it were an awkward ironing board. With her mouth wide open, she tried to catch her breath with her head up, having failed to catch it head down. "I told you . . . and I repeat to you. Apprentice Mediana . . . left us . . . for health reasons."

"That makes no sense. She was the healthiest of all of us."

"Listen, apprentice."

Ophelia was all ears, but she had to wait until Elizabeth was able to speak without suffocating herself.

"It's me who found her, and I can assure you, she wasn't in good health at all. I entered the Memorial through the service door, like every Sunday. Catalogue cards to improve. I punched holes all morning. When I went to the bathroom, I found her lying on the tiles. I don't know how long she'd been there, but it wasn't a pretty sight." Elizabeth wiped her sleeve under her chin, which was dripping with sweat. "Muscles in spasm, convulsions, eyes rolled upwards," she specified. "I alerted security. Lady Septima summoned you urgently, you know what followed better than I do."

Ophelia looked at Elizabeth in the pallid early-morning light. The picture she'd just painted so little resembled the splendid, the indomitable Mediana that her impassivity struck Ophelia as incongruous. Elizabeth was moving the aerial around on her hat to lessen the hissing of the radio broadcast, as if nothing had happened.

"How do you manage not to be afraid?"

"Hmm? Why would I be afraid? Strokes are rare at our age. Statistically, there's little chance of the same happening to me . . . or to you. You'd know that, if you'd read the *Official Journal*. Which, for us Forerunners, must be the sole source from which we garner our information," Elizabeth recited, like a well-learnt lesson.

"I don't know much about statistics," admitted Ophelia, "but don't forget Mademoiselle Silence. A heart attack and a stroke in the same location, fifty days apart, that seems improbable to me."

It was Elizabeth's turn to look at her with incomprehension, from the shade of her half-closed eyelids. "I don't know where you're from, or what you've experienced, but here, in Babel, illnesses and accidents are the only causes of death. If Lady Septima tells us it's a coincidence, then it's a coincidence."

Ophelia was tempted to retort that this woman she put on a pedestal didn't set great store by powerless people like her. And that she probably wasn't telling them the whole truth. The Lords of LUX had doubled the security staff at the Memorial; it was no longer possible to enter or depart without being checked.

And then there was Professor Wolf, his mysterious accident, his research stopped from one day to the next. He, too, was a regular at the Memorial, and he, too, had suffered a great traumatic shock.

No, it definitely wasn't a coincidence. It was a crime. Three crimes. And the fact that that word was forbidden by the Index made no difference. Having accepted this hypothesis, Ophelia could no longer disregard Fearless's message to Mediana. "He who sows the wind shall reap the storm." Was it he who had tried to take her life, along with the lives of Professor Wolf and Mademoiselle Silence? If so, by what means and, most of all, why? What did an expert on wars, a senior censor, and an apprentice Forerunner have in common, apart from the fact that all three worked at the Memorial?

"Aspiring Virtuoso Elizabeth, Apprentice Eulalia, please complete your obligatory circuits!"

Ophelia turned her glasses toward the stadium's watchtower, from which the command had come, and then back toward Elizabeth, who still hadn't caught her breath.

"The best of all possible worlds, didn't you say?"

They continued their run, side by side. Their two bodies were in perfect dissymmetry, Elizabeth's being as long and flat as Ophelia's was short and plump.

"You know . . . I didn't like you . . . at our first meeting." Elizabeth had casually panted this remark between two strides, her long, tawny plait thumping her back.

Ophelia agreed. "I'm not sure I thought much of you, either."

"And now?"

They exchanged questioning looks, and Ophelia finally outran Elizabeth on the stadium's track. The truth was, they could have become friends, had Eulalia really existed. But Ophelia was under no illusion: if the aspiring virtuoso discovered that she was lying about her identity, she would denounce her to Helen and Lady Septima without the slightest hesitation.

When she had completed her obligatory circuits, Ophelia went to the changing room. She bumped into Zen, who was just leaving, smelling of camellia oil. They stammered apologies. They might share the same dormitory and attend the same classes, but they had never exchanged more than one sentence. Zen was the oldest of the whole company, but she was more of a doll than a woman, always ready to hide her almond-shaped eyes behind her thick, black fringe. It seemed to Ophelia, however, that this habit Zen had of avoiding her was down to something other than shyness.

To fear?

Once alone, Ophelia collected the uniform and boots she had deposited at the laundry the previous day. She then went to the communal showers and there, after placing her clothes, gloves, and glasses on a chair, she stood still for a long while. She waited until her heartbeat, taxed by the run, had returned to normal. But it didn't happen. Her entire flesh seemed to be pulsating to a single chaotic rhythm.

This evening, she would see Thorn again.

She had spent these recent weeks not allowing herself to think of it, remaining focused on everything that wasn't him. She had virtually neither slept nor eaten. Her emotions were so muddled, it was impossible for her to untangle them. She wanted to be with Thorn right there, right now. She'd wanted that every second of every minute of every hour, for almost three years. And him, the best he could come up with was to impose three additional days on her! Learning Mediana's translation off by heart? It was nothing but a disjointed, incomplete, and abstruse text that had given her no insight into Thorn's ulterior motives. How had he become Sir Henry? Why had he joined LUX? What was he seeking, through the reading groups? What had stopped him, all this time, from giving a sign of life? Ophelia had given in to the temptation of reading the notes not merely with her eyes—after all, she had become their official owner—but those metallic gauntlets Thorn was wearing when he'd handled them had prevented him leaving any trace on the paper.

Reading the notes with her hands had taught her nothing about Mediana, either, no doubt also due to work gloves having been worn. The Seer had certainly duped her. All that time, she had known that Sir Henry was the man Ophelia was looking for. Would she have ultimately revealed it to her?

Ophelia unfolded a shower screen, threw her running gear over it, and yanked the water pull-chain. She kept her eyes wide open, despite the gush of boiling-hot water. The moment she closed her eyelids, even briefly, she saw Thorn's expression again, imprinted on her eyeballs. His lack of expression, in fact. As though, really, all playacting aside, Ophelia meant nothing to him.

While washing her hair, she tugged on her curls. She kept them short herself, with wary snips of the scissors, but never with the help of a mirror. Surely she hadn't changed that much, had she? She squinted at her skin, tanned by the sun. Suddenly, she felt naked in a way that, never before, in all her life, had she felt naked. This abrupt awareness, ridiculous as it was, made her feel an apprehension she couldn't really fathom.

"You hate being treated like a child," Mediana's voice mocked, in her memory, "but in front of a man, you remain an inexperienced *bambina*."

Familiar clicking sounds cut through the noise of the shower. Ophelia released the pull-chain and wiped her dripping eyelashes. As nearsighted as she was, she could make out, under the screen, shadows on which there were glimmers of silver. The winged boots of the Forerunners.

"You will listen to us."

"You will not scream."

"You will say nothing."

When the Seers spoke in the future tense, ensuing events generally proved them right. So Ophelia stood silently and waited to hear what they had to announce to her.

The answer came in the form of a bucket, pouring a crystalline torrent over the top of the screen. Ophelia barely had time to protect her face with her arms. In an instant, her whole body was grazed with hundreds of scratches. Once back to her senses, she contemplated the fragments of glass scattered over her damp body, and a few seconds later, the blood tracing a vast network of tributaries across it.

"That, *signorina*, is for our cousin."

That sentence, even more than the pain, shocked Ophelia. Zen's fearful attitude and Octavio's insinuations suddenly appeared to her under a devastating new light. Her fellow students didn't subscribe to the coincidence theory, either; they thought that *she* was the guilty one.

Ophelia opened her mouth, but the Seers' hissing voices didn't give her a second to stick up for herself:

"First Signora Silence, and now Mediana?"

"She sure moves *presto*, the new girl!"

"You're no longer *benvenuta* in the Good Family."

A silence ensued, during which Ophelia heard nothing but the drip-drip of the showerhead and the crunching of glass under her bloodied feet. She was shaking. The winged boots were still there, beneath the panel of the screen.

"This evening, *signorina*, you will go to the Secretarium."

"This evening, *signorina*, you will again meet the automaton."

"This evening, *signorina*, you will hand in your wings to him."

It wasn't a prophecy. The Seers' power didn't allow them to see the future beyond three hours. Ophelia still took the warning very seriously. Once the boots had departed with a jangling of silver, she remained standing in the middle of the glass, her blood mingling with the water from the shower.

# THE AUTOMATON

Ophelia moved stiffly along the gangway. She hoped the bandages under her uniform would stop the blood from reappearing, at least until she got through what awaited her. Every movement pulled at the cuts in her skin. They weren't deep, but they reopened at the first opportunity.

In actual fact, she felt no pain. Right now, she was conscious of just one thing: the globe of the Secretarium, in front of her, kept getting bigger as she moved forward. Even the void that stretched beneath her feet seemed abstract to her.

She was going to see Thorn again.

When she reached the globe's reinforced door, Ophelia glanced over her shoulder at the transcendium at the other end of the gangway, where Lady Septima had entered her key to allow her access.

She was going to see Thorn again, in private.

Ophelia entered the Secretarium. As on her first visit, there was that same bizarre sensation of moving inside a replica in miniature of the Memorial. An identical atrium, an identical cupola, identical galleries, and, floating weightlessly in the air, a terrestrial globe that was the same, in every respect, as the one containing it. Ophelia knew perfectly well that this globe was purely decorative, but she couldn't help imagining that there was another globe inside it, containing yet another one, and so on, *ad infinitum*.

She walked on, in the cold light of the bulbs. The freezing-cold room reserved for consulting fragile documents lay straight ahead. Was Ophelia supposed to go straight there to study the manuscript? She would be incapable of concentrating on anything at all until she had, at last, had a proper conversation with Thorn.

She ran her eyes along the stories of galleries encircling the atrium. In the eastern hemisphere, the glass cabinets of ancient collections glimmered between the columns. From the Secretarium's western hemisphere there arose a click-clicking chorus: it was the thousands of cylinders of the database rotating on their axles, processing all those bibliographical-note punchcards.

As she was looking for Thorn, Ophelia jumped on hearing his voice right behind her: "Coordinator Room. Last gallery on the left." The instruction had come from an acoustic pipe.

Ophelia went up, following the vertical wall of a transcendium. The wings on her boots clattered like spurs with her every step—wings she was supposed to hand in to Sir Henry, along with her resignation, if she didn't want to suffer the reprisals of her division, but right now, that was the least of her worries.

She was going to see Thorn again, properly this time.

Although she knew the temperature of this place was strictly maintained at minus eight degrees, Ophelia felt as if it were fifteen degrees warmer. Never in her life had she cared about appearances, and yet she ran a nervous hand through her hair to tidy it up. She came across a few splinters of glass, and quickly got rid of them.

Once on the top floor, she went past the tall rows of cylinders; the mechanical racket they made hurt her ears. She finally spotted a door, with bolts and a sealed frame like the entrance to a submarine cabin. Instead of a cabin, Ophelia discovered a vast office, all wood and copper, and, at the far end of this office, a back.

Thorn's back.

He was sitting on a swivel stool, with radio headphones over his ears, facing an immense console riddled with holes. It was the Coordinator, the only machine in the world capable of searching a database. Thorn was continually disconnecting and reconnecting a tangle of cables, lowering a switch here, lifting another there, like some instrumentalist tackling the most complex of scores.

Ophelia knocked on the door to announce her arrival, but Thorn didn't appear to hear it. She was afraid of distracting him. She was afraid, period. Afraid of what would happen here when, at last, they would both be able to express their true feelings, freely.

She was afraid, yes, but she wouldn't have wanted to be anywhere else.

Turning her attention back to her surroundings, Ophelia observed that the Coordinator Room was barely more welcoming than the Secretarium's industrial galleries. There was no chair to sit on, other than the stool at the machine, nothing pleasing to look at except for shelves overloaded with documents, punched paper, and an array of time dials. This perfect fusion of austerity and organization was undeniably reminiscent of the Treasury, in the Pole.

Thorn suddenly swiveled his stool, checked the yellow tape that a mechanographic machine had just punched, and pressed the button of a microphone.

"The reference requested is 'note No. 8.174, civil-engineering collection, 1S067.' Over."

As a tiny voice was responding through his headphones, he noticed Ophelia's presence and indicated the sealed door to her, which she rushed over to bolt. With every turn of the crank, the deafening humming of the database outside became increasingly distant, finally becoming inaudible. Soon, there was total silence in the room.

"The apprentice virtuoso has just arrived," Thorn then announced. "I have instructions to give her. I will return to processing the bibliographical requests as soon as that is done. Over and out."

He switched off the microphone, removed the headphones, and finally turned his stool around. His stillness was so abrupt and so prolonged, Ophelia wondered whether he was waiting for some initiative from her, but then realized that he was studying her in detail, from head to toe. He lingered on the braid of her uniform and the wings pinned to her boots. That piercing gaze made her feel as if her cuts were reopening, one after another, under the bandages, as he examined her.

"Why are you in Babel?"

An "r" crunched like ice, consonants as hard as stone: Thorn had regained his Northern accent. He had articulated his question slowly and methodically.

When Ophelia realized that it was actually to her, and not to Eulalia, that he was speaking, it completely threw her.

"I couldn't bear to stay at my parents' any longer." Of all the stupid answers.

Thorn remained stony-faced on his stool, waiting to hear more. Ophelia's throat was throbbing so hard, it felt as if her heart was stuck there. She felt like a funnel; intense as the emotions seething inside her were, when it came to expressing them, all that emerged was a pitiful drip-drip.

"I was astonished to discover that you were Apprentice Mediana's replacement," Thorn then continued. "Rather more than that, even."

Ophelia found that really hard to believe. His inscrutable

face gave nothing away. "Well that makes two of us. If I'd known that you were the famous Sir Henry, I would have . . . "

"You could have been God," Thorn interrupted her.

This remark caught her entirely off her guard. Her hands, which had gone limp, dropped the notes written by Mediana that she'd brought along, and they scattered around her feet in an avalanche of paper. "You think that I . . . that I'm . . . "

"You could have been. I could have been, too. God knows our faces."

It was so elementary, Ophelia felt ashamed not to have thought of it herself. "You're right. Luckily for us, God is a very poor impersonator. If you had welcomed me with a smile, I can assure you, I would have been suspicious."

Thorn made no comment. Ophelia had hoped to ease the strained atmosphere with her joke, but it had been a total failure. This reunion was a total failure. It wasn't supposed to go like this at all, she really must say something more intelligent. Finally find the right words. *Now.*

"Click-click!"

It was the fob watch. Ophelia pinched her fingers trying to extricate it from her pocket. "Here's a witness above all suspicion who should convince you that I'm not God."

Ophelia felt ashamed of her shaky voice. From the moment she'd entered this room, she'd behaved like a scared little girl. Back when she didn't know Thorn, and had every reason to fear him, she hadn't felt half the apprehension that was now tying her in knots. This man had breached something within her that made her unbearably vulnerable.

And he was doing nothing to put her at her ease.

He stood up. This movement of bones unbent his endless spine and triggered a grating of steel from his leg. Ophelia preferred him sitting down. She felt intimidated enough like that; she really didn't need to feel crushed by his size.

Thorn took back his watch without taking a single step toward her—from a distance and with his fingertips.

"It's not telling the right time," Ophelia apologized. "It spent all its time looking for you. I'm no expert in watch psychology, but it's sure to return to its senses, now it has found you."

The watch snapped its cover, again and again. Thorn looked at it suspiciously, as if he doubted ever having owned such a noisy object.

If Ophelia had hoped to move him with that, it had failed.

"How is my aunt doing?"

"Oh . . . in fact, I haven't seen Berenilde since the Doyennes made me return to Anima. But I did receive some news. You can count on her to hold strong. And to await your return," she thought it best to specify, with an awkward smile.

Ophelia refrained from making any allusion to the Compass Rose episode. Doing so would have meant having to mention Archibald, and the last thing she wanted was to put Thorn into a bad mood. One couldn't say he was overflowing with enthusiasm right now.

"My return?" he repeated.

"Things have changed in the Pole. Farouk has changed. I'm sure that, one day, you will be able to return home with head held high, and at last make your case." Ophelia had stated that with conviction, hoping that those words at least would reach Thorn's heart. He merely closed his fist around his watch to make the incessant click-clicking stop.

"Did you come to Babel alone?"

"Er . . . yes." Ophelia did her utmost not to think of the scarf right then.

"Is there no risk of the Doyennes discovering that you are here?"

"I think not."

"Is the 'Apprentice Eulalia' cover watertight?"

"I have papers." Her reply was drowned out by an awful grinding of steel. Thorn had wanted to change position, but the mechanism serving as an exoskeleton to his leg had jammed, mid-movement. He gripped the console of the Coordinator just in time to avoid losing his balance.

"I can manage on my own," he said, noticing Ophelia make a move. His tone was final. As he leant to unblock the mechanism behind his knee, Ophelia took the chance to look at him more closely. She suddenly noticed all sorts of details that she would have spotted earlier had she not been so obsessed with her own nervousness. Thorn, too, had changed. The deep furrow between his eyebrows had grown even deeper. His hair had receded, making his forehead even broader than before. His face was so pale, his scars barely showed. And there was that strong smell of surgical spirit he gave off, as if he religiously disinfected every inch of skin, clothing, and metal.

And yet his entire body seemed to be electrified by a powerful energy, a determination so fierce, it was almost palpable.

Thorn unblocked the mechanism of his caliper with a ghastly grating sound, and stood up to his full height. "It's your turn, if you have any questions. Not about my leg, preferably."

Ophelia tensed. Of course she had some! In fact, she had so many she didn't know where to start. She couldn't stop herself from glancing at the sun emblem pinned on Thorn's shirt.

"I make use of LUX as much as LUX makes use of me," he said, preempting her. "I was unable to measure up to God by attacking him from the outside. Consequently, I reconsidered my whole strategy."

"By becoming a Lord yourself? Are they all God's accomplices, then?"

"Just as your Doyennes on Anima are, and my mother's

clan in the Pole were. Somewhat more than that, even. LUX possesses considerable influence and means. These Lords are Guardians *par excellence*: they keep a tight rein on their family spirit, and have made the city of Babel the model that God would like to enforce on every ark."

Ophelia swallowed hard. A world where one always has to watch what one says and what one does was no place for klutzes like her.

"It must have been some feat, joining their ranks," she muttered. "Like everything you've achieved since your escape, in fact."

Thorn glanced at his watch and, since its hands were all pointing at him, turned to the numerous clocks in the room, as if wanting to time how long they spoke. "It's a long story. You should at least know this: I came to Babel due to the pointers you gave me in prison, and I became Sir Henry thanks to the Genealogists."

"The Genealogists?" Ophelia asked, surprised. "You spoke of them last time, with Lady Septima, and didn't particularly want to have dealings with them."

A quiver shot across Thorn's jaw. It was the first sign of emotion he'd shown since the start of their conversation. It was a sign Ophelia knew how to interpret. She had noticed it so often in the past, whenever Thorn was trying to protect her from his own secrets, that she was relieved to see it once again. This man would return to being the gruff bear she'd come to know. He would order her to return to Anima, to stop meddling in his affairs, to leave him to confront the danger alone.

As for her, she firmly intended to impose herself on him. "Thorn, I will remain in Babel, whether you want me to or not. Whatever Lady Septima says, there are some things going on here . . . really disturbing things. I don't yet understand what

you're up to, but before you oppose my decision, know that
I have . . . "

"I won't oppose it."

The response had been so swift, Ophelia mis-swallowed,
and her fine speech degenerated into a coughing fit.

"I agree with you," Thorn went further. "There are things
going on here. I need some eyes outside the Secretarium, and
you need some eyes inside. We will both gain from collaboration. Does that suit you?"

Ophelia nodded her head stiffly. She should have been
delighted, but Thorn's detachment, his way of ridding their
conversation of all sentimentality, made her feel increasingly
hollow inside.

On the Coordinator console, the radio headphones emitted
a murmur, indicating that someone was trying to reestablish
communication. The voice was Lady Septima's.

"The microphone is switched off," Thorn said, seeing Ophelia
draw back. "She can't hear us."

"Does she know who you really are?"

"No one knows that, apart from the Genealogists. I don't
know whether Lady Septima knows of God's actual existence,
but she is convinced that she's serving a noble and worthy
cause. Only the Genealogists are aware of the whole truth.
They are the most powerful Lords of Lux. So powerful, indeed,
that they can no longer bear the thought of having to explain
themselves to God. That's the only common denominator I
share with them," he added, with a distaste he couldn't conceal, "but it enabled me to join their ranks. They created a
new identity for me, from scratch, making me a respectable
citizen of Babel, and then put me in charge of the Secretarium.
God is, of course, unaware of my presence here. We must be
vigilant, you and I, and never betray our past in front of the
others. Including the Genealogists. They are my allies only

because I can be useful to them. They wouldn't take kindly to you interfering in their little affairs."

"But why did they entrust the Secretarium to you?" Ophelia insisted. "What have the catalogue database and the reading groups got to do with their 'little affairs'?"

"They have everything to do with them. The Genealogists have asked me to find a very particular document."

"The manuscript Mediana was translating?"

"That will be for you to confirm to me. I will say no more to you so I don't distort your judgment. I need a fresh approach."

Lady Septima's voice became louder through the headphones, insistently repeating "hello!" Thorn returned to his stool with mechanical rigidity, but didn't switch the microphone on yet. He opened a drawer, and out of it unfurled a stream of punched tape, which cascaded down to the floor. "Let's not waste any more time," he said, handing it energetically to Ophelia. "Here is a list of bibliographical references. I suggest you consult all these books, without exception, as soon as possible. They will prove useful for your evaluation."

Then, ignoring how Ophelia's face had fallen, Thorn returned to sorting out the Coordinator's tangle of cables with obsessive care. He might seem uneasy on his legs, but his hands had the precision of arrows.

"You should go to the cold room without further delay," he advised. "The manuscript awaits you and Lady Septima would deem it unacceptable if you hadn't already started your work. Be prepared for her to be on your back. We will consider meeting alone when her vigilance has abated. Then, and only then, I will give you further information."

Thorn had spoken with the speed of a typewriter, not noticing the effect his words had on Ophelia. On her glasses, in particular. They had turned completely yellow.

"The thing is . . . I was considering leaving the Good Family."

Thorn now swiveled his stool slowly around to her. Nothing in his countenance expressed disapproval, and yet Ophelia suddenly felt chilled to the bone.

"It will be easier for me to assist you that way," she assured, twisting the punched tape. "The conservatoire is very restrictive and allows me little freedom of movement. It was mainly a pretext for accessing the Secretarium, but since you are here, you can . . . get me in secretly. No?"

Thorn's eyes, steady and piercing as an eagle's, made Ophelia lose any remaining composure.

"No. There's much more to be gained from your position within the company of the Forerunners. And that will be even more the case when you become an aspiring virtuoso."

Ophelia was flabbergasted. He spoke of this as if it were a mere formality! For a moment, she was tempted to mention the threats, the blackmail, and the shards of glass, but she abandoned the idea. She didn't want to appear weak in front of Thorn. For a reason she didn't yet understand, a gulf had opened up between them, and she wouldn't allow it to widen.

"That's fine," she said, putting the tape into her uniform pocket. "I'll continue with my apprenticeship at the conservatoire, and I will evaluate that manuscript."

Much to Ophelia's annoyance, Thorn betrayed no sign of satisfaction. "You will submit a written report of your progress to me, just as Apprentice Mediana used to before you. Don't forget to pick up all this before you go."

He indicated the translation notes that had remained scattered on the floor, and returned to his connecting and disconnecting of cables, as if the conversation was over.

"Is that it?" Ophelia murmured. "You have nothing more to say to me?"

"I have, actually," Thorn muttered, not stopping all his connecting. "From now on, until we find out what really happened to Mademoiselle Silence and Apprentice Mediana, avoid isolating yourself. Always stay close to your fellow students; their company will be your best protection."

Ophelia stifled a nervous laugh. She kneeled down, trying her best to ignore the pain under her bandages, which returned with her every movement. When she had finished collecting the pages, she noticed that Thorn wasn't moving anymore. Hunched on his stool, he was holding his radio headphones, undecided about putting them on. His metal gauntlets gleamed in the light from the Coordinator's bulbs.

"And you?" he finally asked, in turn. "You have nothing more to say to me?"

Ophelia had thousands of things she could have said to him. Not one of them passed her lips. Talking to Thorn's back was even harder than talking to him to his face.

As she didn't reply, he put his headphones over his ears. "You will close the door after you."

Once out of the Coordinator room, Ophelia stood still in the middle of the din of the cylinders. She bit her glove with all her might, stifling the sob that threatened to explode between her ribs.

"By the way, I love you." Where had they gone, those six awkward words Thorn had whispered into her ear just before disappearing from her life? Had absence sufficed to erase them, like chalk?

Resolutely, Ophelia wiped her eyes. No. The most important thing was having found him. The rest would be a matter of time, for him as for her.

"To work!" she muttered, heading for the cold room.

# THE CARETAKER

Sultry showers gave way to dusty winds. The Babelian summer was nearly over, but the air was barely less hot.

Ophelia didn't notice the change of season. To do so, she would have needed the time to tilt her glasses up at the sky. She woke before dawn for the pre-morning chores, did her obligatory circuits of the stadium, ran from the amphitheater to the laboratory, gobbled up her bowl of rice while revising her notes for the side, and wasn't allowed to go to bed before completing her evening chores. The slightest delay had repercussions for the whole week. On top of all that, Lady Septima had almost doubled the hours for the Memorial reading groups. She had instigated a ruthless grading system based on individual productivity; the higher the apprentice's grade, the greater his or her chance of obtaining the rank of aspiring virtuoso.

The grade-awarding ceremony was imminent.

Every minute counted when working at such a furious pace, and that much the Seers had fully grasped. Since Ophelia had refused to withdraw from the competition, they targeted the most precious thing she possessed at the conservatoire. Her time. They slipped sleeping pills into her bedside carafe of water; bunged up the toilets when it was her turn to clean them; stitched one leg of her trousers to the other; blocked the mechanism of her bed—they would stop at nothing to slow her down.

At first, Ophelia saw her position plummet in the ranking system. Replacing Mediana was a poisoned chalice, and not just because it had riled her classmates. The extra hours Ophelia spent in the Secretarium's cold room came on top of a timetable that was full to bursting.

And it had to be said: the manuscript she had to evaluate for Thorn was no piece of cake. It was a thick caretaking register kept during the last decade before the Rupture. It was written in an ancient regional dialect of Babel, with an alphabet not used for centuries: complete gibberish to Ophelia. Mediana's start at translating it had only brought to light merchandise accounts, equipment lists, fixtures inventories, health and security instructions. Nothing that appeared worthy of interest.

Ophelia had gotten ahold of the books Thorn had recommended to her, but they were so erudite, she was unable to make use of them.

She could rely only on her hands.

Unfortunately, the edges of the pages in the register had been worn away by time, and they were the parts most likely to have been fingered. In other words, she was deprived of the part most favorable to a reading with hands. Moreover, she had to follow the scientific procedure imposed by Lady Septima. This methodology was more taxing than anything she'd ever had to do at her little museum: progressing from one page to the next took an inordinate amount of time. Ophelia examined every tiny bit of paper meticulously, and when a vision finally came to her, she hastened to record it in her report.

Little by little, she built up a basic profile of the author. The caretaker was a man. He suffered from a severe nervous condition, but didn't lose his cool, for all that. Despite his mistrust, which permeated the register, he was keen to do his work conscientiously. Great rigor, an acute sense of discipline, traumatic aftereffects: a soldier who has returned to civilian life. Ophelia felt great discomfort in her jaw whenever she came across an imprint. The caretaker was probably a severely disabled ex-serviceman.

Putting all this in writing demanded the utmost precaution. Since the Index forbade the use of the words "soldier" and "war," Ophelia had to resort to endless circumlocutions, such as "individual who served in a large unit for the preservation of the nation," or "situation of conflict between several countries using equipment that is harmful in the extreme."

Ophelia was both hoping for and dreading the moment she would meet again with Thorn to give him her report. As he had predicted, they no longer had a single opportunity to meet in private: Lady Septima ensured that she was present for every meeting, so she could judge for herself how her pupil was performing. Elizabeth was also often present, coming and going between the reading cubicles and the Secretarium, reviewing the coding or bringing endless improvements to the Coordinator.

So Ophelia had to remain forever on her guard, call Thorn *monsieur*, and keep her eyes lowered. It was painful every day, knowing that he was so close, and yet so inaccessible. Ophelia felt as if she hadn't really found him again. She was so afraid of not living up to his expectations that she took the mission he had assigned her very seriously; so afraid of increasing the distance between them that she maintained the discretion he had demanded of her religiously. Every time she dared to glance surreptitiously at him, she was struck by the cold determination that spurred him on. Thorn had already set himself the objective of thwarting God back when he had sought to read Farouk's Book, but from the start he had accepted the possibility of failure. Ophelia had watched him gradually exhausting himself, becoming stooped as the weeks went by, crushed by the weight of a burden that was too much for him.

Not anymore. His tirelessness was that of a man determined to succeed. Or rather, that of an automaton. Thorn never showed impatience, never a sign of satisfaction, never an attempt at humor, as if all human emotions hindered his productivity. Methodically, he made use of every new detail, however insignificant, that Ophelia brought to light through her evaluation. And that's why she saw the piles of documentation accumulating, evening after evening, right across the Coordinator room. One had to wonder where Thorn found the energy to read all that on top of his work on the database! Ophelia better understood why he never left the Secretarium.

In the meantime, the weeks went by and she still didn't know what exactly he was looking for in this caretaking register, or what his alliance with the Genealogists really consisted of.

"You still haven't seen them?" asked Blaise with amazement, when Ophelia was asking him about them. "They're real celebrities in Babel. Their every public appearance is *vraiment* an event."

He was perched on a ladder to tidy up some shelves in the Memorial. Two meters further down, Ophelia pretended to consult a dictionary; she had given lexical research as an excuse to leave her reading cubicle for a moment. They were talking in hushed voices, almost without moving their lips, or looking at each other, each giving the illusion of concentrating on their work.

"I rarely get the chance to go out," she said, turning a page of the dictionary. "Do they have as much power as people say they do, these Genealogists?"

"*Mon Dieu*, yes. They run a prestigious club that allows

them to gather personal information on every inhabitant of the ark. In the general interest, they assure. They know practically everything on virtually everyone. Sooner or later, you'll get an opportunity to see them at the Memorial. Avoid attracting their attention, *mademoiselle*," Blaise whispered, turning his big nose in all directions. "They . . . They are people who are not as disinterested as it might appear."

The concern evident in his voice touched her heart. She had been so relieved to see that Blaise hadn't held their subterranean misadventure against her. Even if they had never mentioned it again in public, this secret had become the kernel of their friendship. Ophelia didn't often have time to talk with the assistant, but every smile exchanged in a corridor kept her going.

This time, however, Blaise wasn't smiling. He came down from his ladder, eyes wide with fear. "May I just give you some friendly advice, *mademoiselle*? I know that Forerunners like you have got information-gathering in the blood, but . . . maybe you should curb your curiosity. After what happened to your classmate . . . *eh bien* . . . I wouldn't want to see you joining her over there."

Ophelia trapped her fingers as she put the dictionary back on its shelf. "Over there? You know where they took Mediana?"

Blaise ran his hand through his hedgehog hair uneasily, as though regretting having said too much. That was the last thing Ophelia saw. Night descended upon her, accompanied by a incredible splattering sound. It took her a few seconds to realize that she was covered in ink. The dark, thick liquid was streaming through her hair, over her face, down her neck.

"*Sacrebleu!*" Blaise exclaimed. "I can't believe it, my bad luck has struck again!"

Ophelia removed her splashed glasses and looked up. Just above her, hazy upside-down figures hastened stealthily away.

That was no bad luck. That was a balloon thrown with enough force to defy the ceiling's gravity and land bang on target.

"Don't touch me," she warned, as the assistant quickly handed her a handkerchief. "You're likely to get inky, too. Check that the books are alright, I'm going to clean myself up."

Ophelia spent a considerable time in the Memorial's restrooms. She had to wash her face, glasses, and hair several times, and left her frock coat to soak in the basin. That band of Seers was seriously starting to annoy her. Requesting a new uniform would mean extra chores, and she really didn't need that. While the material released its ink, Ophelia contemplated her reflection in the mirror. Her short hair stuck to her cheeks in dark spirals. She never got to look at herself at the Good Family as there were no mirrors there.

She looked different.

She could see it deep in her eyes, at the corners of her mouth, and even in the shaking of her body under her vest; a strain that wasn't there before.

"I am Eulalia," she murmured.

"I am Ophelia," she thought.

But for Thorn, who was she really?

With a furtive glance, she checked there was no one else in the bathroom. She took a deep breath to calm herself, and placed her palm on her reflection. After a while, the surface of the mirror finally softened and the hand entered it, only to reemerge through the mirror of the neighboring basin. Then, slowly and in reverse, Ophelia pulled it out.

She was shaking.

The mirror had acquired the consistency of mud, as though it had tried to resist this intrusion. Would the double life Ophelia led in Babel end up making her lose her power? Or could it be a deeper identity crisis?

She pulled herself together when she heard the door creak
and a step ringing on the tiles.

"My mother is looking for you, Apprentice Eulalia."

Ophelia recognized Octavio's voice. She held his gaze
through the mirror for as long as he observed her through
the black strands of his fringe. With the reading groups' hours
having been increased, the two divisions' sessions were now
combined. It hadn't helped matters. Octavio was as mistrustful
of her as she was of him.

"She finds your lexical research a touch long," he added,
not without a touch of sarcasm.

Ophelia would have liked to throw him out, but he had
every right to be there. All the communal areas were mixed
in Babel, including the restrooms. She pulled the plug in the
basin and, as the water drained away with a loud gurgle, dried
her frock coat. Luckily, the midnight-blue of the material prevented the ink stain from being too noticeable.

"You're not afraid of being alone with me?" she mocked.
"It's here that Mediana was found in a state of shock."

Octavio's circumflex eyebrows went up. This slight lift took
the golden chain linking his brow to his nostril with it. "I
never claimed that you had attacked her."

"No, just that I had been quick to take her place."

"It's rare to see you being so caustic."

She chose not to react. Behind her, impassive as a sphinx,
Octavio was studying her with almost scientific interest.

"What happened to your uniform? And to your arms?"

Ophelia quickly put on her frock coat, even though it was
still soaked. Most of her cuts had healed, but a few had left
marks that were quite obviously (especially to a Visionary)
recent.

"What happened to them is that I don't have my mother
at the conservatoire to have my back."

Octavio's eyes widened and their fire instantly returned. She had touched a sensitive point. This young man wasn't quite the extinct volcano he wanted to seem. Provoking him was perhaps not a good idea.

"I'm going back to my cubicle," Ophelia announced. "I wouldn't want to keep Lady Septima waiting any longer."

Octavio restrained her by the wrist as she was about to leave. "For your information, I have received no favorable treatment from my mother. My good results are purely down to my own merit. I simply want to ensure that the same is true for every future virtuoso. Including you."

With these words, he let go of Ophelia and turned his face away, as if he suddenly felt ashamed of his action. Relations between men and women were, like everything in Babel, highly regulated. Close contact couldn't occur without the consent of a higher authority. At the Good Family conservatoire, it was, quite simply, forbidden.

For the first time, Octavio's eyes avoided hers. "I'm a good person," he blurted out, reluctantly. "I'll prove it to you."

When Ophelia returned to the shelves where the ink balloon had burst, Blaise was no longer there. Instead, an automaton was finishing cleaning up the mess, endlessly repeating: "A LITTLE GIFT GOES A LONG WAY BETWEEN FRIENDS."

Pensively, she wondered what Octavio had meant by what he'd said to her.

That evening, in the Secretarium's cold room, Ophelia seriously struggled to concentrate on the manuscript. Her eyelids were burning. Her days allowed her no respite, and sharing her privacy with fifteen hostile men didn't help with getting a good night's sleep. She could keep sliding her fingers over the old register, where the paper barely held together, but the caretaker was no longer speaking to her. Facing Thorn empty-handed was unthinkable, but it was no good—there was just endless tattered text, and no more Mediana to finish the translation.

After persisting a long while, Ophelia let her hands fall by her sides. She dozed off without even realizing it, standing there, at the consulting lectern. It lasted but a fraction of a second, a fleeting moment during which she saw herself floating weightlessly above the old world, so high up she could see the horizon taking on the curve of the planet.

Then, in the blink of an eye, she was reading:

"Soon that blasted rainy season, and that blasted dome leaking like a sieve, yet again, and that blasted jungle invading all me bedrooms, and them blasted brats not returning. What's the point of sending them to that blasted city? What are they going to learn there, except that our blasted world is rotten? And what if they get lynched over there, despite their blasted powers? Dammit, how empty this blasted school feels without them."

Ophelia felt no surprise at the time. Plunged into an altered state, she suddenly found it entirely natural to understand what was written in the register. She started to turn its pages, in one direction and then in the other, no longer following procedure, just her instinct. There, in the margins of the inventories, beside the columns of accounts, were the caretaker's comments. They were the real substance of the manuscript.

"L. is getting on my wick with his blasted lights in the middle of the night. Curfew means curfew!"

"Them blasted brats have been quarreling all day. The war was a piece of piss compared with the shambles they've left me. School of peace, huh? Best of blasted luck to their future offspring."

"Shit, J. has disappeared. For real, this time. With his blasted power, it was bound to happen. Shit."

"False alarm, they've found J. On another blasted island. In perfect health. They're indestructible, them blasted brats."

"Little A. cadged a chat off me today. Couldn't twig a blasted word she said to me. She did me a drawing. I think she's after a telescope. Don't know if these kids are going to rule the world one day, but learning the local lingo would be a darned good start."

"Shit. Lost J. again."

Ophelia turned the pages, unable to stop. She was in a trance. She felt as if she could almost hear the caretaker's voice, grumbling in her ear, and she could sense, behind the abrasive words, immense affection. He had loved them, those "blasted brats." Truly loved them.

The register ended abruptly on a final comment:

"He's watching me closely. That blasted way he has of looking at me scares the pants off me. As if I was a blasted intruder in their blasted school. He ain't like them blasted brats, that one. Must have a word with the head about it."

Ophelia stared wide-eyed behind her glasses, totally awake this time. The text instantly returned to being impenetrable. It was, once again, nothing but a string of nonsensical letters. A language totally foreign to her.

"Apprentice Eulalia, your session is over," the voice of Lady Septima announced through the acoustic pipe.

Ophelia turned to her still-blank report page, placed on a corner of the lectern. She felt not the slightest hesitation. She had to find a way of speaking to Thorn in private.

# The Unsaid

When Ophelia came out of the cold room's lift, Lady Septima awaited her.

"You took your time. Let's get going, apprentice."

As usual, they crossed the Secretarium's circular galleries together. Ophelia did her best not to show the excitement that made her want to run all the way to Thorn. She couldn't resist a glance at the decorative globe floating weightlessly in the middle of the atrium. This evening, the old world had revealed a tiny fraction of its secrets to her.

Lady Septima entered the Coordinator room and handed the evaluation to Thorn, unconcerned about interrupting him in the middle of his plugging and unplugging. Normally, Ophelia merely lowered her eyes. Not this time. She stared intently at him as he opened the envelope, unfolded her report, and took in its contents with systematic impassivity. His eyes briefly met Ophelia's, and then he turned to Lady Septima.

"Leave us alone."

"*Pourquoi?* If my pupil has made a mistake, I need to know about it and take the appropriate measures." Imperiously, she held out her hand for the evaluation report, but Thorn put it away in one of the Coordinator's drawers. Away from prying eyes, however powerful they might be.

"If you don't mind, *monsieur*, I would like to take a look at

274

it," Lady Septima insisted. "I undertook to find you a translator; my responsibility . . . "

" . . . is not in question," Thorn cut in, "since there is no
mistake. The fact is, you just don't need to know the contents
of this report."

"I beg your pardon?"

Ophelia clenched her toes inside her boots. It was curious
to note how four words could take on the opposite meaning,
depending on how they were said. Lady Septima was mor-
tally offended. Octavio was really just as fired up inside as his
mother: behind their self-restraint, they were consumed with
pride.

As for Thorn, he was an iceberg. Totally still on his stool,
he showed nothing more than a cold indifference. The metal
tips of his fingers were drumming on the wooden console of
the Coordinator. It had taken a while for Ophelia to understand that those gauntlets he always wore were made of an
alchemical alloy that prevented electrocution. Plugging and
unplugging cables all day long wasn't a risk-free occupation.

"The evaluation of that manuscript was commissioned by
the Genealogists," Thorn said. "I received instructions; so did
you. You had to find an interpreter and you fulfilled that task
well beyond your duty. All that will be said in this room today
will be of the utmost confidentiality."

Lady Septima pointed at the stripe on Ophelia's shoulder.
"This inexperienced apprentice, who may never even become
a Forerunner, would be better informed than me?"

Thorn stood up. Lady Septima, who usually looked down
on people from on high, suddenly appeared tiny.

"If you have any objection to that, I would advise you to
speak directly to the Genealogists."

This prospect succeeded in convincing Lady Septima to
swallow her pride. She clicked her heels, made for the exit,

and then turned one last time toward Ophelia. Her complexion had turned pale and, conversely, her fiery eyes had become incandescent. She seemed to be using her family power to sear into this apprentice who dared to know something that she herself didn't. Ophelia did her best to withstand this intrusive glare, but was relieved when Lady Septima finally left, closing the door behind her.

Thorn turned the crank until the Coordinator room was totally soundproof.

"A blank sheet of paper?"

Ophelia bit the inside of her cheek. There was no reproach in his voice, but that meant nothing. Whether his accent was Babelian or Northern, and whatever the circumstances, Thorn's tone was so monotonous that it was impossible to tell what he was thinking.

"I'm so sorry. You asked me not to draw Lady Septima's attention to us, and I've just done the exact opposite."

Thorn didn't respond. He remained standing and observed her at a distance. He was waiting for her explanation.

"The author of your manuscript," Ophelia began. "He lived right here, in the Memorial, at the time when it was still a school. He . . . I'm certain that he knew the family spirits. I mean when they were children. And I have every reason to think," she added, after a gulp, "that he knew God, too." She watched for a change in Thorn's demeanor. He didn't bat an eyelid.

"What else did you learn?"

Ophelia certainly hadn't expected him to swing her around in the air, but she would have appreciated a sign of approval, however small.

The floorboards creaked under her feet as she went over to the glass-fronted shelves, upon which there were rows of files and dials. She didn't even glance at them. She saw only her hazy reflection, and far, far behind her, Thorn's scarecrow silhouette.

"That I'm not really myself anymore. I don't know when it started. Is it from having read Farouk's Book? Is it from having absorbed some of your family power? Is it from having released that Other, the very first time I passed through a mirror? I sometimes feel as if I'm haunted by a second memory."

Returning to an old habit, she gnawed at the seam of her gloves, and what she saw then, in the glass of the cabinets, didn't please her. A small woman who, deep down, was afraid. Half a woman. "A *bambina*," Mediana's mocking voice whispered to her.

Ophelia turned away from her reflection and looked straight at Thorn. "I read the manuscript. Not just with my hands; with my eyes, too. For a brief moment, I understood what the caretaker had written. As though a part of me had suddenly remembered how to do it."

She proceeded to tell Thorn all she had retained from her reading. The school of peace; the training sessions; the departure to the city; L.'s light; A.'s telescope; J.'s disappearances; and particularly, most particularly, the caretaker's last words: "He ain't like them blasted brats, that one. Must have a word with the head about it."

"So?" she asked. "Was that what the Genealogists asked you to find?"

"Is there anything else in that register that you might have missed?" True to character, Thorn had asked his question in a methodical tone. He didn't seem to notice that his every word reinforced her unpleasant impression of not having come up to his expectations.

"My trance didn't last long, but I think I covered the essentials."

"Would you be able to repeat the procedure?"

"I don't think so. I have no control over such visions; some-thing has to trigger them. I . . . I'll give it another try," she couldn't help but promise, faced with Thorn's intense stare.

She suddenly realized that there wasn't much she would have refused him, had he but asked. It was ironic to see how much the roles had been reversed. Had he also experienced it, in the past, this state of permanent instability?

There was a grating of steel when Thorn suddenly ended his stillness. "That won't be necessary," he said.

He went over to the back of the room and opened a door; it was so well concealed within the wood-paneled wall that Ophelia had never noticed it. Thorn hadn't asked her to follow him, but as he was taking a long time to return, she finally joined him.

The door led to accommodation that went with the job, decked in the same wood and copper as the Coordinator room. The furnishings proved equally austere: a wardrobe, a table, a lamp, and a bed. Ophelia noticed two phantogram facilities. One was a garbage chute, allowing waste to be dis-posed of outside the Secretarium. The other contained a dish, which itself contained a nondescript gruel. Did they phan-tomize Thorn's food?

There was not a crease in the sheets, not a speck of a dust on the furniture, not a forgotten sock on the floor. There were, however, pharmaceutical bottles lined up in serried ranks on every shelf, like in an apothecary's dispensary.

Thorn had folded up his body on a chair, facing the ward-robe, its doors wide open. With an elbow planted on each knee, and chin perched on linked hands, his attention seemed to be totally focused on the inside of the wardrobe. Ophelia's eyebrows rose when she saw that he had pushed the shirts on hangers to either side. They rose further when she discov-ered an amazing quantity of punched tapes, pinned up like a collection of butterflies. They were book references generated by the Coordinator. Each one was marked with a black cross.

"So, what's this hidden bibliography all about?" Ophelia asked.

Thorn rose as she approached, so abruptly that he almost jammed the contraption on his leg. Maybe it was to allow her to take a good look, but she thought it more likely that he wanted to maintain a distance between them.

"The Genealogists know neither the title nor the author of the work they have asked me to track down," he replied. "On arrival, I understood that it would be statistically impossible for me to locate it using the old catalogue. I needed a database worthy of the name. The more the reading groups add to the new catalogue, the more the Coordinator's searches gain in precision, and the more likely I am to accomplish my mission. You are looking at the selection I had put together. As you can see," he said, indicating a tape on which the ink of the cross wasn't yet dry, "the caretaking register was my last contender."

Ophelia slipped the tapes through her fingers. She now knew by heart the language of those punched holes, and could decipher, almost without difficulty, the references they represented. Apart from their printing dates, which were all pretty ancient, the works here were quite different: memoirs, essays, handbooks, certificates, etc.

"It's not feasible," she muttered. "You can't find one book among hundreds of thousands without a single guideline."

"In fact, I do have one."

In her surprise, Ophelia yanked a bibliographical tape from its pin, damaging the sequence of punched holes. She quickly tried to put it back in place, but Thorn hadn't noticed a thing. He was releasing the clasps on his gauntlets, one by one.

"This document the Genealogists are after isn't about any old subject. It would contain some very specific information.

Information," he said, releasing the final clasp, "that would allow the person who knows it to become God's equal."

Ophelia considered Thorn for a long time, without blinking, without speaking, without breathing.

"Needless to say," he continued, "you must repeat that to no one. Lady Septima, in particular. She thinks my research is only for the sake of the catalogue, and that's how it must remain."

Feeling dizzy, Ophelia sat on the bed. "What do you mean by 'become God's equal'?"

"I don't know. For the moment, at least."

"And you're saying that such information would exist here, at the Memorial, in full sight of, and accessible to, everyone, with no one realizing it?"

Thorn laid his gauntlets down and pulled the stopper out of a bottle of surgical spirit. The nauseating smell instantly pervaded the room.

"Almost no one. If the Genealogists know of the existence of this document, someone must have told them about it."

Ophelia frowned. Could that be the "ultimate truth" mentioned by Ambrose, the day he'd brought her to the Memorial for the first time? She had found no strongroom in the Secretarium, and not for want of searching, so she'd ended up accepting that it must all be folklore.

"The Genealogists told me nothing else," Thorn concluded. "If I want to find out more about it, first I'll have to prove myself."

"And you imagined that such a secret was to be found in the caretaking register." Ophelia better understood now why he hadn't jumped for joy when she'd told him of her discovery. In the end, she had informed him of what he already, more or less, knew.

"I was convinced of it. You confirmed it for me. I must inform the Genealogists about it."

With that, Thorn began to disinfect his hands meticulously, over a bowl. Ophelia noticed that every time he mentioned the Genealogists, or was on the point of doing so, he would knit his brows even more, gathering shadows in the middle of his face. He really didn't like them.

"Who wants to become God's equal?" she asked him. "Them . . . or you?"

"I will not depose one god for another. I have had but one aim since my escape: finding the weak point of this coward who conceals his true face from the world." The shadows between Thorn's eyebrows had become even heavier.

"I doubt the Genealogists share your vision of things."

Ophelia didn't know which prospect was the more terrifying. A world governed by God, or a world governed by men who think they're God.

"Indeed," Thorn said, through gritted teeth. "They don't share it."

Silence fell, during which Ophelia resisted the selfish question she was itching to ask. What about her in all this? This mission Thorn had set himself, what place did it leave for her?

"That boarder the caretaker spoke of," she said, "the one he considered different from the family spirits. What if that was him, the Other. Maybe he had become too dangerous. Maybe that's why God imprisoned him in a mirror? You have no looking-glass here," she suddenly noticed, gazing around the room.

Thorn shook his head. He had rolled up his shirtsleeves to rub surgical spirit on his forearms, as if he wanted to erase all the scars on them.

"But didn't you become one?"

"One what?" he muttered.

"A mirror visitor."

"Even though your power enabled me to escape from

prison I haven't made a habit of using it. Indeed, you, too, should also keep well away from mirrors," Thorn added, putting down the spirit bottle.

"Why? Do you think there's still an 'Other' that I could release by accident?"

"No. I will only believe in the existence of that 'Other' when I have encountered him or her. In the meantime, God, for me, will be solely responsible for our world's state of decay. The fact is that he took on your appearance; he probably absorbed your family power, and we don't know what use he might make of it. As far as I'm concerned, I'd rather he didn't turn up in my bathroom."

Ophelia made an effort to think about it. Passing through mirrors demanded great intellectual honesty, and, from what she had seen of him, that wasn't a quality she would ascribe to God. This thought led to another:

"That night he visited us in prison, I noticed something odd. God doesn't have a reflection. He has thousands of different faces, but in front of a mirror, he . . . " Ophelia hesitated, looking for the right words. "I don't know. It's as if he didn't really exist. Becoming God's equal could come at a price."

Thorn's movements halted over the bowl. "That is odd, indeed."

With that, he returned to his vigorous rubbing. Much as Ophelia appreciated silence, when it fell between them at every pause, it felt like torture. She didn't understand. Why did she feel more alone now than she'd ever felt during those last three years? Why was the emptiness she felt inside deepening in Thorn's presence?

"And reading objects?" she asked. "Has that ever happened to you? Because if you need any advice . . . "

"No need. It has never happened to me."

"Perhaps that's due to your memory. My uncle always repeated to me that a good reader had to forget themselves."

"That would be it," Thorn declared. "I never forget anything. In any case, Sir Henry isn't supposed to be an Animist."

Silence fell again. Ophelia had to face it: she had no talent for making conversation. Thorn shared all the information relating to his research with her, but withdrew into himself as soon as it became personal.

When he seized his bottle of surgical spirit, she thought he was at last going to replace the stopper and put it away. Instead, he disinfected his hands for a second time, as if they really were repulsive.

They weren't in Ophelia's eyes. From a distance, she took in the network of veins under the skin, the long, curved fingers, the bone that rose up on each wrist, and suddenly, she felt something like pain in the pit of her stomach. She hadn't the slightest idea what was happening to her, but looking at those hands made her want to scream.

She turned away when Thorn, until then absorbed in his disinfecting, looked straight at her.

"I have told you all that I know. You should return to your company now. Every minute you spend here with me is fuel for gossip. I prefer to use this time exploring new leads."

There was a stiffness in his voice. Ophelia got the feeling that it was to him, more than anything, that her presence was a problem. She stood up, knocking the bedside table as she did, and knocking over the lamp that was on it. To her great astonishment, the lamp righted itself, the bedside table straightened itself, and the sheet smoothed itself until not a crease remained. Maybe Sir Henry was not supposed to be an Animist, but that didn't stop his personal fixtures and fittings from reproducing his habits . . . It was strange for Ophelia to think that, despite their being apart, a small aspect of her at least had rubbed off on Thorn. She thought of the fob watch. Since she had returned it to him, she'd never seen him using it. Had he got rid of it because it didn't work? Ophelia hoped not. Losing the scarf had been painful enough.

"What are you expecting of me now?" she asked, indicating the punched tapes pinned to the back of the wardrobe. "Must I evaluate new documents until I discover the one that holds God's secret? I no longer have much time, myself. In a few days, either I will become an aspiring virtuoso, or I will hand back my wings. I know you're really counting on my making the grade, but . . . let's say that the future is uncertain."

Thorn put his metal gauntlets back on. "I'll inform you tomorrow, I still need to think. In the meantime, keep a low profile around Lady Septima. What I revealed to you today exposes you to danger. Don't isolate yourself, watch your back, and, if you notice the slightest unusual thing, report it to me as a matter of urgency."

Ophelia was tempted, just for a second, to tell him about the problems she was encountering with the other members of her division. She decided to keep quiet. Thorn no longer treated her like a fragile little kid that has to be hidden in the shadows. He entrusted her with responsibilities. He spoke to her like an equal. She'd lost everything else; she refused to give that up, too.

"Will do." Ophelia had no desire to leave. If remaining with Thorn was a source of permanent frustration, leaving was even worse. She found it very irritating, having to come up with ploys to see him in private, and then to time their every meeting.

As she was placing her hand on the handle of the door, a word stopped her in her tracks.

"Ophelia."

It was so surprising to hear herself being called by her real name, after going by someone else's for months, that she felt her stomach lurch. Was Thorn finally going to say them, those words she so needed to hear?

Leaning with both fists on the table, he inflicted his most intense stare on her. "Are you really certain you have nothing to say to me?"

Caught off guard, Ophelia just kept clinging to the door handle.

A spark then flashed deep in Thorn's eyes. "You know where to find me," he said, indicating to her to leave.

# THE REMINISCENCE

Ophelia spent the night tossing and turning in her bed, surrounded by the snoring of the dormitory and the whining of the mosquitoes. She no longer understood Thorn at all. What was that question he'd asked her supposed to mean? Did he think she was hiding information from him? She had run away from home to look for him; she had changed her identity on an ark where lying was a crime; she had chosen to put up with Mediana's blackmail rather than betray him; she had remained at the Good Family because he had asked her to; and never, at any time, had she complained.

Wasn't it rather up to Thorn to tell her in what way, exactly, she was so disappointing?

Exasperated by the heat, Ophelia pushed off her sheets. She should have been furious with him, but it was with herself that she was most annoyed. Three years ago, she had failed to help Thorn when he had really needed her. And the past was repeating itself: now more than ever, she felt useless.

Maybe the only words he was expecting from her, in the end, were those of apology.

Ophelia finally dozed off. She flew above the old world, lost somewhere between the past and the future, dreaming and reality. Beneath the clouds, she caught sight of a town in ruins, scarred by bombardment, and then there was the sea, as far as the eye could see. No, it was much more than a sea: an ocean. It was strange to think that one day, all this water would be swallowed up entirely by the void. By focusing, Ophelia managed to distinguish the underwater curves of a coral reef, and, somewhere in the middle of a lagoon, a tiny patch of greenery.

An island, well clear of the coast.

"That's me blasted home."

It was then that Ophelia noticed a man who was sitting to the side of her, right on the edge of a cloud. She immediately recognized him. It was the caretaker whose register she'd read. The muslin of his turban barely concealed his disfigured face. His mouth resembled a badly healed wound. And yet, Ophelia understood him perfectly when he raised his small, round spectacles towards her and spoke to her in a language she'd never heard before:

"Watch it with that other. He ain't like them blasted brats, that one."

"What other?" Ophelia asked.

The caretaker's only response was to return to contemplating his island, and to twist what remained of his mouth. "If you seek E. G., the other will find you."

Ophelia woke up with a start. Dawn hadn't broken yet, but she no longer felt at all tired. In the neighboring bed, swaddled in her sheet, Zen was anxiously watching her in the half-light, as she would have done a raving lunatic preparing to leap on her.

Once she'd tracked down her glasses, Ophelia slipped on her uniform and boots behind the screen, and then ran down the transcendium. The clatter of her wings filled the silence of the Hall of Residence. She inserted her apprentice card in the turnstile of the telegraphic booth. It was a shame to waste hard-won points to send a simple message, but she just didn't have the patience to hang around.

"To Mr. Blaise, Babel Memorial, Department . . . um . . . for the classification of collections," Ophelia dictated into the receiver. "I need to see you later for . . . um . . . some advice. It's about the books . . . um . . . that you mentioned to me at the bazaar. From Eulalia . . . um . . . of the second division of the company of Forerunners."

After a few seconds, the counter's mechanical arm swiveled on its stand. Its copper finger tapped out pulses, some short, some long, on a telegram machine. Ophelia hoped it wouldn't transmit all her "um"s.

How could she have forgotten E. G.'s books? Mademoiselle Silence had destroyed them without permission, just before dying of a cardiac arrest, and not for a second had it crossed Ophelia's mind to tell Thorn about it. She must rectify this mistake as soon as possible.

She spent the rest of the day counting the minutes. The atmosphere at the Good Family had become stifling. Torrid winds made all the buildings' windowpanes rattle, and hurled sand right into the atriums. Every time Ophelia went near a window, she searched through the swirls of dust for the Memorial, standing on its distant little ark. If only the flight could not be canceled today! She remained shut away for the afternoon, with her fellow students, in the evaluation laboratory, surrounded by a seething silence. The Seers left her out of all the group activities, and Zen changed places so she wouldn't end up sitting beside her. Octavio, who usually never took his eyes off her, had been avoiding meeting hers since their conversation in the restrooms. As for Lady Septima, she didn't honor Ophelia with a single comment during the practicals; she assessed, advised, critiqued everyone, except for her.

Total ostracism. Spontaneous and unanimous. Just a few days from the grade-awarding ceremony.

Ophelia was greatly relieved to see the winds falling as the sun set. The airship reserved for the company of Forerunners took off at dusk, into a scorching, sulfurous sky. Ophelia looked for a seat where she wouldn't prompt a disapproving cough. Strange as it might seem, there were times when she almost missed Mediana. In disappearing, the Seer had left a great void that just kept widening all around Ophelia.

She found herself at the back of the airship, beside Elizabeth, who was calmly writing notes in her notebook, seemingly oblivious to both the pervading animosity onboard and the distress of her neighbor.

"How did you manage to become an aspiring virtuoso?"

"Hmm? Thanks to lots and lots of coffee."

"Please," Ophelia sighed. "I began my apprenticeship after the others, and I've turned Lady Septima against me. I have little time left to make a good impression. Some advice would be welcome."

Elizabeth continued to send her pencil racing across the paper, stringing together numbers, letters, and symbols that apparently made sense to her. "Remain neutral," she finally declared, placidly. "Observe without judging. Obey without arguing. Learn without taking a stand. Take an interest without becoming attached. Fulfill your duty without expecting anything in return. That's the only way not to suffer," she concluded, crossing out a series of instructions. "The less one suffers, the more efficient one is. The more efficient one is, the better one serves the city."

Ophelia looked at Elizabeth's hands, with their constellation of freckles. They were writing, crossing out, starting again from scratch, without flagging.

"Do you never feel alone?"

"We are always alone."

When the airship landed at the Memorial, Ophelia disembarked more disillusioned than when she had boarded.

The catalography session seemed interminable to her. She had to meet her quota as quickly as possible if she wanted to garner herself enough time before her meeting with Thorn at the Secretarium. Her head was buzzing with so many questions that, in the meantime, it was hard for her to concentrate. Why had Mademoiselle Silence secretly destroyed the complete works of E. G.? Was it linked to Thorn's research? Why would an author of old books for children be in the possession of some information that allowed one to be become "God's equal"? Was what happened to Mediana and Professor Wolf in any way connected to this secret?

*If you seek E. G., the other will find you.*

Of course, it was only a dream, but Ophelia tended to take seriously all that rose to the surface of her subconscious. This memory that she shared with God seemed to know much more than she did.

So who was that *other* whom the caretaker had feared so much? Was he the same as the one Ophelia had released from the mirror? And there again, what was the connection with E. G.?

She absolutely had to speak to someone. She glanced over the latticed partition of her cubicle, in the hope of spotting Blaise, but her eyes met only those of the Seers in the neighboring cubicles. Beneath their brilliantine-slicked moustaches, smiles played on their lips that made her feel uneasy. When she had finished her catalography and rose from her chair, their voices murmured in unison: "Evening forecast: heat wave alert."

Ophelia ignored them. She hurried to deposit her books at the Phantoms' counter, and then to punch her cards in the basement. When she consulted the watch of the mechanical statue in the hall, the one that welcomed visitors with low bows, she let out a sigh. She had just enough time to find Blaise.

It didn't prove as easy as expected. The Memorial always closed its doors later on Saturdays, generally for the temporary exhibitions, but this evening there were more visitors than usual. In the large atrium, automatons were maneuvering a crane to install a gong of monumental proportions. These preparations were for the inauguration ceremony for the new catalogue, to take place on the same day as the conferment of grades. Ophelia trod on a number of toes as she paced up and down the transcendiums and topsy-turviums. She turned around every time she came across a Memorialist uniform, but it was never Blaise. She would have found it extremely frustrating to have beaten her own catalography speed record for nothing.

Around a corner in one library, she fell on the last person she was looking for. A man with long, silvery hair was sitting on a leather sofa. He sported a white frock coat and pink glasses.

The inventor of the automaton-servants. The famous ark-trotter. The father of Ambrose. Lazarus!

Ophelia grabbed the largest tome within reach and pretended to be engrossed in it. This man had shaken her hand in the Pole: he knew who she was . . . and who she wasn't. Luckily, Lazarus hadn't seen her. He was deep in conversation with the old sweeper of the Memorial, who was flicking a feather duster over the shelves of books, one inch at a time.

" . . . and that's why one must prepare for the future, *mon ami*!" Lazarus exclaimed, enthusiastically. "You should cast aside your brooms, which are unworthy of you, and make the most of a well-deserved retirement! Why not go on a big journey? The world beyond these walls is *absolument fabuleux*, and believe me, I do know what I'm talking about!"

Walter, his inseparable mechanical butler, was leaning over the sofa to comb his master's long hair. He marked every word Lazarus said with a nod of his faceless head.

The old sweeper responded with a shrug, and went back to his dusting. Ophelia couldn't make out his expression, behind his triple layer of beard, fringe, and eyebrows, but she felt exasperated for him. Couldn't he just be left to work here, if that pleased him? She observed Lazarus on the sofa, legs casually crossed, shaking his top hat like a conjuror, singing the praises of the future and modernity with emphatic, sweeping statements. On their first encounter, she had found him irresistibly charming. She realized that, now, she was wary of him, and not only because he could unmask her. He had turned up at the Pole at almost the same time as God, and like God, had shown persistent interest in Mother Hildegarde's family power.

"Psst! Mademoiselle Eulalia! Over here!"

It was Blaise, who, with his usual bad timing, had just appeared between the rows of bookcases, at the other end of the gallery. He was gesticulating to Ophelia in a way that he probably thought discreet. She had no choice but to join him, her face still buried in her book, sensing the old explorer's intrigued eyes on her.

"Wasn't that Monsieur Lazarus next to you?" Blaise whispered to her. "He's been back in Babel for months now, but I still hadn't come across him."

Ophelia frowned. For months? Had Ambrose started to avoid her because of his father's return?

"You don't seem very happy to see him here," she observed, as they walked off.

Blaise had started pushing his trolley with a heavy step, shoulders hunched, as if, suddenly, he were wheeling a coffin. "Oh, you're quite mistaken," he sighed. "I feel much admiration for Monsieur Lazarus. Gratitude, too. He was formerly a teacher at the college where I did my classes, and he was much kinder to me than to any other adult. My bad luck, my clumsiness, my . . . *eh bien* . . . my tendencies, none of all that ever seemed to put him off. He found me interesting. I almost felt as if I were *spécial* when I spoke with him," Blaise murmured, mustering a faint smile. "Between you and me, it's his automatons that I don't like. They replaced almost all of the maintenance staff; if Monsieur Lazarus is here today, maybe it's because he has new models to propose to the Memorial. Models capable not just of cleaning, but also of . . . of classifying books and advising visitors."

Blaise was rubbing the "assistant" badge pinned to his uniform so anxiously, Ophelia clenched her jaw. No, she definitely didn't like Lazarus anymore.

"Did you receive my telegram?" she asked, gently.

Blaise blinked his big, watery eyes several times. "*Quoi?* Oh, yes, yes, I received it. I'd be lying if I told you that your request didn't surprise me. And worry me, too. After what happened to Mademoiselle Silence . . . Anyway, I hope you're not going to get yourself into any more trouble. What did you want to know?"

Ophelia checked with a glance that they weren't within eavesdropping distance of anyone. Apart from the majestic statues that served as pillars to the bookcases, there was no one in this gallery. Neither on the ground nor on the ceiling.

"Could you show me exactly where E. G.'s books were to be found, prior to their removal?

"*Bien sûr!* Follow me."

On the way, the trolley lost a caster, and when Blaise leant over to put it back in place, the seam of his trousers split open. Ophelia had to admit that he really was unlucky. In the young readers' section, she recognized where they had met that very first time. She saw herself once again picking up the books by E. G. that she'd caused to fall. To think that she had held them in her hands, on that day, barely a few hours before their destruction . . .

"Mademoiselle Silence practically accused me of stealing," she recalled, in a hushed voice. "She even wanted to search my bag."

Tugging the back of his jacket to hide the tear in his trousers, Blaise indicated with his chin the top shelf, on which there were rows of books bound in many colors. "The complete collection of E. G.'s works was up there. And it's from up there that Mademoiselle Silence fell," he added, wrinkling his nose with a nauseated grimace. "I can still smell her fear."

Ophelia noticed an elegant ladder on a rail. A sign read: "Children are not permitted to remove books from top shelves."

"Is that the ladder Mademoiselle Silence used?"

"No, this one is new," Blaise replied. "We got rid of the old one after the accident. The structure was sound, but when in doubt . . . "

This was no good for Ophelia. Reading an object associated with a violent death was distressing, but the object could be the sole witness to the event. "And you told me that Mademoiselle Silence returned here after destroying the books?"

Perplexed, Blaise ruffled his spiky hair. "*En effet*, right in the middle of the night. I still can't fathom why. Nothing was out of place when we found her here in the morning."

Ophelia slid the ladder along its rail and climbed the rungs to reach the highest shelves. There was nothing but recent editions of alphabet primers up there.

"Nothing was *any longer* out of place," she corrected. "Maybe what Mademoiselle Silence had come to look for had already been taken by someone else." The moment Ophelia uttered this sentence, she was struck by an intuition. "Does the Memorial keep a written record of books destroyed by the chief censors?"

Blaise offered Ophelia a helping hand to come down, but

then tripped on an uneven floorboard and almost knocked her off balance. "Oh, *désolé*! To reply to your question: yes, in the archives of the censoring department. Mademoiselle Silence must have recorded everything over there. She undoubtedly took too much initiative, but she always respected procedure."

"Could you take me there?"

Blaise checked the gallery's clock. "I can open it for you, but I won't linger. I've finished my shift and, unusually, my parents have invited me for supper. I mustn't keep them waiting," he said, concealing the tear at the back of his trousers. "They're so ashamed of me, they're just waiting for the first excuse to disown me."

# THE TREACHERY

Ophelia had not yet been to the censoring department. It was located in the Memorial's other hemisphere, the one that had been entirely reconstructed after the Rupture; you couldn't walk there without thinking of the void beneath the tons of stone. The department was deserted and looked more like an industrial site than an administrative office. Naked bulbs cast a harsh light on piles of cardboard boxes, reaching right up to the ceiling. The heat inside was overwhelming.

"It's the incinerator," Blaise explained, pointing at the smoked-up porthole on a pressurized door. "I'm . . . I'm strictly forbidden from going near it."

"It's operating at the moment?" Ophelia asked, with surprise. "I thought that no items were to be destroyed as long as the new catalogue wasn't completed."

"Books, yes, but not garbage. The Memorial welcomes hundreds of visitors every day, not to mention all its staff. You'd be amazed at the number of bin-loads we chuck into there each evening. The archives are this way, *mademoiselle!*"

Blaise opened another door, the handle of which came off in his hand. The archives room was no different from the rest of the department: nothing but boxes everywhere. If the old catalogue was a reflection of this setup, Ophelia better understood why Thorn had started compiling it again from scratch.

"I'm going to leave you," Blaise said. "I mustn't miss my birdtrain. I'll trust you to turn off the lights and close the door behind you when you've finished."

"You can count on it."

Ophelia was late herself; she had no more time to lose. She pushed up the sleeves of her frock coat, scanned the labels on the boxes, and then suddenly noticed that Blaise was still standing in the doorway. A tormented expression contorted his face.

"Have you considered that Fearless might be behind . . . all this?"

"I have considered it, yes." Fearless hated the censors; Mademoiselle Silence had died while doing that very work. Fearless had seen Mediana as an enemy; she had ceased to be a Forerunner from one day to the next. He was a man who was far less innocuous than he seemed, extremely well informed and terribly ambitious. Ophelia wouldn't have been surprised if he, too, was searching for this book that enabled one to become God's equal.

"Take care, alright? Don't end up like your colleague. *S'il te plaît.*"

Blaise's voice had become so imploring that Ophelia was truly moved. She didn't know what to say. She never knew what to say at such times.

"The Deviations Observatory," Blaise then declared, gravely. "It's there that she was transferred. *Au revoir, mademoiselle.*"

"I . . . Thank you."

The words had been blurted too late; Blaise was gone.

Ophelia forced herself to get a grip. One thing at a time: first, the boxes. She found one on which the date corresponded to that of Mademoiselle Silence's death, and flicked through the records it contained.

"Here we are," she whispered. On one of the records there was an entire column of "E. G."s under the heading "author."

Ophelia scanned the titles: *Journey Around the New World*; *The Adventures of the Little Prodigies*; *A Fine and Wonderful Family*, and so on. These books reeked of righteousness, rendering their destruction even more incomprehensible.

Under the heading "grounds for censoring," Mademoiselle Silence had simply written: "Vocabulary condemned by the Index and lack of educational content."

E. G.'s books carried no publication date, as was common in older editions, but according to the record, their date of printing was estimated at the first century after the Rupture. It was a time when humanity was still rebuilding itself, and in full regeneration; so-called optimistic literature was widely available then.

Increasingly disconcerted, Ophelia pushed her glasses back up her nose. There was really nothing untoward here. Maybe, in the end, E. G.'s oeuvre was a false trail. What if the book she was looking for was in fact a Book, with a capital B? And what if God had been created just as he had himself created the family spirits? If a Book existed that conferred the power to reproduce all of the powers?

By reading the record with her hands and discovering Mademoiselle Silence's state of mind, Ophelia could have been enlightened, but for that she needed the consent of the censoring department. The last time she had used her power without permission, she had violated Professor Wolf's privacy—this misconduct still weighed on her conscience.

Ophelia suddenly noticed an anomaly within the record. All the titles on the list of E. G.'s books had been stamped "destroyed." All, except one: *The Era of Miracles*.

Had one book escaped incineration? So that was what Mademoiselle Silence had returned to find in the middle of the night! And it was death that she found instead. But the book itself, what had become of it?

"Once upon a tomorrow, before too long, there will be a world that will finally live in peace."

Barely had Ophelia finished this sentence before she was wondering why she'd said it. Those were the very words that had entered her mind when she had read the statue of the headless soldier. She had the feeling that she'd already seen them somewhere. That she'd learnt them off by heart, and then forgotten them.

Suddenly, Ophelia looked up from the record. She could see nothing but boxes of archives all around her, and yet, for a brief moment, she had seen a movement out of the corner of her eye. Like a shadow leaning over her shoulder. She became aware that she was drenched in sweat, and not because of the ambient heat. Her heart was racing. Her glasses had suddenly turned blue.

Ophelia felt as if she had woken from a nightmare that she couldn't even remember.

When she saw the time on the room's clock, she leapt to her feet. It was much later than she'd thought! Everyone, starting with Thorn, must be wondering where she'd got to. She quickly put her box back and switched off the lights, but just as she was closing the premises, she glanced hesitantly at the door of the incinerator. The porthole was glowing red like a hot plate. It was in there that Mademoiselle Silence had destroyed E. G.'s books, apart from just one. But what if *The Era of Miracles* had accidentally remained inside?

Ophelia was hit with a powerful surge of heat as soon as she half-opened the pressurized door. A furnace took up almost the whole room. It radiated such a high temperature that merely lingering in front of it made her feel as if she'd be reduced to ashes. She should have put on protective clothing before entering here, but she no longer had time to look for any. She had a quick look in every corner of the room, under the garbage skips, behind the coal bunker, anywhere a book could have slipped and remained unnoticed.

Nothing.

The only thing she found, when she decided that it was too hot to stay a second longer, was a closed door. On the other side of the porthole, the Seers were running off.

Ophelia worked on the door handle, which was so hot that it burnt her fingers, despite her gloves. It was no good. They had triggered the security lock.

"Evening forecast: heat wave alert."

They knew! The Seers had anticipated this moment from the start. And, as always, they had made themselves the actual enactors of their own prophesies. Much as Ophelia banged on the door and cried for their help, no one came. And she obviously couldn't count on her Animism to release the lock.

The heat from the furnace was unbearable. Ophelia looked for another way out, but she was well and truly trapped. Sweat was dripping off her chin. Her feet were burning in their boots. She pressed her face to the ventilation grille on the wall. She couldn't escape that way—she'd barely have got an arm through it—but it was the least overheated place in the room. Time trickled away, and with it, all the fluid within her body.

She just couldn't believe it. Were the Seers aware that they were putting her in danger? Apart from them, only Blaise knew where she was, and his birdtrain had flown off a long time ago.

Ophelia tugged at her collar. Panic, more, even, than the heat, was suffocating her. She wiped away the sweat that was stinging her eyes; a shadow appeared at the porthole on the door. A click. The handle turned by itself; air rushed into the room.

Ophelia rushed out of it. She coughed until her lungs hurt. Her head was spinning so fast, she had to lean against a wall.

She would have cried with relief, had there still been enough fluid in her body to do so.

Who had opened the door for her? The Seers? Wherever Ophelia looked, there was no one but her in the censoring department.

She stumbled to the nearest restroom. She had to stop herself from drinking water from the tap—it wasn't fit to drink—but she wiped the skin of her face and neck with a soaked handkerchief. She was as red as if she had been sunburned.

She must find Thorn, and fast. He must be urgently informed of the disappearance of the only book by E. G. not to have been destroyed by Mademoiselle Silence. He could be missing the very item that was central to his research.

Ophelia had barely left the bathroom before she went straight back in and vomited the contents of her stomach. Leaning over the toilet and shivering violently, she seriously considered denouncing the Seers. She would have, without a moment's hesitation, if doing so wouldn't mean she'd have to explain what she herself was up to in the censoring department. She mustn't attract the attention of either Lady Septima or any Lord of LUX as she pursued her investigations.

Ophelia encountered not a soul in the galleries, apart from a few automatons cleaning the cabinet windows. The Memorial had closed its doors; the visitors and most of the staff had left. She headed for the reading cubicles to find Lady Septima. She could only hope that Lady Septima would agree to give her access to the Secretarium, despite her lateness.

The Seers were sitting at their tables, quietly bent over their books, as if they'd never left them. They returned her furious glare with ironic half-smiles. There was, however, one among them who had the decency to hang his head, visibly uncomfortable. Ophelia wondered whether it wasn't he who, feeling remorse, had opened the door for her.

She frowned on noticing that Octavio's cubicle, at the Sons of Pollux desk, was empty.

"*Tiens, tiens, tiens!*" said Lady Septima, when she saw her. "Here's our missing person. For nearly an hour now we've been looking for you, apprentice. Not one of your classmates could tell us where you had gone. What is your explanation?"

"I didn't feel well." Which was no lie. Ophelia's hoarse voice, ruddy cheeks, and sweat-soaked hair all backed her up.

"Well, I never. And you didn't think it might be a good idea to let us know? Sir Henry needed your hands for a new evaluation. You made everyone late."

Lady Septima had clicked her tongue as she spoke, but this disapproval was a mere façade. Her eyes glowed with satisfaction. She could serve back to her pupil the humiliation that she, as a teacher, had suffered the previous day. Ophelia was instantly sure that she was perfectly aware of what the Seers had just put her through. Perhaps she was even the instigator.

"I'll make up for it," she promised. "Could you open the access to the Secretarium for me?"

"There's no point, apprentice. Sir Henry found someone to replace you."

The effect these words had on Ophelia was more brutal than the heat of the incinerator. So that was why Octavio's cubicle was empty!

"If you really want to make up for it, follow the example of your classmates," Lady Septima recommended, indicating the Godchildren of Helen desk to her. "Maybe the extra hours of catalography you do will mitigate the bad impression created by what you didn't do elsewhere? What a shame, just a few days away from the awarding of grades . . . "

Ophelia sat in her cubicle, but took up neither something to read nor something to write with. She merely glared at the globe of the Secretarium, with its red-gold earthly crust reflecting the lamps of the galleries that circled it, like planetary rings. Since the cubicles were on the ceiling, Ophelia was seeing it upside down, but she had a direct view of the reinforced door.

Thorn had replaced her.

"Is the *signorina* going to cry?" one of the Seers whispered through the latticed partition opposite. "Would the *signorina* like a hankie?"

Ophelia shut him up with a single look. She was seething with anger.

Thorn had replaced her because of them.

She left her cubicle as soon as she saw the gangway to the door of the Secretarium being deployed. Lady Septima was seated at the telegram counter; if she discovered she'd deserted her post without her consent, it meant certain expulsion. "I request permission to go to the restroom."

"Again?" Lady Septima hadn't even looked up from her notebook, in which she was busy writing notes.

"I'm really not well. I would prefer not to vomit over Memorial equipment." Ophelia didn't have to fake it. She really did feel nauseous.

"You have five minutes," Lady Septima decreed, still writing away. "And it will be reported in your file. A virtuoso must be *totalement* in control of his or her body."

That was the least of Ophelia's concerns. She went off toward the restrooms, and then changed direction as soon as she was out of view. She went along a series of corridors and arrived at the northern transcendium just as Octavio was about to bring the gangway back with a turn of the key in the post.

"I must go to the Secretarium," she told him, breathlessly. "Just for a minute, please."

Octavio frowned with his thick, black eyebrows. At that

moment, his resemblance to his mother was more striking than ever. "Why?"

Ophelia felt impatience taking over. "Because I must speak with Sir Henry. It's confidential."

"You won't find him at the Secretarium anymore. He's just left it. He's going into town, an airship awaits him."

Ophelia reflected that it was decidedly not her evening. Nothing was going to plan. She went down the transcendium as fast as she physically could. Thorn was just striding through the doors of the atrium; for someone disabled, his pace was impressive. The difference in temperature between the cool of the Memorial and the night outside made Ophelia feel as if she were entering hot water.

She only managed to catch up with Thorn as he was passing in front of the headless soldier. An airship, in silhouette, was preparing its approach, its fuselage gleaming in the moonlight.

"Wait . . . "

Thorn turned when he heard Ophelia. It was the first time she was seeing him in the official uniform of the Lords of LUX. Its gold decorations took on a silvery sheen under the haloes of the streetlamps.

"I'm in a hurry. The Genealogists have summoned me."

"I'll be brief. Why have you done this to me?"

"Do not forget whom you are addressing."

The warning couldn't have been clearer. Right now, Thorn was Sir Henry, and, even if only mimosa surrounded them, they were in a public place. Ophelia didn't care. She could no longer contain the seething emotions consuming her inside.

"Why?" she insisted, her voice choked. "Are you punishing me?"

"You weren't available. Waiting for you would have slowed me down in my research."

Thorn had drawn himself up to his full height and was

looking straight ahead. Out of reach. The detachment of his reasoning increased Ophelia's rage tenfold.

"Slowed you down? For your information, I was also doing research of my own. It might interest you to learn . . . "

"Of your own, that's precisely the problem," he interrupted her. "I advised you never to leave your division, and you were supposed to warn me if you discovered anything new. Nothing has changed, you still always make your decisions alone."

"I wanted to help you," Ophelia hissed, through gritted teeth.

Thorn looked up at the airship, now so close to the ark that its propellers were making all the surrounding mimosas quiver.

"I don't want any of your finer feelings. I need efficiency. If you don't mind, I now have a flight to take."

Ophelia's blood ignited in her every vein. "You're an egoist." She had wanted to anger Thorn, and she knew, by the way he had frozen on the spot, that she had succeeded. All the shadows of the night suddenly seemed to have been drawn to the center of his face. He threw Ophelia a look so hard, she reeled from its impact.

"I am demanding, a killjoy, obsessive, antisocial, and crippled," he intoned, in a forbidding voice. "You can put all the defects in the world on me, but I will not permit you to call me an egoist. If you prefer to do things your way, go ahead," he concluded, slicing the air with his hand, "but don't waste my time anymore." Thorn turned his back on her to join his airship. "Our collaboration is over."

Ophelia knew that one move from her would just make things worse for her. And yet she couldn't stop her hand from shooting out to grab hold of Thorn, force him to turn around, stop him from going any further.

She never reached him. A violent pain shot through her arm like an electric shock. Winded, Ophelia only just held onto the statue of the soldier to stop herself from falling. She stared wide-eyed behind her crooked glasses, as Thorn disappeared into the night with a sinister grating of steel, and without a backward glance.

He had used his claws against her.

# SHADOWS

The pencil flew across the blank sheet of paper. It drew large, dark swirls, darted to the other end of the page, sometimes tearing it with its lead, and then swirled again. Victoria stopped her pencil to look at the result through her long, pale hair.

There was more and more black, and less and less white in her drawings.

"You wouldn't like to use your colored pencils, darling?"

Victoria looked up. Mommy had lifted the lace tablecloth to watch her drawing under the sitting-room table. With a smile, she handed her all the pencils she had avoided using for weeks.

Victoria selected a new sheet of blank paper. She placed it flat on the floor and began to cover it, like all the others, with big, black swirls.

Mommy didn't tell her off. Mommy never told her off. She merely placed the other pencils beside Victoria, on the floor. Then she brushed her cheek with a gentle hand to gather her hair over her shoulder, and put the lace tablecloth back in place.

All Victoria could see now of Mommy was her green satin boots. She would have liked to put the green of Mommy's boots into her drawings. She would have liked to put the blue of her eyes, the pink of her skin, and the blondness of her hair into them, too.

She couldn't. The shadows of the Golden Lady were stronger than all of Mommy's colors.

Since Victoria had seen what she had seen, and even if she didn't understand what exactly she had seen, nothing was the same anymore. She slept only to wake with a start. She had lost her appetite. She had fevers that kept her stuck in bed for days, and when she was better, she preferred to play under the furniture rather than on the cushions.

She no longer *journeyed*.

As soon as she started to feel safe, The Golden Lady returned to the house. Mommy opened her door to her, offered her tea, spoke and laughed with her. The Golden Lady never stayed very long and was no longer interested in Victoria, but each of her visits was enough to add new shadows into the drawings.

Mommy's boots rang out on the parquet floor, on the other side of the tablecloth. They set off, came back toward the table, hesitated a moment, and then set off again.

"Heels alive, calm down!" said Great-Godmother's exasperated voice, at the other end of the sitting room.

Mommy's boots stopped in front of the fireplace, where a log fire was humming away. "I'm a bad mother."

Victoria had barely heard Mommy's murmur above the crackle of the flames. The black lead of her pencil was devouring the paper, inch by inch.

"You're an overanxious mother, that's all."

"Precisely, Madame Rosaline. Everything scares me, all of the time. Steps on stairs, corners of tables, embroidery needles, too tight collars, every mouthful of food: wherever I look, I see danger. If anything at all happened to her . . . I'm so afraid of losing her, too."

Mommy's faint voice caught in her throat. Victoria looked

up from her drawing for a moment to watch the patent shoes of Great-Godmother crossing the floor to join the green satin boots.

"She's fine, Berenilde."

"No, she's not fine. She never smiles anymore, she barely eats, she's tormented by terrible dreams. It's because of me, you understand? I know what they say up there, at the court. They speak of her as retarded." Mommy's voice had become even fainter. "The truth is that, on the contrary, she's highly sensitive. She feels what I feel, and me, I just keep contaminating her with my anxieties. I'm a bad mother, Madame Rosaline."

"Look at me."

There was a long silence in the sitting room, and then Mommy's boots turned, one after the other, toward Great-Godmother's shoes.

"You've given up all the mischief of your old life to devote yourself to your daughter. You are a good mother, but you can't create a family all on your own. He has his role to play, too."

"I always thought that, somewhere, deep inside him, he . . . Well, I hoped that for his daughter . . . "

"He will come. He will come because you have asked him to, and because his place, today, is here with you, not with all those ministers. And if he doesn't come, well, it's me, personally, who will go and fetch him!"

Victoria squeezed the pencil in her fist tighter. *He will come?* Were they talking about Godfather? If there was truly one person in the world who could make all the shadows fly away, it was him!

The bell of the house sang out, in unison with Victoria's heart.

"Ah, you see?" Great-Godmother said.

From under the lace tablecloth, Victoria saw both pairs of

footwear hastily leaving the sitting room. A few moments later, snatches of conversation reached her from the music room:

"Our Lord has an extremely busy schedule . . . holding a plenary meeting on the forty-seventh floor . . . which is, may I remind you, still waiting to be ratified . . . "

This voice, drowning out Mommy's soft one, it wasn't Godfather's.

Victoria was tempted, for just a tick-tock from the sitting-room clock, to *journey*, so as to see for herself what was going on. She did not do it. *Journeying* meant seeing things that mustn't be seen.

The conversations in the music room suddenly stopped. Victoria pricked up her ears, her black pencil frozen in the middle of her drawing. The strip of parquet she was sitting on suddenly rocked, like a wave of water. There was a loud creaking of wood, soon followed by a second one. Someone was walking in the room.

Victoria knew who it was even before seeing, beyond the lace tablecloth, the two big, white boots that were moving slowly, very slowly, across the sitting room.

It was Father.

Victoria hoped, as hard as she could, that he wouldn't notice her presence under the table, but then Mommy pulled her out of her hiding place. She sat her in an armchair close to the door, combed her hair, smoothed her dress, gave her a final, fond smile, and then went back into the corridor, where a man was repeating: "Our Lord has an extremely busy schedule." Had Victoria been able to speak, she would have screamed to them not to leave her alone with Father.

He moved slowly, very slowly to the other end of the sitting room, as far away as possible from Victoria's armchair. He was so tall, he knocked into the crystal chandelier, but there was nothing funny about it. He went over to a window, and its weak light made his profile expressionless, and his over-the-shoulder plait and fur coat even whiter than they already were.

Father looked like the lovely statues in the garden that he was now looking at. He had the same blank eyes. Eyes that, to Victoria, seemed to be absent.

"How old are you, now?"

Once, Victoria had brought both hands down on the lowest keys of the harpsichord in the house. Father's mouth produced an even deeper sound.

"How old are you?" he repeated.

Victoria understood the question; answering it was another matter. Father didn't like her, and he would end up liking her even less. Mommy had stayed in the corridor to ask Mr. Schedule just to wait.

Father finally pulled a notebook from inside his big, white coat. He leafed through the pages, one by one. After an interminable silence, he declared: "Ah, yes. You don't speak."

He returned to perusing his notebook for many tick-tocks from the sitting-room clock. Had he forgotten Victoria altogether?

"Your mother wrote this to me," he suddenly said, placing his finger on a page, "that your health causes her concern. You don't look that sickly to me."

Father's majestic figure didn't move, still facing the window, but his face swiveled round like a screw, as if his neck could turn entirely on itself. The moment he laid his expressionless eyes on her, Victoria got a terrible headache.

"If one excludes the fact, of course, that you are incapable of talking and walking."

The more Father looked at her, the more Victoria's head hurt. He was punishing her, and if he was punishing her, she must be at fault. She was afraid. Afraid that he would never like her.

She felt a tear rolling down her cheek, but didn't dare wipe it away. Father stared in amazement, before turning his eyes back to the window. The pain immediately stopped.

"It wasn't deliberate. My power . . . You're probably not yet ready to endure it. This meeting is premature."

Victoria didn't know what Father was trying to explain to her. She didn't even know whether he was actually talking to her. He always used words that were too complicated.

"I'm not going to impose my presence on you any longer." At the precise moment he uttered this sentence, the bell of the house rang again. There was the sound of footsteps and stifled whispers. A prisoner in her armchair, Victoria waited with Father. Her dress had stuck to her body due to perspiration.

She froze when a strong perfume prickled her nose.

"My Lord! I was making a little courtesy visit to my dear friends, but I had no idea you were here. I just wanted to pay you my respects."

Victoria was shaking, violently. The Golden Lady was there, right behind her. The pendants on her veil were tinkling ever louder as she moved through the sitting room.

"And you are?"

Father had asked his question without a glance at the Golden Lady. He seemed to find the candy jar on the windowsill more worthy of interest.

"It's Madame Cunegond, my Lord. One of your finest illusionists." Mommy's arrival in the sitting room did nothing to calm Victoria down. She was terrified. The Golden Lady had just placed a hand on her armchair, her fingernails digging into the velvet like long, red knives.

"You're sorry . . . or rather, it's I who should be sorry. I didn't mean to disturb your little family reunion." The Golden Lady stroked Victoria's white hair. It was with that very hand that she had closed the eyelids of the Second Golden Lady. She was so close that she had plunged Victoria entirely in her shadow.

In her shadows.

Victoria ran to hide under the table. She had *journeyed* out of panic, abandoning the Other-Victoria in her armchair and her sweat-soaked dress. The Golden Lady's glittering veil was still visible from under the tablecloth, beside Mommy's green satin boots and Great-Godmother's patent shoes. The pounding of the Other-Victoria's heart had become as distant as their conversation, but the fear continued to scream inside her, with all the strength of its silence.

A new pair of shoes invited themselves into the sitting room. Even though the *journey* had shaken her up, Victoria recognized the voice of Mr. Schedule:

"I can't apologize enough for hurrying you like this, my Lord. You are expected at the meeting. It's just that, my Lord has an extremely busy schedule!"

Victoria heard the parquet cracking like a burning log. Father's big, white boots moved slowly, very slowly toward the table. To Victoria's horror, the parquet creaked even louder as Father leaned forward. With the tips of his fingers—giant fingers—he lifted the lace tablecloth.

"Oh, they're only drawings," Mommy said. "The little one often settles there to play. Don't you, darling?"

Father's eyes, pale as porcelain, were interested neither in the Other-Victoria in her armchair nor in the drawings on the floor. They were focused only on the real Victoria, hiding under the table.

Could Father see her?

"My Lord," murmured Mr. Schedule, with an impatient little cough. "Your meeting . . . "

"Leave."

Father had barely moved his lips. He was still bending

forward, tablecloth pinched between fingers, long plait flowing like milk to the ground.

"Immediately."

"My Lord?" Mommy inquired anxiously. "Has something vexed you?"

Huddled under the table, Victoria was staring at Father in amazement. She had always believed that he didn't like her, but never had he looked at her the way he was now looking at the Golden Lady.

Thanks to her *journeying* eyes, Victoria could see Father's shadow. A shadow even bigger and even more clawed than Mommy's when she was angry. A shadow whose spikes all bristled in the Golden Lady's direction.

"I don't know who you are," Father said, stressing each word, "but never enter this residence again."

Since he was still holding up the tablecloth, Victoria could observe the astonished faces of Mommy, Great-Godmother, and Mr. Schedule, all turning toward the Golden Lady. She was smiling with those red lips, but she had stopped stroking the Other-Victoria's hair. Her own shadows were swarming around her feet like an enraged mob. There were so many of them! Were they going to attack Father?

"As I please. Or, I should say, as you please."

To a chorus of jewelry, the Golden Lady left the sitting room, and all the shadows left with her.

Victoria didn't listen to the exclamations that erupted in the room after her departure. She had taken back the Other-Victoria's place in the armchair, and now only had eyes for Father. With slow, very slow movements, he gathered up the drawings and pencils under the table, and then he handed them to her, paying no attention to all the questions Mommy, Great-Godmother, and Mr. Schedule were asking him.

Victoria looked at the shadows she had scrawled a bit earlier. She turned her page over. On this side, the paper was pure white.

As white as Father.

# THE DUST

Ophelia had come across several waiting rooms in her life, but none of them resembled this one. A eucalyptus tree stood bang in the middle of the carpet, and there were budgerigars chirping on the backs of benches. The Deviations Observatory certainly was a most astonishing place.

When Blaise had mentioned it to her, Ophelia had imagined some sinister hospital. She now found it to be a building full of color, in which the jungle was integral to the design. Its pagodas, bridges, conservatories, and terraces formed such a sprawling complex that the observatory took up a minor ark all to itself. She had no idea what exactly the "deviations" observed here might be, but those responsible for the place clearly had considerable means.

Ophelia didn't have to wait long. She had only just sat on a bench when an adolescent came to greet her. Wearing a yellow silk sari, pince-nez with dark lenses, and long leather gloves, she had a mechanical monkey on her shoulder. Ophelia would never have taken her to be a member of staff had she not indicated that she should follow her.

"Welcome to our establishment, Mademoiselle Eulalia! The patient has been taken to the visitors' conservatory; allow me to take you there. You're the first person to visit the poor

316

Mademoiselle Mediana," the adolescent whispered, once they had left the waiting room.

"I'm using my Sunday off to visit my classmate."

"Unfortunately, we can't allow you more than five minutes with her. I'm sure it will do her good to see the face of a friend."

Ophelia refrained from disillusioning her. "It was Lady Septima who left her in your care?"

"And who took on all the treatment costs. A real saint, that Lady Septima! Praised be the Lords of LUX!"

The young Babelian spoke with true religious zeal. Her every smile was like a ray of light across her night-dark skin. As Ophelia followed her along a corridor, she found herself envying her. For her part, she felt as if she would never smile again.

*Our collaboration is over.*

She banished Thorn's words from her mind. Above all, no thinking. Action.

"What exactly is Mediana suffering from? I was told something about a stroke, but it wasn't entirely clear."

The adolescent's smile widened and her eyes twinkled above the dark lenses of her pince-nez. "*Désolée, mademoiselle*, I'm not authorized to reply to that question."

"But isn't that the specialty of your observatory, cases like hers?"

"*Désolée, mademoiselle*, I'm not authorized to reply to that question." On the adolescent's shoulder, the mechanical monkey suddenly made a move, handing her a notepad.

"Aha, I see we already have a file in your name, Mademoiselle Eulalia."

"In my name?" Ophelia asked, with surprise. "It must be a mistake."

The adolescent burst into laughter as she leafed through

her notepad. "We never make mistakes, Mademoiselle Eulalia, we're very well informed. We have our own Forerunners at the conservatoire," she added, with a knowing glance at the wings on Ophelia's boots. "To return to your file, it would seem you had a medical checkup when you entered the Good Family conservatoire. Your test results were communicated to us and, from what I read here, they appear . . . interesting. You have five minutes," the adolescent reminded her, opening a glass door. "I'll be in the corridor, if you need me."

Ophelia just stood there. Medical tests the day of her admission? All she remembered was having done some pointless movements, and fifteen laps of the track, which had almost killed her. She really couldn't see how that could be of any interest to anyone.

She put it aside as she entered the visitors' conservatory. Huge stained-glass windows turned the sunlight into a rainbow. The colors bounced off the tiles, mingled with the branches of the palm trees, and skimmed the water of the fish pools. The serenity of the place almost made one forget the wind outside, rattling every pane in its frame.

Mediana was seated on a bench. She was hunched over, legs drawn up, eyes wide open. She didn't react to the familiar sound of Forerunner wings as Ophelia approached and sat beside her.

"Hello."

Mediana didn't respond. At first, Ophelia thought she was gazing at the stained-glass window opposite the bench, but her eyes were transfixed in their sockets. What Mediana was looking at was within herself. She was barely recognizable, in her baggy pajamas. Her muscles had wasted away, leaving her just skin and bone. Where had her strength gone? Where had her grace and pride gone? The light of the stained-glass window made the precious stones embedded in her face glimmer; so many colors on this soulless body, it was almost indecent.

Feeling awkward, Ophelia struggled to find the right words. "You're probably wondering what brings me here. Your departure from the Good Family was so sudden . . . You left many questions in your wake."

Mediana still didn't respond. With her arms wrapped tightly around her legs, she continued to stare into space, like a stone gargoyle.

"You know that you're still causing me problems?" Ophelia murmured. "Your cousins are giving me a hard time. You always said they detested you, but, believe me, they're making me pay a high price for having taken your place."

Still no response whatsoever.

Ophelia turned on the bench. There was no one but them inside the conservatory, and yet she had the continuous feeling of being watched behind her back.

"What happened in the Memorial restrooms?" she then asked, in a tiny voice. "Who did that to you?"

Still silence.

"I really must know," Ophelia insisted. "Did you discover something about a book? A book by E. G., perhaps?" she suggested, to Mediana's expressionless face. "*The Era of Miracles?*"

Still nothing. Ophelia took a breath; she had one last card to lay on the table. "'He who sows the wind shall reap the storm.' It was Fearless who asked me to give you that message. Was he the one who put you into this state?"

She waited a long time for a reaction, hoping that at least that name would have some effect, but Mediana didn't even blink. A fly settled on her bottom lip, as though she were now but a corpse. Ophelia had promised herself never to feel sorry for her, not after her blackmailing and manipulating. And yet, seeing her like this upset her.

"So, is that it?" she chided her, quietly. "You're going to spend the rest of your life in pajamas on a bench? You were dreaming of becoming a Forerunner, you wanted to know everything. The Mediana I knew would already be looking for a new secret."

"Mademoiselle Eulalia?"

At the other end of the conservatory, the adolescent had opened the door and, with a big smile, was indicating to her to leave. "*Désolée, mademoiselle*, your five minutes are up."

Ophelia rose reluctantly from the bench. Or rather, attempted to rise. Mediana's hand clutched at her frock coat to stop her. Nothing in her demeanor had changed. The same wide-open eyes staring into space, the same rigid body, but her lips mouthed two words: "An other."

"Sorry?" Ophelia leaned toward Mediana, to look her, at last, in the eye. All she saw there was a terror so intense, her own stomach clenched.

"An other . . . there's an other one."

"An other what?"

Mediana's only response was to let go of her and sink back into her silence.

"Mademoiselle Eulalia!" the adolescent called out, cheerily. "The visit's over!"

Ophelia had come to the Deviations Observatory to get answers. She left it with an additional question: so what was this new "other"? One thing, at least, seemed clear to her, as she descended the big marble staircase leading to the birdtrain stop. Mediana, Mademoiselle Silence, and Professor Wolf now really did share one thing in common: terror.

The wind proved particularly fierce around the platform's belvedere, due to the proximity of the void. It whipped up eddies of dust so dense, one could see and hear practically nothing. The Deviations Observatory wasn't a frequently served destination; one had to be patient between one birdtrain and the next. And patience was something Ophelia felt short of. As soon as she stopped doing things, thoughts returned with a vengeance.

*Our collaboration is over.*

Thorn had pushed her away. With his words and with his claws. Ophelia felt drier than the dust stinging her eyes. She missed him. She'd never stopped missing him, even when beside him. She'd not managed to keep her position of collaborator; she'd not understood at all what he really expected of her. She had hoped to get from him what he could no longer give her. Even now, she was clinging to her inquiry and delving into Babel's hidden corners, when, in fact, it was still Thorn she was looking for.

Ophelia stiffened. Through the flurry of dust hitting her glasses, she discerned a figure on the platform. It could be just another traveler, but he seemed to be watching her intensely. Suddenly, the figure made straight for her, with rapid steps. Suddenly, Ophelia became conscious of the void's proximity. In a flash, she thought of the misfortune that had struck all those whose mysteries she wanted to unlock. Mediana's fear, Mademoiselle Silence's fear, and Professor Wolf's fear became her own fear.

"What are you doing here?"

Ophelia recognized the voice, full of mistrust, through the din of the wind. The figure before her was Octavio. He had lifted his jacket over his head to protect himself, which made him seem bigger than he really was. His gift as a Visionary had allowed him to recognize Ophelia, despite the belvedere's poor visibility.

"You followed me?" he asked, insistently. "What do you want of me?"

"That you calm down. I came to visit Mediana. And you?"

There was a long, tense silence, and then:

"Don't tell my mother you saw me here."

It could have seemed like an order, but Octavio's voice had gone from hostile to anxious.

"You, you're asking me to lie? I thought honesty was a civic duty in Babel." Ophelia was spluttering more than speaking; she swallowed dust with every intake of breath. She jumped at the screech of the birdtrain's wheels as it landed on the track beside the platform. Perched on the carriage roofs, the giant birds remained heroically docile, despite the storm.

Ophelia and Octavio dived inside. They each punched their card, sat on a bench, and spent several minutes dusting down their clothes, without exchanging a word or a look. There was just one other passenger in their carriage, and he was so soundly asleep that his turban had toppled at his feet.

"Lying is a sin," Octavio declared, once the birdtrain had taken off. "So I'm going to ask you what I asked the staff at the observatory. If my mother questions you, tell her the truth. In such a circumstance, I would appreciate your discretion."

She sneaked a few glances at him. The long, black fringe he usually hid behind was in a mess. His face had lost its imperial serenity. Even his eyes, resolutely turned to the window, had a less proud glint to them. Octavio was clenching his fists on his thighs, as if he suddenly felt in a position of inferiority. Humiliated.

Ophelia had always seen him as a replica of Lady Septima. Knowing that he was capable of disobeying his mother, a Lord of LUX what's more, made him seem less disagreeable to her. She wasn't ready to trust him, all the same.

"If I must help you to hide something, I would at least like to know what it's about. What were you doing at the Deviations Observatory at the same time as me?"

"It's rather you who were there at the same time as me," Octavio remarked, haughtily. "I go there every Sunday." He bit his lip, as though hesitating to reveal any more. "I was visiting my sister."

Ophelia had been ready for all sorts of revelations, but certainly not that one. "You have a sister?"

"She's called Second. She is . . . different. She always has been."

Octavio turned abruptly from the window to look straight at Ophelia, defying her to mock him.

She had no desire to do so. "I, too, have a little sister who is different. She barely speaks, but she knows exactly how to make herself understood, all the same. There's no shame in that."

She realized, just as she was confiding this, that she'd been talking as Ophelia, and no longer as Eulalia. At least her sincerity had the merit of calming Octavio, whose fists had relaxed on his thighs.

"And your father?" she asked, cautiously. "Does he also forbid you from seeing your sister?"

"*En fait*, I haven't spoken to him in years. He left my mother shortly after Second was born. As my parents saw it, giving birth to an imperfect child cast dishonor on all of Pollux's descendants. My mother finally decided that the best place for Second was this observatory, where they can study her case. So my sister serves the city in her own way."

"You disapprove."

Ophelia had only made a simple observation, but it was like a slap in the face to Octavio, who glared at her with renewed defiance, his golden chain swinging from his eyebrow.

"It's not for me to approve or disapprove. My mother has always placed herself at the service of family interest."

Ophelia wiped her glasses on the equally dusty sleeve of her uniform. To what extent was Octavio aware of the forces actually hiding behind this "family interest"? He'd been endowed with phenomenal powers of observation, but as soon as Lady Septima was involved, he became blind.

"Anyhow, I wasn't asking for your opinion," he added, straightening up, stiffly, on the bench. "The fact is that my mother deems it preferable that Second and I live our lives separately. All I ask of you is to say nothing to her of my visits, unless she asks you questions, *directement*."

"I will say nothing to her," Ophelia promised. Even if she does ask me any."

They both went quiet. During this awkward silence, all that could be heard was the beating of the birds' wings, the grating of sand against the windows, and the snoring of the third passenger. Ophelia couldn't shake off the unpleasant feeling of a presence behind her back, but however often she turned around, there was no one on that bench.

"The conservatoire students are all using their last day off to make a final effort," Octavio suddenly resumed. "And you, you visit Mediana. I never got the feeling you were on such good terms with her."

Ophelia shrugged. "I can't see the point of revising, since there's no actual exam to become an aspiring virtuoso. Lady Helen and Sir Pollux judge us on our overall performance."

"I was told that Mediana is no longer able to communicate. What did you want from her?"

Ophelia sensed Octavio's insistent stare on her. She wasn't going to shake him off just like that. "I'm trying to figure out who did that to her and why. I presume that you, like your mother, are going to tell me that there's nothing to figure out."

"You presume wrong. I believe that we're all in danger. My mother included."

Ophelia stopped rubbing her glasses to put them back, dirtier than ever, on her nose. Octavio's eyebrows had gone from circumflex accents to grave ones. He looked very serious.

"Professor Wolf," she recalled. "You knew that he had been threatened. You warned me that it could happen to me, too."

"I didn't know it, but I supposed it. What happened to Mademoiselle Silence and Mediana only confirmed my suspicions. There's someone who is taking malicious pleasure in mistreating those who get too involved with the Memorial."

"Fearless-and-Almost-Blameless?"

"*Bien sûr*, who else? That agitator flouts our most sacred laws with his incitement. He implants in people's minds what the Lords of LUX have strived to purge for decades: unwholesome, aggressive, and degrading ideas. It's that individual who should find himself in the Deviations Observatory."

Octavio had spoken with supreme composure, but Ophelia wasn't fooled. His eyes were glowing red as if, through the sides of the carriage and the miles of clouds, he were pursuing Fearless in person. He was consumed from within by embers just waiting to burst into flame.

Ophelia wondered if he was aware of this, but the question that came to her lips was completely different:

"Have you ever read E. G.'s books?"

She instantly regretted her imprudence. Too often, her curiosity impelled her to ask the right questions to the wrong people.

"Those old children's tales?" Octavio asked, with astonishment. "I browsed through them when I was a kid. You'll find the entire collection at the Memorial."

Either he was a great actor, or he was unaware of the fate Mademoiselle Silence had reserved for those books.

"And what did you think of *The Era of Miracles*?"

"It's not the best book in the collection. It's a tale that describes the beginnings of the new world. That 'E. G.' was an author of no great originality. Why are you interested in those books? Surely Sir Henry hasn't asked you to evaluate them, has he?"

At this mention of Thorn, Ophelia felt a sudden crack between her ribs. She focused on the metallic rumbling of the birdtrain, to allow the pain to pass.

"And what if we paid a visit to Professor Wolf?" she suddenly suggested. "We could ask him whether, yes or no, Fearless used scare tactics on him."

"Together?"

Octavio seemed completely taken aback. Ophelia was no less so. Before this moment, she'd never envisaged associating with the son of a Lord of LUX, but, on reflection, it wasn't such a crazy idea. Octavio had more influence than she did; maybe he would open doors that would have remained closed to her. Starting with Professor Wolf's.

"Yes, together."

# THE RED

They alighted at the next station to take a public gondola. The Zephyr sailing it had enough experience to channel the wind and bring them across the sea of clouds with no turbulence, but Ophelia was still relieved to return to terra firma. Professor Wolf's neighborhood was unpaved, and wind and sand became so intermingled, they formed burning fumaroles. The sun was now reduced to nothing more than a pale moon in the middle of the sky. So suffocating was the atmosphere, there were neither passersby nor dodos in the streets.

Ophelia crossed the courtyard of the building, a sleeve pressed to her nose to avoid breathing in the dust. Her glasses seemed to be smeared in volcanic soot. She could only just make out the foliage-shrouded facade before her. The ground-floor door's knocker didn't strike of its own accord at her approach, as it had on her first visit. For such a paranoid door, this was unexpected.

Indicating to Octavio to stand clearly in view of the spyhole, she gave three cautious little knocks.

"Professor Wolf?"

She didn't feel proud to be visiting him once again. This Animist, cantankerous as he might be, had helped her to procure some reader's gloves. And she, she had thanked him by rummaging in his wastepaper basket. So it was no surprise to see the door remain closed.

"Professor Wolf?" she insisted. "We need to speak to you, it's very important."

Ophelia pressed her ear to the door. She heard not a sound from inside the apartment.

"His landlady assured me that he never left his home," she said. "Try your luck, he may think better of you."

Octavio did no such thing. He moved back a few steps. With hair reddened with dust, and frock coat flapping in the wind, he was studying the building's facade with great concentration, as the red glow of his eyes intensified.

"Pointless," he finally declared. "He's not at home."

"You can see through walls?"

"If I adapt my vision, I can detect the radiation of warm-blooded creatures. There's nothing of that sort here."

"So we're stuck," she sighed.

Octavio frowned as he slowly swiveled around, this time scanning the cloud of dust. "And surrounded," he muttered.

It took a moment for Ophelia to see them herself: white figures were emerging from all four corners of the courtyard. Each one carried a gun.

"Prohibited items," Octavio remarked, disdainfully. "The powerless have fallen pretty low."

A roar of laughter greeted this statement. It reverberated across the walls of the old buildings, as though coming from all directions at once. Ophelia tensed, from head to toe. To her knowledge, only one man was endowed with vocal cords that powerful. Fearless's form detached itself from the red blizzard as he moved calmly toward them. He wasn't armed. He didn't need to be. The giant saber-toothed tiger served as his escort.

"How do you recognize a Lord's son?" Fearless shouted to the assembled company. "It's *vrrraiment* easy! It strolls around all high and mighty, makes its pretty boots jingle loud and clear, and still manages to play it condescending!"

His voice was so loud, it rose above the storm, but when he stopped in front of Octavio, the latter made it clear that he wasn't remotely impressed. He faced him without batting an eyelid, back straight and chin high, just as if there weren't several guns pointed at him.

"So you're the man who calls himself Fearless-and-Almost-Blameless? I'm disappointed. I've often heard you bragging on the radio; I imagined you to be less ordinary."

A carnivorous smile briefly uncovered Fearless's teeth. He might look like a puny, balding man, but there was a wild beast crouching within him, and it was no less fearsome than the Beast now growling beside him.

Ophelia's eyes darted in all directions. The building's court-yard was a dead end; they were cornered. The billowing dust allowed brief glimpses, here and there, of the silhouettes of the armed men. Ophelia counted them. Four, six, eight . . . at least ten. Plus a giant tiger. She tilted her glasses up at the walls surrounding them; the few shutters she could make out were closed. There were doubtless people watching, eyes pressed between the slats, but none of them, not even the landlady, seemed inclined to get involved.

Ophelia was starting to regret having dragged Octavio here. Thorn was right, she really did have a preternatural predisposition to disasters.

"What do you want?" she asked.

Fearless's eyes barely registered her, as if she were insubstantial. Only Octavio was of interest to him.

"That's my question. You seem *vrrraiment* keen to chat with me. Unless, of course," he added, with a mocking pout, "you fear I will contaminate you with my 'unwholesome, aggressive, and degrading ideas'?"

Octavio's eyes blazed even more. "Those are my exact words. You spied on us?"

"I'm going to tell you something, *garçon*. When one is an old pirate of the airwaves like me, one picks up little habits. I have a tendency to scatter my microphones here and there. You make me *vrrraiment* laugh, you Forerunners! You claim to know everything, but you know nothing. The censors are just siphoning out your brains!"

Fearless was standing so close to Octavio that he spat the last word right in his face. He reveled in the disgust he aroused in him.

"Did you threaten the lives of Professor Wolf, Mademoiselle Silence, and Apprentice Mediana?"

Ophelia looked at Octavio with both admiration and exasperation. He had asked his question straight out, in a supercilious tone, as if he dictated the rules. He didn't flinch when Fearless flicked at the gold chain that signified his filiation to Lady Septima.

"You already see yourself as a Lord, but you're not even a man. You'll never be one as long as you haven't shoved your fist into someone's face. Did she never teach you that, your mommy? Too unwholesome, aggressive, and degrading for you? Admit it, though, you're *vrrraiment* itching to do that right now!"

Fearless's voice produced such strong vibrations, Ophelia could even feel them in her stomach. He really couldn't fear anyone, to insult a Son of Pollux like this, in the middle of a public place.

Octavio took a handkerchief from his frock coat and wiped the spittle from his skin. "I won't lower myself to respond to such provocation. I command you, you and these gentlemen, to face justice and, in future, behave like 'decent citizens.'"

Fearless's burst of laughter sounded like an actual powder

keg exploding. A moment later, he had returned to being deadly serious. He made a sign to his men to lower their arms, and then, in a flash, he ripped the chain off Octavio's face. Ophelia heaved on seeing the blood spurt out.

"You've *vrrraiment* got a nerve," Fearless growled, with a look of disgust. "Do you have the slightest idea of the insult you're inflicting on these people by strutting about in your fine uniform? Your future is all mapped out. They don't have one, and do you know why? Because it's the spoilt-rotten brats like you who end up governing the city. And it's them, also, who choose to give work to machines rather than to 'decent citizens.'"

Octavio refused the hand Ophelia had rushed to offer him. He straightened up, proudly, clenching his jaw so as not to cry out with pain. A lump of flesh was missing from his brow and his nostril was torn in two. His blood mingled with the dust on the ground, but its redness was nothing compared with that glowing in his eyes.

"I can see it," Fearless goaded him, twirling the gold chain around his fingers. "The violence that you so despise, its rumbling away inside you. You can cover it up all you like with your fine manners, it will always be there. You're like me, deep down. A wild beast."

Octavio wiped his bloodied face just as he had removed the spittle shortly before: with an attitude full of superiority. "Do not compare me to you."

"That's enough," Ophelia whispered to him. "We're going."

Fearless looked her up and down, without a word. The howling of the wind, scratching of the dust, and growling of the tiger took over during this brief silence.

"That's fine," he finally decided. "I'll let you clear off. On one condition."

His hand shot out, fast as an arrow. He grabbed Ophelia by

the hair and forced her to her knees. She felt as if the skin of her scalp were about to tear.

"Take off your uniform, lambkin."

She couldn't see clearly anymore. Her glasses were dangling across her face. She wanted to get back on her feet, but Fearless forced her to stay on her knees. He was pulling her hair with an astonishingly strong grip for someone so slight.

"Take off your uniform," he repeated. "Frock coat, shirt, trousers, boots, *tout*! If you're a good girl, I'll leave you your reader's gloves."

Ophelia wasn't particularly modest. She dressed and undressed every day in the Good Family changing rooms. And yet, the thought of being forced to do so here, in such a position and in front of all these men, made her feel sick. Even Octavio was left speechless.

"Take off your uniform," Fearless roared, shaking her, "or I'll ask my friends to see to it."

Ophelia's vision blurred, and it wasn't just down to near-sightedness. Why didn't her claws repel this hand that was hurting her? Why were they never activated when she most needed them? The answer hit her right in the stomach. Because she was frightened. The claws were linked to her nervous system. Anger galvanized them; fear paralyzed them.

Fearless had got it right. She was just a lamb. All the ordeals she'd endured in the Pole, far from hardening her, they had made her more fragile.

Ophelia straightened her glasses with what dignity she still had, and unbuttoned her frock coat. Thanks to her incurable clumsiness, this simple daily activity always demanded great perseverance. Shaking didn't help; Ophelia had to struggle with each button. She hoped Fearless wouldn't notice—she had no desire to give him that satisfaction.

The wind scratched at her bare arms when she let her shirt fall and was left in just a vest.

"Your trousers."

Ophelia battled with nausea as she felt Fearless's order vibrating the length of her spine. That voice hurt her even more than the fist pulling her hair. Just as her fingers were getting caught in the buckle of her belt, she was thrown by the exasperated sigh let out by Fearless.

"I'm *vrrraiment* hoping the spectacle will be worth the wai . . ."

Fearless didn't finish his sentence. Octavio had just hit him square on the jaw. There was a cracking of bone so loud, it seemed to come from both fingers and teeth. The strength of the punch threw them both to the ground. Quick as a flash, Octavio crouched over Fearless to pin him to the ground, and then brought his fists down on him again and again. His face had completely disappeared under a mass of black hair. His body was now just rage in its raw state, as wild as the elements all around him.

The harder he hit, the more Fearless roared with laughter. "Splendid, *garçon*! Go for it! Let the wild beast out!"

Ophelia leapt to her boots, but didn't get a chance to intervene. The saber-toothed tiger, which until then had been still as a statue, stretched out like a spring; its enormous paw sent Octavio rolling into the haze. Ophelia ran over to him. He was curled up on the ground, red with dust and blood. The fire in his eyes had gone out. He had no obvious serious wound, but the blow had stunned him.

Fearless's voice crowed over the commotion of the wind: "He *vrrraiment* did it! Ha, ha, ha! He crossed the red line!"

Ophelia swiftly removed the wings from both her feet and Octavio's, and slipped them into her pocket. Now that hostilities were open, they had to escape. Their enemies were lying in wait, somewhere within the storm. They would locate them from the slightest clatter.

Just as she was slinging Octavio's arm over her shoulders, a gunshot rang out. The bang echoed all around the smoke-filled courtyard, rebounding on the facades of the buildings. Ophelia didn't think she'd been hit, but her veins were throbbing at such a pace, she was no longer sure of anything.

"Who fired?" Fearless bellowed. "I said: await orders!"

He was no longer laughing at all. His men's voices protested, each one asserting that it wasn't him. Ophelia didn't understand what was going on, but was determined to take advantage of this diversion. She led Octavio, feeling her way forward. Still dazed, he was struggling to walk straight. She herself could see no more than three steps ahead. She was disorientated. She swallowed sand whenever she breathed in.

A scream stopped her in her tracks; a howl of horror such as she'd never heard in all her life.

Fearless's voice. It ripped through the air like an explosion, eclipsing the wind and the dust. Ophelia and Octavio put their hands over their ears. The entire courtyard was now reduced to one long, never-ending scream.

Then the voice went quiet.

Octavio showed Ophelia a lofty form looming in the haze. The saber-toothed tiger was there, right in front of them. It was prostrate on the ground, ears flattened back, coat bristling, eyes round as two headlamps.

Terrorized.

Ophelia tripped on a body lying on its back. It took a few heartbeats before she recognized Fearless. The skin on his face was distorted, like an ancient mask of tragedy. His mouth screamed in silence. His bulging eyes stared at nothing.

"Dead," Octavio whispered.

"Killed," a voice behind them corrected.

Professor Wolf suddenly appeared through the storm, eerie as a specter. He was clad all in black, his neck brace making him stiff as a cadaver, and his goatee smelt strongly of singe-ing. Slung across his shoulder was an old blunderbuss, the muzzle of which seemed to have exploded. It must have come from him, that gunshot.

He handed Ophelia her frock coat, having picked it up on his way. "Follow me, you two," he ordered between his teeth. "The person behind this could still be around. Believe me, you don't want to meet him."

# THE DATING

Professor Wolf guided them through the dense haze. When Ophelia lost sight of him, she followed the crunching of his shoes. She could trust only her ears. There was not a sound, not a cry anymore, beyond the wind. What had become of Fearless's men? Had they run away? Were they dead?

And the killer? Was he still here, somewhere in the courtyard?

Ophelia bit into her sleeve to stop herself from coughing. The dust was suffocating her, blinding her, deafening her . . .

She bumped into Octavio when he suddenly stopped in front of her. The professor had led them to the wall of a building. "Climb up," he muttered. "Quickly."

Ophelia saw the safety ladder that led up to the roof. She clambered up the rungs, one by one, slipping on the moss, buffeted by the squalls. The higher she got, the less thick the dust became. When she reached the final rung, she was out of breath, but breathing freely again. She helped Octavio to hoist himself up in turn; the blood seeping from his brow and nose was congealing down one side of his face.

The roof was a vast terrace of lavender, undulating in the wind like a sea. Professor Wolf waded warily through its waves. His black clothes, hair, and goatee were like an ink stain against the surrounding colors. With his neck brace preventing him from turning his head around, he turned instead on his heels to indicate to Ophelia and Octavio to hurry up, and, at the same time, to check they weren't being followed.

The various roofs were linked to each other by stone arches. There was a bit of everything growing on them: rosemary trees, bay trees, lemon trees, but also nettles and creepers. Seen from the ground, the neighborhood was but a world of dust; seen from up there, it became a labyrinthine jungle.

The professor went up some stairs leading to a raised old greenhouse. Its door was so rusty, he had to force it open with his shoulder, and he muttered many an Animist curse before successfully closing it behind them. He then blocked the entrance with his blunderbuss. The greenhouse had been invaded by weeds and flies. Rags of many colors plugged the gaps left by missing panes of glass. The wind whistled through all the cracks, but that sound felt like silence after the commotion outside.

Ophelia collapsed onto the edge of an empty sink. She massaged her still-painful scalp; her curls had taken on dramatic proportions.

"Are you going to tell us what . . . "

"Be quiet now," Professor Wolf cut in. "I'm trying to concentrate."

He had pressed his eye to a telescope to observe the courtyard, which the greenhouse overlooked from high up. Ophelia peered through the dirty panes: all she could see of the world below were red whirlwinds, swelling, undulating, collapsing, and rising up again in a relentless dance. She almost couldn't believe that they had been trapped down there just moments ago.

She rinsed her glasses under the sink's tap. Around her she noticed an arsenal of old weapons among the plants, as well as a camp bed, cans of food, china, and piles of books.

The professor had turned this abandoned greenhouse into a bunker.

Ophelia was concerned about Octavio's silence. He had slumped in a corner, legs drawn up, in the middle of some ferns. Clutching his knees with both hands, he was trying to control the shaking of his fingers, which were swollen from punching. His fringe concealed his face, like a curtain.

Ophelia looked for a container. Here, just as in Professor Wolf's apartment, objects were as shy as those crabs that scuttle into rock cavities. She just caught hold of a tin bowl, as it tried to hide behind a cactus. She filled it to the brim with water and then, holding it down, dipped a handkerchief in it for cleaning up Octavio's blood. He let her proceed without protest; his eyes stared at a particular spot, to one side, studiously avoiding meeting hers. All of his pride seemed to have been torn from him, along with his gold chain.

"Thank you," she murmured to him. "I won't forget what you did for me."

Octavio's mouth twisted into a bitter smile. "I'm not half as heroic as you suggest. I wanted to hit him the moment he stood in front of me. *Vraiment* wanted to. Even now that he's dead, I still want to. Because he saw through me more clearly than my own eyes do. If my mother were to hear about what I did . . . She will hear about it," he immediately corrected, a look of profound self-disgust etched on his face. "I'll tell her about it myself."

Ophelia stared at the reddened water in the bowl, which was still resisting her grip. How many secrets, how many thoughts had she concealed from her own mother to avoid being judged? She took out the wings she'd kept in her pocket, to return them to Octavio.

"It's true," she said. "You're a good person."

Professor Wolf suddenly turned from the window, his

telescope closing itself up with a loud click. "The Family Guard has just arrived. Someone must have alerted them. There will be an inquest that will conclude, as usual, that it was an unfortunate accident. After all, crime doesn't exist in our lovely city."

Octavio looked over the ferns to give him an offended glare. His frowning instantly made his torn skin bleed again. "You're verging on unpatriotic, professor. I won't denounce you if you come to testify with Apprentice Eulalia and me. We must describe the events exactly as they unfolded."

In truth, Ophelia wasn't that keen to do so. If she gave evidence, her identity would be checked and she'd be asked a whole lot of questions that she'd rather avoid.

The problem vanished when Professor Wolf seized a rifle from his collection of weapons and leveled it at his two guests.

"You're going nowhere," he hissed. His weapon was as ancient as the blunderbuss that had exploded in his hands, but he didn't seem that concerned. His charred goatee made him look fearsome. "What were you up to in front of my door? Who sent you?"

Octavio's complexion went from bronzed to leaden. He hadn't flinched before Fearless because, then, violence was an abstract notion to him. He had since experienced it with his own body.

As for Ophelia, she didn't see the professor's rifle. She saw only the fear lurking deep in his eyes. A fear even greater than that she had felt herself in the courtyard.

"We came of our own volition," she replied. "We needed your help. And I, personally, needed your forgiveness," she added, after a sudden inspiration, "for having flouted the readers' professional code under your very roof. You have every right to consider me an enemy, but the reverse isn't true."

Professor Wolf's lips twitched. Although he didn't put his

rifle down, he did lower the barrel slightly. "Why would you need my help?"

"You are the only person alive who understands what is really going on. Or who is able to speak about it, at any rate," Ophelia specified, with a thought for Mediana. "The person who killed Mademoiselle Silence and Fearless, you've already encountered him, haven't you?"

The professor's eyes, sharp as pistol bullets, darted from Ophelia to Octavio. "You two . . . you haven't the slightest idea what you have just come up against. Some good advice: stop nosing around. For my part, doing so brought me only trouble. The less you know, the better off you'll be."

Octavio, who had remained huddled in his corner up to now, slowly stood up, dusted down his uniform, and threw his shoulders back. "We are apprentice Forerunners. It is our duty to have the know-how and to make known."

Professor Wolf sniggered without loosening his grip on his rifle. There was, however, increasingly less anger in his demeanor. The muscles in his face and arms were sagging, gradually yielding under the weight of too heavy a burden.

Ophelia decided that the time had come to carry it with him. "Have you read the books of E. G.?"

She could feel Octavio's eyes searing into her; it was the second time he was hearing her pipe up with this question.

Professor Wolf clutched at his neck brace, as if Ophelia had just winded him. "How did you . . . What do you know?"

"Little and too much, all at once. If I must be afraid, I would at least like to know why. I need to know the truth. Your truth," she concluded, gently.

After endless hesitation, Professor Wolf sat down on his camp bed, and laid down his rifle. He suddenly seemed terribly weary. "My truth," he growled, still stroking his neck brace, "is that I'm a coward. Take a seat. We're going to converse for a while."

Barely had he grunted these words before two garden chairs emerged from the bushes and minced forward. They were so timid, Ophelia had to sit with all her weight on hers to prevent it from retreating. At last, she was going to see the pieces of the jigsaw puzzle fitting into place.

The professor let out a long sigh as he contemplated his black reader's gloves. "I am a specialist in the wars of the old world. I was already one before that word was put on the Index," he said with annoyance, seeing Octavio frown. "Maybe not a virtuoso, as you will become one day, but one of the top experts in the dating of objects. The Memorial is somewhere that has always fascinated me due to its past as a military academy. There was a time when I was allowed into the Secretarium and could read the original collections. I witnessed my discipline being steadily discredited with every new law and decree. The Lords of LUX withdrew my access overnight. Weapons, medals, witness accounts, letters," he listed, unfurling his fingers, one by one, "all the collections relating to war were removed from the Memorial, like garbage. And then it was the turn of the books. Spy stories, crime thrillers, swashbuckling tales, they all disappeared from the shelves. A veritable purge!"

Professor Wolf looked daggers at the two apprentices in front of him, as if they were personally responsible for these events. Ophelia understood him without being able to tell him so; the purging of her own museum had felt like an amputation to her. As for Octavio, he made no comment. From the moment he had sat in his garden chair, he had crossed both arms and legs, defensively.

"The Memorial of today bears no comparison to the one that I haunted as a student," Professor Wolf continued. "It

341

became ever harder to find the resources for my research. I witnessed, impotent, the impoverishment of documentation, archives, and historical literature. In fact, it was worse than that. That accursed Acoustic . . . Mademoiselle Silence . . . Her ears followed me everywhere. The moment she heard me leafing through a work, she sent it straight to the censoring department. She watched my every move at the Memorial, as one might watch a vulture hovering over a carcass. From her point of view, if a specialist like me deemed a book worthy of interest, then that book was inevitably subversive. I spent my time avoiding her, walking on tiptoe to avoid being heard by her. And that's how I ended up, out of pique, resorting to the children's department."

A squall, stronger than the rest, shook one of the panes of the greenhouse. That was all it took for Professor Wolf to leap to his feet, rifle at the ready. His wide-open, staring eyes under his bushy black eyebrows made him look slightly mad.

Ophelia couldn't stop scanning the weeds surrounding them herself. She'd doubtless been affected by this man's paranoia, but she couldn't shake off the feeling of being watched.

Once he realized that it was a false alarm, the professor sat back down, heavily, making the bed's rusty springs creak. He passed his hand over a face that was haggard from insomnia, strained from anxiety.

"I . . . I wasn't immediately interested in E. G.'s books. Like all self-respecting young Babelians, I had clambered up the ladder forbidden to children of my age once or twice, keen to reach these tales that were stored too high up. And, finding them deadly boring, had promptly returned them to their shelf."

Octavio nodded, without uncrossing his arms or legs. On this point, at least, he agreed with Professor Wolf's opinion. Faced with their shared reaction, Ophelia's curiosity was at its zenith. "How did that change?" she asked. "What did you discover about these books that you didn't know as child?"

Professor Wolf grimaced as if he had just gulped curdled milk. "At first, absolutely nothing. They were still the same right-thinking stories, with the same fusty style, in the same dated language as I remembered. All those tales seemed to have been written with but one aim: praising the new world. How the twenty-one family spirits became wonderful parents of humanity!" he proclaimed, rolling his eyes. "How the arks were miraculously repopulated with their descendants! How the family powers were successfully passed on through the generations! How the 'masters of objects,' 'masters of space,' 'masters of gravity,' and the rest of the gang, had all appeared! How peace had replaced wars—in short, that kind of clap-trap. I would never have gone any further had there not been . . . something else."

He swallowed under his neck brace. Hanging on his every word, Ophelia was leaning so far forward on her garden chair, she finally tipped off it.

"If E. G.'s tales aren't worth a bean," Professor Wolf continued, his voice tight, "his books did intrigue me as objects. You see, we're not talking about reprints here: they are all publications from that era, and I found them remarkably well preserved. Too well preserved, in fact. I am an expert in dating," he reminded them, with a sarcastic grin. "I was convinced that the Memorialist who had catalogued them had made an enormous mistake. Those tales couldn't have been printed barely a century after the Rupture, they had to be more recent! My conscientiousness told me to offer my services as a reader to the Memorial, to evaluate this collection properly. No," the professor murmured, more to himself than to Ophelia and Octavio, whom he no longer seemed to see. "Not my conscientiousness. My arrogance. I wanted to make them regret having so misjudged me." He laughed, joylessly. "Not only did I receive a categorical refusal, but on top of that I attracted Mademoiselle Silence's attention to E. G.'s books."

Ophelia held her breath. The jigsaw puzzle was starting to come together before her glasses. So that was why Mademoiselle Silence had tried to destroy the entire collection: due to the interest Professor Wolf had shown in it!

"So, what did you do?" she asked.

"The most stupid thing of my entire life. I stole a book."

Octavio said not a word, but his eyes reddened like embers once again. In Babel, theft was an extremely serious crime.

Ophelia didn't share his disapproval. "That book, do you still have it? It's *The Era of Miracles*, isn't it? Could I see it?"

"No."

The professor's response had been fast as a whip.

"No?"

"No, you can't see it. No, it isn't *The Era of Miracles*. No, I no longer have it in my possession. If you want to hear 'my truth,'" he said, losing patience, "you'll have to button it, young lady."

Ophelia closed her mouth to contain her questions.

"I stole a book," Professor Wolf reiterated. "I picked one in haste from E. G.'s collection, hid it under my jacket, and left, avoiding Mademoiselle Silence's ears. I'd barely got home before I was appalled at what I had just done," he muttered, looking away. "I never felt guilty about saying words that are in the Index, or collecting forbidden objects, but stealing . . . I had proved right all those Memorialists who considered me a man unworthy of being called 'Professor.' I thought of telegraphing Sir Henry to make amends, explain my motives to him, and denounce Mademoiselle Silence. That Lord isn't known for being sentimental, but he has always opposed the destruction of books."

Ophelia swallowed her saliva with difficulty. Whenever Thorn was mentioned, she felt herself cracking even more.

Professor Wolf's face creased into a nasty smile that uncovered his bottom teeth. "I didn't do so. I didn't contact Sir Henry. I denounced no one. Instead, I read the book with my hands."

The professor fell silent so abruptly that Ophelia and Octavio finally exchanged a look. He had turned very pale. His black side-whiskers were dripping with sweat. The closer he got to the denouement of his story, the more the muscles of his jaw seized up. His shaking spread to the wood of his neck brace and the springs of the bed.

"*Et puis?*" Octavio encouraged him. "The book that you . . . purloined, was it as recent as you thought? Were you right?"

His questions made Professor Wolf pull himself together. "No, young man. I was wrong. Wrong beyond all that I had imagined. E. G.'s books are a great deal older."

Professor Wolf slid a hand under the mattress of his camp bed. He pulled out a packet of cigarettes that he must have bought on the black market. It was seeing the lighter flame glowing in the half-light that made Ophelia aware that dusk had just descended on every pane of the greenhouse. All around there was total silence: not a puff of wind anymore, not an insect's chirr.

"E. G.'s books weren't written after the Rupture," Professor Wolf then declared, in a cloud of smoke. "They were written before it."

Ophelia felt a shiver coursing up her spine, like an electric current.

"That's impossible," whispered Octavio.

Professor Wolf's cigarette crackled. His voice took on the same ghostly quality as the smoke he was exhaling. "That's what I thought, too. I cut a piece off a page to submit it to one of my colleagues. I gave him no indication of the source of this sample. He confirmed my evaluation. The very composition of the paper resembles nothing we're familiar with, its longevity defies the imagination. In other words," Professor Wolf stressed, "E. G.'s tales never described the new world. They anticipated it."

Ophelia was seized by sudden dizziness, as if she'd just discovered that her chair was dangling over the void. The last time she had felt that way was when she had read Farouk's Book.

"The Rupture, the arks, the families, the world as we know it today . . . " Professor Wolf elaborated, "it was all planned. And E. G. knew it."

"Impossible," Octavio repeated. His eyes gleamed like those of an animal in the evening. The light was fading fast in the greenhouse. The silhouettes of the plants barely stood out against the indigo of the glass.

The tiny glow of the cigarette disappeared when Professor Wolf stubbed it out. His utterances became telegram-like: "E. G.'s books are dangerous. My life was turned upside down because of them. Literally. From the top of my ladder."

"Who?" Ophelia pressed him. "Who pushed you?"

Professor Wolf's breathing quickened in the dark. "*He* didn't push me. *He* didn't need to do so. *He* simply appeared before me . . . appeared from nowhere. *He* didn't need either to touch me or to speak to me. His mere presence made me . . . "

He went quiet. He didn't need to say it. The terror was constricting his voice.

"And do you know the most ironic part of the whole affair? It's that I can no longer even remember what *he* looks like. I can see myself again going up the ladder. *He* was waiting for me at the top of the steps. And then . . . I don't know . . . it was like falling in a nightmare . . . no . . . into the very substance of the nightmare. Not an image, not a sound. Just an abyss of absurdity. All the horror of nothingness." Professor Wolf inhaled slowly, deeply, to steady his panicky breathing. "It was my landlady who found me, at the foot of the ladder, the following day. Broken in body and soul. The book I had stolen, I realized later that it was no longer in my home. I learnt afterwards that it had been put back on its shelf at the Memorial. No one seemed to have noticed anything over there. In Babel, people only see what they want to see."

The professor stood up, to a creaking of springs.

"So there you have 'my truth,'" he said, sounding disillusioned. "I have nothing else to tell you that wouldn't be even more pitiful. When I learnt that there had been further attacks at the Memorial, I fled from my apartment and shut myself away here, like a coward. I was afraid, viscerally afraid, that *he* would return to pay me a visit. I don't understand either who *he* is, or what *he* wants. The only thing I'm convinced of," he spat out between his teeth, "is that you drew him here."

The words in her dream came crashing back to Ophelia: *If you seek E. G., the other will find you.*

"I think I know what he wants," she whispered. "Mademoiselle Silence threw all of E. G.'s tales into the incinerator, and that's surely what caused her to be . . . um . . . terrified herself. All the tales," she said more loudly, to stop Octavio and Professor Wolf, already opening their mouths, from interrupting, "apart from just one. *The Era of Miracles.* That book escaped destruction and disappeared from circulation. If your mysterious visitor is protecting E. G.'s oeuvre, as I believe he is, then that's what he's looking for. Maybe Mediana and Fearless got in his way unwittingly?"

Ophelia's question remained hanging in the air. The silence between the three of them was as heavy as the night that had

347

finally descended. Octavio's wide, staring eyes were now the only source of light in the greenhouse.

Professor Wolf's shadow eventually made a move. Ophelia jumped when he threw a basket onto her lap that smelt strongly of figs.

"Eat and sleep while I keep watch. You won't find a single birdtrain at this hour to take you back to your conservatoire. Be sure not to go near the bed," he muttered as he left. "If anyone other than me lies on it, it will snap shut like an oyster."

# THE SUMMONS

Ophelia spent the night staring up at the stars through the dirty panes of glass. Occasionally, a red glow would appear inside the greenhouse when Professor Wolf dragged on a cigarette, telescope still pressed to eye. She had found his revelations rather disappointing. The Rupture and the foundation of the families having been planned in advance was a terrifying concept. But Ophelia still didn't know who E. G. was, where *The Era of Miracles* was to be found, and whether, yes or no, it was the work Thorn was looking for. She was equally in the dark as to the identity of the killer who had traumatized so many people around her.

It seemed to her that, once again, she had ended up with more questions than answers.

Ophelia was just dozing off among the ferns when Octavio shook her and pointed at the sky: dawn was approaching. In turn, they splashed water on their faces in a dubious-smelling washroom. Their uniforms could have done with a visit to the laundry.

Professor Wolf stubbed out his final cigarette without saying a word to them. He put on his black morning coat, removed the blunderbuss blocking the greenhouse door, and guided them across the roofs to the safety ladder they had climbed the previous day. "This is where we part," he declared. "You go. I stay."

He shook the hand Octavio offered him half-heartedly, watched him climb down, and then held Ophelia back by the shoulder.

"Do you trust him?"

"Yes."

She was the first to be surprised by this spontaneous reply. Two days earlier, she considered Octavio an enemy. The professor's fingers tightened around her shoulder, making his gloves creak.

"He's still a Son of Pollux, all the same. Everything we spoke of yesterday, he will repeat it to the authorities. If I were you, I wouldn't trust people who manipulate the collective memory, especially now that you know what I know."

Ophelia nodded in agreement.

"I have one request," he continued. "You certainly owe me a favor, young lady."

She nodded again.

"Do you know an assistant at the Memorial by the name of Blaise?"

Another nod, but with less conviction this time. She knew she was indebted, but if the favor involved compromising a friend, that was different. Professor Wolf, however, seemed to feel as awkward as she did. He had started to tug at what remained of his charred goatee, twisting and untwisting his mouth, as if he wanted to chew his words well before uttering them.

"Could you . . . just tell him to watch his back?"

Ophelia stared at him over the top of her glasses, and was suddenly struck by the obvious. The man in Blaise's life was the one standing before her right now.

"Does he know?" she murmured. "Is Blaise aware of what really happened to you?"

The professor instantly frowned again. With his ill-combed

hair, ill-shaven chops, and ill-humored expression, he was definitely more wild animal than respectable scientist.

"No," he growled. "If he finds out, he'll want to help me, and if he tries to help me, he'll cause trouble for himself. Believe me, he's jinxed enough without that. Can I count on you? Put him on his guard, but not a word about me."

Ophelia gripped the security ladder and carefully placed her boots on the top rung. "I think Blaise would have preferred to hear it from your lips."

She went down the ladder with record-breaking slowness. Synchronizing her movements, both left and right, at various levels was, for her, fiendishly hard. She felt strange, setting foot again in the old courtyard. Only yesterday, this place was a maelstrom of dust. Today, the dawn was limpid as a lake. The air and the weather seemed quite still, as though nothing had ever happened.

Ophelia found Octavio in the middle of the courtyard, busy searching the ground. She couldn't have said where Fearless's body had lain, but there remained not a trace of it. Pollux's guard had cleaned the place up. Ophelia suddenly thought of Fearless's son. Would he be appropriately informed of what had happened to his father? Did he have any other family?

"Let's go," Octavio announced. "There's nothing left to see here."

They went to the quayside, boarded the first gondola heading for the sea of clouds, and once in the city center, asked a whaxi to take them to the birdtrain landing stage. The sun was barely rising when their transport finally took off, but the benches were already packed with passengers.

Sitting beside him, Ophelia observed Octavio out of the corner of her glasses. His fringe covered half his face, its shadow obscuring the wounds on brow and nose. His only visible eye was almost covered by an eyelid puffed with tiredness.

His arms were crossed, defensively, and his thumb rubbed the apprentice-virtuoso stripe stitched to his sleeve. Ophelia sensed that something had changed in him.

"What are you thinking of doing?" she whispered to him.

Octavio continued to lean against the carriage window for a long while, his attention lost to the void, before whispering between his teeth: *"Eh bien* . . . I've hit a man, seen a murder, and witnessed more forbidden things in one day than in the rest of my life. I will tell the whole truth to my mother, after classes. She will know which decision is fairest. What do you think of that?"

While saying that last sentence he had given Ophelia a questioning glance. It was then that she understood what had changed. This Visionary had always looked imperiously on the world, sure of the place he would have in it, and the role he would play in it. Now, quite simply, he had doubts.

"What I think of it," she replied, after some thought, "is that you should decide yourself what seems fairest to you."

Octavio stared at her with sudden intensity. "I wonder if I'm not starting, a little, to love you."

Ophelia took off her glasses to stop them turning crimson on her nose. She felt grubby and smelly; this was the last declaration she had expected!

"Octavio . . . "

"Don't bother to make some great speech," he instantly cut in, sounding resigned. "Even if you were interested, there would be nothing between us, and not just due to the rule. Our lives are going to be complicated enough as it is. And," he added, with a touch of irony, "you're too blurry a person for me."

When Ophelia put her glasses back on, Octavio's profile regained its clear contours, his dark skin and hair standing out against the light from the window. He was looking straight ahead, already focused on the future. She found herself admiring him then. He was almost the same size as her, but to her, he seemed much bigger because he had the courage to own his thoughts, feelings, and transgressions.

"Too blurry, huh?" Ophelia thought, relaxing against the back of the bench. It was well deserved.

They finally landed at the Good Family platform. Barely had they set off along the main path to the conservatoire when the watchtowers' loudhailers bellowed in unison: "Apprentice Eulalia, Apprentice Octavio, you are urgently requested to go to Lady Helen's office."

They exchanged tense looks. Spending the night away was a misdemeanor worthy of punishment, but the principal would never have made an apprentice miss a class, unless the circumstances were beyond her control.

They crossed the maze of gardens and walkways, their silence underlined by the cicadas that suddenly stopped singing as they passed. When they walked along the Godchildren of Helen amphitheater, they spotted, through the high windows, a crowd of heads turned toward them. A summons was certainly more exciting than Monday's radio lessons, and it might mean fewer competitors in the race for promotion.

Ophelia held her breath on seeing an airship tethered near the entrance to the administrative building. A giant sun with a human face was painted in gold on its white surface.

"They've beaten us to it," Octavio remarked.

After a series of colonnades and stairs, they arrived at the principal's office. As always, semidarkness prevailed, and Ophelia took a moment to adjust to the abrupt change of light. Helen's elephantine form was enthroned behind the marble desk; for once, all of her chair's articulated arms were still. There were three other people in the room: a family guardsman with helmet under arm, a photographer with sticking-out ears, and Lady Septima. The last barely batted an eyelid when she saw her son's injured face.

"Knowledge serves peace," Octavio and Ophelia both said in greeting, standing to attention.

"Knowledge serves peace," the guardsman responded. His beard was like a soaring wave, every bristle glistening like silver against his brown skin. Going by his leonine nose, and its forceful inhaling, he was an Olfactory.

"I present my utmost apologies in advance to Lady Septima's son for the inconvenience caused by this summons. I know the grade-awarding ceremony is imminent, you hardly want any interruption to your lessons."

"I see," Ophelia thought. "For me, it's not important." At least the tone was set.

"Here, Octavio is not my son, but one apprentice among others," Lady Septima stated, with indifference. "Just as here, I am not his mother, but Sir Pollux's official representative. Question him as your duty demands."

The guardsman assented and, without further ado, deposited an object that tinkled on the marble of the desk. "Apprentice Octavio, does this belong to you?"

It was the gold chain that Fearless had torn off. Ophelia felt her stomach contract on noticing that a small piece of flesh remained attached at one end.

"It does belong to me, *monsieur*," Octavio confirmed.

"We found it yesterday, in the courtyard of a building in a neighborhood of the powerless, close to the body of an agitator whom our forces have been actively pursuing for years. Is it that man who did that to you?" the guardsman asked, indicating Octavio's injuries.

"It is indeed, *monsieur*, but I'm not responsible for his death."

The guardsman's face broke into a kindly smile that

made his silvery moustache shoot up on both sides. "No one is. Don't worry, my lord, the cause of death isn't in question."

Ophelia wondered what more he needed. She recalled the bulging eyes, gaping mouth, convulsed body. In Babel, people only see what they want to see. Professor Wolf was right.

She considered Helen's gigantic body on the other side of the desk, motionless in its chair, long, spiderlike fingers pressed up against each other. Her optical appliance was directed at her visitors like opera glasses, but she didn't seem inclined to relinquish her role of spectator.

"What we wish to establish," the guardsman continued, "is whether Fearless-and-Almost-Blameless was well and truly guilty of violence. It's sad to say, but that troublemaker enjoyed a popularity—only relative, certainly—among the weakest and most easily influenced elements in our city. We will not allow his death to turn him into a heroic figure," he grunted, nostrils flaring with indignation.

A bright flash of light cut through the gloom of the office. The photographer with sticking-out ears had just taken a headshot of Octavio. Ophelia didn't doubt for a second that, tomorrow, the *Official Journal* would publish a close-up of his injuries.

"That will be all," the guardsman said, donning his golden helmet. "Thank you for your cooperation."

"I, too, was guilty of violence."

Octavio's statement made time in the office stop still. Lady Septima's impassive eyelids allowed a spark to filter through them. The photographer froze while putting away his equipment. Helen remained immovable as a mountain.

Octavio himself put on a calm front. Standing just behind him, Ophelia saw that he was clasping his hands behind his back to stop them shaking. She almost gave in to the impulse of telling all, but, with a sidelong glance, he dissuaded her. This was a battle he had to fight alone.

"You must have found bruises on the body," he insisted. "They're the marks of the blows I dealt him."

After a moment's hesitation, the family guardsman consulted Lady Septima with a glance, and then wound his moustache around his index finger. "That is regrettable, *en effet*. I do not, however, consider that detail of sufficient relevance to feature in my report. I bid you an excellent day."

The guardsman and photographer bowed and left the office. Octavio watched the door closing behind them with an expression on his face that Ophelia had never seen before. Nothing, of all he had lived through over the past twenty-four hours, had shocked him as much.

"A detail?" he repeated. "Mother, I don't understand, shouldn't I, too, be answerable for my actio . . . "

Lady Septima cut him short with just a look. "Here, I am not your mother, Apprentice Octavio. And it is not for you to pass judgment on the decisions of the representatives of law and order. Apprentice Eulalia, are you behind this excursion to the neighborhood of the powerless?"

Her tone had become as scathing as the look in her eyes. From that moment, Ophelia knew for certain that Lady Septima hated her. She was the foreigner who had led her oh-so-perfect little boy off the straight and narrow. They now had personal business to settle.

"Yes."

"Did you encourage Apprentice Octavio to join you?"

"Yes."

"Did you deliberately instigate an encounter with Fearless-and-Almost-Blameless?"

"No."

"But can you assert that there was no likelihood of encountering him over there?"

Ophelia's jaws tightened. Lady Septima's way of twisting her questions made them incriminating. Helen followed this questioning in silence, as though she had no say in the matter. Didn't Ophelia's case come under her jurisdiction, rather than that of a representative of Pollux? Was this family spirit, in the end, as easy to manipulate as her twin brother?

"I can't assert such a thing, but I didn't know . . . "

"Are you aware that the awarding of grades is taking place soon?" Lady Septima continued, not allowing Ophelia time to elaborate.

"Yes."

"Are you aware that you have jeopardized your classmate's apprenticeship, on top of putting his life in danger?"

"Y-yes."

Ophelia hadn't managed to prevent her voice from betraying her. Every word from Lady Septima injected her with a little more guilt.

"I request permission to present my version of events," Octavio intervened. "I accompanied Apprentice Eulalia of my own free will. We conducted an inquiry jointly, as Forerunners. What we discovered is more important than what we're discussing here. If you would allow us a chance to explain to you . . . "

"Your testimony has already been heard," Lady Septima hissed, her tone final. "Apprentice Octavio, I order you to return to your division immediately. You will stop at the infirmary and the cloakroom on the way. You are presenting a lamentable image of this establishment."

The son's eyes held the mother's for a long time, like two conflicting fires. Ophelia saw Octavio's flame gradually go out. Even when his chain had been torn from him, he hadn't shown such suffering. Of all his illusions, he had just lost the one that was most precious to him.

He slammed the door behind him. Helen's ogreish mouth grimaced at the noise.

"*Madame*," Lady Septima continued, turning on her heels toward her. "Since this concerns one of your Goddaughters, the choice of punishment is up to you. I do, however, take the liberty of recommending to you expulsion with immediate effect."

"I refuse!"

The words had erupted from Ophelia along with her anger. For the first time, she was fully conscious of the claws that extended her every nerve ending. A primal instinct whispered to her how she could use them to wound Lady Septima as painfully as she herself had wounded Octavio.

She just needed to link her own nervous system to hers.

She just needed a single thought.

Ophelia turned her glasses away, took a deep breath. The following second, she succumbed to the temptation she had felt.

"I refuse," she repeated, in a more controlled voice. "I refuse to be expelled without being allowed to say what I have to say."

"I am listening."

Helen's voice had a mineral resonance, as if the inside of her body was fashioned of the same marble as her desk. It was the first time she had spoken since the start of the summons. With just three words, she had reasserted her presence in the room.

Ophelia focused all her attention on the optical appliance that was trained on her. She had to disregard Lady Septima; if the woman was so keen to get rid of her a few days from the awarding of grades, she must fear seeing her become an aspiring virtuoso, and thus deem her capable of doing so. Ophelia had let Thorn down with everything else, she owed it to him to fight for this.

"I am grateful for the opportunity I was given to join the Good Family. I received quality training here that allowed me not only to hone my family power, but also to broaden my knowledge. I endeavored to make my contribution in return by working hard for the reading groups. Just as I endeavored to prove myself worthy of the trust placed in me by taking over from Mediana at the Secretarium."

Ophelia cleared her throat and straightened her back to relax her diaphragm. She wouldn't allow her little voice to take over. Today more than ever, it was time to make herself heard.

"If there is one thing I have retained from my apprentice-ship, it is that Forerunners don't wait for information to come to them; they have to go and look for the information. And that is what I did. I discovered that some unique volumes had been incinerated at the Memorial, and I led an inquiry to understand why. Apprentice Octavio assisted me. We assumed Professor Wolf would be able to throw some light on certain parts of our investigation, but we didn't find him at home. It was in those circumstances that we unintentionally came across Fearless-and-Almost-Blameless."

All the events that Ophelia had just described were strictly true, but she had chosen to skip the most important ones. She didn't trust Lady Septima enough to risk making any further revelations. And yet, going by the slight jerk of her eyelids, her surprise was sincere.

With pachydermic slowness, Helen turned her chair. "Is that correct? Were books thrown on the fire? Isn't that contrary to the very purpose of the Memorial?"

"I wasn't aware of it," Lady Septima admitted, reluctantly. "But that by no means excuses what you have been up to,

Apprentice Eulalia. You should have come and told me about it."

Ophelia moved a step forward, purely to make the wings at her ankles clatter. "We didn't have all the elements at our disposal. We wanted first to return to the source. Just as you taught us to, professor."

It was most satisfying, turning Lady Septima's own teachings against her. Ophelia found her suddenly less dazzling, despite the fine gold decorations on her uniform.

Helen unlinked her endless fingers, snatched a fountain pen, and scribbled a note.

"Apprentice Eulalia will not be expelled. She will have the right to present herself at the conferment of grades, just like all the apprentices, and, like them, her candidature will be admissible for the status of aspiring virtuoso. However," she added, just as Ophelia was about to thank her, "the pride and lack of judgment she has shown in this affair are the opposite of what I expect of my Forerunners. For that reason, Apprentice Eulalia will be locked in the isolation chamber until the day of the ceremony. She will not complete her apprenticeship at the conservatoire; she will not be able to communicate with anyone; and her misdemeanors will be recorded in her file. You will use this time profitably for reflection, apprentice," Helen concluded, in a lugubrious voice. "The isolation chamber is the ideal place for that."

Ophelia could no longer hear her. Her blood was pounding in her ears like the drum of a washing machine. The only reality of which she was cruelly aware was Lady Septima's triumphant smile.

# THE GAP

Although Ophelia had never seen the isolation chamber, she had heard all about it. The most dreaded room in the conservatoire, it was reserved for rebels. It was said that just a single hour in it felt like a whole day, and staying in it too long sent one mad. Ophelia had doubted its existence, but could no longer do so as Elizabeth led her to the very back of the gardens, where the jungle was but a tangled web of creepers. They arrived in front of a statue of a woman sitting cross-legged, her head that of an elephant. It was monumental enough for trees to be nestled in its crevices, their sinuous roots spilling over the stone. Elizabeth climbed the stairs of the pedestal, and then, clearing away the brambles with the tip of her boot, she uncovered a circular trapdoor in the stone.

"Open it, Apprentice Eulalia. That's the tradition."

Ophelia turned the handle several times. It had to be forged in some Alchemist's rustproof alloy because, despite its obvious age, it put up no resistance. She found it harder, however, to lift the trapdoor: it was thick as her body! Her glasses blanched on discovering a dark well plunging several yards down within the stone of the pedestal.

"I really have to go down."

It was more an acknowledgment than a question. Ophelia

knew that she had no choice. Contesting the ruling of a family spirit would amount to making oneself an outlaw.

Casually, Elizabeth dropped the basket of dried fruit she had brought with her. The wicker echoed strangely as it hit the bottom of the well. "You'll find sufficient water and light down there. At least, so I'm told. I've never been into the isolation chamber. I'll come to collect you at the end of the week, to escort you to the ceremony. Be sure to ration out the food; no one's going to bring you any."

Ophelia thought Elizabeth would add her usual "I'm joking," but it seemed that, for once, she wasn't. The thought of finding herself alone at the bottom of this well for several days and several nights triggered a sudden surge of claustrophobia.

"Would you . . . would you explain the situation to Sir Henry?"

"Don't worry about him, apprentice. He'll replace you, just as he replaced Mediana before you."

Ophelia tried not to show how painful it was to hear those words. "Do you think I still have a chance of becoming an aspiring Forerunner, like you?"

"I don't think so, no."

Much as Ophelia was used to her perpetual neutrality, she would have appreciated her forgoing it today. As she climbed down the rungs of the well, Elizabeth leaned over, pushing the hair clinging to her cheeks behind her ears. "But I have faith in Lady Helen. You should, too."

With this advice, Elizabeth closed the well's trapdoor. Her freckles were the last thing Ophelia saw of the outside world. Just as her voice was the last sound: the cries of birds, monkeys and insects were replaced by a stark silence. Ophelia felt her chest pounding as anxiety overwhelmed her again.

She did not want to stay here alone.

She fought the impulse to bang on the trapdoor and beg

Elizabeth to reopen it. She took a slow, deep breath. The air wasn't particularly fragrant, but it was breathable. She unclenched her fingers from the rungs, and, one foot after the other, made her descent.

A few Heliopolis bulbs cast a cold light at the bottom of the well. The isolation chamber was furnished with basic conveniences: a toilet pan, an unscreened shower, a basin, a medicine cabinet, a mattress, and mirrors. Many mirrors. Every wall was a mirror. The ceiling was a mirror. Even the floor was a mirror. When Ophelia picked up the basket of dried fruit Elizabeth had dropped down the well, her movement was endlessly multiplied. She saw herself from the front and the back at once, her reflections forever shrinking. She felt as if she were not in a confined space, but in the middle of a multidirectional tunnel populated by thousands of other Ophelias. And she couldn't escape from a single one of them.

There was neither a telephone nor a periscope, and nothing, either, to occupy the mind. Nothing to read, nothing to write with, nothing to fill the emptiness and the silence. There was only her. An infinity of her.

*An ideal place for reflection.*

Ophelia sat in a corner of the isolation chamber, drew her legs up, and buried her face in her arms. Time crept over her like glue. She had no notion of the hour—there was no clock, either, in the chamber—but the longer she remained slumped, the drowsier she became. After two sleepless nights in a row, she needed to sleep. But she couldn't. Every time she was about to doze off, her body sent her an electric shock that made her jump. She didn't dare leave her corner of the room, tormented by the eyes of her countless reflections. It wasn't comfortable, but the stench from the mattress was worse.

When had Elizabeth closed the trapdoor? Today? Yesterday? Was it nighttime, up there? If Ophelia could have at least heard the sound of the gong . . . The only sounds here were organic, coming from the plumbing and from her stomach.

Gnawing at the seams of her gloves, one by one, her thoughts veered in all directions: to God, to the Other, to E. G., to LUX, to the Rupture, to that mystery person who spread terror in his path.

Ophelia tried to order her thoughts, but the chamber's mirrors distracted her. She was a mirror visitor. She should have felt in her element here, but anxiety was crippling her. The last time she'd tried to use her power, it had been distressing. She was afraid of confronting her reflection again, and she knew that the mere fact of being afraid made any mirror passage impossible.

Because Octavio was right. Because she'd become too blurry a person.

Where would she have gone, anyhow? To her knowledge, there was no other mirror on the Good Family ark. The closest one in which she'd been reflected was in the Memorial restrooms, and she was incapable of covering such a distance.

Ophelia curled up even tighter. The real question wasn't "where to go?" but "why go there?" Thorn no longer expected her. He'd put an end to their collaboration. She had thought she could hand him the book he was looking for on a platter, but despite everything that had happened, despite all she had learnt, she had made no progress. On the contrary, she had compromised her chances of becoming an aspiring virtuoso.

She had failed to help Thorn. Again.

Exhausted, Ophelia let herself slide onto the floor. Lying on this great ice-cold mirror, she saw her myriad reflections on the ceiling as strange celestial bodies. And then she saw nothing. Her thoughts became diluted, sleep soaked her up, and she felt herself sinking.

When Ophelia awoke, she was floating in a haze in which she glimpsed fragmented images, fluctuating colors, distorted sounds, as if she were drifting beneath the surface of a lake. She felt neither fear nor amazement. In fact, she had rarely felt so calm. She felt as if she were sliding on the tensile web of space and time. She knew this place, tiny and vast, from having passed through it hundreds of times without ever stopping in it. The floor of the isolation chamber had swallowed her up while she slept and she hadn't resurfaced. She was nowhere. She was everywhere.

She was in the gap between the mirrors.

"Why are you in Babel?"

Thorn's voice vibrated on Ophelia as on a tuning fork. He wasn't physically here with her, inside the gap, but his question was only too real. It was the first thing he'd said to her on the evening of their reunion. This echo from the past now returned to her with the inevitability of a pendulum's swing.

Why had Thorn asked her why? Wasn't it obvious that he was the only answer to his own question?

Barely had this thought occurred to Ophelia than she understood the reason for her being within the gap. This space was the very reflection of her inner state. Neither child nor adult, neither girl nor woman, she had remained stuck on the cusp of her life. She had expected words and gestures from Thorn that she had never offered him. At no time had she said "we." At no time had she reached out to him. At no time had she laid herself bare.

The truth, the only truth, was that she had been cowardly.

This realization ran through her like a fissure; the surface of her being felt as if it were shattering, like eggshell. It hurt, but Ophelia knew that it was a necessary pain. Her suffering soared when her old identity shattered.

She could feel herself dying. She would finally be able to live.

*

When she was little, Ophelia had once amused herself by running backwards in the garden, to see the world go by the wrong way. Her foot had then skidded on a ball, and she had felt herself tipping backwards, no longer able to tell up from down.

This was exactly what she felt as she left the gap. She fell backwards with a feeling of unreality. Her back suddenly hit the ground. Her lungs emptied from the impact. For several long seconds, she was no longer breathing. Dazed, she stared through her glasses at the maze of spiderwebs glistening above her. A glimmer, pale as a moonbeam, came through an opening in the middle of a vaulted ceiling.

Ophelia may have left the gap, but she hadn't returned to the isolation chamber.

She got entangled in the spiderwebs as she got to her feet. The place she found herself in was bathed in a nebulous twilight. Apart from the small opening in the ceiling, there was no apparent door or window. An old mirror in the room was, however, producing a vague reflection. Its surface was coated in a thick layer of dust, except for where Ophelia's body had emerged: that dust was still floating in the air in the wake of her fall.

Where was she? How could she have passed through a mirror in which she had never been reflected? It defied every law of Animist physics.

Ophelia soon noticed that that wasn't the only particularity of this mirror. It was hanging in the air. It wasn't in a state of levitation, as one often saw in Babel. Getting closer to it, one could make out that it was surrounded by a panel that was both transparent and—from the way Ophelia could pass her hand through it—ethereal. Of the wall it had been fixed to, all that remained was a ghost.

Ophelia had a quick look around the room, and up at the ceiling, the source of the ray of light. And suddenly she knew where she was: at the heart of the Memorial, in the Secretarium, inside the weightlessly floating second globe. This mirror before her belonged to one of the top floors of the original building. It hung exactly where the other half of the building had collapsed at the moment of the Rupture. For some reason, it hadn't fallen into the void with everything else. It had remained absurdly anchored in the air. Someone had had the globe constructed around this anomaly to conceal it. Was that, there, the work of God? How many people today knew of the existence of this suspended mirror?

'The strongroom,' she then realized. 'The ultimate truth.'

With her glove, Ophelia gently rubbed away the dust that had settled on the mirror. If she was right, this object was several centuries old. No mirror could survive that long without losing its silvering. Normally, she shouldn't have seen her reflection in it.

And, indeed, it wasn't her face that was reflected. The woman facing her had the same small stature, the same brown hair, the same glasses, but it wasn't her.

Their lips moved at the same time:

"I am Ophelia," said Ophelia.

"I am Eulalia," said the reflection.

Ophelia closed her eyes, and then reopened them: her image had become her own again. She unbuttoned her gloves, put them in her pockets, and rubbed her moist palms together. She understood nothing that was happening to her, but she was sure of one thing: she had to read this mirror.

She eliminated her thoughts, one by one, blowing them out like countless candle flames. When she felt ready, she pressed her bare hands against those of her reflection. The first vision to come to her was of her own fall through the mirror, as was entirely logical. From then on, nothing proceeded as expected anymore.

Ophelia felt as though she were making her own reflection suck her up. Her memory turned itself inside out, like a glove. Ancient memories, from a different era, fulminated deep in her consciousness. The memories were so forceful that Ophelia tore in two, just as the building had once done. One half of her had suddenly become a stranger to her.

That half looked exactly like the little woman she had seen instead of her own reflection. The woman was tapping away on a typewriter, facing the big mirror, at the time when there was still a wall for it to hang on. Ophelia saw through her eyes, like a spectator at the theater. Her hair, dark and unruly, hadn't been washed for so long, it was sticking to her forehead. Her nose kept running, obliging her to use her handkerchief with one hand, while still typing with the other.

"Soon," she muttered to the mirror. "Soon, but not today."

Ophelia observed the scene through the eyes of the woman, with the mirror in between. At least, she tried to. The woman's eyesight seemed to be as poor as hers, and she hadn't put her glasses on. No one else was in the room, but there was crumpled paper all over the floor.

There was a knocking on the door. Ophelia immediately stopped typing to pull a thick curtain across the mirror, covering it entirely.

"What is it?" she asked.

The door opened, allowing a vague silhouette to be seen, which Ophelia recognized as she got closer to it. It was the caretaker whose register she had evaluated. As in her dream, he was wearing small, steel-rimmed spectacles and a turban, its scarf attempting to conceal his war-injured jaw. He couldn't refrain from frowning on noticing the paper and handkerchiefs strewn across the floor. His rigidity was a vestige of the military man he had once been.

"No reflective material," Ophelia reassured him, after conscientiously blowing her nose.

The caretaker removed his spectacles in an efficient manner. But that didn't stop his old hands from shaking. "We've got a blasted problem."

The dialect he spouted was unfamiliar to Ophelia. And yet she understood it without the slightest difficulty. She was even courteous enough to reply to him in his language:

"Oh dear, what's he done now?"

"He's killed all our blasted sparrows, that's what he's done. I didn't want him going into that aviary, but he couldn't stop himself. One day, I swear it'll be me he kills."

The caretaker glanced nervously behind him, toward the door, as if fearing a presence on the other side.

"Be patient," Ophelia sighed. "He'll learn to control himself like the others."

"He ain't like them blasted brats, that one."

The caretaker disappeared from her field of vision. She rubbed her eyes, wearily. Thanks to typing without her glasses on, her eyes were smarting. And her chronic sinusitis didn't help, either.

"His role is different," she said. "He protects the school."

"And I protect this blasted school, too," the caretaker grumbled, through his deformed lips. "If those blasted soldiers reach our blasted island, I'll chuck them right back into the blasted briny."

Ophelia rolled her handkerchief into a ball and threw it over to join the others on the floor, prompting an exasperated grunt from the caretaker.

"You're just a man," she told him, gently. "And I'm just a woman. We're limited, you and I. He isn't. Between now and the coming of the new humanity, he'll protect us all. Have faith in him."

*Have faith in him.* Those four words resonated through Ophelia as the old caretaker, the paper, the handkerchiefs, the typewriter, and the entire room faded away, like rings in water. When she was firmly back in the present, she was stretched out in the middle of the isolation chamber, frozen and burning at the same time, like some drowned person thrown up by the sea.

She had left the Memorial's second globe and crossed the gap in the opposite direction, without even realizing it. For a long time, she just stared at her reflection on the ground, blurred as it was by the drops of sweat dripping from her face. Her family power still quivered right across her skin.

She had never felt so different. She had never felt so much herself.

She knew everything. She knew where the book was that allowed one to become God's equal. She knew who protected it and why. Or rather, she knew that she knew. She could glimpse all the answers pulsing through her veins, but didn't yet have access to them.

Ophelia got undressed, took a shower, and then ate some fruit. She experienced each sensation with a new acuity. She didn't put her gloves back on; for once, she felt like touching the world without putting up a barrier. The omnipresence of her reflections no longer disturbed her.

When she felt sufficiently rested, Ophelia sat in the middle of the mirrors and linked her hands tightly. This time, it was her own body she had to learn to read.

She listened attentively to the ebb and flow of her breathing. She listened attentively to all her thoughts, even the most trivial. She listened attentively to the silence of the isolation chamber, which, little by little, became her own. Time disappeared.

She forgot herself the better to remember.

A flood of light poured into the isolation chamber, bouncing off the mirrors with the force of a river. It carried on its waves the sounds and smells of the jungle.

The trapdoor up above had reopened.

"Still alive?" Elizabeth's phlegmatic voice called down.

Ophelia got up slowly, blinded by the brightness of the daylight. A parcel immediately dropped into her arms. It was a fresh uniform.

"Get ready, apprentice. The ceremony awaits us."

She did as requested. She knew exactly what she still had left to do.

# THE CEREMONY

A squadron of luxurious airships, flying whaxis, and Zeph-yrian gondolas had descended on Babel's Memorial. They were tethered there like gigantic fairground balloons, festooning the sky with a constellation of colors. Extra birdtrains had been laid on, but the minor ark was too small to accommodate them all; each had to stick to its allotted time at the station to avoid an accident.

Ophelia alighted from one of them with the members of her division. No one had said a word to her during the jour-ney, and for good reason: the Seers were staring at the toes of their boots. Maybe she was imagining it, but they all looked disappointed.

They passed through the tall, glass doors of the entrance. Forerunners, lawyers, engineers, scribes, guardians, artists: all the Good Family companies were gathered in the huge atrium. So tightly packed were they, in their rows, that their uniforms appeared to be stitched together to create a vast, single length of midnight-blue fabric, embellished with silver. Apprentice and aspiring virtuosos faced the ros-trum on which the giant, twin family spirits were standing. Helen was as strangely disturbing, with her optical appli-ance and crinoline-on-casters, as Pollux was splendid. The latter was winking away benevolently at the faces turned toward him, but patently without the slightest idea of who anyone was.

Ophelia was sent quite dizzy by the crowds that had invaded every gallery, every trancendium, every topsy-turvium, every bit of surface that could accommodate a pair of babouches. After the silence of her interlude in the isolation chamber, the contrast was disconcerting. Wherever she turned her glasses, there were people—in front, behind, upright, and upside down. The scholars from neighboring academies formed a sea of university gowns on their own. The reverberations of their whispering made all the glass of the cupola shake. Ophelia wondered whether the architectural balance that, miraculously, enabled the Memorial to straddle the void wouldn't finally give way due to this surplus of visitors.

Obliged to remain in her place, within her row, she discreetly looked for Thorn among the Lords of LUX lined up behind the family spirits. She didn't find him, but she did spot Lady Septima, who was watching the statue-automaton's clock as if expecting someone's arrival.

On the rostrum there was a golden dais, its megaphones awaiting their orator.

Ophelia caught the eye of Octavio, in the Sons of Pollux division. It was the first time she was seeing him since their summons. He had stitches on his eyebrow and nostril, but they were less obvious wounds than those he bore inside him. His strained face told of the merciless conflict within. He ignored the signs of support from members of his own division, who were attempting to flatter him to the very last minute, in the hope that he would remember them the day he became a Lord. There was no question that Octavio would reach the grade of aspiring virtuoso today, but he no longer seemed that keen.

As for Ophelia, she did want that stripe. Even if her chances

were minute, her dearest wish was to become an aspiring virtuoso, and for Thorn to be there to witness it. She looked up at the
Secretarium, floating like a planet above them. Would he come?

Suddenly, Ophelia had the feeling of being watched. It
wasn't just down to nerves. Rather, it was as if something
viscous was clinging to her skin. There was a spectator in the
midst of the crowd who was focusing all attention on her,
and on her alone. Someone had been watching her from the
shadows for days, weeks, maybe even longer. She never saw
them, but she was becoming increasingly acutely aware of
their existence.

Who?

She noticed a movement. Blaise was making broad gestures
of encouragement in her direction, from among the Memorialists who had come to watch the ceremony. She smiled at
him, and then bit her lip as he accidentally whacked his neighbor. With all that had happened, she still hadn't managed to
give him the message from Professor Wolf.

The Memorial's automatons were among the front row of
the staff. Even though the ceremony hadn't yet begun, they
were already applauding, making a metallic racket. The old
sweeper was no longer among them. "It's the spoilt-rotten
brats like you who choose to give work to machines rather
than to 'decent citizens.'" Fearless was certainly no angel, but
Ophelia couldn't help feeling that a much-needed voice in
Babel had died with him.

One person who wasn't noticeable by their absence, on the
other hand, was certainly Lazarus. Seated on a private balcony,
he was smiling modestly for the photographers bombarding
him with chemical flashes. With his white-satin frock coat and
vivid-pink spectacles, he reflected back all the lights. Ophelia
hoped that, from where he was sitting, he wouldn't recognize
her. Ambrose wasn't at his side.

Ambrose . . . Ophelia now knew with absolute certainty that their paths would have to cross again soon. Very soon.

She was starting to wonder what everyone was waiting for when the sound of an engine drowned out the murmuring. All heads turned like weather vanes toward the main entrance at the precise moment when, to Ophelia's astonishment, an aeroplane appeared through the tall, glass doors. It was a biplane that seemed to have come straight out of a museum of the old world! It swooped above the atrium, circling the globe of the Secretarium. It plunged so close to the crowd that screams and turbans flew up. Ophelia gripped her glasses to see more clearly: two people were sitting casually between the wings of the biplane. There was a gasp across the entire Memorial when they tumbled out, as the plane was performing an aerobatic stunt under the cupola's vast glass canopy. Two parachutes opened up. The acrobats slowly floated down the hundred or so yards between them and the ground, to thunderous applause. After a final loop, the plane flew back out of the entrance, just as it had arrived, forcing all the apprentices in the atrium to duck down. When Ophelia got back up, her hair a complete mess, she reflected that it was the most dangerously stupid thing she had ever witnessed.

The two parachutists maneuvered so as to land in each other's arms, right on the rostrum's scarlet carpet. They kissed passionately, as though alone in the world, and then removed their flying helmets with such a flourish that the applause doubled throughout the Memorial. Their exhibitionism shocked no one. Ophelia wasn't close enough to the rostrum to see them properly, but she was no less dazzled by their gold-painted hair and skin.

The old gong sounded to restore calm.

The couple went up the steps of the dais, hand in hand.

The loudspeakers broadcast their voices as though they were but one voice: "Knowledge serves peace."

"Knowledge serves peace," everyone in the Memorial responded in unison.

It was right then that Ophelia realized that these strange creatures were in fact the Genealogists. They little resembled how she had imagined them. Looking closely, they weren't that young, but their presence was as dazzling as their makeup. They saw themselves as suns, and, in truth, their radiance had totally eclipsed the presence of Helen, Pollux, and all the Lords on the rostrum, as if they were the true family spirits of Babel. Lady Septima herself was looking intently at them with a veneration Ophelia had never witnessed before from her. These people didn't want to become God's equals; they already considered themselves to be so.

Thorn was really playing with fire by allying himself with them.

"Today is a great day for our city!" the woman's sensual voice proclaimed into the microphone. "We are celebrating a double dawn: the new catalogue and the new virtuosos."

"We are witnessing the reconciliation of the past and the future," the man continued, with such perfect synchronicity, he seemed to be a natural extension of his partner. "The modernizing of research techniques has been effected in the service of our ancestral heritage. The human and the machine," he declared, as the woman Genealogist made a point of indicating the automatons, "have attained a level of cooperation never equaled to this day. We must extend this model across the whole of Babel!"

"To do so, we need citizens who are both knowledgeable and competent," the woman seamlessly continued, this time looking lovingly at all the companies of virtuosos. "We need citizens of the caliber of Professor Lazarus, who is honoring us with his presence today, and who was once one of your own. We need citizens like you, Goddaughter of Helen!" she concluded, fixing her gaze on Elizabeth. "Your work on the database has been nothing short of remarkable. Come forward, Forerunner! Come and collect your third grade, which makes you forever a virtuoso citizen of Babel!"

There was a certain voracity about this invitation that Ophelia found rather disturbing. Elizabeth, unusually flushed, went up onto the rostrum.

It dawned on Ophelia that the Genealogists had made no mention of Thorn in their speeches. And yet he had been at the very nerve center of the project. Was that to protect his cover as Sir Henry? Or was it because they hadn't obtained the only book they were interested in from him?

Ophelia raised her glasses toward Lazarus's balcony, just as he was ordering his mechanical butler to photograph the scene. If they knew what she, *she* knew . . . !

"Thank you, Forerunner!" the Genealogists continued, once Helen had handed Elizabeth her silver stripe. "You are proof that Babel is the ideal city, where descendants of the twenty-one family spirits, and also non-descendants, can work together for the best of all possible worlds! As a mark of our gratitude, please also accept this prize for excellence. Come, Goddaughter of Helen, join us!"

Elizabeth went up the steps of the golden dais, where the even more golden Genealogists were holding out her trophy, also golden. Cornered by the couple, she clung onto her prize with both hands. Her long, flat body seemed to want to become even narrower, to lose what contours it had, to escape from the thousands of eyes focused on it. It wasn't the first time Ophelia had noticed a vulnerability behind Elizabeth's mask of indifference. She felt uncomfortable for her when the Genealogists pushed her gently, but firmly, toward the microphone.

"Hmm? Oh, I . . . We just needed a management system . . . a standardized language . . . an algorithm for the instructions . . . that kind of thing. It's really nothing but a simple research program. A bit like . . . like a memory. Our collective memory. The most important thing is the data itself. I wouldn't have got anywhere without the reading groups and without Sir Henr—"

"Bravo once again, citizen!" the Genealogists congratulated her, smiling warmly. "You may return to your place."

So it wasn't that they had forgotten, thought Ophelia, as Elizabeth descended the steps of the dais, hiding behind her trophy. Thorn had been deliberately sidelined. Once again, she searched for him in the crowd at the Memorial, without finding him.

"We are now going to proceed to the awarding of the other grades. Among all the apprentice virtuosos here present, alas, rare will be the chosen few. Tradition requires that just one Son of Pollux and one Godchild of Helen be promoted to aspiring virtuoso in each company, and, believe us, the choice was not always easy. Each file was examined with the utmost attention by the Lords of LUX, and, of course, by Lady Helen and Sir Pollux. Please come up to receive your grade when your name is called. Company of Scribes: Cornelia and Erasmus!"

Two apprentices left their rows to make for the rostrum. Their radiant faces contrasted with the jealous expressions of their classmates, who forced themselves to applaud them, half-heartedly.

As the Genealogists called up the apprentices, tension spread to Ophelia's every muscle. Right. The decisive moment had finally arrived. In but a few moments, either she would become an aspiring virtuoso, and could continue to be seen beside Thorn in public, or she would return to being anonymous, and Babel's every door would remain closed to her.

She observed, one by one, the classmates whose lives she had shared these past months. Zen was so anxious that her uniform kept shrinking and then expanding around her oriental-doll's body. As for the Seers, they were still staring glumly at their boots. Did they already know the results? Ophelia would never see them again, and she almost felt a twinge of sorrow on realizing that she wouldn't miss a single one of them. Her only real thought was for Mediana, whom she had left on that bench, hunched in front of the stained-glass window at the Deviations Observatory. Despite all her faults, it was here, within their ranks, that the Seer should have been found today.

"Company of Forerunners," the Genealogists finally called out. "Octavio and Zen!"

At this announcement, Ophelia did not bat an eyelid. And yet she felt as if her entire consciousness had suddenly retreated deep inside her. She saw herself, from afar, turning her head toward Zen as she stifled a cry of surprise. She saw herself, from afar, applauding her with the rest of the crowd. She saw herself, from afar, watching her as she went timidly up to the rostrum, with Octavio, to collect her stripe.

Zen was a serious and competent woman. She had relentlessly honed her family power for months. Her ability to miniaturize and deminiaturize fragile documents, without ever damaging them, would certainly enable the Memorial to improve the storing and circulation of its information.

She deserved to succeed.

So why did Ophelia not accept defeat? Why did Lady Septima's sly smile, from the rostrum, anger her this much? Because Zen wasn't a true Forerunner. Because she didn't have any real curiosity. Because she wasn't driven by a thirst for truth; and especially, most especially, because she didn't need that stripe like Ophelia needed it.

"What do I know about it?" she promptly asked herself, shocked by her own thoughts. "We never really talked, she and I; I barely know her."

Just for a moment, Ophelia imagined herself, instead of Zen, on the rostrum, as if they were the reverse reflections of one and the same person. Then she stared at her boots, just like the Seers surrounding her. She was no longer just ashamed of having failed. She was also ashamed of having let herself be contaminated by that competitive spirit that had pushed them all mutually to hate one another. If the isolation chamber had helped her to grow up, it was certainly not to become that kind of adult. In one way, Ophelia was relieved that Thorn hadn't been present to see her like this.

She applauded Zen, sincerely this time. Never mind. There were infinite possible futures; it was up to her to choose another one for herself.

"Congratulations to the new virtuosos!" exclaimed the Genealogists, once the last grade had been awarded. "As for all the rest of you, you may continue your lives without your prestigious uniform, but it will always be part of you, through your know-how and making known. Knowledge serves peace!"

All throats in the audience combined to sing Babel's anthem, all fists on chests. It was then time for the slow procession of failed apprentices, who now had to lay their insignias at Helen's and Pollux's feet. Ophelia was swept along in this parade. She went up the steps of the rostrum, like so many before her, and once she reached Helen's vast crinoline, she kneeled to unfasten the silver wings from her heels. "Thank you," Ophelia said to her.

Of all the family spirits she had encountered until then, none had commanded her respect as much as this ogress of nightmarish proportions. She would have liked to garner a final look from her, and never mind it being filtered through a convoluted optical appliance, but Helen remained stony-faced when Ophelia's wings clattered onto the pile of insignias.

Lady Septima pretended not to notice her, either. However, the spark between her eyelids betrayed jubilation in its purest form. Ophelia didn't thank her.

Up on the dais, the Genealogist couple had completely lost interest in what was taking place on the rostrum. They had switched off the microphone and were exchanging sweet nothings with lips so close together, they appeared to be kissing. Their long tresses were as closely entwined as the fingers of their hands. This passion that radiated from their gold-painted bodies transfigured their aged faces. Ophelia couldn't help but find them fascinating. Whether or not they were God's equals, theirs was already an immortal heartbeat.

"Apprentice Eulalia?"

Ophelia turned to Octavio, who was waiting for her at the bottom of the steps. She had almost not heard him due to the fourteenth verse of the interminable family hymn of Babel.

"Aspiring Virtuoso Octavio, I'm no longer an apprentice."

"Sorry. Just a habit."

He looked so uncomfortable that Ophelia rallied a little. She pointed at the new silver stripe on his sleeve, which he was rubbing like an annoying itch. "Congratulations. You deserve it."

"That's what people keep repeating to me," Octavio muttered, looking away. "When it's you saying it, I'm almost tempted to believe you. Would you follow me, please?"

Without giving her time to respond, he crossed the atrium, cleaving through the crowd of apprentices. Despite Ophelia elbowing her way through, she almost lost him. She would have preferred to remain as visible as possible for Thorn, but was he even looking for her? She had the feeling that, conversely, Octavio wanted to escape from the ultrapowerful sight of his mother, on the rostrum.

THE MEMORY OF BABEL

Ophelia frowned on seeing him enter the northern transcendium. He ignored all the hands reaching out to compliment him, and took a key out of his pocket that she immediately recognized.

The gangway to the Secretarium sprang out as soon as Octavio activated it from the post. "Let's hurry up," he said, through gritted teeth. "Sir Henry wants to see you alone. There's such a crowd here today, I wouldn't want any visitors to join us by accident."

Ophelia didn't hear his last sentence. Her mind had remained lodged on "Sir Henry wants to see you alone." She had to concentrate to catch what Octavio was now saying as he walked ahead of her along the gangway:

"My mother wouldn't hear of any of it. She won't budge: what happened to Mademoiselle Silence, to Mediana, to Fearless, all nothing but a series of accidents. Professor Wolf's testimony? Ramblings. She shows so little goodwill, I almost thought she was . . . it's awful to say it . . . she was hiding things from me. But I think what's worse is that she really believes in her own assurances. She's so obsessed with the perfection of our city that, quite simply, she can't conceive that the reality might be different. Just like with my sister," Octavio concluded, all in one breath. "It's for that reason that I decided to tell everything to Sir Henry. I think that he, at least, took me seriously. He gave me his own key so I could open the Secretarium to you after the ceremony. I think he wants to hear your version of events."

Ophelia opened the reinforced door of the terrestrial globe. So Thorn knew everything. Everything, except the most important thing.

"Good luck to you," she said to Octavio. "I'm sure you'll put your wings to better use than you think you will."

After the stiffest hesitation, he shook the hand she offered him. "You, too, you deserved your stripe, Eulalia. I won't bid you farewell. I have reason to think that we'll end up seeing each other again."

He turned on his heels, with a sudden clattering of wings, and set off at a swift pace, which reverberated all along the gangway. In the palm of Ophelia's hand there now lay the key to the Secretarium, and also a little piece of paper, folded into four.

On the paper, there was a very badly written note:

*Come and see me sometime, your hands and you. Helen.*

# THE WORDS

Ophelia crossed the inner court of the Secretarium with the certainty that she was doing so for almost the last time. The celebrations outside took on a sonorous resonance in there, like a refrain from an old record player. She looked up at the globe of the old world, floating in the middle of the light shaft. It was an exact replica of the one she was in, and yet the secret it enclosed surpassed that of all the collections put together.

A hanging mirror.

A mirror caught between two different ages.

A mirror that had witnessed a primordial event.

Ophelia still couldn't understand how she had managed to make such a transition, but she was grateful to that object for all that it had taught her. She took the closest transcendium. The fitful beating in her chest merged with the clicking of the database cylinders.

"Sir Henry wants to see you alone."

She gave two little knocks on the door before entering the Coordinator Room. When she banged into a pyramid of cardboard boxes, she wondered whether she hadn't made a mistake. A flickering half-light hovered in the room, and Ophelia understood why the moment a flash of light hit her in the glasses: a projector placed on a stool was transferring spectral images onto one of the walls, changing transparency every ten seconds with a mechanical clunk. They were all enlargements of printed texts.

"Don't stay in the light."

Thorn's voice had come from the back of the room, among the towering piles of boxes, where the shadows loomed largest. His long, angular body, hunched over a microfilm viewer, twisted like twine, was at one with the stool he was perched on. The machine's binocular lenses covered his eyes, which he raised just once every ten seconds, with uncanny punctuality, to take a quick look at the projection of a new transparency on the wall. Carefully, and very gradually, his fingers turned the rotating knobs that made the spool of film unwind through the lens of the viewer.

"Take a box," he added, without stopping.

It wasn't exactly affectionate, and yet Ophelia instantly felt her eyes, nose, and throat flooding uncontrollably. She suddenly realized how much Thorn had scared her by rejecting her, and how reassured she felt seeing him again. She smothered a sniffle as best she could with the sleeve of her uniform, and then opened a box at random, from among the dozens cluttering the room. It was full to the brim with spools of microfilm, each bearing a faded old label.

"If you can make out a date, put the oldest to one side," Thorn instructed.

With surgical precision, he replaced the spool in the viewer with another one. Ophelia would have appreciated him taking a break from his work, but he seemed more time obsessed than ever. The light of the viewer made the silvery blond beard creeping over his face shimmer. Ophelia might have been on the other side of the room, but she could feel the raw energy radiating from him, like an electric field. How long had he been perched on this stool? Was he even aware that the awarding of grades had just taken place, right under his Secretarium?

Thorn frowned when, as he glanced at a new transparency on the adjoining wall, he noticed that Ophelia hadn't started her sorting. "I am aware of your altercation with Fearless-and-Almost-Blameless; of your edifying conversation with Professor Wolf; and of your research into E. G.'s books after they were destroyed by Mademoiselle Silence," he reeled out in one breath. "You had an excellent lead there. If we had discussed it the other evening, rather than both getting agitated, we would have saved time. All the micro-documents you see here were created for the Interfamilial Exhibition of sixty years ago," he explained, peering once again through his binocular lenses. "They have never been sorted since then. It would be reasonable to suppose that a copy of E. G.'s books might be found somewhere in these cardboard bo—"

"I won't be a virtuoso," Ophelia interrupted him. At this moment, she couldn't care less about E. G.'s books: nothing mattered more than the urgent need to have, right here and right now, a real conversation with Thorn.

"I suspected as much." He had responded to her without lifting his nose from his viewer, or slowing the winding of his spool. "I gave an unfavorable opinion on your promotion," he continued, sounding businesslike. "I presume that must have had some influence."

"You did what?" Ophelia stammered. "But I thought you wanted . . . "

"I changed my mind. It recently struck me that the Genealogists were a little too interested in the future Forerunners. I shouldn't have encouraged you to obtain that grade. Your cover wouldn't have fooled them for long."

"In that case, you could have . . . "

"Spoken about it to you first?" Thorn completed her sentence for her. "You were not exactly reachable these last few days."

Ophelia went quiet. She felt such a jumble of emotions, it was hard for her to decide whether she was enormously relieved or dreadfully disappointed.

She took a deep breath. "There is something else I must tell you. That I should have told you before, in fact."

"It can surely wait a bit longer," he muttered, between his teeth. "At the rate of a transparency every ten seconds and a microfilm every four minutes, I will have found what I'm looking for between now and dawn." As he said this, he changed the spool of his viewer and clamped his eyes back on the binocular lenses.

Ophelia crossed the room, taking care not to knock over any boxes, which wasn't the easiest task. Thorn was so absorbed in his microfilms that he didn't notice her approaching him. She had no choice but to contemplate the huge curve of the back he insisted on turning away from her. She was now just an arm's length away from him. The last time she had attempted to close this gap—this gulf—between them, Thorn had turned his claws on her.

Timidly, she raised her hand toward the shoulder, its joint rolling under the shirt with every knob rotation. She wanted all of Thorn's attention as she finally released the words so long trapped inside her: "I love you, too."

She jumped. Thorn had spun around, fast as lightning, to block her wrist. His reaction was so abrupt, the glint in his eyes so hard, Ophelia thought he was about to push her away once again. With a totally unpredictable opposite movement, he pulled her toward him. The stool tipped over. Ophelia felt as if she were landing with all her weight between Thorn's ribs as they fell together, to a clattering of steel and an avalanche of boxes. The viewer exploded into fragments of glass on the floor beside them.

It was the most spectacular and baffling fall Ophelia had

ever experienced. Her ears were humming like hives. The frame of her glasses was digging into her skin. She could no longer see a thing, could barely breathe. When she realized that she was crushing Thorn, she wanted to extricate herself, but couldn't. He was imprisoning her in his arms so tightly that she could no longer distinguish between the beating in their chests.

Thorn's bushy beard became buried in her hair as he said: "Above all, no sudden gestures."

After the way he had just flung them both to the ground, this warning was somewhat incongruous. The arm vise relaxed, muscle by muscle, around Ophelia. She had to lean on Thorn's stomach to get back up. Half-slumped on the floor, his back against a bookcase, he was watching her with extreme tension, as if expecting her to trigger a catastrophe.

"Never do that again," he said, stressing each syllable. "Take me by surprise. Never. Have you got that?"

Ophelia had too much of a lump in her throat to reply to him. No, she hadn't got it. She was starting to wonder whether he had even listened to her declaration.

She was dismayed at the sight of bits of metal scattered on the carpet. There wasn't much left of Thorn's leg brace.

"Nothing that can't be repaired," he commented. "I have some tools in my bedroom. This, on the other hand, is more problematic," he added, glancing at the shattered pieces of the microfilm viewer. "I'll have to get myself another one."

"I don't think that is a priority," Ophelia snapped.

She bit her tongue when Thorn pressed his mouth against hers. At that moment, she no longer understood a thing. She felt his beard pricking her chin, his disinfectant smell going to her head, but the only thought that crossed her mind, a stupid, obvious one, was that she had a boot stuck in his shin. She wanted to pull away; Thorn stopped her. He cradled her face with his hands, his fingers in her hair, pressing against the nape of her neck with an urgency that knocked them both off balance. The bookcase showered them with papers. When Thorn finally pulled away, short of breath, it was to look sternly straight through her glasses.

"I warn you. The words you said to me, I won't let you go back on them." His voice was harsh, but underlying the authority of his words there was some sort of crack. Ophelia could see the quickened pulse in the hands he was awkwardly pressing to her cheeks. She had to admit, her own heart was swinging to and fro. Thorn was, without doubt, the most disconcerting man she'd ever met, but he did make her feel wonderfully alive.

"I love you," she repeated, firmly. "That's what I should have replied to you every time you wanted to know what I really wanted to say to you. Of course, I do want to unlock God's mysteries and regain control of my life, but . . . you're actually part of my life, actually. I called you an egoist, and at no time did I ever put myself in your shoes. Please forgive me."

Ophelia had wanted to come across as resolute, but she heard her own voice treacherously cracking at those last words. Thorn stared at the tear rolling onto his thumb; his eyes were opened so wide that his scar just kept expanding.

"I must insist," he muttered, increasing his fingers' hold around her face. "Never again accost me from behind my back, or from any of my blind spots. Don't do any movement that I can't see coming in advance, or then warn me out loud."

The transparency projector continued to flash sporadically. With each gleam, Ophelia saw Thorn under a new light: his withdrawing, his sidestepping, his reclusive existence, that distance he carefully maintained between himself and the rest of the world. "You no longer have control over your claws?"

Thorn narrowed his nostrils and pursed his lips. His entire

face seemed to have shrunk at once. "I can contain them if they don't see you as a threat. Which is why you must follow my instructions and avoid triggering defensive responses. You can't afford to be absentminded with me, it's as simple as that."

"But how did it happen?" Ophelia stammered. "Could the injection of my Animism have destabilized your family power?"

Thorn's eyebrows quivered. "Does it disturb you?"

Ophelia knew then that this loss of control was more humiliating to him than his physical handicap. Thorn hadn't deliberately used his claws against her that last time. He hadn't even been aware of it.

She promised herself never to tell him about it.

"No," she replied, looking him straight in the eye. "Now that I know, I'll be careful."

Thorn stared at her with an almost brutal intensity. Ophelia was suddenly acutely, painfully aware of that emptiness she had felt gnawing inside her for the past three years. She began to shake. She was not afraid—she was *no longer* afraid. It was a vibration rising from the very roots of her being. The pressure of Thorn's fingers on her hair first strengthened, and then suddenly relaxed, as his hands fell. He cleared his throat.

"You . . . My toolbox is under the bed in my room. Could you bring it to me? I must find a new microfilm viewer and get back to work, but to do that," he said, grimacing as he tried to bend his knee joint, "I'm going to need my leg."

Ophelia's most self-centered side took over. "Is there really such a hurry?"

For the first time in an eternity, Ophelia saw that slight twitching of Thorn's lips that she'd never known how to interpret. To her surprise, from one of his pockets he took out the old fob watch, which opened and then closed its own cover to show him the time.

"In fact, there is. A bit more than that, even. I have got until the end of the inauguration ceremony to find the book the Genealogists asked me for. Beyond that deadline, if I have nothing to offer them, they will make Sir Henry disappear from circulation. Could you bring me my toolbox?" he asked again, putting away his watch.

Ophelia stared at Thorn in disbelief. "They will make Sir Henry disappear from circulation," she repeated, in a subdued voice. "You are Sir Henry."

"It's merely an identity the Genealogists created for me. They can withdraw it from me at any moment, and hand me over to God, or even worse. Which they will do without the slightest hesitation if I don't give them what they expect from me before dawn. My toolbox, please."

"You knew from the start that your days were numbered, and never mentioned it to me?"

"It would have been counterproductive to tell you about it."

Ophelia didn't know how Thorn did it, but he had a knack for turning her upside down. A moment earlier, she was resisting the desire to throw herself into his arms; now she was resisting the desire to slap him. "But why ally yourself to people like that? Why always put your life in danger like this?"

As he tried, with difficulty, to lift himself up against the bookcase, Thorn suddenly seemed to notice the scattered paper, metal, and glass all around him. Compulsively, he checked his cuff links, and then his shirt collar, as if he feared being contaminated by this mess.

"Because my life is the only thing I feel I have the right to put at stake. My toolbox, if you please. And a flask of disinfectant, while you're at it."

"But why?" Ophelia asked, impatiently. "Why inflict that on yourself? Why force yourself to defy forces that are beyond you? And don't talk to me again of a sense of duty. You owe nothing to the world. What's the world ever done for you?"

Thorn's constant frown suddenly relaxed; but not enough to remove the furrow down his forehead.

"You think it's for the world that I'm doing this?"

The tension electrifying his body immediately intensified, tightening his jaw and hardening his eyes. It was then that Ophelia realized that what she had always taken for determination was, in reality, true rage.

"God said he would keep his eye on you," he muttered, in a choked voice. *"Right in front of me.* I make a lamentable husband, but I permit no one, particularly him, to persecute my wife. It's impossible for me to tear you away from God, but I can tear him away from you. And that's what I'm going to do at once, as soon as you deign to bring me that confounded toolbox. If a book exists that contains God's secret, and allows his invulnerability to be punctured, I will find it."

Ophelia held Thorn's stare in a stubborn face-off, and then got up and went to fetch the toolbox under the bed in his room.

"Repair your brace and forget your microfilms," she said, as she brought it to him. "I know where that book is."

# THE DRAWER

Ophelia cut through the crowd, against the tide. She had been first to leave the Secretarium; being seen in public with Thorn would have attracted attention, and there were still too many people in the Memorial. The visitors who had come for the ceremony were now following the Genealogists through the collections. Their silence was so respectful that, despite their number and the vastness of the place, one could hear the couple's sensual voices from the other end of the atrium. They were taking it in turns to ask the Memorialists highly technical questions about how the new catalogue worked. The launching celebration was turning into a veritable inspection.

Ophelia thought she could see Lazarus's big, white top hat beside the couple. She hoped he would remain there for another hour or two, long enough for she and Thorn to do what they had to do.

She made for the exit, carefully avoiding meeting Blaise, Elizabeth, or Zen, who might have felt obliged to say a few comforting words to her over the loss of her wings. She would try to say goodbye to them properly once this book business was finally over.

Before going through the main doors, she had a last look at the golden figures now going up the southern transcendium, hand in hand, like two solar stars. Thorn may have had no choice but to ally himself with them, but the more Ophelia saw of them, the more convinced she became that they were dangerous. Giving them the book would solve one problem, only to create a new one in the future. "Never mind," she thought, leaving the Memorial. "We'll deal with that when the time comes."

*We.* Just that word produced an unexpected shiver in the small of her back. She sat down on one of the entrance steps to wait for Thorn. She could still feel the irritation on her chin left by his beard. She lifted her nose while taking a deep breath of the warm evening air. The sunset's rays glimmered on the leaves of the mimosa trees and on the constellation of aircraft. The stormy sky had the changing consistency of some concoction in which contrasting colors combined but never managed to blend. Ophelia was about to put herself back in danger, and yet, at that precise moment, she was feeling unbelievably good.

"Do we know each other?"

She turned her head. Sitting on the same step as she was, on the opposite side of the staircase, a giant man was staring at her with an awkward smile. It was Pollux. Ophelia had taken him for one of the bronze statues. The dusk brought out the night of his skin and the fire in his eyes. His huge hands were distractedly leafing through the cutaneous pages of his own Book, like some fellow would have flicked, half-heartedly, through an unfathomable novel. He looked more like an abandoned child than a venerable patriarch. There was something surreal about this scene, when hundreds of his descendants were on the other side of the doors.

"You remind me of someone," Pollux insisted. "Generally, no one ever reminds me of anyone. I find it hard enough to remember the name of my own twin. But you," he said, with a note of melancholy in his cello-like voice, "the more I look at you, the more familiar you are to me. Do we know each other?"

"Not personally," Ophelia replied. "I'm a descendant of Artemis."

"Artemis," Pollux murmured. "I believe I do indeed remember one of my other sisters who goes by that name. Is it her you remind me of? I no longer even know why exactly I got this out," he said, casually turning a page of his Book. "I'm so absentminded . . . "

When Ophelia came over, Pollux stared at the tiny gloved hand she held out to him. His smile became hesitant, almost concerned, but, finally, he obediently handed his Book to her. This tome, which seemed so light in the family spirit's fingers, required Ophelia to use the strength of both arms to hold it. She scanned the writing tattooed onto the skin of the pages, that code to which no one in the world, except God, had the key.

"There," she said, indicating the barely visible edge of a torn-out page. "That was your memory. That's what you were looking for. You won't find it because someone tore it away from you a long time ago. I'm so sorry."

Ophelia returned the Book to Pollux, whose big eyes were blinking with stupefaction. "Do we know each other?" he asked again.

She didn't reply to him, but his distraught expression moved her. Shortly, he would have forgotten this conversation. Maybe it was better that way. Maybe it was better to maintain the family spirits' ignorance of what they really were.

Ophelia was relieved to see Thorn emerging from the Memorial at last. He had buttoned the prestigious LUX uniform over his shirt, and, judging by the stick he was using to support his steps, he hadn't managed to refine the mending of his brace.

She followed him at a respectable distance as he headed for the ark's platform. They waited each in their corner, looking in opposite directions, and once aboard the birdtrain, each chose a different bench. These precautions were perhaps excessive given the few passengers traveling at this time, but, publicly, Sir Henry and Eulalia were mere acquaintances.

Ophelia noticed, with a tightening in her throat, how Thorn positioned himself so as not to have anyone around him. They exchanged not a flicker of a look throughout the journey, and yet she had never felt so close to him. He sat as he usually did, rigid and impassive, but Ophelia could tell how nervous he was from every tap of his index finger on the chrome knob of his stick.

She would have liked to sit beside him, to reassure him, to tell him that she knew exactly what she was doing, even if that wasn't entirely true. She might know the location of the book, but she still didn't know what it contained.

As the birdtrain prepared to land on the terminus tracks, rocked by a squall and rattling from every carriage, Ophelia got that feeling again: the unshakeable impression of being watched. It was much stronger, even, than an impression. Her ears started ringing loudly. An icy chill coursed down her back. She turned on her bench to inspect the last passengers. In the Pole, Ophelia had already been tailed by an Invisible. This feeling wasn't remotely comparable. To her, it felt as if Terror itself, after following hot on her heels, had melted into her shadow. Was the killer who had terrorized Mademoiselle Silence, Professor Wolf, Mediana, and Fearless there, with them, in one of the carriages? Ophelia knew for certain that she knew him personally, without being able to put her finger on his identity.

She wasn't sorry to leave the birdtrain.

She followed the metallic clicking of Thorn's stick along the platform, avoiding, like him, the halo of the lamps. Night had fully fallen. They were both nothing but black silhouettes against an inky backdrop. The darkness enhanced the resinous scent and rustling of the needles from the umbrella pines around them.

"From here on, we will walk," Thorn announced in a low voice. "We must avoid the inspection patrols. You are not supposed to wear the virtuoso uniform anymore, and the dress code is no joking matter for these people."

Ophelia agreed. She had retrieved her false papers before leaving the Good Family, but she'd left her civilian toga there.

"I've only been to Lazarus's place once. I'm not sure I can remember the way."

"I can," Thorn said. "I memorized the maps of the whole city on my arrival in Babel. That address isn't next door, let's not waste a second."

They crossed a succession of badly lit building sites without encountering anyone but opossums. The city was as deserted at night as it was bustling during the day; Babelians were all as virtuous as well-behaved children. Ophelia turned around several times to check they weren't being followed, but the anxiety that had gripped her onboard the birdtrain had disappeared.

"Are you annoyed?" she asked. She couldn't see Thorn clearly in the gloom of the neighborhood they were now walking through, but there was something about his stony silence and the relentless banging of his stick that was a bit more than impatience. Ophelia might have sound legs, but she found it difficult to keep up with the rhythm he was imposing on them. It seemed barely believable that this man, of whom she lost sight around every street corner, had kissed her two hours earlier.

"I'm thinking," Thorn muttered, without slowing his pace.

"You've been looking all this time for a book that I swiped. You have every right to be exasperated."

Two sparks in the dark indicated to Ophelia that Thorn had just turned his eyes toward her.

"If you hadn't removed it from the Memorial, Mademoiselle Silence would have destroyed it, and with it my only chance of survival. What bothers me about your story is strictly mathematical in nature."

"Mathematical?"

"It took me more than two years to set up qualified reading groups in order to examine all the collections closely. The first book you inadvertently take is the right one. Your propensity to distort statistics is alarming."

Ophelia frowned. She recalled that great day when she had discovered the Memorial with Ambrose. She saw herself again knocking over and then picking up the books by E. G. that had been on Blaise's trolley. She felt as if she could almost— almost—remember that fleeting moment when she had slid *The Era of Miracles* into her traveling bag. Was that why Mademoiselle Silence had been so insistent on checking inside it? Had her ears recognized the characteristic sound of the book inside?

"It wasn't really inadvertent." She kneeled on the pavement to retie a lace that kept tripping her up. "I mean, part of me didn't pick that book by chance. Part of me recognized it. Part of me wanted to appropriate it."

"Your other memory," Thorn commented.

"I try hard to understand where it comes to me from and what it wants to tell me. I would have liked it at least to bother to explain to me what this children's book knows of God. But that," she concluded, doubling the knot in her lace, "we are going to find out very soon for ourselves."

Thorn stared at her with such piercing intensity, she lost her composure. Above them, lanterns buffeted by the wind cast a shuddering light.

"When this business is sorted out, we must talk, you and I."

"Must talk about what?"

"When this business is sorted out," Thorn simply repeated. With the steel-tipped end of his stick, he pointed at the columns of a portico on the opposite side of the square they had just reached. Ophelia recognized the star-reflecting pools of water lilies surrounding the property. They had arrived.

"I hope Ambrose will be at his father's," she whispered as they walked along the columns. "It was to him that I entrusted my bag; he'll return it to me without a fuss, if I ask him to."

She refrained from mentioning the adolescent's sudden change in attitude once she had entered the Good Family. He hadn't even deigned to turn around, deliberately ignoring her calls, the last time she'd seen him, on the birdtrain platform.

When Thorn hammered one of the entrance doors with the knob of his stick, an automaton came to open.

"Is Ambrose here?" Ophelia asked.

"NOTHING IS IMPOSSIBLE TO A WILLING HEART."

Thorn marched in. "We will manage on our own."

Ophelia looked around the atrium, where modern appliances blended in with historic architecture. The lamps attracted swarms of moths. There were only statues there, and the portrait of Lazarus, twinkling mischievously behind his pink spectacles.

"Ambrose?" Ophelia walked through the extensive series of rooms, their marble echoing her every step. Returning, after all these months, to the first house to have welcomed her in Babel gave her an indefinable feeling. Thorn accompanied her, walking stiffly and leaning increasingly heavily on his stick.

"I find them disturbing," he muttered. All the automatons of the residence had gathered to follow them at a distance. They seemed unsure of the correct approach toward these visitors who invited themselves like this into their masters' home.

There was nothing hostile in their behavior, but sensing such a crowd of faceless mannequins behind one didn't feel very comfortable.

"Ambrose?" Ophelia called out again, entering another room. Thorn indicated to her to listen carefully. There was a noise coming from the back of the property. It didn't really sound like Ambrose's wheelchair; Ophelia thought it more likely to be the juddering of a washing machine.

The further they advanced into the building, followed by the silent procession of automatons, the louder the noise became.

Ophelia recognized the checkerboard floor and elegant, low wardrobes of Ambrose's dressing room. It was right here that he had presented her with a toga, as worn by the powerless. To her great surprise, the noise wasn't coming from a mechanical washing machine, but from a drawer. It was shaking violently, as if trying to escape from its chest.

"It might be my bag," Ophelia whispered, hesitantly. "I didn't have it in my possession for long, but I could have animated it without realizing it."

"Just one way to find out."

Thorn took out a handkerchief with which to hold the knob of the drawer, as if germs were a more fearsome life form than anything this piece of furniture might contain. Ophelia jumped when something leapt out of the drawer and wound itself around Thorn's arm. Her first, utterly terrifying thought was that it was an enormous snake. Her second, perfectly incredulous thought, was that it was a knitted snake.

Thorn didn't flinch. With his hand still gripping the knob of the drawer, he carefully studied the creature strangling his arm with its three-colored coils. "It's definitely not your bag. It's your scarf."

"I had lost it." The words fell from Ophelia's lips like stones.

She stared at the scarf that was clinging to Thorn. It was definitely the one she had knitted, stitch by stitch, the one she had animated, day by day, and yet she couldn't accept its tangible presence here, right before her. "I had lost it," she said, again.

Cautiously, she stretched out her hand. The scarf immediately unwound itself from Thorn's arm to wind itself around hers, and then wrapped itself around her neck with a sulky possessiveness. It was only when she felt that familiar weight that Ophelia fully realized that, no, the scarf wasn't roaming the city's gutters, and, yes, they were finally reunited. The guilt that had been burning inside her for months rose to her mouth tasting of salt. She buried her nose in the scarf.

"I had lost it," she repeated, her voice muffled.

Her joy was immediately tempered. How had Ambrose gained possession of her scarf? And why had he hidden it in his chest of drawers? Couldn't he have returned it to her? Sent her a telegram, at least, to reassure her? The more Ophelia tried to understand it, the less she was able to. The trust she'd so readily given him, the hurt she'd felt when he had begun to avoid her, all that was starting to disintegrate inside her chest.

Thorn observed her, sternly, and finally said out loud what she didn't want to put into words:

"This Ambrose, are you sure he's definitely a friend?"

"You should leave."

Thorn and Ophelia turned around. A wheelchair, surrounded by a throng of automatons, was silhouetted in the doorway. Ambrose approached with a mechanical purr. The play of shadow and light in the dressing room accentuated the strangeness of his body, with its reverse symmetry, the dazzling whiteness of his clothes, and the velvety darkness of his face.

His inverted hands were convulsively gripping the wheel-chair's armrests. "Leave"

Ophelia swallowed with difficulty. It wasn't an order. It was an entreaty that Ambrose was addressing to her, and to her alone. His voice had become so beseeching that she no longer had any idea what she was supposed to feel.

She tugged on the scarf to uncover her mouth. "I came to fetch my bag. But what has happened to you? I don't recognize you anymore."

Ambrose's antelope eyes widened. The day they had met, he had shown only a kindly curiosity toward Ophelia. Now, he was looking at her as if she were the most improbable thing he had ever seen.

"What has happened to me is that you are not who you claim to be."

Ophelia's heart skipped a beat. How had he seen through her deception? Was it the scarf that, in one way or another, had betrayed her?

Her embarrassment must have been written all over her face because Ambrose looked profoundly disappointed. "So, I wasn't mistaken. From the first moment, I detected in you . . . But, all the same, I didn't think . . . " He went quiet, breathed in slowly, and then repeated with infinite gentleness: "You must leave, *mademoiselle. Je vous en prie.*"

"Or what?"

Thorn had spoken this question without losing his calm, but his eyes were as Polar as his accent. Ophelia tensed. If he was no longer speaking as Sir Henry, it meant that a line had just been crossed. The atmosphere of distrust hovering in the dressing room made the stuffiness of the place even more suffocating.

"Or it will end very badly," Ambrose replied. His fine features contorted with pain as he implored Ophelia with his eyes. "In any case," he added, in a tense whisper, "it can only end very badly. After all, *mademoiselle*, it is you who will cause the disintegration of the arks."

Ophelia's glasses blanched on her nose. The last person to have addressed those words to her was . . .

Thorn let out an exasperated snort. "I'm going to save us some time. You are in the service of God, aren't you?"

Barely had he uttered that last sentence before all the automatons, who, until then, had just been standing around behind the wheelchair, were on the march. In a slow procession, they took over the dressing room, surrounding Thorn, Ambrose, and Ophelia, and then linked hands like children—large children with no mouth, nose, or eyes—to form a ring around them. The moment the circle was closed, there was a flash of steel that made Ophelia's scarf shudder. Dozens, hundreds of sharp blades had just burst through the mannequins' clothes. What little humanity they had possessed had disappeared: they were now nothing but an impenetrable barrier of thorns. A trap.

Ambrose rested his elbows awkwardly on his chair. "That is most regrettable," he sighed. "You should not have said that."

"Call them off," Thorn ordered.

Ophelia shot him an anxious look. He had neither raised his voice nor made a move, but so clenched were his fingers around the knob of his stick that their knuckles had gone white. His claws felt threatened and he was doing his best to contain them. The dressing room wasn't spacious enough for him to distance himself from Ophelia and Ambrose without skewering himself on the automatons' blades.

"Ambrose, please," Ophelia intervened. "I know you don't want to do us any harm. Call off your servants and give me back my bag."

The adolescent shook his head with an unhappy expression. "I cannot, *mademoiselle*."

Ophelia felt her skin bristle as if lightning were about to strike. Thorn seemed to be tightening every muscle in his body to prevent the Dragons' power from bursting forth. His claws would have no effect on the automatons, but they could cut up both her and Ambrose like paper.

"Call them off," Ophelia insisted, drilling her eyes into Ambrose's desperate face.

"He cannot."

The voice that had just sung out those two words echoed through the building's colonnades. It was as light as the flutter of a butterfly.

Lazarus's voice.

"But I can. Fall out, *garçons!*"

The instant this command was issued, the automatons withdrew their weapons with a metallic clatter, broke up their ring, and left at a calm pace.

Lazarus stood on the threshold. He took off his huge top hat, creating a silvery waterfall of hair as he bowed.

"Mr. and Mrs. Thorn, I'm delighted to welcome you to my home! If you had waited for me at the Memorial, I would have happily offered you a lift in my aircraft. Please follow me to the drawing room," he suggested, putting his hat back on with a theatrical flourish, "we are going to have a most interesting chat!"

# THE NAME

Lazarus's teaspoon tinkled musically in his porcelain cup as it stirred the sixth sugar he had plopped into his tea. The tip of his tongue poked out between his teeth. He looked like a studious schoolboy. The old man's ways made him unintentionally amusing.

He didn't make Ophelia feel like laughing whatsoever.

Sitting on the very edge of the sofa, with the scarf snuggling possessively between her arms, she touched neither the tea nor the macaroons that Walter, the mechanical butler, served her. She could feel Ambrose's distraught eyes on her; his lips had remained sealed since his father's return. From the corner of her glasses, she checked Thorn to know what tactic to adopt. He was sitting stiffly among the profusion of cushions on the sofa, gripping the knob of his stick, which he had planted between his legs like a sword, and never taking his eyes off Lazarus. He had regained control of his claws, but they were still lying in wait, on the surface of his nerves, ready to lash out at the first false move. For Ophelia, merely sitting close to him prevented her migraine from completely lifting. When Thorn, in turn, was served a cup of tea by Walter, he promptly tipped the contents into the pot of a rubber plant.

"Come, come, I would never poison my guests under my

own roof!" Lazarus commented, with amusement. "I can't even squash a mosquito without feeling frightfully guilty."

Silence descended again, thick as tar. Ambrose was watching Ophelia who was watching Thorn who was watching Lazarus.

"*Bien!*" the last exclaimed, making his cup chime against its saucer. "I'm going to lay my cards on the table. Yes, I know you-know-who, and yes, I've been working for him for some time. I was a young aspiring virtuoso when I encountered him for the first time. *En fait*, to be accurate, it's he who came to recruit me. It was an experience that was . . . how can I describe it?" With his little finger, Lazarus pushed his pink spectacles onto the bridge of his nose as he searched for the right word. "Disconcerting. A bit like suddenly discovering that I had a twin brother. You-know-who appeared to me with my own face, my own voice, my own uniform—the very one you're wearing today, young *demoiselle*," he pointed out, with a knowing wink at Ophelia. "He graciously furnished me with considerable means to enable me to fulfill my dreams of exploring the world. He asked me for just a single, trifling thing in return . . . *La barbe!*"

Walter had poured him more tea, making his cup overflow and boiling-hot liquid spill over his fine white trousers.

"What in return?" Ophelia encouraged him.

Forgetting the tea burn, Lazarus broke into a beaming smile as he leaned emphatically forward on his pouffe. His eyes, his lenses, his teeth, and the golden tip of his nose glinted in the half-light of the room. This old man had the vitality of a young man. Ambrose, serious and still in his wheelchair, seemed the older of the two. For a father and son, they weren't very alike.

"Something *extrêmement* simple in return," Lazarus confided, an excited tremor in his voice. "I had to look."

"Look at what?"

"Whatever I deemed worthy of interest, young *demoiselle*! And since I deem absolutely everything worthy of interest, I have spent every second of the rest of my life looking on Go— on you-know-who's behalf."

Carried away by his own enthusiasm, Lazarus had stopped himself just in time. He looked around to reassure himself that the automatons, who were dusting the nooks and crannies of the drawing room, weren't moving back into their circle of blades. He then pulled a notebook, triumphantly, from his frock coat, waving it like a magician's wand. "I wrote notes on my travels! So many notes that they could rival the miles I covered on all my peregrinations."

In other words, Ophelia thought, stroking her scarf in an effort to stay calm, this man was God's pawn. The situation was not looking good. She glanced furtively at the large bay window, which the drawing-room lamps had turned into a mirror. It reflected all four of them, five if one included Walter's faceless form. If God had no reflection, it was at least comforting to note that neither Ambrose nor Lazarus were imposters right now.

"A mere handful of years later, you-know-who returned to see me," Lazarus continued, after noisily downing a gulp of his tea. "He entrusted me with a new mission, and new means to carry it out. An *extrêmement* tricky mission. To find the unfindable LandmArk! Or, failing that, to find an Arkadian. The only one I almost encountered," he sighed, looking regretful, "is poor Mademoiselle Hildegarde. It would seem she disappeared in highly dubious circumstances."

"She self-destructed."

Ophelia turned her glasses up at Thorn, who had just spoken these words. His razor-blade profile revealed nothing, but in the pause that followed there hovered an unspoken accusation: *she self-destructed because of you, because you harassed her, because God coveted her family power, and because she preferred to sacrifice herself rather than render him more harmful than he already is.*

With his white-gloved fingers, Lazarus stroked his beardless chin.

"A mighty sad exit for so brilliant an architect. I still can't understand how the situation could have taken such a turn . . . If at least I had managed to see her, speak to her, I certainly would have been able to convince her of the validity of our enterprise. You see," Lazarus gushed, joining his hands as though in prayer, "you-know-who is much more than the father-creator of the family spirits and the new humanity. He seeks neither glory nor gratitude. He aspires to just one thing: to become the incarnation of each one of you. Even I who am but a powerless person, I was touched to the soul by the beauty of his work, by the greatness of his cause! My birth dictates that I will never, alas, belong to his big and beautiful family, but I will use all my energy to make this world—his world—even more *parfait*! And so what if the Lords of LUX don't deem me worthy of joining their ranks. As long as they are satisfied with my automatons, and help me to combat the servitude of man by man, I'm a fulfilled citizen!"

Lazarus expressed himself as if each word sparkled on his tongue. Ophelia was struck by both his sincerity and his credulity. As for her, a single encounter with God had sufficed for her to have no intention of ever putting herself at his service. She observed Ambrose on the sly to gauge whether he was as indoctrinated as Lazarus, but the adolescent was staring into the amber surface of his tea in profound melancholy. His father's presence seemed to negate his own.

"Since we've mentioned LUX," Lazarus then added, giving Thorn's gilded uniform a telling look, "what the devil did you do to become one of them? The last time I heard of you, you were a disgraced Treasurer of the Pole, and here you are today, a Lord of Babel!"

Thorn shrugged his shoulders. "I have an assignment from the Genealogists. Address your questions to them."

Ophelia admired the ease with which he covered up his nervousness. It wouldn't have been wise to reveal that he had allied himself with the Genealogists in order to thwart God, after all that Lazarus had just told them.

"*Sapristi,* that's the last thing I'd do!" the latter guffawed, polishing his spectacles on his frock coat. "My level of initiation is nowhere near theirs. The Genealogists are not permitted to reveal what they know to me, and the same goes for me. Without wishing to offend you, Mr. Thorn, Sir Henry, or whatever your name is, my main concern, anyway, is for the fate of your companion."

Ophelia clenched her hands in her scarf, one end of which was whipping the air like the ruffled tail of a cat. Lazarus put his spectacles back on with a dramatic flourish to shoot a rose-tinted look at her. Just one word from him, and all the automatons in the house, maybe even in the city, would turn into a prison of thorns. Or worse. As her migraine intensified, Ophelia understood that Thorn's claws were ready to go on the offensive should the situation so demand.

"And in what way does my fate concern you?" she asked.

Lazarus leaned so far forward, he knocked his knees on the copper tray of the tea table. "In your opinion, young *demoiselle*, why did you-know-who ask me, from one day to the next, to find Arkadians? Why does he urgently need to possess their mastery of space today? Don't see this as a reproach on my part, but it's because of you. Because you shattered the fragile equilibrium of our world," he explained, with a benevolent smile. "And you-know-who will do all in his power to resto . . . "

"Don't denounce her." All heads, including Walter's faceless one, turned toward Ambrose. He had spoken in an impulsive, barely audible whisper. His chin was so drawn in, his turban threatened to topple onto his knees, and his hand shook around the cup his lips hadn't touched. Judging by his wide-eyed stare, he was the first to be shocked at having interrupted his father. "Don't denounce her," he repeated, all the same. "She . . . she helped me. I promised myself to help her in return."

Ophelia felt as if a weight had lifted from her chest only to end up deep in her stomach. She had helped him? Did Ambrose mean that time she had freed his wheelchair from the cobbles?

"My scarf. You purposely looked for it?"

Ambrose nodded without looking away from his cup. "It seemed to be very important to you, *mademoiselle*. During your trial period at the Good Family, I questioned the tram guards. I had to insist a bit. I finally discovered that your scarf had been deposited at the lost-property office. I imagine it must have been panicked at losing you; because it wasn't being . . . *eh bien* . . . very cooperative, the employee had placed it under seal. A fine had to be paid to retrieve it. I wanted to return it to you, I assure you, along with your bag, in fact."

Ambrose finally looked up at Ophelia, and then subtly glanced at his father. "There was an unforeseen event. I thought it best to hide your belongings until I found a solution."

"*Sapristi!*" Lazarus cried out, with a big, quizzical smile. "Am I the unforeseen event, Ambrose? Is it my return to the house that . . . ? It was clear to me that you weren't quite yourself these past few months, but if I'd had any idea! Why not have simply explained it to me . . . Just a minute," he broke off, suddenly, staring at Ambrose and Ophelia in turn with an increasingly flabbergasted expression. "This young *demoiselle*, who do you think she is, *exactement*?"

Ophelia raised her eyebrows and Thorn frowned even more with his. Long seconds of silence ensued, during which a night wind lifted all the mosquito nets from the windows, carrying with it the song of the frogs and the heady scent of the lily pools.

"She who will cause the disintegration of the arks," Ambrose finally whispered, in a high-pitched voice. "That 'Other' you have so often spoken to me about, Father."

Lazarus leaned with both hands on the tea table, spilling spices, milk jug, and sugar bowl in spectacular fashion. He began to peer at Ophelia with intense curiosity over the top of his spectacles, as if he wanted a view of her that wasn't rose-tinted.

"Well I never," he said, "that's darned interesting!"

"I am not the Other," Ophelia protested.

"She is not the Other," Thorn growled.

"You are not the Other?" Ambrose asked, with astonishment.

"She is not, *en effet*," Lazarus asserted, with total conviction. "But she is the one who released him. She bears the indelible mark, and I am dismayed not to have noticed it for myself," he said, punctuating each syllable with a gleeful slap on the copper top of the table. "You, too, are inverted!"

He scrutinized Ophelia from head to toe, as if she were a major archaeological find. She wasn't sure whether to feel flattered or insulted. Thorn pressed the steel-tipped end of his stick against Lazarus's chest to make him move back again; his fiery outbursts were sorely testing Thorn's claws. Obediently, Lazarus sat back down on his pouffe, while still staring avidly at Ophelia.

"I am one myself!" he announced proudly to her. "Have you never heard of *situs transversus*, young *demoiselle*? It's the name doctors give for anatomies like mine. It's certainly not as obvious as in my son's case," he said, patting Ambrose's deformed hand on the armrest of the wheelchair, "but if you could see inside my body, you would observe that all my internal organs are reversed. My heart is on the right, my liver on the left, and so on. I was born like that. In releasing the Other from the mirror, your symmetry inverted itself, in a certain way, *n'est-ce pas*?"

Ophelia nodded, cautiously. Thorn took out his fob watch, which was getting restless, and opened its cover to remind them of the time. This was all well and good, but it still didn't tell them where the bag was. Soon the event at the Memorial would be over, and the Genealogists were expecting the book that would make them God's equals.

"We're the same!" Lazarus proclaimed, with gusto. "You, me, my son, we are peas in a pod! This idiosyncrasy of ours makes all three of us *extrêmement* receptive to . . . to certain things. I'm not surprised you became such an excellent reader. Ambrose has amazing sensitivity, and I, without wishing to boast, I have intuitions that make me an authentic visionary. Did you know that the left-handed were once persecuted?" he asked, out of the blue. "They were called 'sinister' due to the perception that people had—that we have—of the universe that surrounds us! Thank goodness, they are no longer persecuted today. You will even be amazed to learn, young *demoiselle*, that here in Babel, we have an institution that specializes in cases such as ours."

"The Deviations Observatory," Ophelia said, her heart lurching.

"Oh, you already know of it?"

"I went there once. They even have a file on me. Well, on Eulalia. They deem me to be interesting."

"*Bien sûr!* You are interesting!" Lazarus was speaking so

passionately that his long silver hair was becoming messier by the minute. He was looking at Ophelia as if stifling the irresistible urge to dance with her.

"Where is this digression leading us, exactly?" Thorn asked, as his watch snapped its cover as a stern reminder.

"It's no kind of digression. *En fait*, we are right at the very crux of our 'problem,'" Lazarus said, miming the quotation marks with his fingers. "After all, I'm sure you would like to know whether or not I am going to speak about you two to God. My loyalty to him would compel me to send a telegram to him on the spot, but I'm starting to think that maybe that won't be necessary."

"Er . . . Father?" Ambrose timidly interrupted him.

Lazarus hadn't noticed, but at the mention of "God," all the automatons in the room had dropped their feather dusters to move toward them.

"*La barbe!*" Lazarus cursed. "Back to your work, you lot! Not my best invention," he admitted with an exasperated sigh, as each one returned to its place. "It's the only solution I found to ensure that certain secrets don't leave my house. As I was saying to you," he resumed, instantly recovering his smile, "I am not totally obliged to hand you over to you-know-who. His main priority, and consequently mine, too, is to find the Other. Now, young *demoiselle*, you are linked to this Other, and, sooner or later, you are bound to cross his path again. Personally, I am convinced that you are more likely to succeed in doing that in time if no one is keeping you on a tight rein."

Ophelia looked deep into the woolly folds of her scarf to hide the anger darkening her glasses. Lazarus was speaking to her of her shared destiny with the Other, and of the disintegration of the world, as if they were irrefutable facts. To her knowledge, no ark had been reported missing. Ophelia could barely remember that night when she had released the creature from the mirror; she sometimes even found herself thinking that she had dreamed it. This old fool was making them waste untold time over what were perhaps merely ravings!

An old fool who commandeered an army of automatons.

When Ophelia looked up at Lazarus, her glasses had regained all their transparency. "That's agreed," she said, trying her best to ignore Thorn tensing up beside her. "We will help you to find the Other, on the condition that you leave us free to follow our own initiatives. For now, please be so kind as to return my bag to me and loan us your aircraft."

Lazarus burst into such fits of laughter that his huge top hat toppled backwards. "*Formidable!* You can count on my total cooperation. Ambrose, would you go and fetch what this young *demoiselle* is asking you for? Walter!" he shouted at his butler, while stretching his own legs like two springs. "Let's go and get the Lazaropter ready for our new partners!"

Ophelia had to admit, as she saw them suddenly leaving the drawing room, that she had been expecting tougher negotiations. If Lazarus took her at her word, without demanding any guarantee from her, then he was as naive as he seemed to be.

The moment they were alone, Thorn collapsed against the back of the sofa, as if his long spine refused to support him a second longer. When he unclenched his fingers, one by one, from his stick, Ophelia saw that the form of the knob had imprinted itself on his skin. He winced when he tried to stretch his leg out a few inches, causing a clattering of steel and one bolt to drop off.

"Are you in pain?" Ophelia asked, with concern.

"I didn't save you from the Genealogists just for you to strike a deal with Lazarus."

"He seems neither very fearsome nor very informed. He doesn't even know what we really came to his house to find."

As she said these words, Ophelia wasn't, however, as relieved as she would have liked to be. For one moment, she had almost believed that it had been Lazarus who had gone for Professor Wolf, Mademoiselle Silence, Mediana, and Fearless. If he had nothing to do with this series of attacks, the real threat remained unidentified.

"The Genealogists are eminently corruptible egocentrics," Thorn said. "Lazarus is an idealist who places the wider interest above his own. He won't be as easy to manipulate as you think."

"I secured an aircraft from him. Don't underestimate me."

This was clearly said tongue-in-cheek, but Ophelia was taken aback by Thorn's deadly seriousness as he looked down at her. "I will never underestimate you."

In one gulp, Ophelia downed all the tea she had avoided until then, unconcerned at spilling some on the scarf, which shook itself, furiously. The tea was cold, but it helped to get rid of the lump that had suddenly lodged in her throat. Who would think of making such a declaration with such seriousness? She felt more intimidated now, on the cushions of this sofa, with Thorn's knee brushing against hers, than she had when faced with all the automatons' blades.

When she looked up from her cup, Thorn was looking away. He was studying the patterns on the carpet with inordinate interest. Since they had left the Memorial, something unspoken had hovered between them and she couldn't quite put her finger on it.

"You warned me earlier that we had to talk, you and I."

"Yes," Thorn concurred, stiffly. "It will, indeed, be necessary."

"I'd really like to know what it's ab . . . "

"Your bag, *mademoiselle*." Ambrose had just reappeared, accompanied by a mechanical whirr. "I'm so sorry to have

THE MEMORY OF BABEL

avoided you the way I did," he muttered. "I'd so convinced myself that you were the Other, I thought it was for the best. I . . . I hope we will remain friends?"

After all that had just been said in this house, Ophelia's thoughts were too muddled to give him an honest answer. She didn't, in any case, get the chance. The piercing look Thorn shot at Ambrose prompted the latter to reverse his wheelchair to the other end of the drawing room.

Ophelia took a deep breath before releasing the straps on her bag. Inside it she found her little grey dress, her winter boots, the sparkling-water siphon, some moldy biscuits, and the postcard her great-uncle had given her before her hasty departure from Anima.

Then she pulled out a book for children with a crimson cover and gilded lettering:

CHRONICLES OF THE NEW WORLD
THE ERA OF MIRACLES
WRITTEN AND PRINTED IN THE CITY-STATE OF BABEL
E. G.

Ophelia couldn't stop the slight tingling in her fingers, despite her gloves, as she opened this book that had engendered such covetousness and such misfortune. On the flyleaf she found the Memorial's stamp. She was no paper expert like Aunt Rosaline, but she was intrigued at the book being so well preserved. It was hard to believe that it dated from before the Rupture. Did it possess the same mysterious properties as the mirror hanging inside the globe of the Secretarium?

As she glanced at the opening lines, she wasn't surprised that she could recite them off by heart:

*Once upon a tomorrow,*
*before too long,*
*there will be a world that will finally live in peace.*

*At that time,*
*there will be new men*
*and there will be new women.*

*It will be the era of miracles.*

Ophelia turned the pages, one after another, with an undeniable sense of familiarity, as if she had already leafed through them on numerous occasions in the past. She didn't need to read the story to remember it. Now she recalled that it was divided into twenty short tales, and that each one related the birth of a new family: the masters of objects, the masters of minds, the masters of animals, the masters of magnetism, the masters of vegetation, the masters of transmutation, the masters of charm, the masters of divination, the masters of lightning, the masters of the senses, the masters of thermalism, the masters of tellurism, the masters of the winds, the masters of mass, the masters of metamorphosis, the masters of temperature, the masters of hallucination, the masters of phantomization, the masters of empathy, and the masters of space.

Twenty families, twenty powers.

The tales were just as Octavio and Professor Wolf had described them. Deadly boring. Once one had accepted the revolutionary concept that E. G. had managed to anticipate the advent of the new world at a time when the arks didn't yet exist, his stories in themselves were of no more interest.

There were no instructions to be found for elevating oneself to God's level.

Ophelia was seized by a dreadful, a horrifying doubt. She

handed the book to Thorn, trying hard not to reveal her panic to him. "Maybe . . . maybe the information we seek is coded?"

Thorn didn't respond, entirely focused on the pages he was photographing with his eyes, as he rapidly flicked past them with his thumbs. Once he had reached the end of the book, he remained bowed on the sofa for a long while, rigid as the brace on his leg, before slowly, very slowly turning his aquiline nose toward Ophelia. She suddenly seemed to have become a source of total bafflement to him.

"I think you should read carefully right to the end," he suggested to her, in a voice she'd never heard from him before.

Ophelia pushed her glasses up on her nose to take a good look at the last page, on which she hadn't noticed, due to the ink having faded so much there, a small handwritten inscription:

*"As we await better days, my dear children.*
*Eulalia Gonde."*

Ophelia kept reading and rereading these few words until every particle of her being was imbued with them.

Eulalia Gonde.

Gonde.

God.

Curiously, she didn't feel in the least surprised. She knew it. She had always known it, and she wondered how she could have forgotten something so totally fundamental. The day Archibald had asked her to pick a name for her false identity papers, Eulalia had come spontaneously to her lips. Eulalia, the woman whose memory she shared, that reflection from the past she had seen in the hanging mirror. She saw herself once again, in her seat, tapping away energetically on her typewriter, inventing countless stories for children between one crumpled handkerchief and the next.

Eulalia was God. Or rather, God had once been Eulalia,

before the Rupture. A little storyteller with a mispronounced surname. That didn't explain either why Ophelia shared her memories or how Eulalia Gonde had managed to create the family spirits, smash the world to pieces, and become, over the centuries, an almost omnipotent Milliface, but it did finally explain how a simple book could enable anyone to become God's equal.

"Because it is he who is anyone's equal," Ophelia murmured, stroking the handwritten inscription.

As she was closing *The Era of Miracles*, still shaken by the stirring of her memory, she sensed, at the edge of her glasses, eyes that were staring at them, Thorn and her, with utmost attention. Eyes that she finally recognized. The individual who had terrified Professor Wolf, Mademoiselle Silence, Mediana, and Fearless was right there in the drawing room, right now.

He had never stopped being there.

Leaning on the back of Ambrose's wheelchair, Lazarus gave them a big smile.

"The loaned aircraft for sir and madame awaits!"

# THE TERROR

Ophelia made not a sound as Lazarus, almost dancing, led them between the lily pools. She was pressing Eulalia Gonde's book to her stomach to stifle her trembling. Despite it being a muggy night, it felt as if her blood had turned to ice. She tried to put on a front, but the scarf sensed her fear and was gripping her neck.

Thorn, absorbed in his own thoughts, banged the ground with his stick with renewed resolve. Ophelia would have liked to scream to him that the killer was among them, but she would have hastened their downfall. No. It was imperative that she held her nerve. Looked straight ahead. Didn't arouse suspicion. A plan—unreasonable, full of holes, but still a plan—was slowly but surely coming together in her mind.

"Are you alright, *mademoiselle*?" Ambrose asked, politely. He was maneuvering his wheelchair to remain on her right side, his sweet face looking up at her as if desperately seeking her forgiveness. Ophelia merely nodded.

She was reassured to see Lazarus leaping up the steps of a terrace, the tails of his frock coat flapping like wings. Thorn followed him laboriously, one step at a time, unable to bend his brace at the knee. There was no ramp to access the terrace; Ambrose wouldn't be able to come with them. Not easily, at least. When Ophelia gave him a parting glance from the top of the steps, the adolescent's dark skin and the wood of his wheelchair were subsumed into the darkness of the gardens. Only his white clothes stood out against the shadows, creating the illusion that a ghost was sitting there, in midair.

Ophelia's plan might work.

The "Lazaropter" awaited them on the marble terrace. It was a machine that, with its rotary wings and metal structure, looked, in the lamplight, like the skeleton of a giant dragonfly. Walter was bringing a gangway up to it. The aircraft's propellers produced such gusts of wind that Ophelia felt the air slapping her cheeks and blowing her curls in all directions. She took a deep breath to brace herself and handed *The Era of Miracles* to Thorn as he was making for the gangway.

"The truth we've discovered," she said to him, loudly enough to be heard over the hum of the propellers, "it's probably not what the Genealogists would like to hear."

"I don't care. I've fulfilled my part of the contract." As he seized the book, Thorn closed his fingers firmly around Ophelia's and looked deep into her eyes. The wind, spiking up his hair, made him look even fiercer than normal. "You don't intend to accompany me to the Memorial," he stated. "Why?"

Ophelia's lies had been piling up since her arrival in Babel, often out of necessity, sometimes for simplicity's sake, but if there was one person in the world with whom she wanted to be totally transparent, it was the man facing her right now. And yet, looking him straight in the eye, she brazenly lied to him: "I want to talk with Ambrose. We need to clear up certain things, him and me. In any case, you weren't planning on introducing me to the Genealogists, were you?"

Thorn's fingers squeezed hers even harder. Did he suspect her of not telling him what she was really thinking?

"You don't move from here until I return. People have died for just getting close to the secret of which we're the keepers."

Ophelia almost weakened under his leaden gaze. She wanted to beg Thorn to stay with her on this terrace, but if she gave herself away here and now, then, yes, they would both die in the most horrific way. There was just one option for stopping the killer, and for Ophelia, it involved speaking to him in private.

Somehow, she found the strength to smile. "I won't move."

Reluctantly, Thorn released her fingers, keeping hold of just the book. Ophelia had to stop herself from running after him as he went up the gangway.

Lazarus dived on the hand she had left hanging to shake it, laughing all the while. "I was positively delighted to see you again, young *demoiselle*! We won't talk again that soon, I'm going to have a lot to do over the next few weeks and I surely won't have time to come back to the house tonight. Make yourself at home! I wish you the best of luck in your quest for the Other," he added, speaking right into her ear. "Don't rely on your eyes to find him, no one knows what he looks like, or in what form he will appear to you when the time comes. If you will permit me a final little piece of advice: look closely into the echoes. They're the key to it all. *La barbe!*"

Lazarus charged across the terrace. His white top hat, buffeted by the propellers, had flown off toward the stars.

Ophelia had barely listened to him. "Let them leave with the book," she whispered to the wind as Lazarus now went up the gangway. "It's me you're interested in, isn't it?"

The presence was still there. Without Eulalia's memory, Ophelia would have probably never noticed it. The aircraft rose in a whirl of propellers before disappearing deep into the night. Thorn was safe.

The wind and the silence fell once more. Ophelia swallowed with difficulty, and then turned her head right round. The lamps on the terrace, buzzing with mosquitoes, were doubling the shadow of the man who had remained beside her. For the first time since the start of the evening, she saw him very clearly—despite the triple layer of hair, eyebrows, and beard. Even now, it seemed unbelievable to her that this old sweeper, who looked so harmless, could have terrified so many people.

"That evening I was locked in the incinerator room," Ophelia said to him, with a calmness she was far from feeling, "it's you who opened the door for me."

He didn't respond. It was impossible to make out his expression under such a shroud of hair.

"You were there," she insisted. "You were there when Fearless was threatening me. You were there when Mediana was blackmailing me. You protected me. Just as you protected *my* work," Ophelia stressed, placing all the emphasis she could on the possessive. "You punished Professor Wolf for having stolen one of my books, and Mademoiselle Silence for having destroyed almost all of them."

The emaciated figure of the old man, whose balance seemed shaky without the broom in his hand, slowly straightened at these words. Ophelia felt a drop of sweat slide between her shoulder blades. Her plan relied entirely on her ability to embody Eulalia Gonde in his eyes. He confused her with her. She knew it because she had caused the same confusion to Farouk, to Pollux, perhaps even to Helen and Artemis.

"An other," Mediana had said. "There's an other one."

"You, too, are a family spirit," Ophelia declared, calmly. "A family spirit in obscurity, unknown to the world. Because your own role is different. You protect my school. You protect my work."

The old man didn't move, frozen like a statue. Ophelia wasn't taken in. Wild beasts often stood stock-still before swooping down on their prey.

"I endowed you with a double-edged power," she continued,

in a voice that was just about steady. "That of inspiring either the greatest fear or the greatest indifference. It's a heavy burden I made you carry for centuries. Condemned never really to exist for others unless you were terrifying them."

Ophelia was articulating truths that the old sweeper already knew, but she sensed a kind of hesitation in him. She had to convince him—convince herself—that she was Eulalia right now, and only Eulalia.

She had to use all her willpower not to back away when the sweeper moved sluggishly forward, superimposing his shadow on hers. She felt as if, suddenly, she was far too confined in her own body. She would have liked to untie her scarf, which, increasingly anxious, was half-strangling her, but she could barely manage to move her fingers. If she didn't calm down very quickly, this family spirit wouldn't need to use his power to make her die of fear.

"I'm sorry," Ophelia murmured to him. "You have been alone for such a long time . . . You're not obliged to do all that for me. The school we knew has ceased to exist. Your brothers and sisters are old enough now. My books aren't worth people killing each other over them. Everything that was important in the past no longer is today. You must move on to something else, do you understand?"

Maybe it was a figment of her imagination, but she thought she glimpsed a spark through the old sweeper's fringe. In two slow strides, he covered the small distance separating them, and then, in an almost reptilian movement, vertebra after vertebra, he leant forward until his back had turned into an anatomically inhuman hump. His grotesque, hairy face was now just a breath away from Ophelia's. Except that hers wasn't breathing. Was there even a mouth behind that beard? Were there eyes beneath those bushy brows?

At the first impulsive movement, hostilities would commence.

The old sweeper remained like that for a long while, arched enough to break his bones, in a tête-à-tête that was barely decent. When he finally decided to make a move, it was to unfold his long, bony arm, raise a skeletal hand, and lift up his hair.

The spark Ophelia had glimpsed didn't come from his eyes, but from an aluminum plate bolted directly onto the skin of his forehead. Engraved on it was a minuscule inscription, barely visible in the wan lamplight. She recognized these letters, but couldn't understand them, for all that—Eulalia's memory wasn't that concerned with detail. They were the same arabesques as those in the family spirits' Books, a code describing their intrinsic nature and defining their *raison d'être.*

This plate was certainly less complex than a Book, explaining the old sweeper's primitive behavior, but it was no less his life force. Ophelia was just wondering why he was so desperate to show it to her, when he tapped on it with his big nail.

"You want me to take it off?" Ophelia had got her voice back. Much as she knew that this ancient creature had killed several times, she felt she didn't have either the courage or the right to kill him in turn. Terrified as she was, she felt responsible for him. Eulalia, on ceasing to be Gonde and becoming God, had abandoned him to his fate. If Ophelia had inherited her memory, for whatever reason, hadn't she also inherited her guilt?

"Is that you, Mademoiselle Ophelia? You didn't leave with my father?"

It was Ambrose who, having probably heard her from the bottom of the steps, had exclaimed in surprise. For a fraction of a second, Ophelia had instinctively reacted to the calling of her name. It was but a brief, slight head movement toward the steps, but when she looked back at the old sweeper, she knew she had given herself away. He hadn't moved an inch, still leaning too far forward, one hand lifting his fringe, but the atmosphere around him had suddenly got heavier.

"I must escape," she thought. "Call for help."

She did neither. Her legs felt as if they were embedded in the marble. Every breath made her feel as if she were swallowing swamp water. Her body was no longer obeying her; it was now nothing but a tangle of entrails, every molecule of which was silently screaming in utter desperation. Never before, including in the isolation room, had Ophelia felt so totally alone. As if, with a pitiless snip of the scissors, her link with all that was beautiful and good in the world had been severed. Even her scarf was hanging from her neck like a dead weight, drained of all Animism.

And just as she thought she had reached the depths of terror, the real fear started rising up her body, swelling in her organs, invading and devastating everything until it all exploded.

It took her a few seconds to realize that the explosion hadn't happened within her, but on the outside. With her muscles tetanized and her stomach in spasm, she stared at the face of the old sweeper in front of her.

The plate on his forehead was now punctured with an enormous hole.

Not a drop of blood seeped from it, and for a while, he remained in the same absurd position, stooped into a hump, one hand holding his fringe up. Then, finally, he collapsed onto the marble like a discarded marionette.

Dead.

Ophelia's legs gave way beneath her. She curled up, regurgitated her tea, and only then did she find the strength to turn toward whoever had saved her life.

A shadow was crouching on the terrace's balustrade, hunting rifle in hand. It was so small and lithe that Ophelia thought at first that it was a monkey, but when the silhouette stood up, she saw that it was a child, wearing just a loincloth.

The son of Fearless-and-Almost-Blameless.

Without a word, without a sound, he turned and disappeared into the gardens.

"Mademoiselle Ophelia!" Ambrose's alarmed voice called out. "What was that noise? You're not hurt, are you?"

She looked at the body of the old sweeper, with that hole in the center of his forehead. He was gradually losing any substance, becoming more transparent by the second, and soon the marble he was lying on showed through. A few moments later, he had disappeared altogether. As though he had never existed.

"I'm fine," she finally replied.

Never had she felt so relieved to utter those words.

# FOOLISHNESS

Victoria awoke with a start in her bed. Loud screams reached right through the house. It wasn't long before Mommy turned on the bedroom light; she was wearing just a silk robe, and her hair was covered in curlpapers.

"Don't be scared, darling!" she whispered, taking her into her arms.

Victoria wasn't scared. She hadn't been scared since Father had gotten rid of the Golden Lady and all her shadows. With sleepy eyes, she looked at the fake stars twinkling beyond the window. She was still curious to know the cause of the screams. It sounded like Great-Godmother's voice, and, if it was her, she seemed mighty angry.

"Madame Rosaline? What is it? What's got into you?"

Mommy went down the stairs holding Victoria close to her. There was no one in any of the small sitting rooms, no one in the dining room, no one in the study, but the more doors Mommy opened, the more Great-Godmother's screams hurt the ears.

"What a foolish idea! I might have killed you! You are . . . you are . . . you are more exasperating than a tube of toothpaste!"

Victoria stared wide-eyed when Mommy entered the smoking room with her. The gas lamps were all dimmed, but there was light enough to see. The place was in a mess the likes of which Victoria had never seen before in the house. No item of furniture was in its proper place. The lovely checkerboard table was knocked over, its four legs in the air. On the carpet, the contents of an ashtray were mixed up with the black and white pieces.

Great-Godmother, in dressing gown and nightcap, was standing in the middle of the smoking room with a fearsome expression on her face. One of her feet had lost its slipper.

Victoria clung to Mommy when she spotted a shadow crouching behind the sofa.

"Just turning up with no warning!" Great-Godmother exclaimed, with outrage. "Inviting oneself into people's homes at an ungodly hour! I heard a noise downstairs, I thought . . . I thought it was a murderer!"

The shadow behind the sofa stood up into the light. It was a man who, in fact, wasn't remotely like a shadow. His cheeks and beard shone like the sun, and, in the middle of this blaze of light, a wide, delighted smile sparkled. He was holding a cigar like those lined up in the smoking room's cabinets. With his other hand, he was rubbing—but not managing to make disappear—a strange red mark on his forehead.

"Madame Rosaline whacked me with a waffle spatula. She's quite extraordinary."

Victoria felt herself quivering from head to toe. It was Godfather!

"How did you get in?" Mommy asked.

"Through a little shortcut of my devising. I'll cancel it when I leave." With his cigar, Godfather pointed at the large pedestal clock ticking away at the back of the smoking room. Or rather, that should have been ticking away. The pendulum had disappeared behind the glass; in its place, Victoria thought she could see the cobbles of a dark street.

"Right. I'm going to prepare some tea." Even when woken up in the middle of the night, and finding her home turned upside down, Mommy never forgot her manners.

"Don't worry about that, my dear. We haven't much time."

Godfather leapt over the sofa and sat perched on its back, unconcerned about dirtying the cushions with his shoes. His trousers were riddled with holes, and he hadn't even bothered to pull their braces up over his shirt. His face, neck, hands, every bit of skin not covered in clothes, were all incredibly tanned. Victoria had never found him so handsome.

"In fact," Godfather chortled, in a cloud of cigar smoke, "I don't have the right to be here. But you know me, don't you? The more I'm prohibited, the more I disobey!"

Mommy sat Victoria beside her on a banquette and delicately placed a handkerchief over her nose to avoid her breathing in the cigar smoke. "You're beyond belief, Archie. But your explanations will have to wait a little. First, I must ask you a question of the utmost importance. Did you, yes or no, place an order for an illusion with Madam Cunegond?"

"What an idea! Why would I go and request something that I find repellent?" Godfather had burst out laughing, but Victoria noticed Great-Godmother and Mommy exchanging a nervous look. Neither of them seemed to find his reply amusing.

"So we were dealing with an impostor. When I think that I opened my door to her ten times, and let her near my daughter! Whoever it may be, that person is looking for you, Archie. So I hold you responsible. You put all three of us in danger."

Beneath Mommy's gentleness, Victoria sensed a kind of hardness, but without understanding its nature. Far from diminishing, Godfather's smile became twice as wide.

"If you mentioned my activities in front of this impostor," he said, placing a strange emphasis on that last word, "you're a little responsible yourself. Never mind! I've come to put *all three of you* out of said danger."

From a pocket—likewise full of holes—Godfather took out a ball, which he playfully threw to Victoria. It was so heavy and smelt so good! Mommy immediately confiscated it, as if it were a dangerous object.

"An orange," Godfather declared. "Before your birth, young lady, they graced every table in the Pole. I picked this one barely a quarter of an hour ago."

"You succeeded?" Great-Godmother asked, with amazement. "You found LandmArk?"

"Not without difficulty. We had to cross towns, mountains, and forests to change connection between each Compass Rose! And if it's not easy to reach LandmArk, leaving it is even harder. The Arkadians may be my distant cousins, but they didn't welcome me with open arms." As he explained this, Godfather rubbed the waffle-spatula imprint on his forehead. "Don Janus, their family spirit, gave me express orders not to leave his ark, and to stop using his Compass Roses. Having said that, it would be no great hardship—there are some superb gardens in LandmArk."

Victoria breathed in deeply the scent the orange had left on her little hands. Mountains. Forests. Gardens. For her, these words just meant gloomy illustrations in books from the library, but when it was Godfather saying them, she heard "sky," "trees," "birds!"

"And you promptly disobeyed him," Mommy sighed, gently. "You disobeyed a family spirit."

"Only half so," Godfather said. "I came to the Pole without using a single Compass Rose! It took me a lot of time and effort, but I managed to summon a shortcut between our two arks. It won't last very long, so gather your things together quickly!"

Great-Godmother pressed her nose to the glass of the clock

and wiped away the condensation preventing her from seeing the cobbles. "You mean to say that this . . . "

"No, that's just a street corner, Madame Rosaline. My short-cut to LandmArk is in a different neighborhood of Citace-leste. Come now, I'm saving you a journey of several thousand miles; a little outing's not going to put us off, is it?"

"Why the devil do you want to take us over there?"

Archibald picked up the slipper Great-Godmother had lost and used it like a fan. "Sunshine, coffee, fruit, spices, I hand you paradise on a platter, and you ladies are reluctant to go?"

There was silence, heavier even than the orange resting on Mommy's silk robe, so heavy that Godfather himself suddenly lost all his flippancy. He took a long time to stub out his cigar in an ashtray. His mouth still had that mischievous little kink that Victoria so adored, but his voice was deadly serious when he spoke once more:

"The imposter you had dealings with is a megalomaniac. He's got nearly all of the political institutions in his pocket, without mentioning his ability to assimilate and then repro-duce the family powers of anyone who crosses his path. Men have died, and I very nearly did, too, just because a baron wanted to please him. And that's certainly not an isolated case. There exists just one place in the world, just one, that this megalomaniac hasn't yet managed to get his claws on: LandmArk. And I've finally understood what he's after there, and why the Arkadians keep him well away." There was a flash of light in the middle of Godfather's beard as his smile bared his teeth. "My cousins, you see, possess a most fascinating power. Have you ever heard of the *Agujas*?"

Godfather had pronounced "agujas" like a big clearing of the throat. Great-Godmother frowned, Mommy remained silent. Victoria hadn't really understood the question, but she could tell that neither of them knew the answer.

"They're also known as the 'Needlers,'" Godfather explained. They're a branch of the Arkadians' family tree. I'd never heard of them myself before I met some, and for good reason: they're extremely rare and extremely secretive. Imagine, ladies, being endowed with an internal compass that allows you to find absolutely anyone, absolutely anywhere. Your target might be hiding on the other side of the world, inside the most impenetrable fortress, but he or she would be unable to escape you. Are you with me? That's the power of the Needlers! I leave you to imagine now the use our megalomaniac would make of such a power. No one would be safe from his needle."

Godfather went quiet, as if to savor the stir he had caused. The only word that Victoria had grasped in this long and complicated speech was "tree." It couldn't be an ordinary tree, because both Mommy and Great-Godmother looked pretty impressed.

"If I found LandmArk, sooner or later, he'll succeed in doing so, too," Godfather added, playing with the stub of his cigar. "Which is why I think we should make use of the Needlers' power before he does. And therein lies the whole problem. The Arkadians, starting with Don Janus, care more about their sacrosanct neutrality than anything else. They want no involvement with the world's petty affairs, unless it's lucrative enough. I have spent my whole life being neutral, as my education dictated, and if there's one lesson I retained, it's that 'neutrality' is a nice way of saying 'cowardice.' There comes a time when one has to choose which camp one is in, and, personally, I refuse any longer to belong to that of the puppets."

Mommy applauded with her lovely tattooed hands. Victoria, thinking it was a game, imitated her.

"Congratulations, Archie, you're growing up a little. What's this got to do with us three?"

"I would like to convince Don Janus and the Arkadians

to give up their neutrality, but in their eyes, I'm just an ex-ambassador who is the messenger of only himself. You, Berenilde, you are, in a way, the first lady of the Pole. Your word has more weight than mine. Not to mention your charm."

Godfather opened his eyes wide, eyes bluer than the fake sky outside had ever been. Victoria wished she could fly into them.

"No," Mommy said.

"No?" Godfather repeated, smiling even more.

"You are asking me the impossible. If I followed you, I would have no guarantee of being able to return, and, unlike you, I would never take the risk of triggering a diplomatic incident by disobeying a family spirit."

"But consider . . . "

"I have told you, and I repeat, Archie," Mommy continued, cutting Godfather short, "my place is here. I am surer of that today than ever: our lord needs to have his daughter close to him. He's trying to change, he's trying to change his family, and if he is doing so, it's because he wants to give her a future without fighting clans, without conspiracies, and without assassinations. If we leave, he will forget why he is making all that effort."

This time it was Great-Godmother's turn to applaud. Victoria, delighted by this little nocturnal game, thought it only fair to imitate her, too. She felt as if she were watching one of those operas Mommy sometimes told her about.

Godfather ran his thumb over his smile, which just kept widening.

"The power of the Needlers, Berenilde. Think about it! Persuade them to put themselves at the service of your cause, and they will find Mr. and Mrs. Thorn for you in a snap."

Victoria felt Mommy's body stiffen beside hers on the banquette. When she looked up at her, she saw a kind of pain on her face, as if she'd just burnt herself, but it only lasted a brief moment. Mommy soon had her pretty porcelain mask back.

"I will look for neither Thorn nor Ophelia as long as they do not wish to be found. On the other hand, I do want them to be able to find me here when the time comes. We're staying, my daughter and I. That's my final word."

As soon as Mommy, very upright and very dignified on her banquette, had uttered these words, Great-Godmother held a hand out to Godfather. After a slight hesitation, he returned her slipper to her.

"I have never forced a woman, and it's not today that I'm going to start. Never mind. I must leave you now, the shortcut won't last much longer."

Victoria's heart quickened when Godfather kneeled in front of her to take her hand. His golden chin prickled her fingers. He was smiling at her, but in an unusual way. There wasn't really a smile in that smile.

"I don't know when we'll see each other again, young lady. Between now and then, don't go changing too much, please."

Victoria suddenly felt very cold. She watched Godfather dusting off his big, holey hat, and then shaking it three times above his head, as if saying goodbye to each of them.

She didn't want.

She didn't want to see him leaving already. It was seeing the real sky, the real trees, and the real birds leaving with him. She moved her lips as she saw Godfather disappearing into the smoking room's clock, but he didn't hear her.

No one ever heard her.

Without a glance at Mommy or Great-Godmother, Victoria left the Other-Victoria behind her and went into the clock herself. She found herself on the cobbles of a street full of mist, which her *journeying* made even hazier. Seen from the other side of the clock, the smoking room was now nothing but a tiny patch of light in the middle of a wall. Godfather closed a door, and then reopened it: there was no more smoking room, no more house.

Victoria wasn't scared. She could still sense, in the distance, the presence of the Other-Victoria close to Mommy. And then, Godfather was there. Even if he didn't see her like Father did, she felt blissfully happy being close to him.

This time, she would follow him right up to the real sky!

For the moment, Godfather wasn't moving that much. He remained standing in the middle of the street, hands in pockets, looking searchingly into the mist surrounding him.

"Ah, at last," he said, on seeing a silhouette appear. "Lucky that you were, supposedly, standing guard."

"Thought I saw someone. False alarm."

Victoria recognized the Big-Ginger-Fellow. Even when trying to whisper, his loud voice echoed around the entire street.

"Well?"

"Well, nothing," Godfather smirked, shrugging his shoulders. "There was a time when I could have convinced any woman to accompany me to the ends of the earth. I could have used my old trick," he said, tapping the black teardrop between his eyebrows, "but I promised myself never to use it again on Berenilde. She must be right, perhaps I am starting to grow up. How ghastly . . . "

Victoria leapt from cobble to cobble, trying not to lose sight of Godfather and the Big-Ginger-Fellow. They were walking very fast in the mist. Their murmurings, distorted by the *journey*, were like the bubbles drinking-straws produce in a glass of milk.

They plunged into an alley that was even less well lit. It led only to a brick dead end and mountains of garbage. If Victoria had been able to smell anything when *journeying*, she would certainly have had to hold her nose. It wasn't here, the sky she had hoped to see.

Godfather climbed onto a moldy old crate that enabled him to reach the door of an old carriage without wheels. The Big-Ginger-Fellow watched him do so without asking any questions.

"That's great, it's still there," Godfather whispered, indicating to him to hurry up. "With any luck, Don Janus won't have noticed a thing."

The door had just opened onto a brilliant light, as if the inside of the carriage was on fire. The Big-Ginger-Fellow had to squeeze his broad shoulders to get through the door. Godfather checked with a glance that there was no one around the dead end, didn't notice the little girl right under his nose, and slipped through the door himself.

Without a second's hesitation, Victoria leapt into the light with him.

For a moment, she saw nothing anymore. Neither light nor darkness. One day, Great-Godmother had torn the sleeve of her dress by catching it on the drawing-room door handle. Victoria felt as if, like Great-Godmother's sleeve, she were cut in two. And yet that pain didn't really hurt her, and a second later, she had already stopped thinking about it. She now saw only the sky above her. A ginormous sky. A sky not content to be just blue, but also red, mauve, green, and yellow, with a dazzling sun and great swirls of birds. The real sky! Even distorted by the *journey*, it was the most beautiful thing Victoria had ever seen in her whole little life.

"I told you it was a waste of time."

Victoria turned to the Funny-Eyed-Lady. She was standing right beside her, angrily blowing out smoke from the cigarette hanging from her lips.

"Going over there, that was taking a foolish and pointless risk."

Godfather closed and then reopened the door of a shed

with an exaggerated flourish. "There we are, all over, no more shortcut! Did anything really terrible happen? Did anyone even notice our absence?"

"Dunno," grumbled the Funny-Eyed-Lady. "Me and the cat, we just kept a lookout in the orange grove to stop anyone from approaching your blasted shortcut from this side of the planet."

She threw a reproachful look at the Big-Ginger-Fellow, but he didn't seem overly keen to join in the conversation. He was staring at Twit, who was sniffing his big shoes disapprovingly, as if he could smell that his master had stepped in something not very clean.

Victoria suddenly realized that they were all standing in the middle of a garden in which hundreds of trees—real trees!—were weighed down with oranges just like the one Godfather had given her. The light here was brighter than all the lamps in the house and all the illusions in the gardens.

Victoria's wonderment was soon replaced by a feeling of uneasiness. She could no longer sense the presence of the Other-Victoria in the distance.

"Let's stop moping," Godfather declared, "let's move on to the rescue plan!"

The Funny-Eyed-Lady grimaced. "What rescue plan, Mr. Ex-Ambassador?"

"The one we have to come up with to persuade my cousins to hunt down God rather than running away from him." With these words, Godfather moved off, peeling himself an orange, braces of trousers flapping on hips. Victoria no longer knew what she was supposed to do. Carry on following him? Stop moving, above all? As hard as she concentrated, she could no longer find the way back. She'd never had to make any effort before; returning home had always come as naturally as waking up.

Victoria skipped in front of the Funny-Eyed-Lady, hoping that her strange power would cancel the *journey*, but nothing changed. The Funny-Eyed-Lady spat out a cigarette butt that went through Victoria like a cloud.

"That fool has no idea what he's doing. And you, what's up with you?" she asked the Big-Ginger-Fellow. "Catch a cold in the Pole, or what?"

The Big-Ginger-Fellow didn't respond. He had stopped staring at Twit, who was still sniffing his shoes, to gaze up at the sky.

He was frowning anxiously, all bushy red eyebrows.

"It's the end of the beginning. Or the beginning of the end."

With a terrible shock, Victoria suddenly noticed them: the shadows under the Big-Ginger-Fellow's shoes.

# THE OTHER

The hair dryer was drowning out both the sound of the radio and the patter of the rain, as its big drops hit the window. Ophelia wasn't listening to either, in any case. And neither was she paying attention to the mechanical servant behind her chair, who was spouting the likes of "BETTER AN AGILE MIND THAN A CRAMMED MIND," and "THREE SMILES A DAY KEEP THE DOCTOR AWAY," all while drying her unruly curls. Ophelia had tried to explain to it that a rub with a towel would do, particularly with the stifling heat of the room, but it hadn't given her the choice. Lazarus wouldn't be home for weeks, and Ambrose was out being a whaxi driver; in their absence, best not to annoy automatons that could release hundreds of blades at the first misplaced word.

So she was focusing on her great-uncle's postcard, armed with the magnifying glass Ambrose had lent her. The figures in the crowd at the XXII$^{nd}$ Interfamilial Exhibition weren't easy to make out, but one of them was only too recognizable: an old man on the side, sweeping a Memorial walkway, his face hidden behind an indistinguishable combination of beard, eyebrows, and fringe. In sixty years, he hadn't changed. He had spent entire centuries watching over what remained of the old school that was home to Eulalia and her family spirits. Ever since Ophelia had spotted him on the photograph, she

440

couldn't tear her glasses away from him. He might be dead, but the terror he had provoked was still screaming inside her. She'd had nightmares about it all night, and it had taken several showers for her to wash the acrid smell of fear from her skin.

"And yet I came through it alright," she thought, looking up at the dusty trails of rain on the window. If Fearless's son had waited a second longer to obliterate that plate, she would have ended up—at best—in the same state as Mediana. Had that young boy been spying on her, knowing that she would lead him to his father's murderer? If that were so, Fearless certainly had a worthy successor.

And if the old sweeper she had confronted the previous day was at the Memorial sixty years ago, then he couldn't be that Other whom Ophelia had released from the mirror. She had to admit that she'd seriously considered the possibility, but it didn't fit. And it was one thing terrifying people, and quite another causing the disintegration of the arks.

Ophelia frowned as a smell of singeing came from her own head. "I think that's enough, thank you," she said, with a polite sign of dismissal.

The automaton unplugged the hair dryer, and left with a final "YOU CAN'T PLEASE ALL OF THE PEOPLE ALL OF THE TIME." The sound of rain and radio prevailed again. With its elegant furnishings, huge bed with mosquito net, and lovely standing mirror, the room made a change from the austerity of the Good Family. To think that it was right here that Ophelia had spent her first night in Babel . . . She found it hard to believe that half a year had gone by since then.

She unfolded the little note that Octavio had given her before they had parted.

*Come and see me sometime, your hands and you. Helen.*

It was an invitation she was tempted to take up, but she

thought it best to think twice before going near a family spirit again.

She pressed her nose to the window, and reflected back at her was a tousled head against a background of raindrops. All this dampness was unusual in full dry season. Without really listening, Ophelia heard the radio presenter reporting on the latest Home Improvements Exhibition, taking place in the center of Babel. In the same way, without really seeing, she looked at the lily pools, their water disturbed by that falling from the sky. She fought the urge to open the window, plunge into the rain, and lean from the terrace to keep watch on the entrance portico. Why was Thorn taking so long? Handing over a book didn't take that much time, surely? Had the Genealogists caused him problems?

Ophelia jumped at the sound of two commanding knocks on the bedroom door.

"Would you kindly rid me of this?" Thorn asked, as soon as she opened to him. The scarf had wound itself around his leg. Leaning against the doorpost, Thorn had grabbed it like a cat, by the scruff of the neck, but the wool had caught on his brace.

Ophelia couldn't help smiling as she tried to release him. "And there was I, wondering where it had got to. I think it's developed a taste for independence."

Thorn entrusted his dripping umbrella to the automaton that had guided him there, and then slammed the door in its face. Or rather, in its absent face.

"Where is Lazarus's son?" he asked, sternly scanning the room.

"He's gone out for the day."

Thorn slid the bolt. "Good. We won't be disturbed." He checked there was no one on the little rain-flooded terrace.

Beyond the scarf, Ophelia cautiously observed Thorn's

tense profile. He had combed his hair, shaved his jaw, and mended his leg brace, properly this time. He didn't look like a man who had been mistreated, and yet he was giving off a strong smell of disinfectant.

"What did the Genealogists say to you?" she asked. "Were they disappointed?"

Thorn closed the curtains, unconcerned that he was suddenly plunging the room into semiobscurity. "They were satisfied. A little more than that, even."

"But?"

"There's no 'but.' The book I brought them fully met their expectations. They are ready to give me a new assignment."

"Of what kind?"

"I don't know yet." Thorn's every utterance fell from his lips like lead. Merely by his presence, he made the atmosphere heavier. And yet Ophelia felt lighter now than she had in his absence. More febrile, too.

"And you?" she asked. "Are you disappointed?"

Thorn stared at her in silence, with that intensely serious expression that made her feel exposed. She gathered the panels of her dressing gown around the pajamas given to her by Ambrose. She thought of the automaton and his confounded hair dryer, which had turned her curls into a bramble bush. It was an unusual experience for her, realizing that, suddenly, she would have liked to appear less scruffy.

"No," Thorn finally replied. "I didn't expect to overturn God at the first attempt." He pronounced the word "God" with a cautious glance at the bolt he'd slid earlier. Since no automaton started breaking the door down, he poured himself a glass of water from the bedside carafe, sniffing it suspiciously, and sat down on the edge of the bed.

"And you?" he asked in turn.

Ophelia decided not to tell him about the old sweeper. She

would do so later—she didn't want to hide anything from him, but she sensed that it just wasn't the right moment.

"I feel disorientated," she said, with complete candor. "The closer I get to Eulalia Gonde's past, the more I feel as if I know her, and yet several centuries separate us from each other. The family power you passed on to me shouldn't allow for such a thing, should it?"

"She was punished." Thorn had stated this after taking a careful sip from his glass.

"Punished?" Ophelia repeated. "I don't understand."

"Me neither. I told you once that I myself carried Farouk's recollections, passed on from generation to generation, and from memory to memory, by my mother's clan. Fragmented recollections that are highly subjective. In one of them, it appeared to me that God . . . *Gonde*," he instantly corrected, "was punished. I still don't know by whom, why, or how."

"The Necromancers' cool box-cabinet guarantees perfectly preserved comestibles all year round!" the radio presenter raved. "Sturdy but not bulky, it's the ultimate in practical storage! In practical storage!"

Ophelia looked, pensively, at the radio that had produced an echo.

"Maybe her transformation into Milliface wasn't by choice? Maybe it's a curse? Maybe it is actually linked to the Other?"

"That," Thorn said, "will be for us to find out. If, of course, you are still happy for us to investigate together." He had spoken stiffly, looking deep into his glass.

Ophelia pushed her glasses back up her nose. "You doubt that?"

"For as long as you remain in Babel, however strong the temptation and however great your loneliness, you must have no contact with your family."

"I know that."

"The closer you will get to the truth, the more you will put yourself in danger."

"I know that."

"If you get into difficulty, you may not be able to count on me. My hands and feet are tied by the Genealogists."

"I know that, too," Ophelia said, gently. "Is that what you wanted us to talk about yesterday?"

Thorn finally turned his eyes, from the glass of water, directly at her. His pale pupils glowed probingly through the shadowy light. "Do you recall what I said to you the other evening, in front of the Memorial entrance? That I wanted none of your finer feelings?"

Ophelia nodded with her chin.

"I meant it," he continued, sternly. "I want none of them." He grimaced, as if he had a bad taste in his mouth. He juggled his glass from one hand to the other, before deciding to put it down. "At least, not them alone."

Ophelia moistened her lips. Only Thorn could make her go from chilled one moment to inflamed the next. "You don't . . . "

"No half-measures," he interrupted her. "I'm not and do not wish to be your friend."

"Try the automatic sugar tongs and you'll love them! Love them! Their spring-loaded pincers work at the press of a finger! Of a finger!"

Ophelia promptly lowered the volume of the radio.

"I refuse to live forever feeling that I make you uncomfortable," Thorn continued, brusquely. "If it's my claws that put you off . . . I'm aware that I'm hardly attractive . . . this leg won't stop me from . . . " Exasperated, he swept his brow with his hand, as if enduring a severe verbal challenge.

All Ophelia's nervousness instantly disappeared. She removed her gloves, as though shedding an old skin. Hard knocks had damaged Thorn, and the harm was greater within than without. She promised herself to protect him from all those who could further flay him, starting with herself.

She approached, ensuring that she was well within his field of vision. It was good that he was seated—it put them on the same level. He shuddered when she pressed her bare hands on either side of his face. He was an angular being, both in body and character, with never a friendly phrase, or gallant gesture, or humorous quip, preferring the company of numbers to that of people. One had to have a good reason for looking Thorn straight in the face.

Ophelia had one. She kissed his scars, first the one cutting through his eyebrow, then the one cutting into his cheek, and finally the one cutting across his temple. With each contact, Thorn's eyes widened. His muscles, conversely, tightened.

"Fifty-six." He cleared his throat to make his voice less hoarse. Ophelia had never seen him so intimidated, despite his efforts not to show it.

"That's the number of my scars."

She closed and then reopened her eyes. She felt it again, even more violently, this urgent call from deep inside her. "Show them to me."

The world instantly ceased to be a word and became skin. The gentle shadows of the mosquito nets, the lapping of the rain, the distant sounds of the gardens and the city, none of all that existed anymore for Ophelia. All that she was acutely aware of was Thorn and herself, their hands unfastening, one by one, every restraint, every apprehension, every fear.

Ophelia had spent these last three years feeling empty. She was, at last, replete.

On the pedestal table close to the window, the radio's

volume was down to the merest murmur. Neither Ophelia nor Thorn heard when the report on the Home Improvements Exhibition was suddenly interrupted:

"Citizens of Babel, this is a message of utmost urgency. Major land changes were observed twenty minutes ago in the northwest of the city. Pollux's botanical gardens and the large spice market have . . . are no longer attached to the ark. If you are in the vicinity of the unstable zone, move away and evacuate residential buildings. We ask the entire population to remain calm, we will keep you regularly informed as the situation evolves. *Quoi?* We have just been told that several neighboring minor arks have also seemingly disappeared. Above all, do not panic. I repeat: Citizens of Babel, this is a message of the utmost urgency . . . "

# ACKNOWLEDGMENTS

To Thibaut, my adviser, my reader, my inspirer, my love.

To my family in France and Belgium, who take the woolliest care of me.

To my brother Romain and to Jason Piffeteau, whose feedback was so precious to me.

To Stéphanie Barbaras, Célia Rodmacq, Alice Colin, Svetlana Kirilina: you taught me so much.

To my silver quills and my golden friends who support me across all the arks.

To Laurent Gapaillard, who was able to turn each of my books into a work of art.

To the entire team at Gallimard Jeunesse, thanks to whom Ophelia was able to emerge from her mirror.

To you, finally, dearest reader, who came especially to meet me on the other side.

May the scarf be with you all!

# ABOUT THE AUTHOR

Christelle Dabos was born on the Côte d'Azur in 1980 and grew up in a home filled with classical music and historical games. She now lives in Belgium. *A Winter's Promise*, her debut novel, was a Waterstones Children's Book Prize Finalist 2019, won the Gallimard Jeunesse-RTL-Télérama First Novel Competition in France, and was named a Best Book of the Year by many critics and publications in the US, including *Entertainment Weekly, Bustle, Publishers Weekly*, and the *Chicago Review of Books*. *A Winter's Promise* was also named the #1 Sci-Fi/Fantasy title of the year by *Amazon Book Review*.

TO FOLLOW, THE FOURTH BOOK

OF *THE MIRROR VISITOR*:


The world has been turned upside down. The disintegration of the arks has well and truly begun. Just one way to stop it: find whoever is responsible. Find the Other. But how to do so without even knowing what he or she looks like? Ophelia and Thorn embark on the trail of the echoes, those strange phenomena that seem to be the key to all the mysteries. They will have to delve more deeply into Babel's corridors of power, and into their own memories. And meanwhile, in LandmArk, God may well obtain the power he so covets. Between him and the Other, who poses the gravest threat?